Praise for *Staying at Daisy's*

"Love and laughter prevail in this charming chick lit romp... This screwball romantic comedy piles on the humor and humanity for a clever, absorbing, and very enjoyable read."

—*Publishers Weekly*

"Enduring characters attempting to find true love in the midst of heartache... a very satisfying read."

—*Fresh Fiction*

"Entertaining through and through."

—*Drey's Library*

Praise for *Take a Chance on Me*

"Mansell's characters are quirky, charming, and entertaining, with a supporting cast that is often as enchanting as the hero and heroine."

—*RT Book Reviews*, 4 stars

"Quirky characters, a charming setting, and misunderstandings aplenty make this madcap romantic comedy a fun, light read."

—*Booklist*

"Full of wonder, love, and family... the kind of book you want to savor and reread."

—*Fresh Fiction*

Praise for *Rumor Has It*

"While witty dialogue and wry observations keep the pace brisk, Mansell still manages to tug at the heart."

—*Publishers Weekly*

"Jill Mansell's sleek and sexy style won't disappoint!"

—*Romance Junkies*

"Be sure not to miss this enchanting story. It has everything you could possibly want and more."

—*The Long and the Short of It*

Praise for *Perfect Timing*

"Captivating... The story absolutely bubbles with life... superb entertainment."

—*The Long and the Short of It*

"Elevated by strong characters... the end result is thoroughly enjoyable."

—*Publishers Weekly*

"An extraordinarily witty and at times wickedly sarcastic look at family, love, loss, betrayal, heartbreak, and true friendship. *Perfect Timing* is indeed a page-turner."

—*Rundpinne*

"A smash hit!... Ms. Mansell has just become my favorite British romantic comedic author."

—*Cheryl's Book Nook*

Praise for *Millie's Fling*

"A warm and humorous journey... Just reading it makes you feel good. An absolute delight!"

—*Wendy's Minding Spot*

"A charming romp... Love, it seems, is on everyone's mind... Will all find their soulmates? Mansell's dry humor and engaging story make it an undeniable pleasure to find out."

—*BookPage*

"A pleasure to read! ...A super cute and wicked funny book."

—*Night Owl Romance*

Praise for *Miranda's Big Mistake*:

"A winning read... Miranda's got more than enough irresistible transoceanic charm to promise that this... should net a passionate new audience eager for the more."

—*Publishers Weekly*

"Mansell's novel proves the maxims that love is blind and there's someone for everyone, topped with a satisfying revenge plot that every jilted woman will relish."

—*Booklist*

"A rip-roaring good time... The sexual tension is electric... The dialogue is sharp and the plot will keep readers... on their toes and cheering Miranda on."

—*Savvy Verse & Wit*

ALSO BY JILL MANSELL

An Offer You Can't Refuse
Miranda's Big Mistake
Millie's Fling
Perfect Timing
Rumor Has It
Take a Chance on Me
Staying at Daisy's

to the moon and back

Jill Mansell

sourcebooks
landmark

Published by Sourcebooks Landmark, an imprint of Sourcebooks, Inc.
P.O. Box 4410, Naperville, Illinois 60567-4410
(630) 961-3900
FAX: (630) 961-2168
www.sourcebooks.com

First published in 2011 by Headline Review, an imprint of Headline Publishing
Group, London.

Library of Congress Cataloging-in-Publication Data

Mansell, Jill.
  To the moon and back / by Jill Mansell.
    p. cm.
  1. Widows—Fiction. 2. Traffic accident victims—Fiction. 3. Businessmen—
Fiction. 4. Triangles (Interpersonal relations)—Fiction. 5. London (England)—
Fiction. I. Title.
  PR6063.A395T6 2011
  823'.914—dc22

                              2011015879

          Printed and bound in the United States of America
                VP 10 9 8 7 6 5 4 3 2 1

To Cino, my other half.

We really didn't expect to last six months together, did we?

And now here we are twenty-five years later. One day we should probably think about getting married…

Chapter 1

'WHAT WOULD YOU DO without me?'

Fresh from the shower, Ellie took in the alluring view from the bedroom doorway. Seriously, could anything beat the sight of a drop-dead gorgeous twenty-eight-year-old male wearing nothing but white boxers whilst clutching a steam iron in one hand and a black skirt in the other?

And to think he's mine, all mine. She had the marriage certificate to prove it.

'OK, don't answer that. I know what you'd do.' Jamie bent down and unplugged the iron at the wall. 'Go out wearing a crumpled skirt.'

'Possibly.' She fastened the lime-green bath towel securely around her chest. 'But I don't have to, do I? Because I have you.' Reaching across the ironing board, she planted a kiss on the mouth she never tired of kissing.

'So you're grateful, then?' He gave the edge of the towel a playful tug.

'I am. Very grateful. Thank you, thank you to the moon and back.'

'Because if you feel like repaying the favor, I can probably think of a way you could do that.'

Regretfully Ellie tapped her watch. 'But we don't have time. Look at my hair. I need to get dressed and do my face… *wah*, no, stop it, get away from me!' She snatched the skirt and danced out of reach before Jamie could ravish her. Tonight they were going out separately. Along with a crowd of friends from work, she was heading off to a performance of *The Rocky Horror Picture Show* where dressing up was mandatory. Hence the black skirt, bought in a charity shop last year and cannibalized with garden shears to give it a zig-zaggy hemline for a Halloween party. It had been lying at the back of the wardrobe ever since but would be just the thing for a Rocky Horror outing, teamed with mad hair, over-the-top eyeliner, and fishnets.

'Right then, which shirt should I wear?' Jamie indicated the ones he'd ironed while she'd been in the shower. 'Blue? Or white?' He was off to a school reunion in Guildford.

Ellie said, 'How about the pink one?' and saw his mouth do that turning-down-at-the-corners thing it did when he felt awkward.

'I don't know. Not tonight.'

'Why not?'

'Just… because. I'd rather wear the blue tonight.'

She took the fuchsia-pink shirt out of the wardrobe and gave it an enticing waggle. 'But this is beautiful! Look at that *color*. Why wouldn't you want to wear it?'

'Because I don't want to turn up and have everyone saying they didn't know I was gay.'

'Oh, come on! Just because it's pink?'

Jamie pulled a don't-make-me-say-it face. 'It's a very gay pink.'

OK, maybe it was, but he could carry it off. 'I bought it for you for Christmas! You could have taken it back to the shop and exchanged it.' Ellie shook her head in disbelief. 'But you said you loved it!'

'I didn't want to hurt your feelings. Besides,' Jamie ventured, 'I kind of like it to *look* at. Just not to, you know, *wear*.'

'The color would really suit you.'

'I'll wear it soon, I promise.' He slid the blue shirt off the hanger and shrugged it on.

Men, honestly, what was with them? 'Right, that's it, wait until next Christmas. No presents, that'll teach you to turn your nose up at my choice of shirt. Next year you'll get nothing at all.'

Jamie broke into a grin. 'Does that mean I don't have to buy you anything either?'

'You just wait. You'll be sorry. No, get off me!' Shrieking with laughter, Ellie found herself backed into a corner of the living room. 'I told you, we don't have *time!*'

Jamie snaked his arms around her waist and pulled her against him. 'Sometimes,' he murmured persuasively in her ear, 'you just have to get your priorities right and *make* time.'

DDDDDRRRINNNGGGGGGGG went the doorbell and Jamie clutched his heart, staggering backward as if he'd been shot. 'No, no, not fair…'

'Oh, what a shame. Just as I was about to change my mind too.' Skipping past him, Ellie went to the window and peered down to the pavement below.

Todd waved up at her. She waved back.

'And to think he used to be my friend.' Jamie flung open the window and yelled, 'You're early.'

'I know.' Todd spread his arms wide, evidently pleased with himself. 'That's because you told me not to be late.'

Jamie rolled his eyes. 'The first time in twenty years he's been early for *anything*.' Raising his voice he called down, 'Look, we're kind of busy just now. How about doing us a big favor and just going for a ten-minute jog around the block?'

'Get lost!'

'Or that's something else you could do.'

'Not a chance. Stop buggering about and open the door.' Energetically stamping his feet and rubbing his hands together, Todd called up, 'It's arctic out here. I'm freezing my nuts off.'

———⁓———

'Look at you,' Todd marveled, greeting Ellie with a kiss when she finally teetered out of the bedroom, dressed and ready to go. 'Understated. I like it. Off to church?'

'Ha ha.' She loved Todd, which was just as well, seeing as he was Jamie's best friend. For almost twenty years the two boys had been inseparable. Their personalities complemented each other and their shared sense of humor enabled them to bounce jokes off each other so effortlessly that they never tired of it. Jamie and Todd were known as the double act and Ellie lived in fear of Todd meeting and settling down with a girl she didn't like, because what could be worse than that? How would they cope? It had the potential to spoil everything and she couldn't bear the thought of that happening. All they could do was cross their fingers and pray he'd choose someone great.

'Right, are we ready?' Jamie was driving tonight; rattling his keys, he ushered them toward the door. 'Let's go. Where are we dropping you?'

Ellie gave her back-combed hair one last wild blast of glitter spray for luck. 'Just at the tube station. Everyone's meeting at the Frog and Bucket.'

'You're not going on the tube on your own dressed like that.' He pinched her bottom as she headed past him down the stairs. 'We'll give you a lift to the pub.'

'*Pleurgh.*' Todd smacked his lips together in dismay. 'I've got hair spray in my mouth.'

'Open wide.' Peering in, Ellie said, 'Whoops, there's glitter in there too.'

Jamie grinned. 'That's so when he meets up with the girls he used to fancy at school, he'll be able to make sparkling conversation.'

Ellie brushed a speck of glitter from Todd's cheek. 'God help those poor girls.'

By the time Ellie arrived back at their Hammersmith flat it was almost one o'clock. You knew you'd had a good old Rocky Horror night when your throat was sore from singing and the soles of your feet were on fire. Throughout the show they'd jumped up and joined in with the dancing, bellowing out the words to the songs everyone knew by heart. Then afterwards, on their way back to the Frog and Bucket for last orders, they'd carried on doing the Time Warp all the way down the road.

'That's ten pounds fifty, love.'

She paid the taxi driver, clambered out of the cab, and looked around to see if Jamie was home yet. No sign of the car, but he might have had to park around the corner. And the windows were in darkness, but that could mean he was crashed out in bed.

Letting herself into the flat, Ellie felt the stillness and knew she was the first one home. OK, that was fine, she was still buzzing with adrenaline. If Jamie came back soon she might seduce him, make up for what they'd missed out on earlier thanks to Todd's untimely arrival. Toddus Interruptus, ha. Their very own living, breathing contraceptive. She smiled to herself and switched on the light in the living room. She'd make a toasted sandwich and put on a DVD. Oh, the light was flashing on the phone. Reaching over, she pressed the button and listened to the message from someone whose voice she didn't recognize but whose name she'd heard before.

'Hey, Jamie, what's going *onnnn*? It's Rodders here, man. What happened to you and Todd, eh? You said you'd be here. Give us a bell, mate. You missed a cracking night.'

The call ended. That was it. Rodders was Rod Johnson, who had taken it upon himself to organize tonight's school reunion in Guildford. And he had made the call an hour ago, which made no sense at all unless Jamie and Todd had arrived at the event early, peered through a window, decided it looked like rubbish, and beaten a stealthy retreat before they were spotted.

Because what other explanation could there possibly be for their not turning up?

The only sound in the room, the ticking of the clock Jamie's grandmother had given them on their wedding day, seemed louder now. Ellie fumbled in her bag for her phone, switched off since they'd entered the theatre five hours ago.

Seven missed calls. One message. Her heart juddering against her ribs, Ellie experienced split-screen consciousness. One half of her brain was telling her that this couldn't be happening, there'd been some mistake, everything was going to be fine and any minute now Jamie would be home.

Yet somehow, simultaneously, the other half of her brain was listening to a calm female voice relaying the message that Jamie Kendall had been involved in a traffic accident and could she please call this number as soon as possible…

And now the ground was tipping and another voice, a male one this time, was advising her to make her way to the Royal Surrey County Hospital in Guildford. Jamie was currently in a critical condition, the voice on the phone explained—*No, no, no, he can't be,* screamed the other voice in her head—and he was in the process of being transferred from casualty to the intensive care unit.

Chapter 2

Bip. Bip. Bip. Bip. Bip.

The sound of the heart monitor filled Ellie's ears. As long as it kept on doing it, everything would be all right. With every fiber of her being, she willed the bipping not to stop.

It was four o'clock in the morning but the intensive care unit was flooded with blue-white light. Most of the nursing staff was busy working on an elderly patient at the other end of the ward, calling out instructions and rattling machines across the floor. Ellie shut out the noise they were making. She had to concentrate all her attention on the bips. And on Jamie, who was lying on the bed looking like a life-sized waxwork model of himself.

How can this be happening? How can it?

The left side of Jamie's head was swollen and purplish-blue. He was unresponsive, in a deep coma. His skin was warm but when she held his hand he didn't curl his fingers around hers. Saying his name provoked no reaction. Even when the doctor had rubbed his knuckles hard against Jamie's sternum, he hadn't reacted to the painful stimulus.

For God's sake, he wasn't even able to breathe on his own. A ventilator was doing the job for him. Plastic tubes were running into his body. Every function was electronically monitored. It looked like something out of a film but with ultra-realistic special effects. Except it was real. Already gripped with terror, Ellie jumped a mile when a hand came to rest on her shoulder.

'Sorry,' said the nurse. 'But could we ask you to leave for a short time?'

'Can't I stay? I want to stay.'

'I know, dear.' The no-nonsense nurse shook her head, indicating the increased activity around the bed at the other end of the ward. 'Just for a while, though. Go and have a cup of tea, and we'll call you back as soon as we can.'

She wasn't asking, she was telling her to leave. On wobbly legs, Ellie made her way out just as the doors crashed open and three white-coated doctors burst into the unit.

Time to phone Jamie's dad. Oh God, how was she going to tell him about this? But she had to.

Please, just make it stop.

Outside, the sub-zero temperatures gripped her and her teeth began to rattle. The ground was slick with frost, the puddles were frozen. How had Jamie felt as the car had begun to skid on the ice? What thoughts had flashed through his mind when he knew he'd lost control? She couldn't bear to think about it but she couldn't *stop* thinking about it. Horrific images replayed themselves over and over in her mind. If only there was a button she could press to switch them off. Had he cried out as the car had hit the crash barrier? When he woke up would he remember every detail or would his memory of the accident be blanked out?

OK, just do it, call Tony in LA and tell him what had happened. Would he be able to come over or would he have filming commitments he couldn't get out of?

Ellie's hands shook as she found the number on her phone. The time difference between LA and London was eight hours, so it was eight thirty in the evening there. How should she say it when he answered the phone? Which were the best words to choose? Right, just press Call. Do it. The sooner it was done, the sooner she could get back to Jamie.

Moments later she heard his familiar voice at the other end of the line. *Do it now.*

'Tony?' Aware that she was about to break his heart, her voice cracked with grief. 'Oh, Tony, I'm so sorry. There's been an accident...'

The nurse came out to find her in the relatives' room fifteen minutes later. Making her way back into the intensive care unit where calm had been restored, Ellie saw the curtains drawn around the bed of the elderly man at the far end of the ward who'd been the center of attention earlier.

'All sorted now, is he?'

The nurse said gently, 'We lost him, I'm afraid.'

Lost him?

Did she mean the man was actually behind the curtains, *dead*?

Oh no, that only happened on TV, at a safe distance. Not here, right in front of her, in real life.

'Sit down, dear.' The nurse deftly steered her on to the chair beside Jamie's bed. 'Take deep breaths and I'll get you a glass of water. You have to be strong now.'

Strong? Ellie swallowed; she felt about as strong as a newborn kitten. Jamie was here on a ward where people died and every minute was more terrifying than the last. And she was wearing a Rocky Horror outfit that couldn't be more inappropriate if it tried, but going home and changing into normal clothes was out of the question because she couldn't leave Jamie...

Oh, Jamie, wake up, please just open your eyes and tell me everything's going to be all right.

The dead man was placed in a covered metal trolley on wheels and removed from the unit by two porters. Two new patients arrived, a skeletal, yellow-tinged woman and a teenage boy. Relatives sobbed around their beds and looked strangely at Ellie in her jagged short skirt and fishnets. When none of the nurses had been looking she had kissed Jamie's face but it hadn't felt remotely like his face and now he had bits of giveaway glitter on his forehead and cheek.

'Sorry about the glitter,' Ellie told the nurse when she came back to do his vital signs.

'It doesn't matter a bit. We'll just wipe it off with some damp cotton wool, shall we, so it doesn't get into his eyes. Now, do you want me to see if we've got some spare clothes you can change into, or can you call a friend to bring something in?'

It still felt like the middle of the night, but the clock on the wall showed it was nine thirty. And it was light outside. With a jolt, Ellie realized she was supposed to be at work. Out in the real world, life was carrying on as if nothing had happened.

'Um, I'll call a friend.'

Outside again, she rang work. Paula answered the phone and let out a squeal of mock indignation. 'You lazy bum, I had way more to drink than you last night and *I* managed to get in here on time!'

'Oh, Paula, I'm at the hospital and I need you to h-help me…'

———

Hollow-eyed with lack of sleep and gripped with grief, Ellie stayed at Jamie's bedside. The chemical antiseptic smell of the ward seeped into her skin. Doctors came and went. Various medical tests were carried out. Paula arrived in a taxi and floods of horrified tears, with a change of clothes and toiletries, and a hastily purchased Get Well card for Jamie signed by everyone at work. Not allowed into the unit, she clutched Ellie's hands and kept sobbing, 'You poor thing, I can't *believe* it,' and, 'He's going to be all right though, isn't he? I mean, he's not going to die?'

Numbly, Ellie submitted to the hugs. It was a relief when Paula finally unpeeled herself and left. All she wanted was to get back to Jamie and listen to the bips.

More hours passed, then the nurse came and told her that Todd was outside. This time, in lieu of family and because he was Jamie's oldest and closest friend, the nurses agreed to let him on to the ward.

Ellie's stomach clenched at the sight of Todd as he made his way over to the bed. There were cuts and bruises on his head and hands; kept in overnight for observation, he was limping but otherwise OK. He put his arms around her but she felt herself shrink away. She didn't want to be touched and hugged; her skin was too sensitive. It was like having the flu, when it hurt to even brush your hair. How could two people be in the same car, in the same car crash, and one of them escape with scarcely any injuries at all?

It was unfair. So unfair. Fond though she was of Todd, what had he ever done to get off practically scot-free? Why did it have to be Jamie lying unconscious in the bed? Not that she could say this out loud, it wouldn't be polite and it might hurt Todd's feelings. Anyway, that was the thing about life and fate; it never *was* fair. Horrific things happened to good people and brilliant things happened to bad ones.

And it wasn't as if Todd was even bad. It was just that out of the two of them, he wasn't the one she loved with all her heart.

But he did love Jamie. Sitting back down, Ellie watched him move across to the bed and rest a hand on Jamie's bare shoulder. A muscle jumped in his jaw as he gazed, ashen-faced, at his best friend.

Bip. Bip. Bip.

Bip. Bip.

Bipppppppppppppppppppppp...

'*Oh God, what's happening? No no no—*'

'Don't panic.' The nurse bustled over, reclipped the electrode lead that had popped off when Todd's sleeve had brushed Jamie's clavicle. 'There you go,' she said as the regular bips resumed. 'All fixed.'

'Sorry.' Visibly shaken, Todd backed away from the bed and wiped a slick of perspiration from his upper lip.

When the nurse had left them alone again, Ellie said, 'How did it happen?'

'I don't know.' A helpless shrug. 'We weren't going too fast. The car just took a bend and went into a skid. It was like slow motion, but kind of speeded up at the same time. I said, "Oh shit," and Jamie said, "Oh fuck."' His knuckles turning white with the effort of holding back the tears, Todd said, 'We didn't even know there was ice on the road until it was too late.' His voice broke. 'And then we just… *went*.'

———

Todd had left. More tests were carried out. Jamie's bruises grew bluer. Night came and so did Jamie's father; calling the unit, Tony informed them that he had just landed at Heathrow and was on his way to the hospital. The nurse who spoke to him recognized his voice and put two and two together. Within minutes, word had spread that Jamie was the son of Tony Weston… you know, *the actor*. Behind the professional exteriors, excitement grew. Watching them, hoping against hope, Ellie wondered if this meant they would somehow make more of an effort to help Jamie recover. Because if all they needed was an incentive to try harder, maybe she should offer them cash.

Then a vivid mental image sprang into her mind and she smiled, just fractionally, at the thought of explaining *that* to Jamie when he arrived home, gazed in disbelief at the bank statement, and demanded to know why she'd emptied their joint account.

Forty minutes later, Tony appeared. In his midfifties, tanned, and handsome, he was immediately recognizable to the staff as the respected actor who had moved to America and made his name as the quintessential upper-class Englishman, despite having been born and raised in a two-up two-down on a council estate in Basingstoke. If everyone else on the unit was discreetly thrilled to be seeing him in the flesh, Ellie felt only relief. She no longer had to be the one in charge. Jamie's dad was here and he was a proper grown-up. Tears of exhaustion leaked out of her eyes as he hugged her.

'Oh, sweetheart.' It was all Tony said, all he needed to say. He smelled of airplanes and coffee and expensively laundered shirts; he was also unshaven. Turning his attention to Jamie, he gazed at him in silence and seemed to vibrate with pain. Finally he murmured, 'Oh, my baby boy,' and his voice cracked with grief.

The doctor materialized within minutes and introduced himself. Ellie watched him carry out the various neurological tests the doctors had been performing at regular intervals since Jamie's arrival in the unit. She studied the expression on the man's face, searching for clues, waiting for him to stop looking so grim and break into a smile of relief before turning to them and saying, 'He's really on the mend now, give him another couple of hours and then he'll start waking up.'

Go on, say it.

Please, just say it.

The smile didn't happen. She and Tony sat together in silence at Jamie's bedside and watched the still-serious doctor write something in the hospital notes. Finally he turned to face them and Ellie felt as if her chair had been abruptly pulled away. A great rushing sound filled her ears; was this nature's way of drowning out the words she already knew she didn't want to hear?

The rushing sound was loud, but sadly not loud enough to do that. Fear coagulated like cement in her chest. Next to her, Tony was shaking his head slightly but the rest of his body had turned to stone. One of the senior nurses came to stand close to them, a sympathetic look on her face.

Don't do this, please don't say it, Jamie might hear you...

'I'm so very sorry,' the doctor said, 'but the tests that have been performed are conclusive. There is no remaining cerebral function.' He paused. 'Do you understand what that means?'

No, no, nooooooo…

'You're telling us his brain is dead.' There was a world of agony in Tony's words. 'He's gone. My boy's gone.'

The doctor inclined his head in somber agreement. 'I'm afraid he has.'

Chapter 3

Fifteen months later

'LOOK, ARE YOU SURE you don't fancy the cinema?' It was Friday, it was five o'clock, and Paula was clearing the debris from her office desk, cramming makeup back into her oversized handbag, along with her work shoes, a half-full bottle of Fanta, and a packet of Kettle chips to keep her going on the bus home. 'Because if you want to come along, honestly, that'd be great, we'd love to have you with us.'

Ellie was touched; it was like two balloons inviting a hedgehog along on their night out. Two newly-in-love balloons on their romantic night out, at that. It was thoughtful of Paula to make the offer but she wouldn't dream of taking her up on it. Paula and Dan had only been seeing each other for three weeks and Paula was doing her best to pretend she wasn't completely crazy about him, but it was obvious that she was besotted. It was yet another of the alleged 'secrets' she, Ellie, was supposed to be unaware of in order to spare both everyone else's feelings and her own.

'Thanks, but I'm fine. I want to get to B&Q and pick up the wallpaper I ordered.' Did that sound boring? Oh well, never mind, dull but true.

Paula paused and gave her the sympathetic look she'd come to know so well. Then she said brightly, 'Well, that'll be nice, won't it? When it's done, I mean. Is this for the living room?'

Ellie nodded. There was black mold growing on the living room walls. Since scrubbing it off and painting over it hadn't worked, covering the whole lot with wallpaper appeared to be the next logical step.

'Well, look, if you want some help with that tomorrow, me and Dan could come over and give you a hand if you like. I mean, I've never done any wallpapering before, but it can't be too hard, can it?'

Eek, Paula had enough trouble putting her lipstick on straight.

'You're all right, I can manage it myself.' Grateful for the offer, Ellie slung her bag over her shoulder and gave her a hug. 'Anyway, I won't be doing any tomorrow. Tony's over for a few days and he's taking me out to lunch.'

'He is? Oh, *that's great*.' Relieved to have been let off the hook, Paula said with enthusiasm, 'You lucky thing!' Then she winced and clapped her hand over her mouth. 'God, sorry. I'm so stupid!'

It had happened dozens of times. Maybe hundreds. No matter how often Ellie told her to stop worrying about it and apologizing, Paula kept right on doing it. At work, everyone did; it was a kind of Pavlovian reaction they couldn't control.

'Anyway, I am lucky. We're meeting at the Ivy.'

'Wow.'

'Meeting at the Ivy, eating at McDonald's.'

Paula's eyes widened. 'Really?'

So sweet, so well-meaning, so easy to tease. 'No, not really.' Ellie relented with a smile. 'We'll probably have lunch at the Ivy too.'

'Bloody… bloody… *bloody* useless sodding stuff…' By midnight Ellie was ready to murder the wallpaper. Hanging on to the step-ladder and jabbing wildly at the top right-hand corner of the length she'd been battling to hang for the last forty minutes, she had no hands free to prevent the adjoining section from unpeeling itself and rolling down the wall.

'Right, that's it, I've had enough of you!' Letting out a shriek she launched herself at the first bit, missed, and gave the pasted wall a slap that made her palm sting. OK, now the wallpaper had made her so mad she was turning into Basil Fawlty. Time to stop. It wasn't her fault; she'd just been sold unhangable wallpaper or non-stick wallpaper or something. OK, let it all fall down if that's what it wanted to do. Leave it, just step away from the carnage and get a Kit Kat out of the fridge instead.

Returning from the kitchen, Ellie turned her back on the desperate scene—it had *all* unpeeled itself now—and threw herself down on the sofa. She unwrapped the Kit Kat and began flicking through the TV channels. Ooh, lovely, *Sleepless in Seattle*, how long had it been on?

Then Jamie came into the living room and joined her on the sofa. He was wearing his old jeans and the pink shirt he'd refused to put on for his school reunion. He wore it a lot these days. Ellie loved to see him in it and she'd been right about the color; it *was* great on him. She knew what suited Jamie better than he did.

'Great job with the wallpapering.' He grinned at her, sitting sideways with one leg hooked beneath the other and his bare foot inches from her knee.

'I know. I'm brilliant.' Ellie took in every detail of his face, the sparkling blue eyes, the sun-streaked blond hair, the golden tan.

'You should turn professional. People would pay a lot of money to have their homes decorated like this. You know what this is, don't you?' Jamie nodded seriously, indicating the bare walls, the crumpled, fallen-down paper. 'It's postmodern shabby chic.'

'If you'd bothered to give me a hand I might have had more luck,' said Ellie.

'Ah, but it's so much more fun watching you try to do it yourself.'

'You mean you're too lazy to help.'

He smiled sadly at her. 'Oh, sweetheart, I would if I could. You know that.'

Ellie felt the familiar prickle of heat behind her eyes. Of course she knew that. They'd worked so hard together to make this flat their own. And she *wasn't* going to cry. 'OK, that's enough, you can go now. I'm going to watch this film.'

He turned his head, gazed at the TV screen with suspicion. As well he might. 'Is it a slushy girlie film?'

He knew her so well. Ellie nodded. 'Oh yes.'

Jamie held up his hands in horror; sci-fi and war movies were more his thing. 'I'll leave you to it. Bye, gorgeous.'

'Bye.'

But the film wasn't able to hold her attention tonight. After ten minutes, unable to settle into it, Ellie switched off the TV. She could get Jamie back, but she wouldn't. It was starting to concern her, just slightly, that it wasn't quite normal to be doing what she'd been doing for the last year. Because Jamie wasn't here anymore. And he wasn't a ghost either. All she did was conjure up a mental image of him in her mind, talk to him, and have him talk back as if he were real. At school, her teachers had forever been telling her that she had a vivid imagination. Well, they'd been right. And now she was putting it to good use. Because imagining that Jamie was still around, she had discovered, was actually a really comforting thing to do. Like thumb-sucking or clutching a manky old security blanket, it just made her feel… *better*. At least, it did while she was actually doing it. Sometimes, afterwards, it made her feel worse, bereft and alone and sadder than ever. But most of the time it was good. If Jamie could appear as a real ghost… well, obviously that would be fantastic, but so far it hadn't happened; he hadn't obliged in that respect and she didn't believe in ghosts anyway. Besides, this way she could be in charge of his clothes. If she wanted Jamie to wear a dinner jacket or a tutu there wasn't a thing he could do about it besides complain bitterly.

Ellie wiped her eyes with the back of her hand; sometimes she didn't realize she'd been crying until the tears slid off her chin and dripped down her neck. She missed Jamie so much she sometimes wondered how she'd managed to carry on, but it had been fifteen months now, and one way or another she had. Maybe she was going a bit batty, conjuring Jamie up and having imaginary conversations with him, but it was her coping mechanism and she wasn't ready to give it up yet.

—~~—

Ellie always looked forward to her lunches with Jamie's dad when he came over to England. They had each lost the most important person in their lives and their meetings could so easily have been morbid, but Tony never allowed that to happen. Obviously the grief was still there but, in public at least, it wasn't dwelt on. Instead, they talked about Jamie, celebrating his memory and recalling happier times. They laughed a lot, ate well, generally ended up sinking a couple of bottles of the kind of wine she'd never dream of buying herself, and ended up coming away with precious snippets of information they hadn't known before about the boy they'd both loved.

This was the best bit; it was like discovering buried treasure. Today, amid the busy, buzzy atmosphere of the Ivy, Tony had already regaled her with the story of Jamie's sixth birthday party, when one of the young girls had demanded a kiss in return for giving him his present and Jamie, utterly horrified, had promptly handed the still-wrapped gift back.

'He was never that wild about social kissing.' Ellie grinned, the tale triggering a memory of her own. 'The first time he met the girls from work, one of them gave him a kiss on the cheek at the end of the evening, and you should have seen the look on his face. You'd think she'd *licked* him.' She demonstrated Jamie's reaction at the time, the way he'd grimaced and shrunk back. Then she spluttered with laughter, realizing that the waiter attempting to top up their wine glasses thought she was pulling a face and leaning away from him.

'Speaking of which, anything happening in that direction?'

It wasn't the first time Tony had broached the subject. He raised his eyebrows, nodding meaningfully to indicate that he was talking about her. Specifically, had she kissed or been kissed by another man yet? 'No, no. Nothing.' Ellie shook her head. 'It'll happen.' His smile was reassuring. 'Sooner or later.' Later, then. She wasn't remotely ready for anything like that. Just the thought of it made her feel sick. Apart from anything else, what if Jamie was watching her from somewhere, like through celestial CCTV? *What if he didn't approve?*

Ellie dipped a tiger prawn in hollandaise. Not believing in ghosts was one thing, but heaven was another matter. You could never rule out the possibility that they were up there, looking down. Aloud she said, 'I know. But not yet.'

Timing was Tony's forte. Effortlessly changing the subject, he took an appreciative sip of white wine—the bottle had cost eighty-five pounds!—and said, 'How's the flat? Did those noisy neighbors of yours move out?'

'Oh yes. Two weeks ago, thank God.' She smiled and didn't elaborate; he didn't need to know that the replacements were shaping up to be a hundred times worse. The last family had played Eminem pretty loudly, quite often. The new lot made them look like rank amateurs. In the last fortnight there had been half a dozen major fights, the police had been round most nights, and the family's dogs barked nonstop. Worst of all, Eminem had been replaced by Celine Dion and Josh Groban.

Given the choice, Ellie would have welcomed Eminem back with open arms. But never mind that, seeing as she was highly unlikely to be given the choice. Before Tony could start asking questions about the new neighbors she said, 'Oh, I didn't tell you, I'm redecorating the living room!' See? He wasn't the only one capable of changing the subject. She launched into telling him about last night's disastrous battle with the wallpaper, turning it into a funny story and leaving out the bit where Jamie had turned up, because that was her guilty secret. Lots of people, following a bereavement, talked to the loved one they'd lost. She knew that, had been told many times that it was a completely normal thing to do. What was less normal, it appeared, was having the dead person talk back.

———

Zack McLaren had arranged this lunch meeting with the director of an IT company he might soon be doing lucrative business with. Normally he was able to concentrate on the subject in hand with no difficulty, but today was proving to be different. Earlier, as he'd been standing outside the restaurant taking a phone call, a girl in a pink coat had caught his eye as she headed down the street towards him. Her hair was long and dark, her eyes light brown, her cheeks rosy, and the effect she'd had on him was extraordinary; he couldn't stop looking at her. Whoever she was, he wanted to know more. Heavens, what a weird feeling; he'd never experienced anything like this before.

As she passed him, Zack caught a waft of her perfume, something fresh and herby, unfamiliar but instantly leaving an impression. He turned, watching the back view of her glossy hair, fitted pink coat, and long legs in black tights. Incredible legs, actually. His heart, unbelievably, was thudding in his chest. What was *happening* to him? Then, realizing where the incredible legs were taking her, the thudding turned into a gallop; she was heading into the Ivy…

Hurriedly ending his call, Zack followed her inside. Just in time to see her being warmly greeted by someone he did recognize.

Now, an hour and a half later, he was still struggling to pay attention to what his lunch companion was saying. Across the room sat the girl in the pink coat, now minus her pink coat and wearing a thin wool dress the color of Parma violets. She wasn't the most stunningly beautiful girl he'd ever seen but she was making him feel as if she was. If she'd been having lunch with a female friend, he would have approached her, introduced himself, said something or other—God only knows what, he'd never done anything like that before in his life—and found out who she was. He would have given her his card, asked her to call him, no, asked if *he* could call *her*, found out if she would like to have dinner with him sometime soon, hopefully very soon...

Except she wasn't with a girlfriend, was she? That would be too much to hope for. Instead, she was having a lovely, entertaining lunch with the actor Tony Weston. They were chatting together, laughing a lot, clearly well acquainted, and enjoying each other's company.

Which meant any form of approach wasn't likely to be appreciated. Instead, he was stuck over here, too far away to eavesdrop on their conversation or hear what her voice sounded like, while the company director sitting opposite him droned on about financial forecasts and—

'So what do you think about that, then?'

Shit. Typical. Zack snapped his attention back to the reason he'd come along to the Ivy today. Well, the original reason.

'I think it's... interesting.' He nodded thoughtfully.

'And what's the verdict? Do we have a deal?'

This was ridiculous; he was a professional. Nothing like this had ever happened to him before.

'Ian, I can't come to a decision today.' Chiefly because he hadn't the faintest idea what Ian had been saying for the last hour. 'I need to go over the figures again, have a word with a couple of other people. But I'll get back to you by Monday afternoon, and that's a promise.'

Ian sat back, took a swallow of water, and shot him a suspicious look. 'Everything OK? You seem a bit... distant today.'

What would Ian say if he were to tell him, if he suddenly leaned across the table and said, 'The thing is, there's a girl over there, a complete stranger, but just looking at her is making me feel like I've never felt before in my life'?

How would bluff, ruddy-faced Ian react to that?

Except it was a rhetorical question because they were two businessmen, here to discuss business, and he wouldn't dream of saying any such thing.

'I'm fine. Just a touch of jet lag.' He flashed a brief, reassuring smile at Ian. Apart from anything else, there was such a thing as street cred to consider. He didn't want to become a complete laughingstock.

By the time they left the restaurant it was three thirty. Out on West Street, Tony flagged down a taxi and Ellie gave him a hug.

'Thanks so much for lunch. It's lovely to see you again.'

'I know.' He opened the cab door and said, 'Hop in. I'll drop you home.'

'But it's out of your way.' Ellie shook her head. 'Honestly, I'm fine. I can get the tube.'

'It's raining. Let me give you a lift.' Amused, Tony said, 'It's OK, I can afford it.' Indicating that she should climb in ahead of him, he added, 'Please?'

OK, he was right about the rain. It was starting to come down more heavily now too. Relaxed by the wine, she gave in gracefully and climbed—slightly less gracefully—into the cab. It wasn't until they were on their way to Hammersmith that Tony said, 'Besides, I want to see this wallpapering disaster of yours.'

'Oh no, you can't come in!' The words burst out before she could stop them. She'd already planned for the taxi to halt at the end of her road. Each time she and Tony had met up over the past fifteen months, it had been in restaurants; that was just the way it had happened. He hadn't visited the flat for almost two years. Her skin prickling with embarrassment, Ellie knew he'd be shocked by the state of it now.

'That's not very friendly,' Tony observed mildly.

'I'm sorry, I don't mean it like that.' She shook her head, ashamed. 'It's just… you know, messy.'

He smiled. 'You mean there's washing-up in the sink?'

'It's worse than that.' Ellie felt her cheeks flush. 'The whole place is, oh God, it's all just a bit… yuck. I'd really rather you didn't come in.'

But Tony Weston hadn't got where he was today by giving up easily. He patted her hand and said, 'I'm not going to judge you, sweetheart. What am I, some kind of monster? I just want to have a look at this troublesome wallpaper of yours.'

'Please don't. I messed it up, that's all.'

'When I first left drama school and couldn't get any acting work, I used to help out a friend who was a painter and decorator,' said Tony.

'Oh, I didn't know that.'

He smiled. 'I'm full of surprises.'

'Hmm.' Ellie sank back against the seat. So was her flat.

Chapter 4

'JESUS,' SAID TONY. 'So this is why you didn't want me here.'

'Yes, well. Now you know.' There was nothing like a fresh pair of eyes—and ears—to remind you of what a dump you were living in. Mortified and ashamed of herself for having put up with it for so long, and most of the time not even realizing how bad things had got, Ellie watched him pace around the living room. A year ago, her lovely, gentle landlady, Moira, had died of a heart attack, leaving her son to take over the property portfolio. Less than lovely Ron had wasted no time at all filling the flats with dubious characters. It had been a while before Ellie had discovered that the council were paying him over the odds to take on families who were well known to them, chiefly because they'd caused so much havoc they'd been evicted from their previous homes. This, now, was their last resort but rather than calm down they seemed to want to vie for the honor of becoming the noisiest and most disruptive tenants in Hammersmith, if not the whole of London.

As if to prove it, what sounded like a rugby scrum was currently taking place in the flat upstairs. On bare floorboards, because their putrid carpet was currently occupying the table-sized front garden. Josh Groban was belting out something heartfelt at maximum volume. The two dogs were going mad. The matriarch of the family, a fifty-something woman with a face like a bulldog and a voice like a cement mixer, was roaring, 'If you two fookers don't fookin' stop that, I'll chuck youse through the fookin' window.'

'Is she talking to the dogs?' said Tony.

'Maybe. Or her sons. There are four of them.'

'And get out the way of the TV, ya fookin' junkies!'

'That'll be the two youngest boys,' Ellie explained.

'This is diabolical.' Tony was outraged.

'You get used to it.' Most of the time she managed to tune the worst of the noise out.

'And what happened there?' He pointed to the badly stained ceiling.

'Someone left the bath running.'

'As if the place isn't damp enough already.' Breathing in the musty odor that Febreze hadn't managed to dispel, Tony surveyed the bare wall she'd been working on last night. 'If you managed to put wallpaper over that mold it'd fall down again in no time. For crying out loud, this place is a health hazard. Haven't you asked the landlord to get it sorted out?'

Only about a million times. But why would he bother? Ellie knew Ron wanted her out; packing another family in here would allow him to crank the rent right up. She shrugged and said, 'I have asked, but—'

'Fook off yourself, ya fat cow!' bellowed a male voice, followed by a door slamming and the sound of footsteps thudding down the stairs. Then the front door slammed too. Tony watched from the living-room window as the boy, scrawny and blue-white in color, stood hunched on the pavement and made a phone call. Within seconds a gleaming BMW with blacked-out windows screeched to a halt. A window slid down, money was exchanged for a small package, and the car sped away.

'Don't let him see you,' Ellie said hurriedly.

Too late of course. The boy had already swung round. Spotting Tony at the window he grinned nastily, stuck his middle finger in the air, and spat on the ground before letting himself back in the house.

As he passed her door on the first floor, he yelled, 'Nosy fookers around 'ere, i'nt there?'

Peering down at the tiny front garden, most of which was taken up with spilled-open bin bags and stained carpet, Tony said in disbelief, 'There are syringes lying in the mud.'

'I know.' Ellie's neck prickled again, as ashamed as if she'd thrown them there herself. How must this compare with his multimillion dollar palace in the Hollywood Hills?

'Ellie.' His tone changed. 'In God's name, why didn't you tell me it was like this?'

She shrugged, unable to explain. On the scale of misery, losing Jamie had been a ten. Compared with that, having to tolerate undesirable neighbors had barely scraped a two. And if that made her sound ridiculous, well, too bad. 'You get used to it. It's just noise.' To distract herself, she had got into the habit of conjuring up Jamie and having a chat with him instead. It was just a question of tuning out the rest, the yelling, the door-slamming, the incessant Celine Dion.

'There are used syringes in your front garden. This flat should carry a government health warning. You can't stay here.'

'Fook off, ya gobshite, that's me last can!'

Ellie pressed her lips together. She knew he was right. And if she was a friend she'd be telling herself exactly the same thing. But what Tony didn't understand was that this was where she and Jamie had lived together. They had found the flat, moved into it as ridiculously happy newlyweds, loved and laughed, and had the best time here for over three years. The rooms were filled with memories and she didn't know if she could bear to leave them behind…

'OK, I'm not completely stupid.' Tony's voice softened as her eyes filled with tears. 'This is about Jamie, isn't it?'

Her throat had constricted. 'Yes.' Embarrassingly it came out as a high-pitched squeak.

'So the flat didn't used to be like this. But it is now.'

She nodded.

'You know what I'm going to say next, don't you?'

Wearily, she nodded again. 'Probably.'

'If Jamie could see this place now, he'd be horrified.' Tony's manner was gentle but firm. 'He'd want you out of here.'

'Owwwww, ya bastard, I'll fookin' get you for that!' There was a roar, a crash, and a shower of glass rained past the window, along with a spraying, somersaulting can of lager.

'He'd want you safe,' said Tony. Tilting his face up to the ceiling he added drily, 'Although your neighbors have timing, I'll give them that.'

~~~

Was this another reason she'd done her best to hide the situation from Jamie's father?

Three days after their lunch at the Ivy, Ellie found herself standing outside an imposing Victorian end-of-terrace property on Nevis Street, just off Regents Park Road, in the heart of Primrose Hill village. The outside of the house was painted palest yellow, the sash windows were framed in white gloss, and the front garden was small but well-tended, without a manky discarded carpet in sight.

This was what you called a Seriously Nice Area.

'Well?' Tony stood next to her. 'What do you think?'

'Honestly? I feel sick. I can't believe you're doing this.'

'Listen, I'm not doing it for you. It's a sound financial investment. Every time I come over to the UK, I stay in a hotel. It's a very nice hotel, but it isn't home.' Indicating the building in front of them, he said, 'I need a pied-à-terre, and this looks pretty good to me. But if it's going to be standing empty most of the time, my insurance premiums will shoot up. And I'll spend all my time worrying about squatters. Whereas if I have someone living in the place, keeping an eye on things, I won't have anything to worry about. Makes sense to me.'

The estate agent arrived and let them into the flat, situated on the first floor like the one Ellie had lived in for the last four years but otherwise different in every conceivable way. There were two good-sized bedrooms, each with a bathroom en suite. There was also a small third bathroom, a huge airy living room, and an ultra-modern kitchen. It was like something out of a glossy magazine. Everything was clean and dry, freshly painted, and sweet-smelling. *Immaculate.*

'No mold,' Tony pointed out. 'No damp. No Celine Dion.'

'Just as she was starting to grow on me,' said Ellie.

'Do you like it?'

'Of course I like it.' What was there to dislike? She shoved her hands into the pockets of her red jacket to hide the fact that they were trembling.

'Could we have a moment?' Tony waited until the estate agent had left them alone. 'Sweetheart, now listen to me. I can afford it. We'd be doing each other a favor.' He paused. 'James was my only child. What else am I supposed to do with my money?'

Ellie nodded. 'I know, and I'm grateful. But... it just feels like too much.'

'OK, how about this then? Say I buy the flat anyway. And you don't move in, and squatters take over the place, and they wreck it and cause all kinds of trouble and end up bringing down the whole neighborhood.' He shrugged. 'If that happens, it'll be all your fault. Everyone in Primrose Hill will hate you.'

She smiled. 'No pressure, then. Um, can I meet you downstairs in a couple of minutes? I'd just like to... have another look around on my own.'

Tony followed the estate agent down the stairs. She knew she was being ridiculous, but it was something she just needed to double-check. Ellie closed her eyes, concentrated hard, then opened them again.

'Oh ye of little faith,' said an amused voice behind her.

Turning, she saw Jamie leaning against the closed living-room door. White shirt, clean jeans, arms crossed, head shaking in good-natured disbelief.

Oh, thank God.

'Did you seriously think I wouldn't turn up?'

She exhaled with relief. 'I just wanted to make sure.'

'Well, I'm here.' He spread his arms. 'Ta-daaa!'

'Your dad's been amazing.'

'I know. He gets it from me.'

Ellie searched his face. 'So what do you think?'

'About this place? It's fantastic.'

'Should I say yes, then?'

'I think you'd be stupid to say no,' said Jamie.

Which was cheating really, because the words were coming from her brain. She was making him say them.

Oh well. He didn't seem to mind.

'Right then.' She nodded. 'I'm going to do it.'

Jamie winked and gave her the kind of encouraging smile she missed the most. 'Good.'

Chapter 5

'GOD, LOOK AT THIS place, it's like a dream come true, you're so *lucky*... oh no! Sorry!' Paula clapped her hands over her mouth. 'I've done it again, you're not lucky at all. *Ow.*'

'From now on, every time you say sorry I'm going to have to hit you over the head with a cushion.' Ellie put the gray velvet cushion back on the sofa and gave it a little house-proud pat. Had it only been a month since she'd come along with Tony and seen the flat for the first time? But that was the power of cold hard cash for you; with no need for a mortgage, Tony had simply put his solicitors on to it and the sale had gone through in record time.

And now here she was in her new home, surrounded by packing cases and so far not missing the old Hammersmith flat at all.

Well, it had only been three hours.

'OK, tell me what to do.' Paula made a show of rolling up her sleeves and looking efficient. 'I want to help. Shall we start on these?' Without waiting for an answer, she ripped the tape off one of the boxes and said, 'Just let me know where you want everything to go... oh... oh no, are these Jamie's?' Appalled, she hurriedly bundled the armful of shirts and sweaters back into the box. 'I'm sorry, I didn't mean it! I didn't know!'

Paula left at five. Between them they had done a fair amount of unpacking, and it had been kind of her to give up her day off to come over and help. Ellie was grateful, but it had also been kind of exhausting. Emotional, soft-hearted Paula had welled up on three separate occasions. Unwrapping a silver photo frame containing a picture of Ellie and Jamie on their honeymoon in Cornwall, she'd wailed, 'Oh God, how can you *bear* it?'

Watching from the bedroom doorway as Ellie had packed some of Jamie's favorite clothes away at the back of the wardrobe, she had declared tremulously, 'I don't know how you cope.'

And when she heard about Ellie having lugged three bags of Jamie's belongings down to the charity shop, she had wiped her streaming eyes and hiccupped, 'Oh, Ell, you're so *brave.*'

Like she had any choice. Ellie had found herself, not for the first time, having to comfort Paula.

Not even for the hundredth time, come to that.

———

The next morning Ellie didn't wake up until gone eleven, partly because she was exhausted but chiefly because her alarm clock was still packed away in one of the boxes she hadn't got round to tackling yet. The good news was that she had three days off work, so it didn't matter. In her white terry-cloth dressing gown, she sipped a mug of tea and stood at the window gazing across the street. The sun was shining, glinting off the polished windows of the houses opposite. Tiny wrought-iron balconies bore potted plants, and well-tended window boxes abounded. Even the air seemed cleaner here in Primrose Hill. The street was lined with gleaming upmarket vehicles. A glossy fifty-something brunette in sprayed-on jeans jumped down from a black four-by-four, slung an expensive-looking bag over her shoulder, and sashayed off in the direction of the shops. A yummy mummy pushed a state-of-the-art buggy along the pavement. Further along the road, a black and gold chaise longue was being carefully unloaded from a smart bottle-green delivery van.

Ellie mentally compared this with her old street. Yesterday as she'd been in the process of moving out, she'd seen a used condom lying on the ground by the front gate. Instead of being repulsed, her initial response had been relief that someone had at least bothered to use one.

She leaned against the windowsill and admired the clean, litter-free scene. Now another van had drawn up, a tulip-pink one this time, and a vast cellophane-wrapped bouquet of lilies was being delivered to the house next to the one receiving the chaise longue.

Crikey, was she going to fit in here or would she feel awkward and out of place? What if it was *too* genteel and perfect?

The next moment a taxi drew up, an emerald-green front door swung open, and a blonde raced out of the house directly opposite. For a moment Ellie thought it was a skinny boy in a white T-shirt and low-slung combats, a male hairdresser perhaps, with his hair bleached silver-white and cut in a super-short, choppy crop. But no, it was a female; when the figure turned, she saw the bright red lipstick, dangling earrings, and jewel-encrusted shoulder bag. And OK, maybe that didn't prove anything conclusively, but if it was a boy he'd have taken the trouble to stuff his bra with socks.

As Ellie watched, the girl suddenly screeched to a halt, signaled to the cab driver to wait, let herself back into the house, and reappeared twenty seconds later triumphantly waving her mobile phone and slamming the door shut behind her. Then she threw herself into the back of the cab and disappeared off up the road.

Leaving something small and glittery swinging from the lock on the front door.

Whoops.

Were the residents of Primrose Hill really as relaxed about security as those in village communities in the nineteen fifties?

Just in case they weren't, Ellie left her coffee mug on the windowsill, fastened the tie belt on her dressing gown, ran downstairs to the ground floor, and let herself out.

Better safe than sorry.

The edges of the dressing gown flapped around a bit as she hurried across the road. The tarmac was cold beneath her bare feet. A passing teenager in a gray hoodie, having also spotted the key ring dangling from the lock, had abandoned his bike on the pavement and was heading for the emerald-green front door.

Ellie sprinted past him and snatched the keys a millisecond before he could reach them. Looked like Primrose Hill wasn't so different from Hammersmith after all. Startled, the boy blurted out, 'I wasn't going to do anything, honest. I'd've taken them to the police station.'

He was pale, spiky haired, radiating guilt.

'Of course you were. But it's OK, you don't need to now.' Flashing him a cool smile, Ellie dropped the keys into her pocket. She felt like Wonder Woman. Well, Wonder Woman in a dressing gown and with a scary case of bed hair. 'I'll take care of my neighbor's keys. They'll be safe with me.'

The boy stared at her defensively, an opportunist rather than a hardened criminal. 'They'd've been safe with me too.'

'Excellent, glad to hear it.' She patted her pocket and turned triumphantly to cross the road. Ha, get her, less than a day in Nevis Street and already a pillar of the community! If she hadn't intervened, the girl over the road could have come home to a furniture-free house.

There was a whoosh of tires on tarmac and the would-be burglar sped off. The two men further up the road, who'd now delivered the chaise longue, eyed her state of undress with appreciation. The younger one wolf-whistled and called out, 'Bin sleepwalking, have you, love? 'Orrible, innit, when you wake up and find yourself out in the street.'

Ellie grinned and waved at them before letting herself back into her own flat. It wouldn't do to start lowering the tone of the neighborhood.

Upstairs, she showered and dressed in black jeans, a charcoal sweatshirt, and pink flip-flops. Before getting on with the unpacking she would take the keys along to the police station.

Except, where *was* the nearest police station? And if the girl came home and found herself unable to get in, wouldn't it be quicker and easier for her to pick the keys up from here?

Ellie wrote a note, searched and failed to find any tape, and ended up using the next best thing. Heading once more across the road, she unpeeled the backing off the Band-Aid and stuck the note securely to the doorbell.

Pleased with her own ingenuity, she then returned to her flat.

At two o'clock, Paula called from work to see how she was getting on.

At three, Ellie stopped for a Krispy Kreme doughnut and a packet of crisps.

By three thirty she had a collection of cardboard boxes, emptied and collapsed and ready to go out for recycling.

Twenty minutes later, in the middle of a complicated battle to get the cover on her duvet, the doorbell rang. Struggling backwards on her knees out of the duvet cover, Ellie prepared a cheery smile and went to answer it. Time to meet the girl from over the road and be welcomed to Primrose Hill. Plus, of course, she'd explain all about her encounter with the would-be burglar and how she'd seen him off—

'Hi, you've got my keys?' The voice over the intercom was breathless.

'Oh, hello. Yes, I have! Hang on, I'll just press the buzzer and you can come on up. You'll have to excuse the mess, I only moved in yesterday so it's—'

'Look, sorry, but I'm in a real rush, could you just chuck them down?'

Oh. Oh. Put out, Ellie took her finger off the buzzer and went over to the living-room sash window. Pushing up the lower half, she leaned out and saw the girl with the cropped white-blond hair waiting impatiently on the pavement. The moment she spotted Ellie, she held out her arms and yelled, 'I'll catch them. Quick!'

The keys were on the coffee table, held together by a multi-colored Swarovski crystal key ring. Ellie did as she was told and threw them down to the girl, who promptly missed and let out a shriek as they scooted into the road, inches from the drain.

When she'd retrieved them, she raised a hand in acknowledgment and called out, 'Cheers, you're a star,' before hurrying past the waiting taxi and letting herself into the house.

Never mind thank you.

Oh well.

Ellie exhaled and went back to the bedroom to resume her fight with the duvet. Five minutes later the phone rang in the living room. As she answered it, she saw the blonde girl emerge from her house once more, now wearing a bright red dress and matching spiky stilettos.

'How are you doing?' It was Tony, calling from LA.

'Great.'

'Natives friendly?'

'I don't know.' Ellie watched the girl dive into the taxi without so much as a glance up at her window. 'I haven't met any yet.'

That evening the emptiness closed in and even a visit from Jamie didn't help.

'You've hardly eaten all day,' he pointed out in that maddening way of his. 'Come on, cheer up. Make some pasta or something.'

She looked at him. 'Don't tell me what to do.'

'I'm not telling. I'm making a helpful suggestion. You could do that sauce I used to like.'

Ellie's stomach rumbled. He was nagging her, but he had a point. She made the tomato and red wine sauce, stirred in fried onions and garlic, and left it to simmer on the hob. God, there was nothing to watch on television. She felt herself weakening, her eyes drifting over to the box of DVDs pushed up against the wall.

'Don't do it,' said Jamie, effortlessly reading her mind. Of course he could read her mind; he was *in* it.

'Why not?'

'It always makes you cry.'

'And?'

He looked at her, shook his head. 'I hate it when you cry.'

'Oh well, too bad.' Ellie sorted through the DVDs, found the one she wanted. 'Sometimes I just want to. You don't have to watch.'

Jamie shrugged and left. She bent down and slid the disc into the DVD player.

Was this cathartic or a form of self-torture? Putting the box of tissues within easy reach, she pressed Play and sat back to watch Jamie and herself on the beach in Cornwall two years ago. Not imaginary Jamie, *real* Jamie, actually on the TV screen, captured by Todd with his camcorder as they'd mucked about in the waves, chased each other in and out of the water, and ended up rolling around on the sand. Back when life had been normal and happy, because it had never occurred to them that what they shared could be ripped away without warning and—

Bbbbbrrrrrrrbbbbb.

The doorbell. At eleven thirty at night. For heaven's sake, she hadn't even had time to start crying yet.

Bbbbbbrrrrrrrrbbbbbb.

Was this some kind of joke? In disbelief, Ellie clambered off the sofa and went over to the intercom. Curtly she said, 'Yes?'

'Are you awake?'

She closed her eyes. 'What?'

'Sorry, I know it's kind of late. I saw your light was still on. You weren't asleep, were you?'

'No.'

'Oh good. Now listen, was I a bit rude earlier?'

Ellie leaned against the doorframe, listening to the anxiety in the girl's voice. 'Possibly, yes, a bit.'

'Oh, bugger, I knew it! Did I not even say thank you for my keys?'

'Now you come to mention it, no, you didn't.'

'OK, so will you let me tell you why? The thing is, I was so bursting for the loo that I thought my bladder was going to *explode*. I could hardly speak, let alone make it up your stairs. When you threw the key down and I had to bend over to pick it up, I thought that was it, I was going to flood the road! And I'm not even exaggerating. I've never been so desperate in my life. So that's why I forgot to thank you. And I'm really, really sorry if you thought I was rude.'

Ellie smiled and felt herself relax. 'Apology accepted.'

'Hooray!' The girl gave a little whoop of relief. 'I've got something for you too. OK if I come up?'

'Only if you think your bladder can stand it.'

Chapter 6

Having pressed the buzzer, Ellie opened the door and waited for her visitor to appear.

Within seconds the girl with the cropped, white-blond hair came clattering up the stairs. 'Hi, I'm Roo! I bought you a little thank-you present. Only from the late-night supermarket, but everywhere else was shut.' Up close, she was tanned and goose-pimply in her strappy red dress, bare legs, and skyscraper heels. Bursting into the flat, she said, 'Ooh, smells nice in here,' before dumping her carrier bags on the coffee table and pulling out two bunches of bright orange roses. 'These are for you.'

'Thanks.' Ellie was touched by the gesture. 'You didn't need to.'

'Shut up. Here, this is for you too.' With a flourish she produced a bottle of Chablis followed by a box of chocolate truffles. 'And these.'

Ellie shook her head. 'This is way too much.'

'It isn't, it's to say sorry and thanks. And the reason I wanted you to have them tonight is because if I took them home, I'd end up eating the truffles and drinking the wine.'

There was something weirdly familiar about her voice. Puzzling to work out where she might have heard it before, Ellie picked up the chilled bottle. 'We can open this now if you like.'

'Fab, I love it when people say that!' Eagerly Roo followed her into the kitchen. 'Ooh, pasta sauce. That smells fantastic.'

She didn't have a noticeable accent but the voice was still ringing bells. Now, covertly studying her face, Ellie really felt they'd met before. Probably in her early thirties, slim and toned and with huge dark eyes dominating a heart-shaped face, Roo was strikingly pretty beneath the layers of makeup…

'Ah, the cogs are turning.' Roo took the corkscrew from her and began energetically uncorking the bottle. She tilted her head and said with amusement, 'Managed to figure it out yet?'

'Oh God, now I'm embarrassed. I *knew* I knew you from somewhere.' Time for a wild stab. 'OK, I work at Brace House Business Centre in Twickenham. Are you one of our clients?'

'Nope.'

Damn.

'I knew you weren't. Um, let me think… have you ever worked in a shop?'

'Yuck, no, thank God. Way too much like hard work.' Roo sloshed wine into two glasses. 'Kills your feet too. Unless it was a sitting-down type of shop. That might not be too bad.'

'OK, let me think.' Ellie was floundering. 'Dentist's surgery? Hospital? Hairdresser? Or did we meet at a party? Ooh, ever been to the Frog and Bucket in Hammersmith?'

'No, and I never want to. Sounds too slimy for words. You are stone cold.'

'Sorry, then. You'll have to give me a clue.' This was getting seriously awkward now.

Roo clinked her glass cheerfully against Ellie's. 'OK, picture me with long black hair down to *here*. On TV. Prancing around in a sequined tube top,' she added, 'whilst miming badly into a microphone.'

'Oh my God, I've got it!' Slopping wine on to the worktop, Ellie made the connection. 'You're one of the Deevas!' OK, even more embarrassing; they'd never met before, she'd just seen Roo on TV.

'Don't feel bad. I prefer it when people don't recognize me.' Roo tweaked her spiky white-blond bangs. 'Hence the hair. Anyway, that was way back. We grew up.' She rolled her eyes. 'Well, kind of. And we moved on.'

Crikey, the Three Deevas had been huge seven or eight years ago. Billed as the girl band with claws, they had been sparky, feisty, and full of attitude, the natural successors to the Spice Girls. Their songs had been played everywhere, their first album a triumph. One black girl with blond hair, one white girl with black hair, and one Asian girl with super-long eyelashes and no hair at all.

Ellie searched her memory bank for more details. Dolly, Daisy, and Mya Deeva, those had been the names they'd gone by. Their first single had been the fantastically successful, 'If I Loved You, I'd Remember Your Name'. It had to be bleeped because of the line, 'Men are good for a shag and a new handbag.'

But music was a notoriously tough business. Eight months later, Dolly Deeva had blotted her copybook when she'd flashed her boobs live on children's TV. Then Mya Deeva had fallen off the stage at a benefit gig and broken both legs. Finally, Daisy Deeva had given a tipsy interview to MTV announcing that she couldn't sing in tune, Dolly Deeva wasn't really a vegetarian, and their fat git of a manager needed to come out of the closet.

After that, the magic formula unraveled faster than an old sock. A year after they'd burst onto the scene, it was all over. The Three Deevas broke up and slid back into obscurity, and their fans found new girl bands to idolize.

Fascinated, Ellie said, 'You were Daisy.'

'Just don't ask me to sing.' Roo pulled a face. 'Because I really can't. Anyway, I'd much rather talk about you.'

But first they had to put a pan of spaghetti on the boil, to go with the sauce. As soon as that was done they headed back into the living room. Spotting the azure seas and white sandy beach on the still-frozen TV screen, Roo exclaimed, 'Ooh, what were you watching? *Mamma Mia?*'

Before Ellie could react, she'd seized the remote control and pressed Play. Belatedly, Ellie said, 'No, it's—'

'OK, not *Mamma Mia*.' Gazing intently at the screen, Roo watched as Jamie chased Ellie into the water, pulling her into a jokey Hollywood clinch as a wave broke behind them, showering them in spray. Todd, manning the camcorder from a safe distance, called out, 'You two, get a *room*.'

'That's you.' Roo glanced back at Ellie, then at the box of tissues on the arm of the sofa. Realization dawned. 'Oh no, you were sitting here all on your own, playing home videos, and getting emotional. Who's the guy? Don't tell me, let me guess. You're not together anymore.'

Momentarily lost for words, Ellie said, 'Um, well, no...'

'Ha, knew it! And he's the one who buggered off, that's obvious, because otherwise why would you be watching this stuff? Now look, this isn't doing you any good.' Roo picked up the box of tissues, tut-tutted, and put them on the floor, out of reach. 'Trust me, men aren't worth it. You just have to get on with your life. OK, so he was a pretty one.' She turned back to the TV and pressed Pause, freezing the screen to capture Jamie mid-leap in a game of beach volleyball. 'But he left you, so don't dwell on the good points. Be *critical*. Ask yourself what kind of bloke wears a T-shirt the color of baby's poo. And what about those legs? They're too skinny! And I bet he snored!'

Ellie hesitated, her mind racing. It was already too late to tell Roo the truth about Jamie; she would be mortified. What's more, she would stop being irreverent and funny and treating her like a normal person. It happened every time, without fail. As soon as anyone found out she was a widow, their attitude towards her changed in an instant.

Sorry, Jamie.

Aloud she said, 'OK, sometimes he snored.'

'I knew it!' Roo clapped her hands. 'And spindly little legs like bits of spaghetti. Just concentrate on the bad points and you'll be over him in no time. Trust me, I've had heaps of practice. I should be a relationship therapist.'

'You're right, I'm going to do that. Starting now.' Retrieving the remote control, Ellie switched off the DVD player with a flourish. She sat down and indicated the sofa opposite. 'There, I'm feeling better already. Come on then, your turn now. Tell me what it's like living in Primrose Hill.'

'Spindly little legs? *Like spaghetti?*'

It was two o'clock in the morning and Roo Taylor had just left. She was single, Ellie had discovered, but currently was seeing someone called Niall who looked a bit like Simon Cowell and was brilliant in bed. She loved New Zealand wines, DIY programs on TV, and MAC cosmetics. Her real name was Rosalind but her father had nicknamed her Roo because she'd been a bouncy baby. She still worked in the music industry, writing songs for people who could sing in tune...

'Excuse me? *Spindly?*' Jamie was wearing his bright turquoise surf shorts. Outraged, he pointed to his lower half. 'And you just let her say it! There's nothing wrong with my legs. They're *athletic*.'

Ellie carried the glasses through to the kitchen. 'Your knees are quite knobbly.'

'They have to be! They're knees; it's their job to be knobbly. If we didn't have knees, we wouldn't be able to bend our legs. *And* you said I snored.'

'I said sometimes.'

'Occasionally,' Jamie protested. '*Occasionally* I snore. Like any normal man. And as for her being rude about my T-shirt—'

'I'm not going to say I told you so.' Oh, the argument they'd had in the surf shop when Jamie had insisted that *this* was the one he wanted, and she had complained that it was a hideous cross between khaki and banana. Ellie paused then said, 'But I did.'

Jamie shrugged. 'And you didn't happen to mention I was dead.'

'I know. Are you OK with that?'

'Sweetheart, if it makes things easier, that's fine by me.'

This was the advantage of having a conversation with someone who wasn't really there; you could make them say anything you wanted. It was cheating, but comforting at the same time.

'I'll tell her the truth later.' Ellie finished rinsing the glasses.

'You do that. Are you going to bed now?'

She dried her hands and nodded. 'Yes.'

'OK, I'll leave you to it. Night, sweetie. See you tomorrow.'

'Night.'

She liked him to leave properly; trying to imagine Jamie lying next to her in bed didn't work and was just too hard to bear. She hung the towel over the rail and watched Jamie head out of the kitchen.

Oh, Jamie, where are you really? Haven't I been without you for long enough now?

Please come back.

Chapter 7

'Oh my giddy aunt, did you even listen to a word I *said*?'

In the sunny bathroom, Ellie pulled the flush and washed her hands. When she emerged, Roo was standing in the hallway brandishing the honeymoon photo in the silver frame.

'That was on my bedside table,' said Ellie.

'I know! You and thingy with the skinny legs! Look, it doesn't do any good to keep stuff like this out. You're just making things worse for yourself.'

'What were you doing in my bedroom?'

'Having a snoop around. I'm very nosy. It's OK, I don't go through people's drawers; I just wanted to see what you'd done with the room. And it's looking very nice,' said Roo. 'Apart from *this*.'

Oh well, it had been ten days since she'd moved in; she'd had a good run for her money. Ellie said, 'That was taken on our honeymoon.'

'You were married? You didn't tell me that.' Studying the photo, Roo said, 'Just as well you didn't have kids—they might have inherited those legs.'

'There's something else I didn't tell you.' Ellie took a deep breath. 'We didn't break up, exactly.' Another quick breath, because it was still a hard thing to say. 'He died.'

Silence.

Longer silence.

Finally Roo said, 'Oh God. When?'

'January last year.'

'Oh *God*.' She took another look at the photo. 'And I made fun of his legs.'

'Don't feel bad.' Ellie half-smiled. 'I used to make fun of them too.'

Back in the living room, Roo threw herself on to the sofa and grabbed a handful of Twiglets. 'OK, I'm really sorry about everything I said before. But now you have to tell me all about him.'

Had it really only been nine days since she'd met Roo? The first night they had talked for hours. Since then, Roo had taken to popping over the road most days and now it felt as if they'd known each other for years. The timing had been fortuitous; it probably wouldn't have happened if Roo's best friend Marsha hadn't recently moved to New Zealand, leaving her with a friend-shaped gap in her life. But Ellie was grateful for that; Roo was entertaining company, funny, impulsive, and with an outrageous track record when it came to men. It had also been an education pretending that they were just two single girls, living charmed lives in Primrose Hill, with nothing more to worry about than where to buy the best balcony bras and whether Chanel lipsticks were better than Dior. So she made two mugs of tea and spent the next hour talking about Jamie. She told Roo everything, about how they'd first met, what he'd been like, and how he had died. Roo asked to see more photos and together they pored over an album.

Finally, Roo turned and said emotionally, 'Why didn't you tell me any of this before?'

'OK, keep your face like that. Don't move a muscle.' Jumping up, Ellie took the beveled mirror above the mantelpiece off its hook and brought it over to the sofa. 'There, now just take a look at yourself.' She held the mirror in front of Roo. 'That's why.'

Horror, sympathy, pity... it was all reflected there in Roo's face. Seeing it for herself, she said, 'Oh. Right. Sorry.'

'It's OK. You get used to it. But it's been nice to be treated normally. Sometimes at work it just feels like everyone's tiptoeing through a minefield when they talk to me.'

Roo said at once, 'I won't do that.'

'They don't mean to, but they do treat me differently.'

Vehemently Roo shook her head. 'I promise I won't. It's just not the way I am.'

'Except you've just looked through a whole album of photos,' Ellie pointed out, 'and you haven't once made fun of how we look.'

'Oh well, but that's because it wouldn't be fair. And it might hurt your feelings.' Roo pulled a face, willing her to understand. 'I'd feel *awful* if I said something to upset you, after everything you've already been through...'

'Sshh. This is what I get all the time.' Ellie finished her second mug of tea. 'I'd rather you were normal.' She tapped her watch. 'And it's seven o'clock. Aren't you supposed to be meeting Niall at eight?'

Roo jumped up as if she'd been electrocuted. 'It's *what*? But I haven't done anything yet!' She was still at the stage where getting ready for a date entailed *hours* of painstaking preparation. Having leapt to her feet, she hovered awkwardly and said, 'Oh God, I feel terrible leaving you on your own.'

'*Sshh.*'

'OK, sorry, I'm going.' Roo paused in the doorway. 'Look, are you sure you're going to be all right?'

'*Sshhhh!*'

'Oh I know, but it's just—'

'I'm not three years old,' said Ellie. 'I can cope. Go and have a fantastic time with Niall and tell me all about it tomorrow.'

She saw Roo take this in. Finally. Thank God.

'*All* about it?' Roo said it with a raised eyebrow and a glint in her eye.

'You can be selective, leave out the biological bits.' Ellie relaxed; all she wanted was to be treated normally. 'I've forgotten what any of that mucky stuff's like.'

An email dropped into her inbox at lunchtime the next day. Still at her desk at Brace House Business Centre, Ellie was working her way through a mountain of reports waiting to be typed up. Paula had brought her a coffee and she was eating a sandwich she hadn't ordered that contained off-putting slivers of cucumber. Try as she might, Ellie was unable to understand how anyone could possibly like cucumber. It tasted wet. And green. And just… *eurgh*… cucumberish. Picking the biggest bits out and dropping them in the bin with one hand, she clicked onto the email from Michael, her boss, asking if she could put in a couple of extra hours this evening, to help clear a backlog of work that had built up.

Damn, how could she wriggle out of this? The last time she'd said no, Michael had launched into an interminable story about how, when his messy divorce had been going through, plenty of overtime had taken his mind off the heartbreak. The next moment, a new email pinged up on the screen and her heart gave a squeeze at the sight of it. The subject was Hi, which gave nothing away. And the sender was Todd.

Ellie put down the sandwich that she hadn't wanted anyway. A mixture of guilt and anxiety made her mouth dry. Why was Todd contacting her now? The last time had been four months ago, on the anniversary of Jamie's death. He had written her a brief, stilted email and she had sent an even more stilted one back.

It was all her own fault and she hated herself for it. Todd and Jamie had been so close; Jamie had loved Todd like a brother. And the three of them together had been a team. That they wouldn't stay friends for life had been unthinkable.

But that was then, before the unthinkable thing had happened, altering their lives for ever. Ellie swallowed with difficulty as all the old feelings came flooding back. Following Jamie's death, they had both been overwhelmed with guilt and grief. Todd had blamed himself; with a reputation for turning up late wherever he went, it haunted him that on that night he had arrived at the flat early. It was all his fault; if they'd left at the right time—the late time—the accident wouldn't have happened. He had told her this before the funeral. Up until then, it hadn't occurred to Ellie that it might have made a difference. But once he'd said it, the seeds were sown and resentment had begun to grow. His untimely arrival had interrupted her and Jamie. Thanks to Todd, they had missed out on the last sex they would ever have. And he'd been right about the accident not happening if they'd left the house thirty minutes later, because by then—she knew this for a *fact*—the gritting lorry would have been along to make the road safe.

By the time she'd come to her senses and realized that, of course, Todd wasn't to blame, it was too late. The damage was done, the awkwardness between them had been too much to overcome, and they had done their grieving separately. Three months after the accident, Todd had moved over to the States and Ellie had been relieved. She still hadn't been able to stop wishing that, out of the two of them, Jamie could have been the one to be saved.

It was shameful, unfair, and she hated herself for thinking it, but that was the way she felt. Basically, she was a horrible person.

Unable to bring herself to delete the message without opening it, she clicked on Todd's name and brought his email up onto the screen:

Hi Ellie,

Well, it's been some time, hasn't it? Hope you're doing OK and work is going well.

My news is that I've left my job here in Boston and I'm coming back home next week, going back to work at the London branch. One year was enough. Once I'm back, I wondered if we could meet up. I'd like to see you again, talk about old times.

Hope you'd like to see me too. Let me know. Are you
still in Hammersmith?
Love,
Todd.
P.S. You have no idea how long it's taken me to write
this email. I hope life is as good as possible for you, Ell. I've
missed seeing you.

Ellie sat back. There was that familiar feeling of dread in the pit of her stomach, the one signaling that something was going to happen whether you wanted it to or not. Like opening the post and getting the appointment for your next smear test.

But what could she do? Pretend the email had got lost in the ether? Change her email address? Todd didn't know where she was living now…

Oh, stop, stop. Hiding from him wasn't the answer. Besides, he could find her in five seconds if he wanted to, just by—

'Hard at work, Ellie?'

Shit, Michael was right behind her. Damn those Hush Puppies of his, enabling him to creep silently around the offices.

'Sorry.' Hurriedly she clicked the email off the screen, although he'd probably already read it.

'You know what company policy is where personal emails are concerned.' Michael had an irritating habit of sucking air in through his lower teeth when he was being 'the boss.' Ellie squirmed as he did it now, then squirmed again in response to his hand on her shoulder. 'But under the circumstances, I'll let you off. Todd,' he said. 'That's Jamie's friend, am I right?'

She nodded, bracing herself for the inevitable squeeze. Michael probably thought he was being sensitive and sympathetic but his touchy-feelyness, quite frankly, gave her the creeps. Amongst all the hideous aspects of being a widow, submitting to unwanted hugs was one of the worst. Michael felt compelled to comfort her, and it would be churlish and mean to complain about it. Poor chap, he meant well. What was she going to do, accuse him of sexual harassment? 'So, how about a couple of extra hours tonight?' *Squeeze.*

Plus, he didn't miss a trick.

'Um, the thing is, I'm supposed to be... doing something...' Oh, it was no good; she was rubbish at lying under pressure. Caving in, Ellie said, 'Well, OK, I'll do an hour.'

Michael did the air-sucking thing. 'We really need to catch up. Make it two and I'll give you a lift home.'

She hesitated and glanced out of the window. The rain had been hammering down all day. There were engineering works on the Northern Line. And waiting at the bus stop would wreck her pink suede shoes. 'OK, deal.'

Michael beamed. 'You're a great girl.' *Squeeeeeeeze.*

The moment he'd left the office, Ellie clicked back on to her emails. Come on, get it over with, then she could put it out of her head.

> *Hi Todd,*
>
> > *I'm glad you're well. Hope your trip back home goes OK. I'm doing all right. As well as can be expected, I suppose. Keeping very busy. Doing lots of overtime at the moment so not many evenings free. Maybe we could meet up when things are less hectic.*
> >
> > *Love,*
> > *Ellie.*

She pressed Send. There, done. When Todd received her brittle, stilted reply, he'd know she wasn't ready to see him yet.

Todd wasn't stupid; he wouldn't hate her for it. He'd understand.

Chapter 8

AT EIGHT THIRTY, MICHAEL pulled up outside the flat in Nevis Street. The rain, battering down on the roof of the Honda Civic, sounded like a never-ending drum roll. There wasn't another soul in sight. Everyone else had too much sense to venture out in such a downpour.

The lift home was welcome, the conversation less so. As they'd made their way across the city, cocooned inside the lovingly valeted car that was his pride and joy, Michael had opened up and talked at length about his loneliness. Quite movingly, in fact. Since the breakup of his marriage he had had to watch his ex-wife move on, remarry, and give birth to twin girls. In contrast, his own confidence had nose-dived and his one and only attempt at socializing had resulted in a slow dance at a club on a friend's stag night with a girl who had turned out to be a boy. 'See, nobody else knows how I feel.' His face was pale and earnest under the glare of the street light. 'Except you, Ellie. We're in the same boat, you and me. You understand what it's like.'

Ellie unfastened her seat belt. She was fairly sure she hadn't slow danced with a boy who was really a girl. 'I know, but things'll get better. You'll meet someone else. Anyway, thanks for the lift—'

'Don't go!' Michael's arm shot out and he seized her hand. 'Ellie, you're on your own. So am I.' *Eugh, knuckles being stroked!* 'We deserve to be happy, don't we? So how about being happy together? I'd never hurt you, I promise.' He was hyperventilating and edging closer now. Stunned, Ellie realized his mouth was puckering up, homing in on hers like a heat-seeking missile while his other hand reached out to clasp her by the waist and—

Click.

Phew, saved by the seat belt. Lamentably out of practice when it came to making romantic advances, Michael had forgotten to take his off.

'Michael, no. Stop it.' His face fell as she gently pushed him away. 'I can't do that.'

'No?' Ellie saw him mentally adding this fresh rejection to all the others he'd suffered in his life.

'Sorry. It's not what I want. But it's kind of you to… offer.' Oh God, his chin was starting to wobble, please don't say he was going to cry.

'Fine, I know, I get the message.' Michael sat back, his eyes swimming with tears. 'Loud and clear. I'm not your type.' He wiped his hand across his face and heaved a sigh. 'I'm thirty-five years old and nobody's ever fancied me. I don't appear to be *anyone's* type.'

You could feel sorry for someone, but not sorry enough to personally prove them wrong. Ellie said, 'Oh, Michael, that's not true. Your wife must have fancied you.'

He shook his head mournfully. 'She said she only married me because I had a three-bedroomed house.'

———

'Ugh, that's so gross.' Roo was paying a flying visit on her way out to a comedy night at O'Reilly's bar in Camden. She shuddered dramatically. 'What a creep.'

'He's not a creep, that's the thing. He's just sad and lonely.' Ellie paused. 'It was *slightly* gross.'

'You turned him down. And he's your boss. That's going to make things awkward at work.'

She had a point. Fending off a clumsy, slobbery advance, then having to comfort your manager when he broke down and sobbed on your shoulder wasn't ideal. It hadn't upset her because she hadn't been scared. But Michael was going to be mortified.

'Maybe it's time to start looking for something else.' Ellie had been vaguely considering this for the last fortnight. She had worked at the business center for six years now. Since moving to North London, getting to and from Brace House had become more complicated. Anyway, there was no hurry. She'd see how things went. It might be nice to work for someone who wasn't always resting their hand on your shoulder and giving it a comforting *squeeeeeeeeze*.

'I have to go.' Roo jumped up at the sound of an idling diesel engine outside. 'Are you sure you don't want to come along?'

'No thanks. Have you seen the rain out there?'

'Which is why I prebooked a minicab. Come on, give it a try. It'll be great!'

Ellie shook her head. 'I'm shattered. Being propositioned takes it out of you. I'm having a bath and an early night. But thanks anyway.'

'I hate leaving you on your own.'

Like a decrepit old spinster.

'And I hate you telling me that you hate leaving me on my own. I'm not completely useless.'

'I didn't mean it like that. But will you be OK?'

'Now you're sounding like Paula. I'm fine, I promise.' As soon as Roo was out of here, she was going to have a lovely, long chat with Jamie. That wasn't too weird, was it?

'Yes, but—'

'Go!'

Except Jamie wasn't playing ball tonight. For whatever reason, Ellie discovered she couldn't conjure him up. Probably because she was too tired. It was hard work doing it properly. She took a bath and tried again afterwards, but the concentration just wasn't there.

Then as if to prove her wrong, he turned up just as she was falling asleep, when she hadn't been trying at all.

'You're not being fair.'

Her eyes snapped open at the sound of Jamie's voice. And there he was, sitting at the end of the bed, watching her intently.

'What?'

'You know what I'm talking about.'

'No, I don't.'

He gave her a meaningful look. 'I *know* you know.'

'And you're going to force me to say it? Fine, then. Todd. He sent me an email and I sent him one back. I was perfectly polite.'

'You're not being fair,' Jamie said again.

'Guess what? I don't care.'

'Yes, you do.'

'What are you, my conscience?' OK, stupid question, she might not be firing on all cylinders but even Ellie knew the answer to that one.

'You can't blame Todd for what happened. It wasn't his fault.'

'I'm not listening.' She closed her eyes and rolled over onto her front, pulling the duvet over her head.

'Don't you think he feels bad enough?'

'Shut up.'

'He was my best friend.' Jamie's voice was gentle.

A hot tear leaked out of Ellie's eye. 'Go away,' she mumbled. 'I'm asleep.'

The little blue and white café amongst the row of shops along Regents Park Road was one of Roo's favorite places to spend an hour while she was waiting for inspiration to strike. At least, that was her excuse. The official line was that she was on the hunt for ideas for lyrics whilst also trying out possible melodies in her head.

In reality she just loved the buzzy atmosphere, the people watching, the mugs of hot chocolate, and the cheese and spicy mushrooms on toast.

Yesterday's torrential rain had power-hosed the streets; today the sun blazed down out of a cobalt sky and it was hot enough to sit outside in a T-shirt. Roo, giving her new sunglasses their first outing, was comfortably set up at one of the steel tables along the pavement and tapping away on her laptop. Anyone watching would admire her businesslike manner and air of efficiency. They wouldn't suspect that she was actually scrolling through photos of Richard Armitage, and reading her horoscope, and checking out all the latest scurrilous gossip on *Popbitch*.

But *looking* efficient, which was what counted.

'...So that's that, it's all decided. We're moving to Albufeira!' The dark-haired woman at the next table was proudly relaying her big news to her friend. Both in their late fifties, unshowy, and frumpily dressed by Primrose Hill standards, they were huddled together over cups of tea and plates of lemon cheesecake. 'Roy's going to play golf all day and I'll be a lady of leisure!'

'Oh, how marvelous, you'll have a wonderful time! I mean, we'll miss you being here.' Her gray-haired friend nodded eagerly. 'But you'll have a spare bedroom, won't you, so Jim and I can come and stay with you both! We could pop over every couple of weeks!'

'Well, ye-es...'

Roo hid a smile at the dark-haired woman's less than enthusiastic response. Eavesdropping was one of her favorite pastimes; she just loved observing the way other people interacted.

'So have you handed in your notice at work?'

'Not yet. Zack's up in Manchester today. I'm going to tell him tomorrow. He'll be devastated to lose me, of course. We work so well together. Is this cheesecake a little more *lemony* than usual?'

'Possibly. But he won't have any trouble finding someone else, will he? I mean, he's Zack McLaren. He'll be inundated with offers from girls desperate to work for him!'

The dark-haired woman gave a snort of derision. 'That's not what he wants though, is it? He wants someone capable of doing the job, someone trustworthy who takes pride in their work. Not some simpering ninny in a short skirt.'

Roo, currently wearing a very short skirt, idly typed the name into Google Images and watched as a series of photos popped up on the screen. Zack McLaren, it appeared, was an entrepreneur. Bloody hell, the bossy old trout worked for this man? He was a *looker*. Covertly studying her, Roo took in the sensible slip-on shoes, the 1960s perm, and the hint of moustache on the woman's upper lip. What was he *thinking* of?

Ten minutes later the woman daintily brushed cheesecake crumbs from around her mouth, finished her tea, and rose to leave.

'Well, back to work. Lots to do in the office this afternoon. I tell you something,' she added smugly, 'Zack's going to have his work cut out finding someone who matches up to me.'

Her friend nodded. 'You're right there, Barbara.'

'I'm always right.' Barbara beamed. 'Anyway, I'll be in touch, dear. Toodle-oo!'

How could Zack McLaren have employed someone who said toodle-oo? And whose ankles looked as if they were melting over the top of her shoes? Raising her sunglasses, Roo watched Barbara strut off up the road like a soldier on a route march.

Just before she was due to disappear from view, an idea popped into Roo's head that sent little zings of adrenaline through her fingers. Hurriedly shutting her laptop, she jumped to her feet and set off in pursuit.

Barbara had turned the corner. By the time Roo got her in her sights again she was halfway down Ancram Street. Then she paused, took a key from her bag, and climbed the steps to a white stucco-fronted Georgian-style house with a pillared entrance and a cranberry-red front door.

This must be where Barbara worked. Unless she'd been lying about getting back to the office and was in fact meeting her secret lover for an afternoon of torrid, passionate sex.

OK, it was probably where she worked.

Reaching the house, Roo rang the bell. The box next to the glossy cranberry-red door emitted a squawk and an officious, 'Yes?'

'Barbara? I have a message for you.'

'What kind of message?'

'OK, it's more of a proposal. Except not the marriage kind,' Roo added. 'Can I come in?'

The door was opened seconds later. Barbara stood in the doorway, her gaze flickering over Roo on the top step. Finally she said, 'You were sitting outside the café just now.'

'I was. Well spotted!' Roo beamed; a bit of flattery never went amiss. 'And I couldn't help overhearing what you were saying about having to leave your job.'

'Really.' Barbara didn't invite her in. 'Where's this leading?'

'Well, wouldn't your boss appreciate it if you could present him with a replacement when you tell him you won't be working for him anymore? I think he would,' said Roo. 'And I think it was fate that had us both sitting outside that café today.'

Barbara's pale eyes narrowed. 'Well, it's very kind of you to offer, but I don't think you're quite the type we're looking for.' She was gazing at Roo's abbreviated skirt, silver Uggs, and turquoise T-shirt with I've Had Your Dad emblazoned across the front.

'Oh God, no, it's not *me*. Ha, what a thought!' Roo waved her hands in horror; out of the two of them, it was a toss-up who was more appalled. 'No, no, someone else. The absolute opposite of me, I promise. She works in a business center in Twickenham, but this would be so much handier. And she types like lightning…' She waggled her fingers madly to demonstrate. 'Honestly, you should see her, she'd be perfect for here.'

'How old?'

'Nearly thirty.'

'That's younger than we'd want,' said Barbara.

'I know. But listen, I heard what you were saying earlier about girls wanting to work here. And this one isn't like that. *At all*. She doesn't wear short skirts. She's efficient and hardworking, and she wouldn't go gooey over your boss. I'm telling you,' said Roo, 'you'd be mad not to snap her up.'

Chapter 9

'YOU DID WHAT?' IT hadn't been the easiest of journeys home. Delays on the Circle Line had resulted in far too many commuters being sardined into too few carriages and Ellie had ended up sandwiched between two men who hadn't been introduced to deodorant. Now, convinced that their BO had wiped itself all over her jacket, she peeled it off and chucked it into the washing machine.

'I found you a job.' Roo had been waiting for her to get back. Now she was firing up her laptop. 'Probably. Well, possibly. But you said it was time for a change, so I got you this.' She pulled a card out of her left bra-cup and waved it. 'All you have to do is call this number and fix up an interview.'

'Where's the job?'

'Right here in Primrose Hill. Ancram Street. Five minutes' walk from here.' Persuasively, Roo added, 'Just think, no more getting smeared in other people's skanky sweat!'

'You have a way with words.'

'I know. That's why I'm such a brilliant songwriter. There's nothing worse than skanky sweat,' she extemporized. 'It really made her gag and retch, far nicer than some creep with BO, would be a super-cool guy like Ne-Yo...'

'Your country needs you.' Ellie nodded. 'You should be our next poet laureate.'

'Not many people have a name that rhymes with BO. Anyway, speaking of super-cool guys, take a look at this one.' Roo swiveled the laptop around so Ellie could see the screen.

'Who's he?'

'Zack McLaren. The one who needs a new PA. I'd volunteer for the job myself, only you need to be able to do all sorts of nifty typisty stuff. But what about him, eh? Pretty impressive? He's an entrepreneur! Look at those *eyes*...'

Ellie studied the photo. There was no denying he was an attractive specimen, what with that glossy dark hair and those film-star cheekbones. Beneath the well-cut suit he clearly had an athletic body. Nice eyes too. Next to her, Roo was visibly drooling.

'The thing is, it's like asking a vegetarian to rave about a piece of fillet steak. I can see that he's good-looking but it's wasted on me. All that stuff's just irrelevant right now. I'm not interested.'

'I know, I know, but he doesn't want someone who's going to be all over him, does he? Flashing her boobs and simpering like a teenager. That's what's so great. Because you wouldn't do any of that. You'd be *perfect*.'

'Well...'

'And if things don't work out between me and Niall, this one can be my first reserve.' Roo lovingly stroked the computer screen. 'He looks like he'd be fantastic in bed.'

Two hours later, Ellie reached across the coffee table and scooped up the business card. As she'd been leaving, Roo had urged her again to think about it, and now she had. She had also pulled her just-washed purple jacket out of the washing machine and sniffed it, and still been able to *sense* the body odor clinging to the fibers. This was the downside to having an overactive imagination. From now on, she knew, just the sight of the jacket would be enough to make her feel a bit queasy.

Whereas here was the possibility of a new job, close to home and where her past wouldn't color people's attitudes towards her because they wouldn't know about it.

Really, there was no contest.

It was only nine o'clock. That wasn't too late to call, was it? Ellie picked up the phone and pressed out the number.

Here goes...

―᯾―

The phone began to ring as Zack let himself into the house. After a long day of meetings followed by a three-hour drive back from Manchester, all he wanted was a cold beer and an hour of mindless TV before crashing out for the night.

Except that wasn't an option. Instead, he had a detailed business plan to put together and several letters to dictate. Peeling off his jacket and pushing open the door to the office, he dumped his briefcase on the desk and answered the still-ringing phone.

'Oh, hello, is that Mr McLaren?'

It was a female voice he didn't recognize. Zack kicked off his shoes and reached for a pen. 'Speaking.'

'Hi there! I'm calling about the job.'

'Job?'

'That's right. My name's Ellie Kendall, and my friend persuaded me to call you. I hope you'll consider me, because I really think we could be a good match. I'm local, very hardworking, my typing speeds are brilliant, and I—'

'Hang on, sorry, you've lost me here, I don't know what you're talking about,' said Zack.

'Oh!' She sounded taken aback.

'What kind of job are you applying for?'

'Well, working as your PA.'

'I'm afraid there's been some misunderstanding. I already have a PA and I'm perfectly happy with her.'

'Oh right, but... no, OK, I'm really sorry. My mistake.' Hurriedly the girl said, 'Sorry to bother you. Bye.'

'Wait—' But it was too late; she had already hung up. And what would have been the point in prolonging the conversation anyway? Zack's stomach rumbled, reminding him that he needed to eat something before settling down to the paperwork. An ice-cold beer and a ferociously hot curry, that was his priority now. Then he would dictate the most important letters so that first thing in the morning Barbara could get them typed up and sent out.

~~~

'So there we are. I know this has come as a shock, but rest assured you don't have to worry about a thing. I shan't leave you high and dry.' Barbara's tone was consoling. 'I'm going to devote myself to the task of finding you a worthy replacement.'

Zack looked at the official letter of resignation she had handed him before launching into her little speech.

'Thank you. Well, I'll be sorry to lose you, but it'll be exciting for you. And the Algarve's beautiful. You never know, you might take up golf yourself.'

Barbara shuddered. 'I can assure you I won't.'

He smiled slightly. 'And at least this solves one mystery.'

'Oh?'

'I had a phone call last night from someone applying to be my PA.'

Barbara closed her eyes in despair. 'That dreadful, pushy girl. I'm so sorry. She *knew* I wasn't telling you until today.'

Mildly diverted, Zack said, 'But you told her yesterday?'

'Of course I didn't tell her! She eavesdropped on a private conversation! Then she followed me here and said her friend could take over my job. She was most persistent. I'm afraid I ended up giving her one of your cards, otherwise I'd never have got rid of her.'

'Well, you could call that enterprising.' Barbara's reaction amused him. 'And the friend sounded very keen on the phone. Maybe I should see her.'

'Oh no no no.' Chins wobbling, Barbara vehemently shook her head. 'No no no no, trust me, absolutely not the type of person you'd want to hire.'

'But… hang on, have I got this right? You didn't actually meet the girl's friend.'

'Zack, I didn't need to. This girl had hair like a *punk rocker*, all chopped and dyed. And silver boots!' Barbara shuddered. 'The entire outfit was bizarre. And her T-shirt was obscene. Believe me, you wouldn't want to employ anyone who's friendly with a girl like that. No, no, just leave it to me. I'll find you the right lady.'

To tease her, Zack said, 'Or man.'

'I can assure you, it'll be a lady.' Nobody had ever accused Barbara of having a sense of humor. With a dismissive sniff she retorted, 'Men can't multitask.'

———

It was Thursday evening. True to her word, Barbara had drawn up a shortlist of six eminently suitable applicants for the position of replacement PA. Zack had spent the afternoon interviewing them, and it was safe to say it hadn't been the most enthralling three hours of his life.

All the ladies were super-efficient, incredibly organized, and vastly experienced. But if there was such a thing as crimplene overload, he was suffering from it. Even when they hadn't been wearing any, they still exuded the aura of crimplene. Each of them had been in their mid to late fifties, with sensible hair and minimal—if any—makeup. Smart interview outfits. Below-the-knee skirts. Low-heeled shoes. Clipped, unvarnished fingernails. Basically, Barbara had provided him with half a dozen clones of herself. Zack knew why she'd done it, and in theory he agreed, but the prospect of choosing one of them, it had to be said, didn't fill him with joy.

Fifteen minutes later he emerged from the shower and wrapped a towel around his waist. Heading downstairs to the office, he flipped back through the notepad on his desk until he found the page he was looking for.

There was the number he'd scribbled down, the one belonging to the friend of the unsuitable girl who had so alarmed Barbara last week. Smiling slightly at the memory of her reaction, Zack dialed the number. He knew nothing about the girl, other than that she didn't sound as if she wore crimplene.

It was picked up on the third ring. 'Hello? *Whoops.*' There was a clatter followed by a big thud. 'Sorry about that. Hello.'

'What happened there?'

'I reached over to pick up the phone and rolled off the sofa. Who's that?'

'Zack McLaren.'

'Oh! Look, can I just say I'm so sorry about last week? I really put my foot in it, didn't I? Your poor PA, I hope you weren't cross with her.'

Amused, Zack said, 'I'm never cross. Listen, you sounded pretty enthusiastic before. I just wondered if you'd like to come over for an interview tomorrow morning?'

'Really? Oh, wow, that'd be fantastic! But I can't do tomorrow; I'm catching the first train up to Glasgow.' She sounded genuinely apologetic. 'It's my gran's eightieth birthday and she's having a surprise party and I can't miss it. But I'm back on Sunday night.' Hopefully she added, 'Could we make it next week instead?'

Damn. 'Sorry, I've already seen all the other applicants. I promised to let them know by tomorrow.'

'Oh.' There was a pause. 'Well, I'm not doing anything right now. Apart from falling off the sofa. How about if I just throw some clothes on and come round in thirty minutes?' Another pause. 'Um, that makes it sound as if I'm naked. I'm not naked, I'm wearing pajamas. Oh God, this is too much information. Shall I see you in thirty minutes, fully clothed?'

Zack caught sight of his reflection in the office window. He didn't tell her that apart from the towel slung around his hips, he wasn't wearing anything either. Anyway, that was beside the point. 'I can't do it. I have a business dinner this evening.' He'd called her number on impulse but there was no way he would employ someone without meeting them first. And he was the main guest speaker at tonight's dinner so he couldn't be late. 'Well, we gave it a try, but I guess we'll leave it after all. Just a case of bad timing.' Glancing at his watch, he saw that it was eight o'clock. Seeing as his car would be here in ten minutes, he needed to get a serious move on. 'Thanks anyway.'

'OK.' The girl, Ellie, sounded disappointed. 'Well, thank you too, for thinking of me. It was nice of you to call. It's a shame we couldn't meet up.'

She had an attractive voice, clear and musical, the kind that would be a joy to listen to. *If you had time.* 'I'm sorry too. And good luck with finding another job,' said Zack. 'Bye.'

Chapter 10

'How's your new woman doing?' Next to Zack in the passenger seat, Louisa pulled down the sunshield and checked her lipstick in the mirror. 'Settling in?'

Zack nodded. He'd gone for Christine in the end, out of the six applicants, and she was proving every bit as efficient as Barbara. Christine was in her late fifties and uninterested in fashion; with bushy eyebrows and a penchant for pleated skirts, stylishness wasn't her raison d'être. But she typed so fast her sausage fingers became an actual physical blur. She also brought packed lunches to work and ate egg mayonnaise sandwiches at her desk, swilling them down with weird-smelling herbal tea.

'Still eating the egg sandwiches?'

'Every day.'

'Oh well, maybe she'll move on, give cheese and tomato a try. Can you pull up over here?' Waving her hand at the rank of shops ahead, Louisa said, 'I need a couple of mags for the journey.'

Zack's heart sank a couple of notches. He'd been seeing Louisa for almost three months now and she had a lot going for her—she was confident, glamorous, and strikingly attractive. But stopping at the newsagents, he had learned from bitter experience, meant that she would be spending the next couple of hours reading bits aloud to him from magazines. For some reason she thought he would be as fascinated as she was to hear the items of celebrity gossip, words of wisdom from relationship experts, and which brands of mascara made your lashes look longest. They were heading down the M4 to the wedding of one of Louisa's friends in Bristol and if he tried to listen to the radio she would reach over and turn it down each time she needed to relay some new and vital piece of information, like had he *heard* about Victoria Beckham taking up knitting? And why on earth would Russell Brand be having lunch with Kate Winslet?

He drew up at the curb, parking on double yellows behind a blue Volkswagen. Louisa, in her chic, pale gray wedding suit and pink frilled shirt, jumped out of the Mercedes and disappeared inside the newsagents on Regents Park Road.

Ellie was queuing to pay for her newspaper and a packet of Rolos when she glanced across at the racks of magazines and saw a cover featuring a large black girl in a gold bikini and a white-blond wig. The caption shrieked, 'Dolly Deeva: Bigger, better, and back with a splash!'

Only last night, Roo had been wondering how Dolly was doing these days. Ellie darted out of the queue and reached for the magazine, the last one on the rack. She'd buy it for Roo.

'Whoops, sorry!' Her elbow was jogged by another customer and the magazine almost slipped to the ground. Clutching it to her chest, she smiled apologetically at the elegant redhead in the pink and gray outfit, even though it hadn't been her fault. The redhead graciously accepted the apology with a nod and said, 'Where did you get that mag?'

'Up there.' Ellie pointed to the empty space and the redhead heaved a sigh of annoyance.

'You mean there aren't any more?'

'I don't know.' Was she seriously expecting her to hand it over? Ellie said pleasantly, 'I'm sure they'll have them in another shop.'

A couple of minutes later, having paid at the counter, she made her way out of the newsagents and paused for a moment on the pavement to flick through the pages of the magazine. There was the interview, spread over two pages, with Dolly insisting that her boob-flashing days were behind her and, what's more, she was now a born-again Christian who didn't go anywhere without her Bible. Squeezing between a dark gray Mercedes and a sky-blue VW Beetle, Ellie crossed the road and headed up the hill towards Nevis Street. From what Roo had told her about Dolly Deeva, she'd have a good laugh about that.

———

'There you are! I thought the car was empty.'

Zack straightened up. 'I was just sorting through the glove compartment. Found some CDs I'd forgotten about.' He showed her what he'd unearthed. 'And a bag of Liquorice Allsorts!'

'Ugh, don't eat them, they'll be moldy.' Louisa settled herself into the passenger seat. 'I couldn't get the mag I wanted, some girl grabbed the last one. *So* annoying. Anyway, I found some others instead.' She patted the three glossy magazines on her lap. 'These'll keep me going until we get to Bristol.'

'Good.' Zack slotted his long-lost Gogol Bordello CD into the machine, pressed Play, and started up the car. 'Have you heard this before? It's brilliant.'

Less than two minutes later, Louisa reached out and turned it down. 'Ooh, can you believe it? What a liar!' She jabbed her finger at the photograph of a well-preserved former Bond girl. 'She's fifty-five if she's a day, and she says she's never had Botox!'

———

'Zack, I'm so sorry. I just can't cope anymore. I thought I could, but I can't. It's too much.'

'Really?' Zack's first reaction was amazement; his second, relief. It hadn't occurred to him that he was that demanding an employer. On the other hand, *no more egg mayonnaise sandwiches.*

Thank God.

'It's my husband.' Christine wavered, her pale eyes beginning to swim. 'He's not... himself anymore, you see. He goes to a day center while I'm at work, but it's at night that he's really difficult. Wandering around the house, trying to find a way out. I'm just not getting enough sleep and I'm exhausted. So my doctor's told me to give up work. I can't tell you how bad I feel, letting you down like this when you've been so lovely to work for.'

OK, now he felt ashamed; he was selfish beyond belief. Zack shook his head and said, 'Please, don't feel bad. There's no need to apologize. I'm sorry about your husband. I had no idea. Of course you need to save your energy if you're looking after him.' Riddled with guilt, he realized that she did look exhausted; there were dark circles under her eyes. 'And look, don't worry about having to work out any notice. I can manage.'

Christine gazed at him and fumbled up her sleeve for a tissue as a tear brimmed over. 'Oh, Zack, that's so kind. But I couldn't do that to you. I can't leave you high and dry.'

'Hey, what's more important? A bit of typing and filing, or your health? In fact, why don't you go home now?' Rising to his feet, Zack reached for his keys. 'Come on, I'll give you a lift.'

———

'OK, this is another long shot.' Zack McLaren's voice echoed down the phone. 'You've probably found another job by now. But just in case you haven't, the lady I took on has had to leave. So I'm looking for someone else, and I thought I'd let you know.'

Zack McLaren. Was this fate? Sitting cross-legged on the sofa, Ellie put down her mug of tea and said, 'She had to leave after a fortnight? Does that mean you're the boss from hell?'

He sounded amused. 'I'm not, I promise.'

'So you're inviting me along for an interview?'

'If you're still interested.'

Ellie smiled to herself. Was she? Two weeks ago she'd been determined to escape the friendly but claustrophobic confines of Brace House. Yet once the initial embarrassment of having to see Michael again had been overcome, it had simply been easier to stay where she was. Lassitude, her GP had assured her, was all part of the grieving process. Sometimes you knew changes needed to be made but just couldn't summon up the energy to make them.

But now Zack McLaren was calling her, giving her another chance, and she was going to take it. 'Oh yes, I'm definitely interested. When do you want to see me?'

She heard him say, 'As soon as you like. How about now?'

'You're on.' Ellie was already scrambling off the sofa, shaking pins and needles out of her left leg. She might get there and discover she didn't want to work for this man. But some inner instinct told her she would.

Bloody hell.

Bloody hell.

It was her.

The shock of it jerked Zack back from the upstairs window. He felt as if he'd been punched in the chest... no, it was like someone creeping up behind and performing the Heimlich maneuver on you without warning. It took a lot to shock him but this had managed it. The girl currently making her way along Ancram Street was the one he'd seen at the Ivy. She'd made such an impression on him back then—*when had it been? Over two months ago*—that he could still remember every single detail about that lunchtime. He had even skillfully engineered the ending of his own meeting so that they'd exited the restaurant at more or less the same time. Emerging onto the pavement, he had watched her jump into a taxi with Tony Weston and had experienced an almost uncontrollable urge to yank open the door and pull her back out again.

He hadn't of course. He had controlled himself. Apart from anything else, this was the kind of behavior that got you arrested. Instead, he had stood there in the rain, watching the taxi disappear off up the road and thinking that Tony Weston was old enough to be her father.

But now she was here, walking towards his house when he'd assumed he'd never see her again, and the chances were that in less than a minute she would be ringing his doorbell. Because this girl, in her white shirt and narrow, on-the-knee blue skirt, was surely dressed for an interview.

Which meant she had to be Ellie Kendall.

Zack's mouth was dry. Emotional complications were the last thing, the *very* last thing he needed in his working life. Everyone knew that getting involved with your PA was asking for trouble.

So how was he supposed to deal with a situation like this?

Chapter 11

WHOEVER HAD SAID THAT getting pooed on by a pigeon was lucky had to be deluded. As she climbed the steps to the front door, a dollop of white fell past Ellie's field of vision and landed with a splat on the ground, just inches from her right foot. Darting belatedly to the left, she took it as a hopeful omen. Narrowly avoiding being pooed on by a pigeon was surely what counted as good luck.

She rang the bell and waited. When the door was opened, she knew from the images on Roo's laptop what to expect, but in real life he was taller than she'd envisaged. And undeniably impressive. No wonder Roo had been so enthusiastic. Great eyes, and there were those killer cheekbones. Hopefully he also had a sense of humor. Especially if Roo were to make a less than subtle play for him. At least that wouldn't happen as long as Niall stayed on the scene.

'Ellie, hi. I'm Zack.' He hesitated for a split second, then took her hand and shook it. 'Good to meet you at last. Come along in.'

OK, best behavior, *don't tell him a pigeon just nearly pooed on your head.* Clutching her shoulder bag, Ellie followed him through to the office on the ground floor. He was wearing jeans and a pale gray T-shirt. Roo would approve of that bum too. She might be immune to other males herself, but she could still acknowledge their good points.

'I've brought along my CV.' She took it out of her bag and handed it to him. 'There isn't much I don't know about running an office. My typing speeds and computer skills are good. You can test me on them. And I'm really hardworking.'

'Glad to hear it.' Zack smiled briefly. For the next twenty minutes he explained the nature of the work she would be expected to carry out. He dictated a letter and she transcribed it. He showed her the filing system, which was straightforward. He asked her about Brace House Business Centre and she told him she'd been perfectly happy there for six years but that now she was ready for a change, and it would be nice to work just a few minutes' walk away from her flat.

'Oh, and can I just say something else?' Ellie knew he couldn't ask her the question himself but she'd spotted him glancing at her ring-free left hand. 'I'm not married.' If it helped her get this job, she was happy to reassure him he needn't worry that she might announce she was pregnant and start demanding maternity benefits. 'And I'm not planning on having any babies either. That's not going to happen.'

'Right.' He looked relieved to hear it but was still watching her carefully.

She hesitated, weighing up the options. No, don't tell him about Jamie. The whole point of changing jobs was to make a fresh start and not be treated any differently than other people. *Other normal people...*

'Anyway, so that's it. I'm single.' Having made her point, Ellie changed the subject. 'Am I allowed to ask what happened to the last PA?'

That was when Zack explained about Christine. Concluding the story, he said good-naturedly, 'So if you don't have an invalid husband to look after, that's a bonus.'

This was good practice at being normal. Ellie summoned up a bright smile and said, 'Well, I definitely don't have one of those!'

Then he offered her a coffee and showed her through to the kitchen, which was all sage green and sleek stainless steel, and opened out through French windows on to a small walled garden at the back of the house.

But since it wasn't that warm outside, they headed up the stairs to the living room, decorated in shades of deep red and dove gray and showing reassuring signs of actually being lived in. There were newspapers stuffed untidily into a rack, an empty Coke can on the coffee table, and a jacket flung over one of the chairs.

'Have a seat.' Zack indicated the sofa and sat down on one of the chairs opposite. He was being polite, charming even, and he'd invited her up here for a coffee, but there was still a faint but discernible edge of reserve. Ellie wondered if she already had the job in the bag, or had he not made up his mind yet?

'Thanks.' She concentrated on not spilling her coffee.

'So, you live in Nevis Street. Very nice.'

'I know. And being so close would mean I could be flexible.' Selling herself didn't come naturally but she wanted this job.

'Excellent.' After a moment, Zack said, 'Share with other girls, do you?'

'Um, no.'

'Oh.' He shrugged. 'Just wondering. I mean, there must be a pretty big mortgage on a place like that.'

'I don't have a mortgage.' Ellie prevaricated, caught off guard by the direction this was heading in. She'd never been asked these kinds of questions at an interview before.

'Rent, then. The rent would be high. That would still be manageable, would it, on the kind of salary I'm offering?'

'Well, ye-es.' She felt herself begin to flush beneath his scrutiny. Telling him about Tony would only make matters more complicated, but he was gazing at her so intently now, she had to say something. 'The thing is, I'm not really renting the flat either. I'm just... you know, living there. Kind of... looking after it.' She swallowed and made an audible gulping sound in her throat. 'For a friend.'

There followed what felt like an awkward silence. She felt her skin heat up by a few more degrees. After several increasingly uncomfortable seconds, Zack finally nodded and said, 'Right.'

What had he done? Jesus, what was he *thinking* of?

As he had earlier watched her arrive, Zack now stood at the window and followed Ellie Kendall's progress as she left the house and made her way back along Ancram Street.

He had gone against everything he'd ever lived by. He'd offered Ellie Kendall the job and she had delightedly accepted it. If Barbara were here now, she would have boxed his ears.

But he hadn't been able to help himself, simply because of the way she'd been in his company. The reason he'd taken to hiring women like Bossy Barbara and Crimplene Christine in the first place was because his two previous PAs had developed unreciprocated crushes on him that had been an added complication he could have done without.

The difference was that this time, he appeared to be the one in danger of getting emotionally involved.

What's more, there was a good chance that Ellie was living rent-free in a flat paid for by the actor Tony Weston, who was old enough to be her father.

Zack watched her reach the end of the street and pause for a moment, illuminated in the orange glow of the streetlamp, before turning left and disappearing from view. When he could no longer see her, it almost felt as if the light had been dimmed. Oh God, this was crazy. He shouldn't have offered her the job. If he felt this way about her, he should hire someone else and just call her, explaining why it wouldn't be sensible to take her on and inviting her out to dinner instead.

But he could only call up a girl and ask her out to dinner if there had first been a spark between them, signaling the existence of mutual attraction.

And this was the precise reason he wouldn't have been able to do it. Shoving his hands into the back pockets of his jeans, Zack turned away from the window. He couldn't have done it because on Ellie Kendall's side, there had been no spark of attraction. None whatsoever. Which meant that if he were to call her up and invite her out, the chances were that she would politely but firmly say no.

Which would mean he wouldn't have any reason to see her again.

Which was just... unthinkable.

So unthinkable, evidently, that he'd had to offer her a job instead.

———

'Guess what?' Roo demanded two days later when Ellie met her in Café Rouge after work.

'What?' Did Roo seriously expect her to start guessing? But from the look on her face, the news wasn't fantastic.

'When a man sounds too good to be true... and *looks* too good to be true... the chances are that...'

'He's too good to be true?' For a moment Ellie panicked; did she mean Zack McLaren? Oh God, and she'd handed in her notice at work. Had Roo discovered something about him and was about to tell her? Was he a crook, a terrorist, a convicted fraudster?'

'Spot on. Cor-rect.' Roo was drinking red wine and wearing white jeans, which probably wasn't wise given her current state of agitation. 'Then again, why am I even surprised? This is my life we're talking about, after all.'

Roo's life. Not her own. Ellie slowly exhaled. 'Is it to do with work?' She used the term loosely; Roo's idea of work appeared to involve meeting up with fellow songwriters, singing random lines, and playing chords to each other for a couple of hours, then deciding that today wasn't a happening kind of day, musically, and going down the pub instead.

'No, it's more to do with finding out that my boyfriend is married.'

'Niall?' Oh Lord, and she was crazy about him. Shocked, Ellie said, 'Are you sure?'

Roo was spinning her silver bracelets round her thin wrist. 'Pretty sure, yes. Seeing as he's the one who told me.'

'You mean they're separated? Getting a divorce?' That was OK, wasn't it?

'Nope.' She shook her head. 'They're still together.' Spin, spin, went the bracelets Niall had bought her only last week.

'Oh no, what a bastard.' Ellie's heart went out to her. 'That happened to Sally from work a couple of years ago, except she only found out when the wife turned up one night on her doorstep. She was devastated. It was horrible. Why do men think they can get away with it?'

'Because they're men.' Roo took another hefty slug of wine.

'Well, it's his loss. And you're better off without him,' Ellie said consolingly. 'You don't need crap like that. Trust me, you'll find someone a million times nicer. What a slimy git. Good riddance.'

Roo flinched. 'Don't say that.'

'I bloody well will say it! He's a sleazebag and you're well out of it.'

'You haven't met him, though.'

'I'm glad I didn't! Oh, come on.' Ellie leaned across the table and gave her arm a squeeze. 'You'll be OK. There are loads of fantastic men out there, just waiting for you to meet them. Lovely men, men who don't lie, men who aren't married... ooh, I know, you liked the look of Zack McLaren, didn't you? When I start there next week I'll find out if he's single, then maybe—'

'Sshh.' Roo jumped as her mobile started to ring. Snatching it up from the table, she pressed it to her ear and whispered, 'Yes? Yes. No. No, I know. Yes, me too. OK. Right. Yes. Bye.'

The furtive look on her face told Ellie who'd been on the other end of the phone. 'That was Niall, wasn't it?'

'Yes.'

'And?'

'Nothing.'

'What did he want?'

'Just… seeing how I am.' Furtiveness was now mixed with defiance.

'Is that all?'

'Pretty much.' Furtiveness and defiance combined with guilt. Roo drank some more wine and paid close attention to the glass.

'You're still talking to him, then.' Was this how it felt to be a barrister, cross-examining in court?

'Looks like it.'

'Still seeing him too?'

'Maybe.' Pause. 'Yes.'

'Oh God.' Ellie shook her head. '*Why?*'

'Don't look at me like that,' Roo wailed. 'I love him!'

So this was why Roo hadn't liked her calling Niall a slimy git. Marveling at the power he had over her, Ellie said, 'But he's *married*.'

'Not happily, though!'

'Still married.'

'But it's not his fault.' Roo leapt to his defense. 'She trapped him.'

Ellie gave her a long look. 'You mean, like in a big metal man-trap?'

'Worse than that.'

'So you're telling me they have children.'

Two bright spots of color appeared in Roo's cheeks. 'One child. Only one. Look, he's not a bad person,' she pleaded. 'He's just trying to do the right thing. He was about to finish with her when she told him she was pregnant. He could have walked away, but he didn't. He stayed for the sake of the baby. But she's just been a complete nightmare. She's made his life a misery—'

'The baby?'

'No! The wife! Yasmin.' Roo's lip curled. 'That's her name. Isn't that just so… princessy? And she's a complete bitch, you have no idea. Seriously, he tried so hard to make it work, but it was just impossible.'

'So he's going to leave her?'

'Well, yes, of course he will.'

'When?'

'Soon.'

'Why doesn't he leave now?'

'He can't do it yet, not while the baby's still so young. He has to stick it out until it's a year old. Otherwise it just kind of looks bad, you know?' Roo paused. 'You don't approve, do you? Don't tell me I'm doing the wrong thing. You're not allowed to nag.'

'When it all goes wrong, am I allowed to say I told you so?'

'It's not going to go wrong. He's brilliant. I've waited *years* to be this happy!'

'But—'

'Oh please, don't say anything else,' Roo begged. 'When you meet Niall you'll understand. I *love* him.' She clapped her hand to her chest. 'And it's not my fault he's married.'

Chapter 12

IF YOU WANTED TO make grumpy Londoners talk to you, Ellie had discovered the answer. All you had to do was carry a huge cellophane-wrapped bouquet home from work.

'Those for me, love?' said the newspaper seller outside Brace House as she left the building on her last day there.

'Ah, thanks, you shouldn't have!' a taxi driver yelled out of his window.

'Cheers, darlin', they're my favorites,' said a transport worker on the underground.

'How did you know it was my birthday?' beamed a stranger in the street.

It was like living in Mary Poppins world.

Actually, it made a nice change, having her final commute transformed into such a jolly affair. Maybe lugging flowers around wherever you went should be made compulsory. Reaching Nevis Street, Ellie let herself into the flat. Tony was already here; she could smell his Acqua di Parma cologne.

He came to greet her. 'Hello, sweetheart. Are those for me? You didn't need to do that.' Delighted by his own wit, he relieved her of the cellophane-wrapped bouquet then gave her a warm hug. 'You're looking good.'

'You too.' Tony was over for a few days to meet with film producers and give a few interviews. It was lovely to see him again.

'All settled in now?'

'Completely. It's brilliant here. And on Monday I start at Zack's.'

'Great. How was your leaving party?'

Ellie began unwrapping the flowers. 'Emotional. Paula cried buckets. Everyone kept reminiscing about the past. They're worried about how I'm going to cope without them. I just felt guilty because it was my decision to leave and I'm really looking forward to the new job.' She had already told Tony this over the phone, but it bore repeating. 'He still doesn't know about Jamie, by the way. I'm not going to tell him.'

'That's fine.' Tony nodded. 'Don't look so worried. Whatever's easiest for you.'

He made coffee while she arranged the flowers in a bowl. Before heading out to meet the film producers, he told her about the project. 'They're pitching it as *Lock, Stock* meets *Gavin and Stacey*. They want me to play a lovable gangster who runs a line dancing club, keeps Chihuahuas, and has people shot if they annoy him.'

'I'd watch that.' Ellie snipped a couple of inches off the stem of a yellow gerbera. 'So are you definitely going to do it?'

'Maybe. We'd be on location in London, Cardiff, and Reykjavík. We'll see.' He added sugar to his coffee and stirred. 'By the way, I had an email from Todd the other day. He's living back here now.'

She concentrated on the flowers. 'I know. He emailed me too.'

'Have you seen him?'

'No.'

'Why not?'

'Don't know.' Ellie shrugged and snipped another stem. 'Just haven't.'

'Do you hate him?'

'Of course I don't hate him!'

Tony backed off. 'OK, no pressure. Just asking. So when am I going to meet this new friend of yours, then? The one who lives across the street?'

'Whenever she can tear herself away from her new man. Or when he's otherwise occupied.' Unable to hide her disapproval, she added, 'With his wife and baby.'

Tony said drily, 'Oh dear.'

Damn, what was she saying? Ellie bit her tongue; it was common knowledge that Tony had been unfaithful while he'd been married to Jamie's mother. Hastily she said, 'Roo's not had much luck with men. I don't want to see her get hurt, that's all.'

'What's he like?'

'No idea. Fantastic, according to Roo. Who knows?' The doorbell went and she felt a rush of relief; no more foot-in-mouth moments, no more talk of Todd. 'There you go, that'll be your car.'

At lunchtime on Saturday, Ellie caught the tube to Camden then headed along Parkway in the sunshine. Before leaving the flat earlier this morning to pay a visit to his tailor, Tony had said, 'By the way, I've booked us a table at York and Albany. One o'clock.' And when she'd protested that there was no need, she could rustle up something to eat here, he had shaken his head. 'If I was staying in a hotel, we'd be meeting up somewhere decent for lunch, wouldn't we? So let's carry on doing that.' Straight-faced, he'd added, 'Not that your fried eggs on toast aren't exquisite.'

He had a point. Tony enjoyed fine food and they both looked forward to eating out. As Ellie reached the restaurant, her stomach rumbled. She was ten minutes early, but maybe Tony was already here.

He wasn't, yet. She made her way downstairs to the Ladies', faffed about with her hair for a bit, and redid her lip gloss.

Heading back up the stairs, she saw a new arrival sitting at a table by the window. Her scalp prickled and her mouth went dry. *Oh God, no.* At that moment, alerted by the sound of her heels on the wooden floor, Todd turned to see why the footsteps had so abruptly stopped.

From the expression on his face it was clear he'd had no idea either. He was as shocked as she was. He looked older, more grown up. And he was wearing a dark green shirt and navy trousers that didn't quite go. Gathering herself, Ellie loosened her hold on the banister rail and approached him.

'Hello, Todd.' Did she look older too?

'Hi, Ellie.' He rose awkwardly to his feet. 'Fancy meeting you here.'

'Well, I'm guessing this isn't a coincidence. Tony asked me to meet him for lunch.'

Todd was evidently still wondering if he should try and give her a hug. 'He asked me as well.'

Trust Tony to take matters into his own hands. And he wasn't even here yet. Taking out her phone, Ellie called his number.

'Hi, sweetheart. Is he there?'

'Yes. Are you joining us?'

'Ellie, just have lunch with him. Will you do that for me? And don't worry about the bill.' Tony's voice was soothing. 'All taken care of.'

'You might live to regret that,' said Ellie. 'I'm going to be ordering the most expensive wine on the list.' She hung up and looked at Todd. 'He's not coming. I can't believe he's *done* this.'

Todd eyed her with caution. 'So what happens now?'

'I don't know.' Ellie closed her eyes for a second, hating the fact that she'd been set up. This wasn't a situation she wanted to be in. The last time it had happened had been during Jamie's funeral, when all she'd wanted to do was escape from the church and run and run. That hadn't been an option then, but it was now. If she really wanted, she could just walk out of here…

'What's that noise?' Todd looked incredulous. 'Is that your stomach?'

Stupid stomach, it was rumbling again like a cement mixer. She deliberately hadn't had any breakfast. 'I think I'm going to go home,' said Ellie.

'What did Tony say on the phone?'

'He wants me to have lunch with you.'

Todd said steadily, 'Why don't you want to?'

Ellie's toes curled. 'I just... just...'

'Hello!' The head waiter smilingly approached them. 'Your table's ready if you'd like to come through.'

Todd raised his hand. 'Actually, hang on, there may be a change of plan.'

OK, this was stupid. Todd was looking at her. The head waiter was waiting. The couple standing beside the bar were watching and listening...

Grrrrowwwllllll.

For crying out loud, had they heard that too? Had everyone in the restaurant heard it?

'Fine.' Ellie pressed her hand over her rumbling stomach in a futile attempt to muffle it. 'Let's eat.'

For the first five minutes they concentrated on the menu. Finally, when she'd learned it by heart and couldn't stare at it a moment longer, Ellie said with a sigh, 'Sorry.'

'That's OK.' Todd put down his own menu. 'Sorry about what?'

'You know. Everything.' A huge lump grew in her throat and she gazed down at the cutlery. 'Today. The emails. Not wanting to see you. All of it.'

'Do you know why you felt like that?'

'Because I'm a horrible person.'

He shook his head. 'Come on. You're not.'

'I am.' The lump in her throat was expanding and the pretty waitress was coming over to take their order. Pushing back her chair, Ellie said hurriedly, 'I'll have the duck terrine and the risotto. Just give me a moment...'

She clattered downstairs for the second time, locked herself in a toilet cubicle, and wept silently until the other female customer left the bathroom and she could let out a series of honking great sobs in peace. It was a noisy, messy, undignified business, and it went on for some time, but there was no hope of stopping it. Like a toddler's out-of-control tantrum, it just had to burn itself out.

God, what a state. Ellie eventually confronted her reflection in the mirror and winced. Puffy eyes and blotchy cheeks, just like old times. She hadn't looked this bad in months. Rummaging in her bag, she found her all-in-one compact and trusty lip gloss.

OK, still moderately scary, but it would have to do. If she'd known this was going to happen beforehand, she'd have packed her mascara.

'No need to say it,' she told Todd, resuming her seat at the table. 'I know.'

'Sorry.' He looked awkward.

'Don't be. It was just a bit overdue, that's all. Anyway, I'm feeling better now. Did you order?'

Todd nodded.

She glanced around the restaurant, saw hastily averted eyes. 'People are pretending not to look at me. I bet they're trying to work out what's going on over here.'

He managed a brief smile.

Ellie drank some water. It was no good, she had to say it. 'Can I tell you why I'm a horrible person?'

'Let me guess. Jamie's gone and I'm still here. If one of us had to die, you wish it could have been me.'

Oh God. He knew.

'Yes.' Shamed, she nodded, her knees pressed tightly together beneath the table.

'Ell, you think I hadn't worked that out? From day one?'

'Sorry. I tried not to.' She felt like a wrung-out flannel. 'But I couldn't help it.'

'And there was me, feeling guilty because I was still alive. Because why should I be? It's not a good feeling,' said Todd. 'I knew I wasn't better than Jamie. I didn't deserve to be the one who was saved. I've asked myself that question a million times. Why me?' His eyes were pain-filled, reflecting his anguish. 'And the thing is, there's no answer. So the guilt never goes away. My best friend isn't here anymore and I miss him so much... and I still think that if only I'd turned up late instead of early that night, or if I'd gone for a walk around the block like Jamie told me to, the accident wouldn't have happened.'

He'd been torturing himself with that too? Now Ellie was the one overcome with guilt. She reached across the table and took his hand. 'Oh, Todd, I miss him too. But it wasn't your fault.' She squeezed his fingers to show she meant it and saw the beginnings of relief on his face. 'It really wasn't. And I'm not going to be a cow anymore, I promise.'

Their first course arrived and the atmosphere relaxed. Now that she'd confessed to having wanted him dead and Todd had forgiven her for it, the tension between them miraculously melted away. The food was delicious but they were too busy catching up to do it proper justice. Todd told her about life in Massachusetts and demonstrated his Boston accent, which made him sound like the confused love-child of Loyd Grossman and Dick Van Dyke. Although working there had been interesting, he'd only transferred in an effort to escape his grief. But that hadn't been the answer and now he was back, ready to resume his London life, albeit this time without Jamie in it.

Then it was Ellie's turn to tell him about Tony's shock when he'd visited the Hammersmith flat, and his decision to buy the place in Nevis Street. 'I feel guilty that I'm living somewhere so nice, all because Jamie died.' She hadn't actually admitted this to anyone before; it must be how people felt when they collected life insurance and discovered they could now afford a luxury holiday.

'Tony did it because he wanted to. I bet it's made him feel better,' said Todd.

Maybe. Actually, she knew it was true. Their main courses arrived and Ellie described how trapped she'd felt at Brace House. 'People were nicer to me than I deserved. I just never felt normal. It was like walking around with WIDOW spray-painted across my forehead. So from this Monday it's a new job, a new boss, and a fresh start.'

They carried on eating and talking. She told Todd about Roo. In return he relayed how embarrassing it was, as a Brit in the States, to get into a tricky situation as a result of misunderstanding the meaning of the word pants.

Their wine glasses were refilled.

'Do I look older?' Ellie leaned closer, lifting her chin so he could see her better.

'No.' He smiled. 'You're exactly the same. Why?'

'Because you look older. Sorry.' She pulled a face. 'Maybe it's the haircut. You look… more like a grown-up.'

'I *am* more like a grown-up. I'm more mature. I've even given up watching *SpongeBob SquarePants*.'

Encouraged by this flash of his old humor, Ellie said playfully, 'So how about the girls in Boston? Meet any good ones? Meet any deranged enough to go out with you?'

'Honestly? More than you'd think.' Todd grimaced. 'More than I was expecting, that's for sure. It's the British accent apparently. They're mad for it. They think we're all dead posh.'

'So you're telling me you were inundated with offers.' Of course he had been; Todd was a catch. With his winning smile and cheery, laid-back attitude, what girl wouldn't be attracted to him?

'With offers.' He nodded, holding back.

'What does that mean?'

'You want the truth? OK, I went out with one girl. For a few weeks. She was… fine. Nothing wrong with her. But I just couldn't let myself get involved. Because I felt guilty. It wasn't fair that I could still be doing all that stuff when Jamie couldn't.' Todd shrugged and said simply, 'So I didn't.'

'Do the stuff?'

'That's right.'

'You mean have the sex?'

'Spot on.'

'What, you didn't even try?'

'Didn't want to try.'

'And how did the girl feel about that?'

'She was devastated, thought it was all her fault. Then when I told her about Jamie she thought maybe I was gay.' Todd took a drink. 'So I had to explain that I wasn't. And after that I was a challenge. Girls were falling over themselves to seduce me. And the harder they tried, the more I backed off. Talk about weird.' He shook his head. 'I've never been so popular. Bloody typical that I didn't get to take advantage of it. I bet Jamie was up there laughing his head off.'

How had she kept her distance from Todd for so long? He'd loved Jamie just as much as she had. Ellie said, 'I bet he was too.'

He leaned towards her, lowered his voice. 'Do you ever talk to him?'

Ellie's stomach gave a squeeze. She nodded. 'I do.'

'Me too.'

She put down her fork. 'Does he talk back?'

'No.' Todd looked bemused; the idea had evidently never occurred to him. 'How can he? He's dead.'

'Still speaking to me, then?' Tony greeted them on their return to the flat.

'You did exactly the right thing.' Ellie gave him a hug. 'Thank you.'

He patted her on the shoulder. 'I'm glad it worked out. Just call me Svengali. Todd, come here. Good to see you again.'

Leaving them to their reunion, Ellie went through to the kitchen and put the kettle on. When they rejoined her, she said, 'More like fairy godmother, the way you've been sorting out my problems.'

'Make the most of it, I'm only here until Wednesday.' Tony pinched a biscuit out of the tin. 'Oh, and your new boss rang earlier. Can you call him back?'

'He's changed his mind about taking you on. You're sacked already,' said Todd.

Ellie made the coffee, then phoned Zack.

'Hi, just letting you know I've got a breakfast meeting at the Savoy on Monday morning, so don't turn up at the house at nine. Make it ten instead. I'll definitely be back by then.'

'OK, fine. Thanks.' This was the kind of message she liked to hear.

Zack cleared his throat. 'Who was it who answered the phone when I called before?'

Ellie hesitated; why was he so interested? And to think it was women who were meant to ask all the questions. Anyway, it wasn't as if he could have recognized Tony's voice; it wasn't that distinctive. Easily she said, 'That was just my friend. Right, ten o'clock on Monday. Anything else I need to know?'

'Not that I can think of.' For a moment he sounded as if he did want to say something else but was keeping a lid on it. 'Right, enjoy the rest of your weekend,' Zack said abruptly. 'I'll see you then.'

Chapter 13

It was Monday afternoon, a balmy summer's day, and all human life was out here on Primrose Hill.

Well, not *all* human life. But enough to keep you entertained for hours. Following a morning of press interviews, Tony was enjoying being able to give his voice a rest. From his position on this south-facing bench, possibly the most spectacular view in London was stretched out in front of him. The sun blazed down from an almost cloudless sky. There were dog walkers out in force, and parents with small children playing games on the grass. There was a group of adults practicing t'ai chi. Sunbathers stripped down to essentials were stretched out on the ground, soaking up as many rays as humanly possible. Toddlers ate ice lollies and investigated daisies, teenagers played football, and a grandfather was gamely attempting to teach his grandson how to fly a kite.

Grandchildren. Tony, who would now never experience that particular joy, was speared with fresh grief. He watched the man try and fail to coax the kite up into the still air.

Don't think about it.

A Rollerblader swooshed past with a Labrador on an extendable lead. On a bench further down the hill an old man was feeding the birds with a carrier bag of seed. Straight-backed and lost in concentration, a woman sat at an easel, painting the view. Her hair was very short, her skin was coffee-brown, and she was wearing a long geranium-red cotton dress that covered a generously curved body.

Tony watched as her brush moved confidently across the paper, her bare arm almost dancing as she added color to the sky. One minute she was leaning forward concentrating on intricate detail, the next she was sitting back to survey the results. At one stage she smiled with satisfaction and he found himself smiling too, because the pleasure she was taking in creating the picture was infectious. From forty feet away he couldn't be sure, but he thought she might be singing to herself.

Over the hill behind her came a teenager pushing a buggy and attempting to kick a soccer ball for the preschool boy with her. The baby in the buggy was crying, the small boy running ahead.

'Kick it! Kick it to me!' he yelled.

Distracted, the teenage girl managed to get the ball over to the boy and he aimed a wild kick at it, sending it sailing through the air. In a flash Tony saw what was going to happen next. The ball followed its inevitable trajectory, the boy chased after it, the teenage girl had already turned back to attend to the wailing baby… and with a thud the ball hit the woman in red squarely in the back.

Oh dear. Even from this distance Tony saw the paintbrush go *splat* against the painting and fly out of the woman's hand. The boy, realizing he could be in trouble, abruptly stopped running and looked scared.

But when the woman turned to identify the culprit, she broke into a wonderful smile and bent to retrieve the ball from its position under her folding chair. Beckoning the boy over, she handed the ball back to him then rested a hand lightly on his shoulder as together they discussed the painting. Within seconds the boy was giggling and gazing up at her as if she were his favorite teacher.

As Tony sat and watched them, a gray cloud passed over and the temperature dropped. A couple of minutes later, the first drops of rain began to fall. The teenager called to the boy and he ran back to her with his ball, stopping to wave at the woman in red before they disappeared back over the hill. The woman waved and called out, 'Bye, darling.'

The shower grew heavier as the cloud moved overhead. The woman had already flipped the easel over to protect her painting from the rain. But she wasn't packing up her things or running for cover. Getting to his feet, Tony headed for the shelter of an oak tree. As he passed her, he said, 'Would you like a hand with your things?'

'No thank you, darling, it's fine. This rain isn't going to last long.'

Her voice was beautiful, velvety, and lilting. Tony said, 'You're going to get wet.'

Her smile broadened, lighting up her face. Running her hand over her bare arm, she replied easily, 'No worries, I'm waterproof.'

She was soon proved right; within five minutes the cloud had passed over, the rain had stopped, and the sun was back out. Everyone who had taken shelter re-emerged onto the hill. As soon as the woman in red had tilted her easel back into position and opened the lid on her paintbox, Tony made his way over.

Up close, her close-cropped dark hair glittered with water. At a guess, she was in her late forties, but her good Afro-Caribbean bone structure and unlined complexion made it difficult to tell for sure. She was wearing no makeup. Her eyes were an amazing color, the light golden brown of maple syrup.

Not that she'd actually turned to look at him yet. All her attention was currently concentrated on the painting in front of her. Or, more likely, on the crimson *splat* courtesy of the ball landing in the small of her back.

The rest of the painting was a joy, executed with verve and style, depicting not just the wider view over London but the individual stories of the various characters spread across the hill. Tony smiled, spotting the ancient t'ai chi enthusiasts, the jogger, and the Rollerblader with his excitable Labrador, the pair of them colliding

as the dog's extendable lead wrapped itself around one of the orna-
mental lamp posts along the path.

'Did he ruin it?'

'The little boy? Bless him, he was almost in tears.' The woman
shook her head. 'I told him it didn't matter a jot, and that it might
even make the painting better.' Taking out a pencil, she deftly
sketched around the splat for a minute or two. Then she sat back.
'There, see? How about that?'

Tony leaned closer. In the lower left quadrant of the painting,
a plump lady had materialized, sitting in front of an easel. She was
gazing in dismay at her own painting, which now sported the red
splodge, whilst overhead a guilty-looking seagull flew past clutching
a tipped-up pot of paint.

'Clever.' There was something about the painting that just drew
you in. Utterly drawn, Tony said, 'Do you sell your work?'

'Sometimes. Why, are you interested?'

'Could be. I like a picture that tells a story. How much?'

'One hundred and fifty pounds.'

Tony nodded. 'I'd like to buy it.'

'Really? That's very sweet of you.' Smiling, she continued
adding detail. 'In that case, you don't have to buy it. You may have
the painting.'

'What does that mean?' He was taken aback.

'Tell me, have you ever been given a present you didn't like?'

Tony hesitated. 'Yes.'

'It's a horrible feeling, isn't it? But have you ever given someone
else a present and known for sure that they absolutely loved it?'

'Well… yes.' He nodded.

'And doesn't it feel fantastic?'

'There's no other sensation quite like it.'

Turning at last to look at him, her golden eyes danced. 'Which
is why it gives *me* pleasure to give *you* my painting. If you enjoy it

enough to pay for it, it's yours. On the house. A little gift to you from me. When it's finished, of course.'

There had been no flicker of recognition when she'd looked at him. Years of practice enabled Tony to be able to tell when people were pretending not to know who he was. This woman, with her guileless smile and easy manner, wasn't playing any kind of game.

'That's incredibly generous of you. Thank you.' Tony shook his head. 'But you're never going to make the shortlist for Businesswoman of the Year.'

'Ah, but I know my painting's going to a good home. It'll be properly appreciated.' She loaded a fine brush with topaz yellow. 'That's good enough for me.'

'Do you always give them away?'

'Only when the mood takes me.'

'Where do you exhibit your work?'

'Nowhere fancy. Just the occasional art fair. And online.' Leaning closer to the easel, she painted a child's sundress.

'What's your name?'

'Martha.'

'I'm going to need more than that,' said Tony, 'if I'm going to look you up on the Internet.'

She burst out laughing. 'Sorry, I'm a hopeless case. I'm Martha Daines. Now, are you local? Could you be here tomorrow afternoon?'

'After two, no problem.' He had an interview at twelve thirty.

'See you tomorrow, then. I'll bring it with me. And your name is?'

'Tony.' She didn't have a clue.

'Tony. It's been lovely to meet you. Thank you for liking my work.' Bracelets jangled on her wrist as she waved her paintbrush at him. 'Bye!'

Chapter 14

IT WAS ALMOST THE end of her first day. With all the new information she was absorbing, Ellie felt as if her head was ready to explode. Zack had been in and out of the house, receiving visits from clients and disappearing to meet with others. His working life was chaotic and his phone never seemed to stop ringing. She was typing up reports, fielding calls, making travel arrangements for upcoming trips to Zurich and Madrid, and familiarizing herself with the all-important business diary, as well as the general workings of the office.

Zack was upstairs taking a conference call when the doorbell went at ten past five. Opening the front door, Ellie found herself face to face with a polished, sheeny-looking redhead in a sage green, fitted linen dress.

'Well, hello. So you're the new girl.' Her mascaraed lashes batted as she carried out a comprehensive up-and-down. 'Alice?'

'Ellie.'

'Right. Bit of a change from Barbara. I'm Louisa, I expect Zack's mentioned me.'

He hadn't, but Ellie diplomatically didn't say so. She recognized Louisa from the newsagents the other week and wasn't at all surprised that Louisa hadn't, in turn, recognized her. She didn't seem like the kind of person who would. And presumably she was Zack's girlfriend. Bad luck for Roo then, who had been keen to find out if he was single.

Then they heard footsteps on the staircase and, conference call evidently over, Zack appeared.

'Darling, *hi*.' Louisa moved forward to greet him with a kiss that announced, loud and clear, that he belonged to her. Or she would have done if Zack hadn't leaned back and turned his head slightly, preventing the public display of affection. Or ownership. Ellie wondered if it would save all sorts of hassle if she just said, 'Look, it's OK, you don't have to worry about me, I'm really not after him.'

But no, it was hardly the kind of thing you could announce. Instead she said, 'I've booked the flights and the hotels, and the letters are all ready for signing.'

'Great, thanks. Come on through.' Leading the way into the kitchen, Zack said, 'It's time for you to meet someone you're going to get to know pretty well.'

'Who?'

He grinned. 'The love of my life.'

Ellie guessed who it was by the way Louisa rolled her eyes. During her interview Zack had asked how she felt about dogs. He'd then gone on to explain about Elmo, but she hadn't seen him yet. Now she was about to.

'Geraldine's back from visiting friends in Brighton. She just called to say he's coming over.' Somewhere outside they heard a rhythmic clattering noise. Zack paused then said, 'Five… four… three…'

'He'd better not be muddy,' warned Louisa.

'Two… one…'

Another clatter, this time closer to hand, then the dog flap in the back door swung open and Louisa backed into a corner as a disheveled-looking dog burst through into the kitchen. Yelping with joy, he danced around Zack for a few ecstatic seconds before launching himself into his arms.

'I'm not scared,' said Louisa. 'It's just these stockings are eight denier. They cost a fortune.'

So this was Elmo, Zack's true love. A three-year-old wild-haired terrier cross with attitude, Elmo resembled nothing so much as a teenager after a hard week of partying in the mud at Glastonbury. He had button-bright eyes, lopsided ears, and a jaunty manner. Not to mention bushy eyebrows and a straggly beard. As he squirmed in Zack's arms, he did exaggerated double takes of delight.

Hmm, no wonder Louisa was looking put out.

'I'll wait upstairs,' she announced. 'Don't be long, OK? We're meeting the Drewetts at six fifteen.'

'I'll be up soon.' Was it her imagination or did Zack visibly relax the moment Louisa was out of the room? Turning round, he pointed and said, 'Elmo, say hello to Ellie.'

It would have been extra impressive if Elmo had actually said hello back. But she was still charmed by the way he snuffled and wagged his tail and gave every sign of being thrilled to meet her. Zack lowered him to the ground and Ellie knelt to greet the little dog properly.

'He's gorgeous! Hello, baby, I'm going to be friends with you! You are *fab*.' She blew kisses as Elmo rested his front paws in her hands and excitedly licked her neck. Looking up, she said, 'And he doesn't get confused, living in two houses?'

Because Elmo was a timeshare property. Two years ago, Zack's neighbor Geraldine had said how much she'd love to have a dog, but her bad leg made it impractical. Zack, in turn, had told her that he'd always wanted a dog but the hours he worked and his frequent trips abroad meant it would be unfair on any animal. The next day, in true entrepreneurial fashion, he had come up with the solution and a week after that Elmo had entered their lives.

'It works fine. He has the best of both worlds. Geraldine's at home most of the time. We have matching dog flaps into our kitchens.' Nodding out of the window, Zack indicated the specially lowered section of wall separating their gardens. 'Elmo just hops over when he fancies a change of scenery. If I'm working too hard, he'll go and see Geraldine for a bit of company. If he wants a walk, he comes back here. We share vet's fees and make sure we keep track of who's feeding him, otherwise he'd end up the size of a barrel.' His gaze softened like a proud father's as he watched her scratch the dog's comical ears. 'He likes you.'

'Well, good. I like you too.' Ellie kissed Elmo's whiskery eyebrows and got her chin licked in return. 'You're so… huggy!'

'Zack?' Louisa's voice drifted down the stairs. 'Come on, you need to get changed before we leave. We mustn't be late.'

'So, first day at work. How did it go?'

'Pretty good. Busy.' Ellie was in bed; she put down her book and looked at Jamie, lying on his side across the end of the bed with his head supported on one elbow. 'I think I'm going to enjoy it.'

'You're moving on.' Jamie's gaze was intent.

'Your dad said that. But I don't feel as if I am.' It was hard to explain, but part of her didn't want to move on; the prospect made her feel guilty. 'I still love you. I'm never going to stop. It's a new job, that's all. With people who aren't going to treat me differently because of what happened.'

Jamie said easily, 'Zack sounds all right.'

'He is all right.'

'What's the girlfriend like?'

'Louisa? Confident on the surface, insecure underneath. Wishes I was thirty years older. It's funny, she doesn't trust me. If only she knew.'

Jamie grinned and flicked back his streaky blond hair. 'If only she knew what a sex maniac you are?'

'I meant what a eunuch I am. Zack couldn't be safer with a lesbian nun.'

'I used to know a joke about a lesbian nun.'

Ellie pulled a face. 'I know you did.'

'I can't remember how it went. You'll have to ask Todd.'

'But then he might tell me.'

'Don't be like that. My jokes are hilarious.' Jamie pretended to make a grab for her feet beneath the duvet, because in the old days he would have tickled them mercilessly by way of punishment. But since that couldn't happen now, all he could do was pretend.

'Todd's coming over at the weekend.'

'Good. I'm glad you two are talking again.'

Ellie felt warm and comforted; of course he was glad. Wasn't that why she'd done it, safe in the knowledge that it was what Jamie would have wanted?

'It was your dad. He was the one who set it up.'

'But you did your bit. You made the effort. I'm proud of you.'

'Don't make me cry.'

'Oh, baby. I love you.'

'Me too.' She wiped away the tear that was sliding out of the corner of her eye.

'You're doing OK. Get some sleep now. Night, baby.'

Ellie closed her eyes and felt the aching loneliness well up inside her chest. 'Night.'

Chapter 15

HE COULDN'T REMEMBER THE last time he'd looked forward so much to seeing someone again. It almost felt like a date. As he made his way up the hill, Tony had to force himself to slow down. He wanted to see if she was there but didn't want to be panting and gasping for breath when he reached the top. Or red in the face. Apart from anything else, the color would clash with his purple shirt.

Then he climbed the last section of the hill and there she was, sitting in the same spot as yesterday but this time with her easel facing further to the west. Tony stopped to look at her and felt his heart lift. She was wearing a long emerald-green dress today, with some kind of bright pink necklace around her throat and flat pink sandals on her feet. There was something about the way she held herself, the sense of how supremely comfortable she was in her own skin, that was utterly beguiling. Just looking at her made him want to smile. And not because she was giving him a free painting…

Martha spotted him as he made his way towards her. She waved her paintbrush in greeting and called out, 'Hooray, you turned up!'

Her voice was mesmerizing, warm and velvety and redolent of the Caribbean.

'Did you think I wouldn't?' Up close, he saw that the necklace was composed of huge uneven pebble-shaped beads painted a dazzling shade of fuchsia pink.

'No, I thought you would.' Martha smiled. 'I hoped you would. Otherwise I'd have lugged this thing all the way for nothing.'

Leaning to one side, she reached down for a flat canvas bag lying on the grass.

Tony's heart began to beat faster as she slid her smooth brown arm into the oversized bag and drew out the completed painting, professionally double-mounted on ivory bevel-edged board.

'I still can't believe you're doing this. You didn't have to have it mounted.'

'Oh, shush, that was no bother at all, I did it myself.' Her eyes sparkled. 'I'm a demon with a Stanley knife. Anyway, it finishes it off nicely. You can choose your own frame. Here, take it. Have a proper look. It's yours.'

The added pen and ink detail enhanced the quirky characters she had observed yesterday afternoon. The result was charming, and captivating in every way.

'I have no idea how to thank you.' Tony shook his head. 'This means a lot to me. You don't know how much.'

'I'm just happy you like it. And I certainly do know how much it means.' Reaching up to touch the pink necklace, Martha said, 'I felt exactly the same way when my son made me this.'

OK, that explained the lumpy pink pebbles. Tony wondered how old she was. Had she had her son when she was in her early forties?

'Of course, that was a while ago.' Answering the unspoken question, she said, 'He's twenty-eight now, and a criminal lawyer. It embarrasses him no end that I still wear it. Which is always good fun. But every time I touch this necklace, I see him as clear as day, sitting at the kitchen table in his little shorts, rolling up the clay to make the beads, then painting them with my brand new bottle of nail varnish.'

Tony nodded, a long-forgotten memory flashing up of the day Jamie had rushed home from school and presented him with a clay pot. Glowing with pride, he'd announced, 'It's a thumb pot, Daddy! We made them with our thumbs! You can keep your cufflinks in it!'

What had happened to that funny little blue pot? He had no idea. OK, don't think about Jamie now, don't mention his name, don't announce that you had a son too, but he died. It would only create awkwardness and bring the mood crashing down.

Instead he said, 'It's a great necklace. It has character. I took a look at your website, by the way.'

Took a look. That sounded as if he'd glanced at it, clicking casually through the pages for a few seconds before moving into something else. Whereas in reality he had pored over them for almost two hours. It wasn't the glitziest of sites; indeed, it was a modest, home-built affair with no photos of Martha herself and only the briefest of introductions to her work, along with the gallery of paintings past and present. Potential buyers were requested to send an email. Each of the paintings was a delight, as individual and heart-warming as the one he was currently holding in his hands.

'And...?' She clutched her chest in mock terror. 'I always get nervous when people say that. It's like being back at school and your teacher saying he's read your essay.'

'Well, you get an A plus from me. I'm officially a fan of your work.' Tony paused. 'And I'd like to buy more. But this time you'd have to let me pay for them.'

'Really?' Martha looked delighted.

'Really.'

'Now I feel like a drug dealer. Giving you the first taste for free, making sure you come back for more.' She searched his face. 'Seriously, so long as you aren't doing it just to be polite.'

Tony said gravely, 'I'm very rarely polite.'

She smiled. 'Which ones would you be interested in?'

'The swimmers in Hampstead Ponds. The one with the fireworks on the Thames. Possibly the wedding party.'

'Oh, sorry. That one's sold.'

'Oh.'

'But there are plenty more at home.' Martha brightened. 'I haven't got round yet to putting them on the website. They're still waiting to be photographed.'

'Right.' He nodded slowly. 'Well... I'd be really interested in seeing them.'

'OK, great.' She carried on painting.

What did that mean? Tony said, 'So, will you put them on the website? Or is there some way I could get to see the actual paintings?'

Martha sat back and surveyed the half-finished scene on her easel. 'Is that what you'd prefer?'

'Yes.'

'We can go now, if you like. If you have time.'

'I have time.' It was what he wanted, more than anything. 'Are you sure this is OK?'

She smiled. 'If I wasn't sure, I wouldn't say it.'

Together they packed away her things. He folded up the easel and the collapsible chair. Martha slid everything else into her canvas carrying case. They headed down the hill and she said, 'It's a mile and a half from here. Can you manage that on foot?'

And Tony, who never walked anywhere in LA because... well, because no one there ever did, said, 'Are you calling me decrepit?'

She lived on Lanacre Road in Tufnell Park, in a terraced redbrick house with bright hanging baskets either side of the topaz-yellow front door.

'Why doesn't it surprise me that you have a yellow front door?' said Tony.

'Ah, I'm a lady of color.' Martha opened the door. 'It's one of life's joys. Come along in.'

He inhaled the light summery scent she was wearing as he followed her into the living room. Cleverly, she hadn't overdone the color.

Three walls were white, one was a vivid shade of peacock blue. The sofa was upholstered in bottle green velvet, and there were white rugs on the polished wooden floor. Bookshelves were crammed with books. There were paintings on the walls and bowls of flowers everywhere.

'They're not yours.' He indicated the framed paintings.

'I couldn't hang my work in my own living room. That would be too weird.' Pulling a face as she unloaded her canvas bag, Martha said, 'Like a novelist choosing to read their own book.'

Tony glanced once more around the room. 'You don't have a TV?'

'Not for years now. I listen to the radio. Sing, sometimes.' She smiled. 'Now, I can either cart everything down here or we can go upstairs to see my paintings.'

She genuinely had no idea who he was. Charmed by her manner, by her character... OK, by pretty much everything about her, Tony put down the folded easel and the mounted painting she had given him and said, 'Let's go up and have a look at them, shall we?'

The front bedroom had been converted into a studio. Here were the paintings, propped up against all four walls, some familiar to him from the website, others not. The sun streamed in through the windows, another easel was set up in the center of the room and paint-spattered white sheets covered the carpet.

'They have to be there,' Martha apologized, 'because I'm such a mucky pup. Mind you don't trip on them. Now, let me talk you through the paintings you haven't seen before.' Resting her hand on his arm and leading him towards them, she said confidingly, 'I tell you what, see if you can guess which one's my favorite.'

From that moment on, Tony was lost. It was almost impossible to concentrate on whatever it was she was saying. All he could think of was how close she was to him, how wonderful she smelled, how unbelievable it was that she could make him feel this way. Yesterday he hadn't known her. Now he did. She had a voice like honey and a smile capable of lighting up any room.

'…Well?'

OK, he needed to pay attention. 'Well what?'

She surveyed him with amusement. 'Have you been listening to me at all?'

'That one. That's your favorite.' He pointed to a painting of a picnic on the beach.

'I just asked you what color your walls were. Where you're going to hang them.'

'Oh, sorry. I'm distracted.' Should he say it? Could he? Bracing himself, Tony said, 'By you.'

'Me? Why?'

'Because you're such a lovely surprise.' Did that sound completely ridiculous? Well, it was true. Aloud he said, 'You don't know how happy I am to have met you.'

Martha looked away, then back at him. Finally she exhaled. 'Me too. You're a very nice man.'

'It's not just me, feeling it?'

She shook her head and swallowed. 'Not just you.'

'I want you to know that I don't make a habit of doing this.' Reaching for her hand, he stroked the brown ringless fingers. 'But I want to do it now.'

The next moment she was in his arms and he was kissing her, and it was like being twenty again. Martha's soft body pressed against his, her silver bracelets clinking as she ran a hand through his hair. She was trembling with emotion. He wanted to carry on holding her and kissing her for ever. God, she was *so beautiful…*

'Tony?' Breathlessly she pulled away to study his face. 'Are you single?'

He nodded. 'Divorced many years ago. I've been on my own for a long time.'

'Me too.' He felt her sadness. The next moment it was dispelled. 'And I want you to know that I've never done this before either.'

Another kiss, then she led him out of the studio and across the narrow landing. Her bedroom was smaller, ultra-feminine in shades of cream and gold.

Tony turned her to face him. Wonderingly, he stroked her face. 'You're sure this is all right?'

There was a world of emotion in her golden eyes. Her voice unsteady, she whispered, 'I've never wanted anything more in my life.'

Chapter 16

An hour had passed. Possibly the most incredible hour of his life. When he said, 'OK, there's something I have to tell you,' Tony saw a flash of fear.

'What?'

'I probably should have said this before. But it's all right, it's workable.'

Martha had gone very still. 'Tell me.'

'I don't live here in London. My home's in Los Angeles.'

She sank back against the pillows. 'Oh. That's a long way away.'

'But we can sort something out. I want to keep on seeing you. I hope you want to keep seeing me. I can come over every few weeks. I don't know, maybe you could come out and stay. There's plenty to paint, believe me.'

'You work over there?' She searched his face. 'What do you do?'

'I'm an actor.'

Her eyebrows went up. 'Really? Any good?'

'Pretty good, yes.'

'Successful?'

'Yes. Yes, I am.'

Martha thought for a moment then said slowly, 'Are you famous?'

He nodded.

She broke into a huge smile. 'Well, that explains it, then! While we were on our way back here, I saw a couple of people looking at you. But more than just a normal look, you know? More *interested*.

I thought it was because you were so attractive. But it wasn't, was it? They recognized you. Oh my God, what's your name?'

'Tony Weston.'

'I've heard that name!' Martha clapped a hand over her mouth. 'You *are* famous! You were in that film about the two brothers… ooh, what was it called… *Mr and Mr Black*!'

'That's right.'

'I heard all about it on the radio! They said you were very good.'

Tony smiled. 'They were right.'

'I always mean to go to the cinema, then I never get round to it. You must think I'm completely hopeless. I should have known who you were!'

'Don't be daft.'

'Oh God!' This time she clutched the side of her head. 'I just had sex with a film star!'

'Fantastic sex,' Tony corrected.

'Fantastic sex. Absolutely. God, sorry, I've come over all unnecessary now. This is just bizarre.'

'Can I tell you something?' He traced the tips of his fingers along her collarbone. 'It's the most miraculous thing that's happened to me in years.'

Martha nodded, her eyes filling up. She whispered, 'Me too. When do you go back to the States?'

'The day after tomorrow. You could come with me.' But she was already shaking her head.

'I can't. But thank you. Oh my word, is that the time? I didn't realize it was so late.' Pulling on a white cotton robe, she said, 'I have to be somewhere by six. And you haven't had a proper look yet at the other paintings…'

———

'Oh, wow, look at those. They're so… happy!' Home from work, Ellie encountered the four paintings lined up on the sofa. She pointed to the Primrose Hill picture. 'That's the one you told me about last night. Did she give you all of these?'

Tony shook his head. 'I paid for them. We went back to her house and she showed me her work. I bought the other three.' He kept the rest to himself. Much as he longed to talk about Martha, he was Ellie's father-in-law; there was no way he could tell her what else he'd done this afternoon.

'You should buy paintings more often.' Ellie was smiling at him. 'It suits you.'

His soul was singing. If only she knew. 'I might do that.'

— ⁓ —

The next morning was taken up with meetings, followed by lunch in Soho with an old actor friend he couldn't let down. By two thirty, as the taxi took him to Tufnell Park, Tony's heart was flick-flacking away in his chest. Fifty-five years old, and he felt like a teenager on a first date.

This was unbelievable. It had never occurred to him that something like this could happen. At his age too. Love—or something perilously close to it—at first sight. Martha, Martha, just saying her name in his head gave him a thrill.

They reached Lanacre Road and he paid off the cab. Turned to look at the topaz-yellow front door. Martha. He'd barely been able to sleep last night for thinking about her and reliving every second of yesterday. He raised his hand and rang the bell. What would she be wearing today? It would be their last time together for weeks; would she let him spend the night here? If she did, he'd have to phone Ellie and come up with some plausible fib as to why he wasn't coming home.

The door opened and there was Martha, wearing a violet shift dress and looking... completely different. As if seeing him on her doorstep was the very last thing she wanted. Even her head was shaking fractionally from side to side as she said, 'Oh hello, is this about the paintings? I'm afraid it's a bit of an awkward time.'

'Who is it, Martha?' Behind her, another woman came into view. Older, Afro-Caribbean, taller, and thinner, with gray hair and sensible shoes. Over Martha's shoulder she surveyed him with an unwavering, miss-nothing gaze.

'Nobody, just someone interested in my work…'

What's going on?

'My name's Tony.' He held out his hand to Martha and shook it, then reached past her and said pleasantly, 'Hello there. Tony Weston.'

Forced to shake his hand, the gray-haired woman nodded briefly in return. She had a tight bony grip and a habit of blinking slowly like an owl.

'Could I come in? I've sent my taxi away now.'

Martha swallowed and said fearfully, 'OK, just for five minutes.' The prospect clearly didn't thrill her but she stepped aside. Tony followed the older woman into the living room.

'I'll bring the pictures down.' Hurrying upstairs, Martha said, 'Eunice, why don't you make Mr Weston a cup of tea?'

Eunice raised an eyebrow. 'Are we a café now?'

'It's fine, don't worry.' So much for charming her into submission. Yet again Tony smiled and failed to get a response. 'I'm a great fan of Mrs Daines's work. Are you a friend of hers?' Because if she was, he was going to have to reassess Martha's taste in friends.

'Sister-in-law.'

'Oh.' Did that mean Eunice was the ex-husband's sister? Or was she married to Martha's brother? And could he ask her that? No, of course he couldn't.

In less than thirty seconds Martha was back with an armful of mounted prints. One thing was for sure, she was like a cat on a hotplate. Every minute he was here under this roof was a minute too long. As soon as the paintings were spread out on the table, she said, 'There you are, that's all of them. Which one would you like?'

The tension in the room was palpable, like an overdose of air freshener. Realizing he was in a no-win situation, Tony put her out of her misery and pointed. 'I'll have that one.'

'Excellent.' Martha managed a smile and exhaled with relief. 'Good choice.'

And that was it. Within four minutes of ringing the front doorbell, he found himself being propelled back out onto the pavement. With a painting under his arm and his plans for the rest of the day well and truly scuppered. On his way out he said in desperation, 'Could I have your number, in case I wanted to buy another one?'

Eunice replied crisply, 'She doesn't hand out her telephone number to strangers. Do you, Martha?'

Martha swallowed. 'If you want to contact me about my work, my email address is on my website.'

'Fine, I'll do that then.' Pointedly Tony said, 'I'm going to be out of the country for the next couple of weeks, but I'll be back at the beginning of July.'

'OK. Well, it's been nice to meet you, Mr Weston.' Clearly desperate to close the door, Martha said, 'Enjoy your painting. Goodbye.'

'Or I could give you my number?' It was a last-ditch attempt; he so badly needed to speak to her before he left.

'That won't be necessary,' Eunice coolly intervened. 'Why would she want to phone you?'

Because we spent yesterday afternoon in bed together, you bloody interfering old witch. And I'm in love with her.

But of course Tony didn't say this out loud.

Chapter 17

'CAN YOU GET THAT?' Ellie was busy scrubbing her favorite Havaianas flip-flops in the sink when the doorbell went on Saturday morning.

Todd pressed the button on the intercom and waited.

'Hi, it's me.' Roo's voice echoed tinnily through the speaker. 'I'm heading out on an undercover mission. Want to come along?'

'What an offer.' Todd launched into his Sean Connery impression. 'Shall we go in my vintage Aston Martin?'

A split second of silence, then, 'James Bond, is that you?'

'Shweetheart, I'm afraid that's classified information. I could tell you, but then I'd have to seduce you.'

'Let her in.' Ellie switched off the tap and rinsed the soap off her pink flip-flops. This was going to be interesting; how would her old friend and her new friend hit it off?

Roo bounded up the stairs and into the flat in a black and white checked shirt, white denim skirt, and black Uggs.

'I can guess who you are.' She waggled her fingers at Todd. 'But do you really have an Aston Martin?'

'Sorry.'

'See? Now I'm disappointed. And you don't look like Sean Connery either.'

'I'm younger than he is. I'm funnier,' said Todd. 'Plus, I have hair.'

'What's this mission in aid of?' Ellie finished patting the flip-flops dry with paper towels and put them on her feet.

'OK, Niall came over last night. And while he was in the loo I happened to find a shopping list in his jacket pocket. Nothing exciting, just nappies and baby wipes and stuff. But it was written in girly handwriting on a Post-it note with the name of a beauty salon printed along the top.' Roo narrowed her eyes in a sleuth-like fashion. 'Now, Niall's always refused to tell me where his wife works. So I rang the salon this morning and asked if Yasmin was in today… and she is! And guess what? I've booked an appointment with her for this afternoon! We can go together!'

Ellie pulled a face. How could anyone think this was a good idea?

'Who's Niall?' said Todd.

Roo looked at him. 'My boyfriend.'

'He has a wife?'

'Yes, but she's awful.'

'And there's a baby?'

'That's the only reason he's still with his wife.'

'What are you doing having an affair with a married man?'

'I love him. And he loves me.'

'Where's your self-respect?'

Roo stiffened. 'What's your problem?'

'Look, shall we talk about something else?' Ellie was keen to cool the situation down.

'No, let's not.' Todd turned to Roo. 'When I was a kid, my father had an affair with another woman. He walked out on me and my mum. I just happen to think wrecking other people's marriages is a pretty low thing to do.'

Roo said defensively, 'Trust me, Niall's marriage was wrecked long before I came along.'

'So why have you made an appointment at this place?' said Ellie.

'Because I want to see her. I just want to find out for myself what she's like. I'm not going to do anything,' Roo protested. 'She won't know who I am. Oh, please come with me,' she begged. 'It'll be easier to have a conversation with the two of us. And then you'll be able to tell thingy here that I'm not a complete monster.'

Todd was ice-cool. 'Thingy can make up his own mind, thanks.'
Oh dear. Off to a rocky start.

—⁓—

The salon was in Hampstead. From the outside it was all subtle
shades of rose-pink and cream. Inside it smelled like heaven. Ellie
had never paid a visit to a beauty salon before; given the choice of
how to spend thirty pounds, she'd choose a bottle of bubble bath and
a new top every time. When it came to waxing and manicures she
had always done her own. But never mind that now. They were here
on a mission. Roo was more nervous than she was letting on. And
the woman behind the reception desk with the terrifying ice-queen
face and scraped-back hair could be Niall's wife.

'Twelve thirty… let me see…' She ran a ferocious crimson nail
down the appointments book. 'Yes, there you are. Just take a seat and
Yasmin will be with you very shortly.'

So, not the ice queen then.

They sat and waited and watched one of the other customers
have a pedicure. Within two minutes the door to the salon burst
open and a woman in her twenties rushed in with a multipack of
nappies under one arm and a carrier bag from Lloyds the chemist in
the other.

Having stowed them in the back room, she returned. 'Hello,
sorry to keep you waiting, just had to dash out to the shops. I'm
Yasmin. Gosh, if your hair was different you'd look like that singer
from years ago. What's her name… thingummy… Daisy Deeva.'

'I get that all the time.' Roo pulled a face. 'I saw her once, in
Selfridges. She was buying a really horrible hat.'

'Wouldn't mind her money though, eh?' Yasmin didn't seem like
a nightmare. She was smiling and friendly, with wavy, honey blond
hair and pretty eyes. 'Now, I hear you asked for me specially. Does
that mean you know one of my regular clients?'

Caught off guard, possibly by her niceness, Roo said, 'Um…'

'We were in a wine bar yesterday,' Ellie leapt in, 'and a girl at the next table was telling her friend how great you are at manicures. She had beautiful nails, so we asked her where you worked.'

'Oh wow, how brilliant! I wonder who it was?' Beaming with delight, Yasmin said, 'Let's hope you're happy too!'

The conversation was all about nails for the next few minutes, as she got to work on Roo. Ellie watched as the hands were painstakingly cleansed and moisturized, a scrub containing exfoliating crystals was applied, then some kind of special oil was rubbed into the nails and cuticles. Finally Roo said, 'I saw you with the nappies. Does that mean you have a baby?'

Yasmin grinned. 'Well, they'd be a bit small for me. Yes, we've got a boy, Benjamin. Seven months. He's just adorable.' Her eyes were shining. 'I can't believe the difference he's made to our lives. How about you?'

'Kids? Me? No.' Roo shook her head, then clearly realized a child might come in handy. Indicating Ellie, she said, 'She's got one.'

Oh, great. Thanks a lot.

Yasmin turned to her. 'Have you? Aren't they fantastic? Boy or a girl?'

'Girl.' Ellie nodded and prayed they weren't about to start swapping childbirth stories. 'Five months. Her name's Alice.'

'Ah, that's lovely.' Cheerily Yasmin said, 'Hard work, though, aren't they? Does your chap help out much, or is he as useless as mine?'

Luckily her attention was on the job in hand so she didn't see Roo's eyelashes bristling.

Ellie said, 'Not much. They're all pretty useless, aren't they?'

'Tell me about it! My husband was supposed to be buying those nappies yesterday, and what happens? He comes home at midnight, says he had to work late, but it's just a big fib. He wasn't working. I know exactly where he was!'

Roo swallowed.

'Where was he?' said Ellie.

'Out with his friends, of course! It's that old meet-up-with-your-mates-on-a-Friday-night thing. He just can't give it up. I mean, I wouldn't mind, but he promised to come home with the baby wipes and the nappies.' Yasmin shook her head. 'Still, that's men for you. They can't multitask like us, can they?'

Ellie looked at the narrow wedding ring glinting on Yasmin's left hand. 'What's he like with the nappies?'

Smiling, Yasmin said, 'He changed three-quarters of a nappy once. I'm telling you, that was a sight to behold. You'd have thought he was detonating an unexploded bomb. It was hilarious. There now, let's just wrap your hands in warm towels to let the moisturizers sink in. And you can choose which color nail polish you'd like…'

'But he must do it sometimes.' Ellie frowned. 'I mean, like today, while you're here working.'

'Oh, he's not looking after him now.' More amused resignation. 'Niall likes his lie-ins on a Saturday morning. I drop Benjamin off at my mum's before I come into work.'

'This is interesting,' Ellie murmured when Yasmin disappeared to attend to another client. Roo must be devastated to discover that her boyfriend's wife was so nice.

'See? I told you she was a nightmare,' Roo whispered back. 'She's just a complete control freak.'

—✳—

Todd was waiting for them in the pub watching tennis on the giant TV screen up on the wall.

'Well? How'd it go?'

'I had my nails done.' Roo showed him her hands. 'Actually, she did a good job.'

'Thank goodness for that.' Todd's voice was heavy with sarcasm. 'What was she like?'

'Lovely,' said Ellie.

'Oh please, that's not fair.' Roo shook her head. 'She was *pretending* to be lovely because she was doing my nails. She's at work, I'm her client, of course she's going to put on a good show. But you could tell what she's really like.'

'She was great,' Ellie insisted. 'Cheerful, warm, working her socks off. Do you want my honest opinion?'

'No.' Roo was busy fiddling with her sunglasses.

'Niall sounds like an arse.'

'You're biased.'

'Because he's an *arse*.'

'I wish I'd never taken you along with me now.'

'And Yasmin's like a single mother,' Ellie went on. 'She does everything and he does nothing.' *How could Roo not see it?*

'Because when he does try to do anything, she tells him he's doing it all wrong!'

'He told her he was working last night. But he wasn't, he was with you.'

Roo was defensive. 'If he goes home, all she does is nag him.'

'Probably because she's exhausted looking after the baby on her own!'

'Look, she was exaggerating, making herself sound hard done by to get the sympathy vote.'

Todd, his head swiveling between them, said, 'This is better than the tennis. So come on, are you going to finish with this bloke?'

'Don't be so horrible! I love him!'

He looked exasperated. 'The guy's a liar and a cheat.'

'Everyone tells lies.' Their drinks arrived and Roo took a gulp of hers. 'You should have heard Ellie going on about her baby.'

'What baby?'

Roo spread her arms. 'I rest my case.'

But Todd had missed the joke; he was busy staring at Ellie. 'Are you *pregnant*?'

Ellie spluttered into her glass of wine. 'No! How could I be pregnant? We just pretended I had a baby so we'd have something in common.' She saw the look of relief on his face. 'It was a white lie, that's all. Harmless.'

'Speaking of white.' Roo checked her watch, knocked back the rest of her vodka, and ruffled her spiky white-blond hair. 'I've got an appointment to get my roots done, so I'm off. Have fun watching the tennis without me.' She looked at Todd. 'I'd say it was nice to meet you, but that would be another lie.'

He said pleasantly, 'That's because I'm right and you're wrong. And you know it.'

—⁓—

The tennis had evolved into a tense five-set match that had got everyone in the pub cheering and on their feet. Afterwards Ellie and Todd went out for pizza, before heading off to a club in Camden to see a band.

'That was… loud,' said Ellie three hours later as they made their way back through Chalk Farm to Primrose Hill. 'My ears are ringing.'

Todd nodded in agreement. 'They were so loud I couldn't even tell if they were any good. Is this a sign that we're getting old?'

'We are old. Maybe next time we could stand outside on the pavement, just hear it from a distance.'

'Why stand? We could take a couple of deck chairs along. Get comfy, roll up our trouser legs.'

'Wear knotted hankies on our heads,' Ellie said. 'You can't beat a knotted hankie. In fact, why bother with going to see a noisy old band anyway? What's wrong with watching some nice Morris dancers instead?'

'Now you're talking, Ethel, that's a grand idea. We'll take along a Thermos of tea and a packet of ham sandwiches.' He paused, checking she was OK.

Ellie managed a smile to reassure him she was fine. This had been his and Jamie's thing, taking an idea and running with it, inventing characters, and creating impromptu sketch shows. From time to time she and Jamie had done the same, but it had never happened between her and Todd before. It was a weird experience, like holding your toothbrush in the wrong hand. You knew you were brushing your teeth but it felt all strange.

'God, I miss him,' said Todd.

She nodded, the all-too-familiar hollowness in her stomach expanding like a balloon. Together they made their way up Gloucester Avenue. It was a warm night and music drifted out of open windows. In a doorway, a couple in costumes were having a drunken argument, the woman in the nun's outfit noisily accusing a man dressed as Frankenstein of flirting with someone else. ('She's not Superwoman, she's just a fat slag!') Further along the road another couple were kissing passionately. Up above, stars twinkled in a black velvet sky and an almost full moon hung just above the rooftops. Now they could hear a soaring soul ballad being played nearby. Under other circumstances this would count as a romantic situation. The hollow stomach feeling increased. If Jamie were here now, she would be so happy. Actually, if he was here now, he'd have grabbed her and waltzed her around in circles all the way up the road whilst singing along to the tear-jerking ballad in the manner of Dame Edna.

They reached Nevis Street and Ellie fished out her key.

'Thanks. It's been a good day.'

'I've had fun too.'

'You didn't have to walk me home. You've missed the last tube now.'

Todd shrugged easily. 'No problem. I'll get the bus.'

All the way back to his mum's in Wimbledon. It would take a while.

'OK.' She stepped forward and gave him a kiss on the cheek.

'I'll give you a call. If you're free next weekend, we could do it again. Check out what bands are on, stock up on earplugs.' He hesitated. 'No pressure. Only if you want to.'

Did she want to? Ellie thought she probably did. Over the past seventeen months she'd got so used to not wanting to go out and be sociable that saying no had become her natural default setting. The moment anyone invited her anywhere, her brain began scrambling for plausible excuses as to why she couldn't make it.

But today had been different. She hadn't secretly been longing to be back at home on her own. Which had to be an encouraging sign, didn't it?

She looked at Todd. He was Jamie's oldest friend and now she'd got over her stupid resentful phase she was comfortable in his company.

'Yes, call me. I'd like to do that.' There, that hadn't been too difficult, had it?

'Great.' He sounded pleased. 'I'll buy the earplugs.'

Ellie smiled. 'And I'll bring the Thermos.'

Chapter 18

ELMO WAS DANCING AROUND like a lunatic, chasing dandelion seeds as they drifted like mini parachutes above his head. Keeping an eye on the pair of German shepherds playing together down the hill, Zack stuck his fingers in his mouth and whistled. Like a D-list celeb spotting the paparazzi, Elmo pricked up his ears and came racing back.

'Those two are bigger than you are.' Zack brushed dandelion seeds out of Elmo's Denis Healey eyebrows and reattached his lead. 'They'd eat you for breakfast. Come on, we need to get home now.'

He and Elmo left the hill and made their way back to Ancram Street. Later on this morning he was flying to Amsterdam to meet with a co-investor. He'd be home by eight. Tomorrow he was visiting a shoe factory in Derby. The following day he had back-to-back appointments with prospective partners and the amount of research he still needed to carry out on the companies was ridiculous.

But this was how Zack lived his life. Work came first; it always had. Business was his priority and personal relationships came second. They fitted in when it was convenient and he enjoyed them, of course he did, but they didn't make his heart beat faster like the prospect of a brilliant business deal.

At least they hadn't, before Ellie Kendall had come into his life.

Elmo was busily investigating an abandoned ice-cream wrapper. Zack steered him off the grass and on to the pavement. The situation he found himself in was crazy; it was just ridiculous. Never before had his mind been occupied during important meetings with thoughts of a female who *wasn't even remotely interested in him.*

And to make matters worse, he'd employed her. He'd had to, otherwise who could say when he'd have the chance to see her again?

'Elmo, stop it.' He tugged at the lead as Elmo began straining to sniff the ankles of an old man wearing saggy shorts and Birkenstocks. Simultaneously his phone began to ring.

Louisa's name flashed up on the screen. Should he? Shouldn't he?

OK, get it over with. She would only keep on calling until he answered.

'Hello, you.' She was using her consciously sexy telephone voice. 'Listen, how about if I come over this evening?'

Zack knew it was wrong that the suggestion didn't fill him with joy. Their relationship had started out so well, it had taken a while for the realization to sink in that the Louisa he'd first got to know was something of a front, a beguiling persona created to give a good impression. As time had gone on, she had begun to change and reveal her bossier, more possessive side. They were turning out to have less in common than he'd first thought. 'The thing is, I'm going to be shattered when I get back from Amsterdam.' A lie, but a necessary one.

'I know, that's why I'm suggesting it. I'll cook dinner and spoil you rotten. We'll have you feeling better in no time. Go on,' Louisa purred in his ear. 'You know you want to.'

He really didn't, not tonight. 'Look, I don't want to mess up your evening. I may have to stay on for a couple of drinks with the Van den Bergs. Who knows what time I'll be back.'

'Oh, darling, you're so thoughtful, but I really don't mind.'

And now she was being nice, which only made him feel worse. 'But I do. It's not fair on you.' Pricked with guilt, Zack said, 'Let's leave it for tonight, OK?'

'Oh, right. Well, how about tomorrow then?'

'Tomorrow. Fine.' His voice softened. Anything to keep the peace. He still liked her when she was relaxed and not taking herself too seriously; it was just that those times happened less and less often nowadays. If he was honest, he knew he should probably finish with Louisa but he also knew it was going to be hard work. Louisa was so dramatic, she wouldn't leave without kicking up a fuss. It was a daunting enough prospect that it put him off broaching the subject. When all you wanted to do was concentrate on work, the thought of so much angst and disruption was off-putting to say the least.

Zack ended the call, coaxed Elmo away from an abandoned chicken nugget in a shop doorway, and headed for home. It was ten past nine and Ellie would be there by now. He also knew it was wrong to be seeing Louisa whilst feeling the way he did about someone else. But Ellie's absolute indifference towards him meant it hardly mattered. It wasn't as if finishing with Louisa would make her suddenly change her mind and fall for him. It just didn't work like that.

If it did, he'd already have done it.

Ellie was in the office, smelling gorgeous and with her hair tied back with a gray velvet ribbon to reveal her neck. The post had already been sorted into piles and she was now watering the forest of plants that had taken up residence along the windowsill, courtesy of Barbara.

'Some of these are going funny,' she warned him over her shoulder. 'I told you I wouldn't be able to keep them going. I'm a serial plant-killer. Look at the leaves on this one.'

She was wearing a gray jersey top with a square neck and elbow-length sleeves, and a red skirt. Moving closer, Zack breathed in the fresh, lemony perfume and watched the way her dark hair glinted in the sunlight streaming in through the window. 'Yes, they definitely look like leaves to me.'

'But the edges are going all weird and yellow.' Frustrated, she turned the blue ceramic pot to show him. 'I thought it needed more water so I gave it loads yesterday and now they're even worse. Do you think I should try and dry out the soil?'

The way her eyebrows tilted in concern made him want to kiss her. It was a common-as-muck spider plant, practically a weed, but she really cared about it. But since there was no way he could kiss her, he said, 'How would you do that?'

'I was thinking maybe a hair dryer.' Ellie lifted the blue pot and gave the sodden compost a tentative prod.

'Give it a go. If it doesn't work, at least the leaves'll look stylish.'

She stopped prodding. 'Are you making fun of me?'

Zack smiled; the one thing he knew he mustn't do was flirt with her. 'I'm making light of the fact that neither of us has the foggiest idea how to look after a potted plant.'

'Just as well we don't have kids.' Cheerfully oblivious to the effect this statement had on him, Ellie said, 'Right, I'm taking it outside. Maybe all it needs is a bit of sun to cheer it up. Oh, by the way, there's a message on the phone from someone called... Huggy?' She looked bemused. 'Is that right?'

'Huggy Hill.' Zack held the door open for her, watched as she carefully placed the pot down in a sunny spot against the wall. 'My first ever business partner.'

'First ever? How did it happen? Was that when you were still at college?'

He nodded and followed her back into the office. 'That's right. I was taking a degree in business management. Huggy was a mate, clever in his own way but clueless when it came to business. He'd set up this tiny company selling mobile phones and he started asking me for advice. After a couple of months I saw the potential of what he was trying to do—this was before mobiles went mega—and I took a stake in the business in exchange for all the work I was doing for him. Chiefly because he was skint and it was the only way he could afford to pay me. Then things really started to take off and I realized

I'd far rather be working with Huggy than carrying on with a three-year degree course.'

'So you dropped out of university.' Ellie knew much of the story; he knew she'd been familiarizing herself with his CV. But talking to her was no hardship; maybe she'd even be impressed.

'I did. We built up the business and sold it two years later for crazy money. By then I'd already begun to diversify. I discovered I had good instincts, I could see why other people's companies were failing and what it would take to bring them back up again. I did some stuff with a computer support consultancy that turned it around.'

She nodded. 'Then there was the ice-cream business.'

He smiled. 'I loved that one.'

'And the holiday park in Dorset.'

'You've been doing your homework.'

'And the restaurant with the home-delivery service. Did your friend Huggy start investing in other companies too?'

'No, he moved to the Caribbean, spent his days surfing, and became a professional beach bum. He's still there now. Having a great life.'

'Do you ever wish you were doing what he's doing?'

'Never. I'm happy here.' Did that make him sound boring? Work-obsessed? *Was he boring and work-obsessed?* He said, 'Would you do it?'

Ellie thought for a moment. Finally she said, 'It would depend on who I was with. Living in the perfect place with the wrong person would be horrible.'

Zack couldn't help himself. 'How about living with the perfect person in a horrible place?'

Something flickered behind her eyes for a second. Then she half-smiled and said simply, 'If they're the perfect person, it would still be perfect.'

OK, what did that smile mean? Was she thinking of that actor bloke of hers, Tony Weston? Was she thinking that she *could* live with him in some dump somewhere and be happy about it, but luckily she didn't need to slum it because—hooray!—he'd set her up in a half-million-pound love nest in Primrose Hill instead?

On the few occasions he'd subtly asked questions about her private life she had veered away from the subject. He'd offered her the opportunity to tell him about Tony Weston and she'd chosen not to. Therefore he wasn't going to push it. The only way forward was to back off and leave her to carry on with her life. If she wanted privacy, he'd let her have it. Instinct told him that all he could do for the moment was stay cool and play the waiting game. It wouldn't be easy but he'd manage it if it killed him. Because right now, thanks to that unerring instinct, he knew for a fact that Ellie wasn't remotely interested in him. Which meant he *had* to hold back. No flirting allowed. Not even a *hint* of flirtatious behavior. She worked for him, he was her boss, and there was nothing more hideous than finding yourself the unwilling target of a workmate's affections. He'd encountered it himself before now and knew what a complete turnoff it was. Imagine how much worse it must be for a woman to be on the receiving end of unwanted attention.

So that was that. He was going to hold back completely. Be charming and as nice as he knew how to be. But without flirting at all. It wouldn't be easy but he was going to do it. He had to. Because this was too important to mess up.

'OK, I'd better get changed and head off.' Zack was still in the sweatshirt and jeans he'd worn to take Elmo for his walk. He indicated the folders on the desk. 'There's plenty in here for you to be getting on with. Any problems, give me a call. If my phone's switched off, just leave a message and I'll get back to you.'

'Right, fine. Oh you naughty boy, don't do that!'

If only she could have been talking about him. But it was Elmo, scrabbling madly, probably having spotted a spider and getting himself caught up in a tangle of electrical leads under the desk. Launching herself across the top of the desk in the nick of time, Ellie managed to grab the printer before it crashed to the ground.

'Well held. Here, let me.' Reaching past her to pull it back to safety, Zack's hand accidentally brushed her arm. A *zingggg* of adrenaline jolted through his veins. OK, this was ridiculous; it was like being fourteen again. 'There, all done. Elmo, you stay out of trouble now.' Raising the dog to eye level, he said, 'Behave yourself, OK? Ellie's going to take you for another walk later.'

He'd said the w-word. Elmo did one of his exaggerated double takes and let out a yip of excitement.

'No, no, calm down, we've just been out.' Zack wondered if Ellie secretly thought he was mad, talking to Elmo the way he did. 'Right, see you later. Be good.'

Ellie had started opening the post. She looked up and said cheerfully, 'We'll try.'

Even the shape of her mouth was irresistible; when she formed the word *try*, it created the most perfect pout. And now she was smiling again, but still without anything approaching *that* kind of interest.

Letting himself out of the office, Zack said casually, 'I'll see you tomorrow.'

God, this not-flirting and just-being-friends business was going to be bloody hard.

Chapter 19

WHAT WAS GOING ON? Tony had no idea, but he knew he needed to find out. Over the past fortnight he must have sent Martha a dozen emails. All he'd had in return was a single brief message on the first day. In it, she had apologized and said their encounter had been a huge mistake. They mustn't meet again, she was sorry if she'd led him on, and could he please respect her privacy and not attempt to contact her in any way.

That was it, that was all. Since then, each subsequent email had gone unanswered. Directory inquiries had declined to give out Martha's phone number. Tony, stuck in Hollywood filming an unexciting part in a completely dire movie, had been counting down the days. But in a desperate rather than a hopeful way, because flying over to London to find out what was going on was one thing, but actually persuading Martha to change her mind about him was quite another.

Anyway, he was back now. Another day, another taxi. And no way was he capable of respecting her wish for privacy. As they pulled into Lanacre Road, Tony's chest tightened in anticipation. He didn't even know if she was in the house, but the need to see her again was overwhelming.

The taxi driver said, 'Where d'you want me to stop?'

'Further along. It's the house with the yellow door, up on the left.' As the taxi slowed, Tony said, 'Pull over behind that blue van.'

The next moment the yellow door opened and Disapproving Eunice came out. Followed by Martha.

'Oh God, don't stop.'

'Eh? But you said—'

'Don't stop!' Tony shrank back from the window and hissed, 'Keep going.' Jesus, talk about bad timing. What did Eunice do, *live* there? From the depths of the cab he glimpsed Martha's profile as she turned to lock the door behind them. The taxi trundled on to the end of the road and stopped at the junction.

'Where to now, then?'

'Um…' Peering out of the back of the cab, Tony saw that the two women were heading off in the opposite direction. 'Turn around and wait. See if they get into that car.'

'And then what?' The cab driver twisted in his seat to look at him. 'You want me to follow them? Hey, you don't know how long I've waited for someone to say that and actually mean it!' Chuckling, he expertly spun the steering wheel and swung the cab around. 'You're Tony Weston, right?'

'Yes.'

'Am I allowed to ask what's going on here?'

'I'd rather you didn't,' said Tony.

'They're not getting into any car. Looks like they're walking.' Tony thought fast. Knowing his luck, they were off to the supermarket. But he was here now, and what else did he have to do?'

'Let's follow them.'

'Are you serious, mate? We're in this thing'—the driver indicated his cab—'and they're on foot.'

'You'll just have to go slowly then, won't you? And make sure they don't catch you at it.'

Luckily Martha and Eunice didn't look back. The taxi remained at a safe distance behind them, trundling along at the speed of mud. When they reached the busy main road it got trickier, the cab driver having to stop and start and work hard not to get trapped in the bus lane.

'I'm sure it's supposed to be more exciting than this,' he grumbled. 'Tires squealing, handbrake turns, police joining in, all that malarkey.'

'Think yourself lucky. When that happens,' Tony pointed out, 'the taxi driver tends to end up not getting paid.'

Martha and Eunice weren't window-shopping. They didn't dawdle; this was an outing with a destination at the end of it. Eventually turning off the main road, they made their way down leafy side streets. They weren't speaking to each other, just walking side by side. Where they might be heading was anyone's guess. A church meeting, perhaps. Visiting a friend. Keeping an appointment with the orthodontist.

'There you go,' said the cabbie as the two women finally turned into the driveway of a property set well back from the road.

Tony leaned forward. It was probably a dental surgery. As the taxi drew closer he saw the sign by the gate.

Stanshawe House Nursing and Residential Care Home, the sign announced.

'Mystery solved.' The cab driver sounded relieved; the last twenty-five minutes must have ranked among the most boring of his life. 'They're visiting some old granny.'

'Maybe. Maybe not. They could be visiting anyone.'

'Or else they work there,' the cabbie amended. 'Anyway, what now? Are you going in after them?'

'No.' Tony sat back in his seat; this wasn't how he'd planned to spend the rest of the day. 'Take me back to Primrose Hill.'

—•—

Ellie was still out at work. Back at the flat, Tony looked up Stanshawe House in the Yellow Pages and copied down the number of the place. Then he forced himself to sit and wait, because the one thing he couldn't do was phone them while Eunice and Martha might still be there.

At five o'clock he made the call.

'Oh, hello, I'm calling about one of your residents. By the name of Daines.' It was a shot in the dark, but the only shot he had.

'Sorry, who?' The woman sounded distracted.

'Daines.'

'Could you give me the first name?'

Tony hesitated. No he couldn't, because he didn't know the first name. He didn't even know if it was a male or a female. 'Um, well…'

'Oh, do you mean Henry Daines? Sorry, I'm new here, I've just found him on the list.'

Bingo. 'That's it. Henry.' Tony wondered whether real detectives got sweaty palms when they had a breakthrough.

'Right. And what is this about? Let me take a message.'

'Oh, no message. I'm just calling to… find out how he is.'

'Hang on, I'm just writing this down. Say again?'

God, she was dippy. 'I haven't seen Henry for some time. I heard that he's in your care,' said Tony. 'Could you tell me why he's with you?'

'Ooh no, we're not allowed to do that! Sorry! I tell you what, love, why don't you contact his family? They'll be able to give you all the information you need.'

Typical. 'OK then, can you tell me who his family—'

'Oh my goodness, now the red light's started flashing! What does that mean? Sorry, love, I'm going to have to go, just call his family… OK, bye!'

———

At nine o'clock the next morning, Tony rang the bell and heard the sound of footsteps inside the house.

The topaz-yellow door opened and for the first time in a fortnight he came face to face with Martha. His heart twisted with longing; it was so wonderful to see her again and so unbearable to witness the look of anguish on her face.

He kept his voice low. 'Are you on your own?'

She closed her eyes for a second, then nodded. 'Oh, Tony, don't do this. You shouldn't have come here.'

'I had to. You can't just tell me to leave you alone and expect me to do it. I thought we *had* something…'

'Please, no.' Martha was shaking her head in despair, her fingers clutching the front of her raspberry-pink shirt.

'Can I come in?'

'No.'

'Why not?'

'I told you, we can't see each other anymore.' Across the street a door slammed and she raised a trembling hand in greeting at whoever had just emerged from their house. Her breathing shallow, she said, 'Tony, just go. Do you think this is easy for me? Because it really isn't, I can promise you that.'

'I know, I know, but we need to talk.' He paused. 'Who's Henry?'

She froze, the fingers of her other hand convulsively tightening around the edge of the door.

'Who told you?'

'Is he your father-in-law?'

'No.'

'Brother-in-law?'

Martha shook her head.

'So that means he's your ex-husband.' Tony had already guessed as much; he didn't need to look at her to know he was right.

Except he couldn't help himself; he couldn't tear his eyes away from her face.

'He's not my ex-husband,' Martha said finally.

'You mean you're still married.'

She pressed her lips together, gave a funny, wobbly nod.

'Why don't I come in?' said Tony. And this time she stood back to allow him into the house.

In the kitchen, Martha rubbed her face to get the blood back into it. 'I still don't know how you found out. Was it Eunice?' She shook her head. 'It couldn't have been Eunice.'

Rather than tell her how he had stalked the pair of them, Tony said, 'Just tell me about Henry.'

'How much do you know?'

'Nothing at all.'

'We've been married for thirty-three years. Happily. Very happily.' Her voice began to waver. 'Well, up until six years ago. OK, I'm going to cry now. Don't say anything, just ignore it.' Reaching for the roll of kitchen towel, she tore off a couple of quilted sheets and rested one hip against the kitchen units. 'The thing is, he has Alzheimer's. Well, officially it's presenile dementia. It started seven years ago when he was only fifty-five. Just gradually, you know, losing keys and forgetting people's names. We joked about it at first. Until he made a serious mistake at work and it stopped being funny.' The tears were rolling down her cheeks, almost as though she didn't know they were there. 'Then he saw the doctor and had to have all these tests... well, you can imagine the rest. We got the diagnosis. We were both devastated and I promised to look after him. Henry was a high-powered accountant. Within a year of giving up work he couldn't put together a shopping list.' Martha paused to wipe her eyes. 'It all happened so much more quickly than I thought it would. He started putting his shoes in the oven. He tried to give our microwave to the postman. And instead of eating his dinner, he'd hide it in the loft.'

She stopped again to gather herself, and it was all Tony could do not to take her in his arms. But he stayed where he was, at the opposite end of the kitchen.

'And it carried on going downhill from there,' Martha said quietly. 'I did my best, I swear I did. But it was so much harder than I ever thought it would be. I was twenty-one years old when

I married Henry. He was just the best husband any girl could ask for. I loved him so much… and he could do *anything*, you know? He was clever, he was practical, if anyone had a problem he was the one who'd solve it. One of our neighbors was desperate once when her plumber let her down. I mentioned it to Henry when he came home from work, and he spent the evening plumbing her toilet in.' She shook her head. 'But that was before. Then it all changed and I was the one who had to look after Henry. He started having mood swings, then temper tantrums. It wasn't his fault, he was just scared and frustrated. But it was like trying to keep a six-foot toddler under control. He wasn't… easy. And all the time you know it's only going to get worse. I was having to feed him. And wash him. Brush his teeth.' Martha's voice broke. 'It's horrible. It's so undignified. And I know I'd promised to look after him, but it was just the l-loneliest job in the w-world…'

Tony said, 'That's why you told me you'd been on your own for a long time.'

She nodded, struggling to regain control. 'It is. But it wasn't fair for me to say that. I let you think I was divorced. That was so wrong.'

'It was completely understandable.'

'No, it was… disgusting. And I've never been so ashamed.'

'I interrupted.' Tony made a scrolling-back gesture with his finger. 'Carry on with the story.'

'The story.' Martha grimaced. 'The one with no happy ending. OK, I carried on as long as I could. With help from Eunice,' she amended. 'She's Henry's sister. Very hardworking, very serious. But I owe her a lot. Anyway, a year ago it all got too much for me. I was exhausted, I just couldn't cope anymore. I sold our big house in Notting Hill and bought this little one instead. Thanks to Henry, our finances were in good shape. And how did I repay him?' She heaved a sigh. 'By putting him in a nursing home. That was nice of me, wasn't it? But you know what? If it had been the other way round, he wouldn't have done that, I can guarantee you. Henry would have looked after me.'

'You don't know that.'

'Oh, I do.'

'He's getting the best care. You visit him... who's to say that isn't *better*?'

But Martha was giving him an odd look. Tony held up his hands in surrender. 'I'm sorry. I followed you yesterday afternoon. I had to know.'

She nodded slowly. 'It was stupid of me to ignore you and hope you'd disappear. But you do see now, don't you, why we can't see each other again?'

'It's a terrible situation.' All he wanted to do was comfort her and make the pain go away. 'How is he now?'

'Confused. Sad, sometimes. But he still recognizes me. He knows who I am. He calls me his beautiful wife.' Martha's expression changed. 'And in return I betrayed him.'

'When I saw you that day on the hill, you looked as if you didn't have a care in the world,' said Tony. 'You seemed so happy. That was what drew me to you.'

'I was happy.' She inclined her head in agreement. 'At first, after Henry went into the home, I was relieved. And every time I felt relieved, I felt guilty. My life had become easier and his hadn't. I was ashamed of myself, I shouldn't *be* happy. But as time went on, the guilt started to fade. For the last couple of months I've let myself relax and feel OK about my life. And, I don't know, sometimes it all just comes together. I was outside on a beautiful summer's day with the sun on my face. My painting was going well. That dear little boy came along with his ball and he was just adorable, and I suddenly realized I felt completely at peace. It was the most amazing experience, like having a great weight lifted off my shoulders.' Martha gazed fixedly at the wall. 'And then you came along, and you were lovely too. It was as if you were part of it.'

So that was why she had wanted to give him the painting. The money aspect had been irrelevant, the fact that he'd loved her work was all that mattered.

'And the next day was a continuation of that,' said Tony.

She nodded. 'I still can't believe I did it. You were just... so perfect. It was like taking a holiday from being myself. For a few hours I could be somebody else. I felt normal. No, I didn't, I felt *wonderful*.' Fresh tears sprang into her eyes. 'It was like the best dream ever.' Her fingernails were digging into the palms of her hands. 'And then it was over, and I woke up.'

'But it wasn't a dream.'

'I know that. I wish it had been. I was unfaithful to my husband and I hate myself. Which is why you have to leave me alone and not contact me. Because it's never going to happen again.'

Tony didn't want to hear her saying this. 'I don't think what we did was wrong.'

'That's not true. Of course it's *wrong*.' Martha eyed him sadly. 'You're just trying to justify it.'

'But there *is* a justification.'

'For better, for worse. That's what I said when I made my wedding vows.'

'But that's not—'

'Don't say it.' Martha held up her hands to stop him. 'This is my husband we're talking about. Would you like to ask Eunice if she thinks there's justification? What do you suppose her opinion would be? She lives just across the street, by the way. That afternoon we came back here, I knew she was away visiting friends in Stockport. Then when you turned up the next day, she was here. She'd come back early. And Eunice isn't stupid. She doesn't miss a trick. Which is why you have to go now.'

This was unbearable. Tony said, 'But I love you.'

She flinched, the words hitting her like arrows. 'Don't say that either. It can't happen. We had a moment together, but it was wrong. And it's *over*. You're a Hollywood actor and I'm an ordinary married woman from Tufnell Park.'

'You're not ordinary.'

Martha pressed her lips together and crossed the kitchen. Out in the hall, she pulled open the front door.

'I can't do this anymore. You have your life to live and I have mine.' She sounded as if her heart was breaking, but the look she gave him was resolute. 'If you care about me, you'll leave. Now.'

Chapter 20

A NASTY RIDING ACCIDENT seven years ago had left Dr Geraldine Castle with a broken left hip that had never successfully knitted back together. Now arthritis had set in as well, making the situation that much more difficult. It was, as she put it herself, a complete bugger. Walking was painful now, horse riding a thing of the past. High heels these days were only for looking at.

It didn't stop her buying them, though.

Once a shoe queen, always a shoe queen.

The postman, unable to deliver the parcel next door earlier, had left it with Ellie instead. Now back from lunch with an ex-work colleague, Geraldine had arrived to pick it up.

'OK, you have to see these,' she exclaimed. 'They are just to die for!'

Neither her limp nor her carved ebony walking stick detracted from her glamour. At sixty-one, innate style coupled with the posture of a model meant heads turned whenever Geraldine entered a room. Last year she had retired from a career in medicine, having spent many years in general practice.

In the office, she sat down and unwrapped the parcel.

'Oh, now, *there* you are. Hello!' Having removed the lid of the box, she greeted the shoes like long-lost children. 'Look at you! Aren't you beautiful?' She lifted them out and lovingly stroked the butter-soft lilac leather.

'If a patient told you he talked to his shoes,' Ellie pointed out, 'you'd refer him to a psychiatrist.'

'You know what? I probably would. But these are different.' Geraldine was busy admiring the silver leather flowers on the front. 'They're a work of art. They demand adulation!'

She truly loved them. Sometimes she would even wear them, but only whilst sitting down. Ellie watched her reverently place the shoes back in the box. 'I prefer flip-flops.'

'That's because you're a heathen,' said Geraldine. 'Where's Zack today?'

'Northampton. He'll be back around six.'

'You've been here for almost a month now.' Geraldine's eyes were bright as they searched her face. 'Enjoying it?'

'Definitely. No more getting squashed on the tube,' Ellie said happily. 'Bliss!'

An eyebrow was raised. 'That's all, is it?'

'And getting to see Elmo every day.'

'Well, that goes without saying.' Geraldine looked amused. 'I was thinking more of Zack. Isn't it a bonus getting to see him too?'

Giving up work had left Geraldine with way too much time on her hands and a curiosity that knew no bounds. She was like a couples therapist in perpetual search of problems to solve. Probably because she was a doctor, there was no question she was too embarrassed to ask. It wasn't the first time she had attempted to find out if Ellie was secretly harboring a crush on Zack.

'He's a good person to work for,' Ellie said patiently.

'And don't forget handsome.'

'Looks aren't everything.'

'But you don't have a boyfriend.' Geraldine had found out this much. 'Surely you must find him attractive.'

'OK, he's nice to look at. But that's all.' Ellie shrugged. 'Really.'

'You mean it, don't you? This is so disappointing.' A fresh thought struck Geraldine. 'Ooh,' she said brightly. 'Are you a lesbian?'

The question provoked a bittersweet flashback moment; whenever

Jamie had been in the mood for sex and she hadn't, his standard jokey riposte had been, 'How can you not want me? What are you, a lesbian?'

But that had been then. This was now. Ellie smiled slightly and said, 'No.'

'Oh, *shame*. My friend's daughter is a lesbian. I could have introduced you.'

'Sorry.'

'Zack's so lovely, that's all I'm saying.'

'I'm sure Louisa thinks so too.'

'Oh, *her*.' Geraldine's tone was dismissive; she couldn't summon up much enthusiasm for someone who didn't adore Elmo as much as she did. 'He can do better than that. I was out in the garden last week and I heard her having a panic attack because there were dog hairs on her skirt. You'd have thought it was snake venom, the fuss she was making.' After a moment she added, 'You're far nicer than Louisa. And prettier.'

'But I still don't have any designs on Zack,' Ellie pointed out. 'And he knows I don't. That's why he employed me.'

'You're absolutely right, darling.' Recognizing when she was beaten, Geraldine closed the shoebox and prepared to leave. 'Touché.'

'I wish you weren't married,' whispered Roo.

Niall tightened his arm around her waist and pulled her closer. 'Me too.'

Roo closed her eyes. It was Wednesday afternoon and he'd phoned at midday to say he was on his way over. Thanks to her overactive imagination, she'd managed to convince herself that something momentous had happened, he'd realized he couldn't live without her, he was going to leave Yasmin... or, better still, that Yasmin had decided *she* wanted out of the marriage, because then they wouldn't even have to feel guilty...

But in the manner of happy fantasies, it hadn't come true. When Niall had arrived at the house, Roo had said breathlessly, 'What's going on?'

And Niall, seizing her by the hand and leading her upstairs to the bedroom, had replied, 'I've been thinking about doing this all day.'

Which was flattering, of course it was. The fact that he'd so badly wanted to take her to bed was lovely, and romantic in its own way. It was just that it hadn't quite lived up to expectations because she'd misinterpreted the excitement in his voice over the phone and had geared herself up for something, well, *more...*

But it had still been nice.

'Hey, are you OK?'

One thing was for sure, she couldn't tell him what was wrong. It would make her sound pathetic.

'I'm brilliant.' One of the reasons Niall was so attracted to her was her confidence. Playfully raking her fingernails down his chest, she flicked the tip of her tongue against his mouth. 'I started writing a song about you last night.'

'You did?' He looked pleased. 'How does it go?'

Roo cleared her throat and began to sing: 'Feeling so real when one and one make two... you should know I'm the best thing that happened to you...' She shook her head. 'I'm still working on it. You'll have to wait till it's finished.'

Niall kissed her. 'Sounds amazing. You're incredible.'

'I know.' A breeze fluttered the pale gray linen curtains and all Roo's good intentions flew out of the open window. 'When are you going to leave your wife?'

'Hey.' He tilted her face back towards him, shaking his head slightly. 'I thought we weren't doing this anymore.'

Patience had never been Roo's forte. 'I just want us to be together properly.'

'And we will be. I *love* you,' said Niall. 'But it's a delicate situation. We can't rush it.'

'Why not?' It came out as a bleat but Roo couldn't help herself; she loved him too.

'Because it would go against me. The solicitors would have a field day.' He was checking his watch now, over her shoulder. 'I need to get back to work.'

'What's Yasmin like?'

'I've told you before. Can't we give it a rest?'

Innocently, Roo said, 'Where does she work?'

'Sweetheart, stop it. You don't need to know that.'

Except I already do. A knot tightened in her stomach as he slid away from her and climbed out of bed. 'She might be lovely.'

'She's not.'

'When you get home tonight, what will you do?'

'Honestly? You really want to know?' Niall began to pull on his trousers. 'Fine, here goes the routine. I arrive back at the house, see if there's anything to eat. Occasionally she bothers to cook something, generally she doesn't. So I'll make myself an omelet, open some tin or other, or do a microwave meal. Whatever I do, Yasmin will complain about it. Then I'll spend some time with Benjamin and she'll moan about that too. If I try to load the dishwasher, she'll tell me I've done it all wrong. If I sit down to watch a program on TV, you can guarantee she'll want me to get up and take the bins out. Basically, she criticizes me nonstop. And that's about it, that's our fairy-tale marriage in a nutshell.' His shirt was done up now and Niall was shrugging into his jacket. 'Trust me, my life is no fun.' Ready to leave, he moved back to the bed and bent to kiss her. 'Except when I'm with you.'

Why couldn't everything be straightforward? Why couldn't he be single? Aching at the unfairness of it all, Roo clung to him for a moment. 'When am I going to see you again? How about Saturday?'

'Oh God, I wish I could.' Niall stroked her short ruffled hair. 'But it's Yasmin's birthday. She's been going on about us having some time away. I don't want to,' he went on, 'but I can't get out of it.'

She felt sick. 'You're going on holiday?'

'Not a holiday. Just a weekend in Norfolk.'

'In a hotel?'

'Staying with friends. They've got kids too, so I'll be taking ear-plugs.' Niall pulled a face. 'It's going to be a nightmare. But what could I do?'

Roo gazed at him. Half of her felt sorry for him, the other half felt jealous.

Niall had promised her that he and Yasmin no longer slept to-gether, but she had to ask. 'If it's her birthday, will she want you to have sex with her?'

'What, change the habit of a lifetime?' He burst out laughing. 'Not a chance. And if she did, I'd just pretend to fall asleep. But she won't, I can promise you that. Look, you have a good time this weekend. I'm going to get through it the best I can, and I'll call you on Monday. I could come over in the evening. How about that?'

It was only Wednesday. When you were desperate to be with someone every minute of every day, being forced to wait five whole days before seeing them again was purgatory.

But what choice did she have? He was the love of her life and compared with never seeing him again, it was bearable.

And she would be super-cool about it, to make up for the earlier display of neediness. Looking vague, Roo murmured, 'Monday, Monday... I may have something on...'

'OK then, it'll have to be next Thursday.'

For crying out loud, that was a whole *week* away. Roo crumpled in an instant and curled her arms around his neck. 'Make it Monday.' Between kisses she said, 'I'll cancel whatever it is.'

Niall smiled. 'Good.'

Chapter 21

THERE HAD BEEN SOMETHING different about this evening. The realization had crept up on Ellie gradually; at first she'd thought she was imagining it. But she wasn't.

Well, that was pretty obvious now.

Furthermore, she appeared to be having an out-of-body experience. Todd Howard was kissing her and she was mentally standing back, noting her reaction to the experience with the detachment of an exam steward.

It probably ranked as a medium-strength kiss. Not too wet, not too dry. Not too hard or too soft. It felt completely bizarre, yet you couldn't call it unpleasant. She didn't want to wrench herself free and go *spleeurghhhh*, spluttering in horror and wiping her mouth like a six-year-old caught by a whiskery maiden great aunt.

Actually, that was long enough now. Breaking contact, she drew back and opened her eyes. Todd was already watching her, waiting to gauge her reaction. Had he spent the last few hours gearing himself up for this?

'Sorry.' He was breathing quite heavily. 'Are you OK?'

'Yes.' She still felt like an observer. Easy in each other's company, they'd fallen into the habit of spending time together at the weekends. Today had been no different; shopping on Portobello Road, a couple of drinks in the afternoon, then a walk in Regent's Park followed by a trip to a comedy club in Camden, and a stop-off at a pizza takeaway on the way home. Once back at the flat, they had relaxed on the sofa, washed the slices of quattro stagioni down with white wine, and started watching *Ocean's Eleven* on DVD.

Then halfway through the film, Todd had turned to look at her and said, 'Ell? I want to kiss you.'

And she'd been so astounded she'd said, 'Seriously?'

'Yes.'

'Oh.' And more out of politeness than anything else, she had heard herself say bemusedly, 'OK.'

The next moment, Todd's mouth had descended on hers. *And they were kissing.* This was when the split-screen effect had really kicked in. Half of Ellie had been evaluating the pressure, the wetness, the taste of the kiss, the smell of his skin, and the sensation of stubble gently grazing her cheek. The other half had felt like a mannequin in a shop window.

But it was bound to feel weird. It was eighteen months since Jamie had died, eighteen months since her last experience of mouth-to-mouth contact. And this was an unfamiliar mouth.

It was also saying something. Whoops, she'd been so busy assessing how it felt she hadn't been listening. Ellie shook her head. 'Sorry, I missed that.'

'I just asked if you're sure you're all right.'

'I'm all right.' Poor Todd, he was looking so worried. She smiled slightly to reassure him. 'I'm fine.'

'You had no idea I was wanting to do that? You weren't expecting it?'

'No.'

'But you didn't hate it?'

'No.'

Todd looked relieved. 'I've been plucking up the courage.'

'Oh?' What else could she say?

'Yes.' He nodded, searching her face for a reaction. 'I like you, Ellie. It never occurred to me to think about it before, when you and Jamie were together. But these past few weeks… I don't know, something seemed to be happening. I just really like being with you.' His eyes were bright. 'You're lovely.'

'Am I?' It was bizarre to hear him say it.

'Oh yes.' Gaining confidence, he added, 'Mind you, I can be pretty lovely too, when I put my mind to it.'

Her smile broadened, because that was the kind of banter he and Jamie had engaged in. Before you knew it they'd be off, arguing which of them was the loveliest.

'Look,' Todd went on, 'no pressure. I'm going to go now.' The tiniest of pauses gave her the opportunity to tell him he didn't have to leave. When she didn't say it, he stood up. 'You need time to think this through. The ball's in your court, OK? Give me a call whenever you want. I know it must feel a bit strange. But I reckon we could be good together. We could give it a try, see how we go. If you want.'

She rose to her feet. 'OK, thanks.' This was weird, like a job interview. Were they supposed to shake hands now?

Todd solved the dilemma by giving her a quick, just-good-friends hug. 'I'll wait to hear from you.'

She reciprocated with a polite, just-good-friends kiss on the cheek. 'Right, thanks.' It still felt surreal. She patted his arm. 'Bye.'

'Well, well, who'd have thought it?'

From the bed, Ellie sat with her knees up and studied Jamie's expression. She needed to know how he felt about what had happened earlier. The good thing was, he didn't look outraged. He seemed completely relaxed.

Then again, she was the one making him look like that.

'I know. Took me by surprise. I didn't lead him on at all.'

Jamie's blue eyes were sparkling. 'No need to be so defensive. Leading men on is allowed.'

'Don't you feel funny about it?' He must do, surely.

'OK, a bit.' He lounged against the wall and shrugged. 'But maybe it's better that it's someone I know. I trust him. Todd's not going to break your heart. That has to be a good thing, doesn't it?'

'I suppose.'

'Better than you going out and having a drunken one-night stand with some chancer who wouldn't even remember your name the next day.'

'Damn,' said Ellie. 'I was looking forward to that happening.'

Jamie grinned. 'I know you too well.'

'Anyway, we're not talking about sex.' The prospect of getting naked and actually *doing it* was too bizarre to even contemplate. 'That's not going to happen.'

'Right. Take things slowly.' He nodded in agreement. 'A few kisses and a bit of hand holding, that's enough to be going on with for now. See how you feel.'

'I already know how I feel. I feel *weird*.'

'It's been eighteen months.'

'Oh, has it really?' Mock amazement. 'That long already? I hadn't noticed.'

'One thing. Is he a good kisser?'

'He's OK.'

'Better than me?'

Ellie pretended to consider the question. 'Hm, I'll have to think about that.'

'He'd better not be better than me,' said Jamie. 'At kissing or holding hands.'

She looked at his long, tanned fingers, remembering how they'd felt and how well they'd fitted together with hers. She'd give anything to be able to hold his hand again. Oh great, here come the tears, was this ever going to stop happening?

'Don't cry,' said Jamie.

'I know.' She pulled a tissue from the box on the table next to the bed.

'Does this mean he *is* better?'

He was looking horrified, trying to make her laugh. Ellie smiled and wiped her eyes. 'Don't panic. You're still the best.'

'Thank goodness for that.' He relaxed and pushed his hands into the back pockets of his favorite low-slung jeans. 'But just so you know, I'm fine about Todd. You could do a lot worse.'

Chapter 22

'I'M SORRY, ZACK'S NOT here today. Did you have an appointment?'

The couple on the doorstep looked disappointed. The girl, who was petite and dark-haired, said, 'We just called round on the off chance. Oh, what a shame! We read that piece about him in the *Telegraph* the other day and thought he sounded like our kind of person.'

'Not afraid to take a leap occasionally, if he comes across a proposition he likes.' The man with her was tall, thin, and slightly beaky looking, but in a good way. His hair was Scandinavian blond, his manner was enthusiastic, and he resembled a scruffily dressed tennis player. Eagerly he said, 'And that's what we think we have for him.'

'OK, well, come in for a minute and let's see what we can do.' Ellie ushered them through to the office. Pulling the appointments diary across the desk, she said, 'I tell you what, he's had a cancellation for tomorrow morning. I could put you in for eleven o'clock, how does that sound?'

'We can do that. Brilliant.' They looked at each other and beamed.

'Give me your names.' Ellie reached for the diary and picked up a pen.

'Kaye and Joe Kerrigan.'

'And the proposal's in there,. is it?' She indicated the padded A4 envelope Joe was clutching to his chest like treasure. 'Why don't you leave it here, then Zack can have a look through it before he sees you? That'll save some time.'

'Oh, but...' Kaye looked worried, then stopped herself. 'The thing is, we kind of wanted to talk him through the whole thing...'

Joe put a bony hand on her arm. 'Let her take it. Whatever's easiest for Mr McLaren. We'll see him tomorrow.' He flashed Ellie an apologetic look. 'Sorry. This just means so much to us. You have no idea.'

'It means everything in the world,' Kaye echoed longingly. 'If anyone can make this happen, it's Zack McLaren. We've been reading up on him all week.' Her eyes were shining. 'You're so lucky. He must be fantastic to work for.'

'He's a nightmare.' Ellie broke into a smile. 'No, he isn't, he's great. I'll make sure he gets this.' She reached for the padded envelope. 'And we'll see you tomorrow.'

'Hang on.' Kaye grabbed the envelope before Joe could hand it over. 'Sorry! Just let me give it one last kiss for luck...'

Zack arrived back at four. Ellie brought him up to date with everything that had been happening in the office. Then she passed him the folder that had been inside the padded envelope.

Zack flicked through the proposal for all of twenty seconds, then closed the folder, and Frisbeed it on to the desk.

'You have to read it,' Ellie said.

'Just have.'

'All of it!'

'I don't need to read all of it. I just need to get the gist.'

'And?'

'It's a film script.'

'I know!'

'They want me to be their backer, to provide the finance to get the film made.' Amused, Zack shook his head. 'It's completely crazy. Not my thing at all. No way.'

'But if it took off…'

'It wouldn't. We're talking about the riskiest business on the planet. I wouldn't touch a project like that with a barge pole.'

Kaye and Joe Kerrigan's earnest faces, so filled with hope, swam in front of her. They were going to be devastated. Ellie said, 'What about *Mamma Mia*?'

'The exception that proves the rule.'

'*Titanic.*'

'The other exception that proves the rule.'

'*ET.*'

'And just how much of your own money would you be prepared to bet that this script is as good as the script for *ET*? Look,' said Zack, 'I'm not going to back these people. It would be madness. And don't look at me like that. I'm not an ogre. I just don't want to pack all my hard-earned money into one giant firework and explode it over London.'

'You haven't even read the script,' Ellie protested.

'I don't need to. What would be the point?'

'Oh, come on, you're an entrepreneur. It might be stupendous. You just don't *know*.' She jiggled the pen she'd been using. 'Honestly, this couple has worked so hard on it. You not looking at the script is like… it's like spotting a Lotto ticket on the pavement but not bothering to bend down and pick it up because the chances are that it wouldn't win the jackpot anyway!'

Zack raised his hands in surrender. 'OK, OK. You've made your point. You really want to shame me into reading this script?'

'Yes, I really do.'

'Fine then, you win. I'll read it.'

'Promise?'

'Promise.' His phone burst into life and Zack answered it. 'Robert, thanks for getting back to me, do you have time to run through these figures now? Great, hang on, my notes are upstairs…'

Backing out of the office, Zack pointed to the folder on the desk then pressed his hand to his chest and silently mouthed, 'I *promise*.'

When he'd gone, Ellie opened the folder and detached the film script from the rest of the paperwork. There were just over a hundred loose A4 pages. Crossing the office, she fitted them into the photocopier and pressed PRINT. She might not be a multimillionaire entrepreneur, but Kaye and Joe Kerrigan's enthusiasm had sparked her curiosity.

She was going to read the script, even if Zack wasn't.

'Well?' Ellie demanded the next morning.

'Well what?' Zack was throwing Elmo's rubber ball around the kitchen, bouncing it off the units so that Elmo skittered and slid across the cream marble-tiled floor like something out of a cartoon.

'Did you read it?'

'Read what?'

'The film script.'

'Oh, that. Yes I did.'

'*Woof.*' Elmo barked impatiently, ready for Zack to throw the ball again.

'What was it like?'

'Actually, it was pretty good.' *Throw.*

Ellie filled the kettle at the sink, skipping out of the way as Elmo barreled past in ecstatic pursuit of the ball.

'And?'

'Still not doing it.'

'Woof woof *woof.*' Elmo's tail wagged furiously as Zack dodged behind the table and grabbed the ball a split second before he could reach it.

'Who was the priest?' said Ellie.

'What priest?'

Ha! 'The one in the film script who turned up at the end.'

Zack straightened up; his red polo shirt had come untucked and there was a new rip in the knee of his Levi's. 'Oh, that priest.' He narrowed his eyes in concentration then said innocently, 'Sorry. I don't think I can remember.'

Ellie shook her head. 'You promised.' The one thing she'd thought about Zack was that he was honest. If he said he'd do something, he should do it.

'I was really busy last night.' He was watching her reaction. 'Anyway, how do you know there's a priest in it?'

'I made a copy, took it home last night, and read it.' Meaningfully, she added, 'Unlike some people.'

'Have I disappointed you?' Zack lobbed the ball towards her, over Elmo's head. 'Here, catch.'

Ellie caught it in her left hand as Elmo leapt into the air. 'Yes, you have.'

'Neat catch.' He signaled his approval. 'So what did you make of the script then?'

She threw the ball back to him, sending Elmo into a frenzy of excitement. 'I thought it was brilliant. It *is* brilliant. It's funny, it's moving, and it's original. If it was made into a film, I'd go and see it.'

'Would you?'

'Yes.'

Zack teased Elmo by waving the ball just out of reach. 'And would you cry at the sad bits?'

'Maybe. OK,' Ellie conceded, 'probably.'

'Like when Mary finally meets the son she put up for adoption and discovers it's Father Dermot?'

'Oh God, *yes!*' Belatedly she stopped dead in her tracks. Zack lobbed the ball into the air and she stood there, not even attempting to catch it. One of the stools clattered as Elmo almost brained himself, diving on the ball and triumphantly regaining possession at last.

Zack half-smiled and said, 'It just came back to me in a flash.'

'So you did read the whole thing?'

'I wasn't going to. You shamed me into it.'

'Excellent.' Ellie felt herself flush with pleasure. 'And will you back them?'

'I still can't do that.' He looked regretful. 'It's not my field, the risks are astronomical, I don't have any contacts who'd be prepared to invest in that kind of venture. But I did like the script,' he went on. 'A lot. When they get here, I'll let them down lightly.'

'Right.' Oh well, at least she'd tried.

'And if their film ever does get made,' said Zack, 'we'll go along to the cinema and watch it together. My treat.'

Elmo dropped the ball at his feet, desperate to get the game up and running again.

Ellie said, 'And will I get to say I told you so?'

Zack said good-naturedly, 'Deal.'

The doorbell went at two minutes to eleven. Ellie opened the door to the Kerrigans and saw the naked hope in their eyes.

As she showed them into the hall, Kaye whispered excitedly, 'Has he read the script?'

'He has.'

'We didn't sleep a wink last night! And on our way over here this morning we saw two magpies. Two for joy!'

Oh dear. And now Zack was about to dash their dreams. Ellie led them up the staircase and knocked on the living-room door.

'It's finally happening. This could be it.' Joe Kerrigan, taking deep breaths, briefly touched Ellie's arm as they waited for Zack to appear. 'Wish us luck.'

They were in with him for almost thirty minutes. Ellie, typing away with her ears on elastic, finally heard the door open upstairs, followed by the sound of footsteps on the staircase. If the meeting had lasted half an hour, could that mean Zack had changed his mind?

Then she heard Joe say, 'Well, thanks anyway,' and knew he hadn't.

Zack put his head round the office door. 'I have calls to make, but Joe and Kaye would like a quick word before they go, so I'll leave you to show them out.'

'He can't help us,' Joe explained when Zack had disappeared back upstairs. 'But we just wanted to say thanks for fighting our corner.'

'He told us about you nagging him to read the manuscript.' Kaye was being heartbreakingly brave. 'And he said you read it too.'

'I thought it was brilliant.' They were such a lovely couple.

'That means so much.' Kaye smiled at her.

'You mustn't give up.'

'We won't. We can't,' said Joe. 'We think it's brilliant too.'

'Plus he's modest.' Kaye gave him a nudge.

'I can't help how I feel. This is our dream. It's been our dream for so long.'

'It's just that we're starting to run out of options.'

Joe shook his head. 'We have to keep going.'

Ellie said, 'Look, I don't know anything about getting films made, but do you have to do all this yourself? How about sending the script out to all the big film companies? Maybe one of them will snap it up!'

'We've already tried that. Every company, every last screen agent. They all turned us down.'

'Oh.' OK, now she felt stupid.

'We have enough rejection letters to paper our whole house. It's just so frustrating.' Kaye *sounded* intensely frustrated. 'Most of them don't even bother to look at the script. I started putting hairs between the pages so you could see if they'd been opened. And they hadn't!'

Nice. Ellie wondered how charmed any potential producer would be by the sight of a script full of hair.

'Not a whole head's worth.' Joe grinned. 'Just one hair per script.'

'Glad to hear it.' He had an open, friendly face and an easy manner. Together he and Kaye made a good couple.

'Anyway,' said Kaye, 'you need to be getting back to work. But we just wanted to say thank you for being so enthusiastic and for doing your best with Zack.'

'Don't give up,' Ellie said as she showed them out.

'Don't worry.' Joe paused on the doorstep, then raised a hand in salute. 'We won't.'

Chapter 23

Tony, back from three days in Wales, was watching *Deal Or No Deal* when Ellie arrived home from work.

'I've ordered Indian.' He waved to her from the sofa. 'It'll be here in twenty minutes. How was your weekend, darling?'

Ellie waited until the food had been delivered before telling him what she knew she had to tell him. Tony was flying back to LA tomorrow morning and he deserved to know the truth.

That was, if they didn't burst from overeating before she could get the words out.

'Did I order too much?'

'Maybe a bit.' Faced with a takeaway menu, Tony was famous for his inability to whittle things down. Practically every surface in the kitchen bristled with foil containers and discarded lids.

'I can't help it, I just hate the thought of missing out.' He was helping himself to lamb jalfrezi, peshwari naan, saag aloo, bindi bhaji, and mushroom rice. 'Remember the time I ordered *the* tandoori chicken and they thought I'd said three?' Chuckling at the memory, Tony said, 'Jamie never could resist a challenge, could he? Ended up eating every last one of them.'

Oh no, and now he'd brought Jamie into the conversation. Her heart sinking, Ellie put down the carton of prawn bhuna. How to say it? She took a deep breath. 'Tony, do you think Jamie would be OK about it if I started… um, maybe seeing someone else?'

He stopped spooning mango chutney onto his lamb. There was the tiniest of pauses while he gathered himself.

'Oh, my darling, of course he'd be OK. It's been a year and a half. Haven't I said this before? You *should* be getting out there again. Jamie would be happy for you, I know he would. And I'm happy for you too. So long as it's someone nice, someone who deserves you.' He looked at her sideways. 'Is it someone nice?'

'Yes.' *Tell him, tell him…*

'I think I know.' Tony's smile was compassionate. 'Are we talking about Mr McLaren?'

What? God, what a thing to say. 'Zack? No, it's not Zack!'

'Oh, sorry, my mistake. Go on then, who's the lucky man?'

Ellie braced herself. *Just tell him.*

'Unless it's a woman,' Tony said hastily. 'That's fine too. It doesn't have to be a man.'

Ellie snorted with laughter and the tension was broken. 'The look on your face!'

'I know. Sorry.' He shook his head. 'It's all this bloody political correctness. Of course I'd rather it was a man.'

'Well, that's good, because it is a man.' *For crying out loud, just spit it out…* 'It's Todd.'

Another pause. Then Tony broke into a broad smile and said, 'Really? Even better! Sweetheart, that's great news. I had no idea.' He seemed genuinely pleased.

'Me neither. I thought we were just friends. And now it seems as if it might be… you know, turning into something else.' Hurrying to reassure him, Ellie said, 'It's very early days, though. He only told me on Saturday. Nothing's happened yet.' Way too much information probably, but she needed Tony to know she hadn't been cavorting here in the flat behind his back.

'Trust me, Jamie would want you to live your life.'

Hopefully he was right. 'I'm doing my best.'

'And no need to feel guilty either.' Tony was perspicacious. 'You're not being unfaithful.'

'I know.' She dolloped a spoonful of rice on to her plate. 'But it still feels funny.'

'Bound to.'

Now that she'd started, Ellie discovered she couldn't stop. 'It kind of feels like an arranged marriage.'

'Oh, sweetheart, it's just a question of getting used to the idea. So long as the basic attraction's there, you'll be fine.'

Hmm, that was the other thing she wasn't so sure of. *Was* there a basic attraction? How could she even tell when she was this much out of practice? Since Saturday evening she had given it a lot of thought. Like the kiss itself, the prospect of becoming emotionally involved with Todd didn't fill her with abject horror. Whereas if she turned him down, his feelings would be hurt. Consequently she had decided to go along with the idea for the time being. If nothing else, it would be nice to be part of a couple, to just feel normal again.

Well, relatively normal.

Anyway, take things slowly, see how they go. And at least she'd told Jamie's dad now. That was one hurdle out of the way.

Their plates were both full. No longer even hungry, Ellie picked hers up and said, 'Shall we go through?'

In the living room, keen to change the subject, she launched into the story of Kaye and Joe Kerrigan's unsuccessful meeting with Zack.

'It's tough.' Tony nodded in agreement. 'You've got more chance of being struck by lightning than you have of getting a film made. In LA,' he went on drily, 'you've got more chance of being struck by lightning than you have of finding someone who hasn't written a film script.'

'This one's really good, though.'

'Thousands of scripts are really good. Tens of thousands.'

'But they tried sending it to agents and film companies and they didn't even bother to read the thing!'

'That's because they get sent thousands of unsolicited scripts.

Literally. If they sat down and read them all, they'd never get any-thing else done. Sometimes they'll look at the first page.' He said this as if that made it better.

Ellie said frustratedly, 'That's so unfair, though.'

'Like I said, it's a tough business.'

She swallowed a mouthful of bhaji. 'I know. It's ironic, though, isn't it, that so many films do get made and turn out to be crap.'

—〜〜—

The next morning Tony was up early, packed and waiting for his car to arrive and deliver him to Heathrow. Carrying his cup of coffee through to the living room, he flicked through the jumble of news-papers and copies of *heat* in the magazine rack in search of something to take with him to read on the plane. *TV Guide*, nope. *Cosmopolitan*, not likely. Cheap-and-cheerful holiday brochures, no thanks. Argos catalogue, just kill me now. Then he came to the screenplay Ellie had been banging on about last night. At one stage she'd even pulled it out of the rack and tried to persuade him to read it himself. What she lacked in slick salesmanship she more than made up for with enthusiasm, but he'd retaliated by arguing, 'Is there a part for me in this nonexistent movie?' And when her face had fallen and she'd said, 'Well, not really,' he had replied, 'So that would be like asking an alligator to be interested in a dandelion sandwich.'

Ellie had abandoned her campaign after that. Instead, they had watched *The Apprentice* on TV, made fun of the contestants, and chatted about his weekend in Wales with the cast of the upcoming *Gavin, Stacey, and Two Smoking Barrels* film.

Now Tony straightened and glanced out of the window. His car had pulled up outside. Fine, he'd pick up a few magazines when he reached Departures, but he could still do with something to pass the time on the way to the airport. A closer look out of the window confirmed that he'd yet again drawn the short straw on the driver front; Malcolm was a good soul, but his never-ending cheerfulness, garrulousness, and terrible impressions of celebrities were a bit too much to bear at this hour of the morning.

Tony drained his coffee cup, picked the screenplay out of the rack, and surveyed the title page: *My Long-Lost Irish Daddy* by Kaye and Joe Kerrigan. With a God-awful title like that, was it any wonder it hadn't been taken seriously by the professionals?

Right, he'd take the thing with him and read through it on the way to Heathrow; that way maybe noisy Malcolm would lay off the Tom Jones impersonations and leave him in peace. He zipped it into his hand luggage and paused in the hallway, wondering whether to knock on Ellie's door. Should he wake her up to say goodbye?

Sanity prevailed. It was six o'clock. In the months following Jamie's death, Ellie had suffered terribly from insomnia, not to mention the dreaded waking up at four in the morning and not being able to get back to sleep again. Her sleeping routine was only now returning to normal.

To disturb her would be an act of cruelty.

He'd just go.

—◦◦◦—

Another weekend, another Saturday out with Todd, another awkward moment at the end of it.

And three—three!—kisses this time; one when he'd arrived at the flat, another while they'd been walking through Regent's Park, and now this, the goodbye one on her doorstep at the end of the evening.

Ellie did her best to make her muscles go loose. She'd been trying to just let herself relax into it, but it still felt weird. Her whole body was uncomfortable. Worst of all, she was now unable to banish from her mind the idea that Jamie was up there somewhere, looking down at them, watching her, and finding her ineptness and lack of engagement hilarious.

It was all so off-putting. No wonder she couldn't concentrate.

'I've had a really good time.' Todd stroked the side of her face, smoothing back a stray strand of hair.

'Mm, me too.'

'Sure?' Jamie's voice was in her head, as clear as anything. 'Because you never used to kiss me like that.'

Shut up, shut up, shut up.

'If you've forgotten how to do it,' Jamie added helpfully, 'maybe you should sign up for evening classes.'

For crying out loud, was it any wonder she couldn't relax?

Todd was still doing the smoothing thing with her hair. 'Are you OK?'

Could he stop doing it now? 'Yes, fine. Just a bit tired, that's all.'

'Oh dear, oh dear.' Jamie tutted with amusement. 'Now that's definitely not true.'

Bugger off, will you?

'Tired,' echoed Todd, clearly equally unconvinced.

'Sorry.' She could tell from his expression that he knew what she was saying. Basically, if he'd been entertaining hopes of staying over, it wasn't going to happen. Again.

'No problem.' As before, Todd hid his disappointment well. 'You have a good night's sleep.' He gave her a final hug. 'I'll call you tomorrow. And don't forget about Mum's barbecue, whatever you do.'

Ellie suppressed another qualm. Her very first invitation to a social event as Todd's girlfriend. It was his mum's sixtieth birthday the week after next. On that Wednesday they were having a big old party at home with a barbecue, dancing in the back garden, and friends and relatives from all over to celebrate the occasion. When Todd had broken the news to his mother that he and Ellie were an item, Maria Howard had evidently clapped her hands in delight and cried, 'Oh, how wonderful. I'm so *happy* for the two of you!'

So that was it; in eleven days' time Ellie would be introduced to everyone and officially welcomed into the family. What's more, there was nothing to be nervous about because she had it on good authority that they were all lovely people and looking forward to meeting her.

'A week on Wednesday.' She nodded and smiled reassuringly at Todd. 'I'll write it on my calendar. I won't forget.'

'I can't wait for you to meet everyone. It's going to be great.' Todd gave her one last kiss on the mouth.

'*Mwah*.' Oh well, she liked parties and she liked people. Maybe actually being introduced as Todd's girlfriend would make it feel a bit more… real.

Chapter 24

'What's this? I didn't send you this.' Tony's agent had called by the house in Beverly Hills to get a sheaf of contracts signed and show off his fresh-from-the-showroom lime-green Ferrari. As long as it 'pulled the chicks'—Marvin's own excruciating words—it didn't bother him that the color clashed with his brick-red face. Now, out on the shaded terrace, he homed in on the screenplay lying on the table next to the water jug. 'Where d'ya get this thing, Tone? Jeez, that's the crappiest title I ever heard in my life.'

'I know. But the script's bloody good. In fact it's amazing,' said Tony. 'Don't pick it up.'

'Bluddy good, bluddy good, *amaaayzing*.' Marvin chuckled; it cracked him up to imitate Tony's accent. 'So who wrote it?'

'No one you know. Just leave it. Here, have a drink. Are you hungry?' Oh, it was so easy to wind Marvin up. Reverse psychology was a wonderful thing. Tony covertly watched as his agent picked up the script and turned to the first page.

In all honesty, it wasn't the best first page in the world. Ninety-nine percent of agents would have given up. Then again, ninety-nine percent of agents didn't have Tony Weston saying, as if he meant it, 'I'm serious, Marvin, put it down, it's nothing to do with you.'

What could be more enticing than that?

Tony got on with signing his way through the contracts Marvin had brought over. And he waited. When several more minutes had passed, he said, 'Well?'

'Interesting. Different.' Marvin's Prada shades were pushed up on to his shiny red forehead. If it had been physically possible, he would have been frowning. 'There's no part in it for you.'

'I know. But I have a real feeling about this script. You know how sometimes you just get that? And it never does any harm to be the person who introduces the right script to the right producer. I have a few contacts that—'

'Hello, mission control? Who has more contacts in this business? You or me?'

'Yes, but—'

'Cor-*rect*.' Marvin pointed a stubby finger at him. 'I do. Who works for one of the biggest talent agencies in the country? Oh, wow, would ya believe it, me again. Tone, do the right thing here, wouldja? Just let me take care of this, let me take it back to the agency and show it to Stephen. If anyone can get a buzz going, he can.'

Tony hid a smile. In the space of a few minutes he hadn't done such a bad job on the buzz front himself. But that was this industry for you. Appear desperate and you're dead in the water. Tell someone they can't have something and they'll snap your hand off. Even now, Marvin was flicking through the pages of the screenplay with a greedy, acquisitive glint in his eye.

Welcome to Hollywood, baby.

—✦—

'Darling, come on, just say yes. You know you want to really.'

OK, the time had come. Zack prepared himself for the imminent fallout. He hadn't actually planned for this to happen this evening, here in Louisa's flat, but she had forced his hand. Throughout dinner all she'd talked about was holidays. Friends of hers had rented a luxury villa in Tuscany in late August and were keen for Louisa and Zack to join them, but they now needed a definite answer by tomorrow, presumably so that if they were turned down they could move on to the next couple on the list.

Zack also presumed that since it was already mid-July, he and Louisa hadn't been anywhere near the top of it.

But Louisa had been enthralled by her friends' offer and was longing to go. Now, desperate to persuade him that he did too, she was giving him her playful, encouraging look. 'Think about how fabulous it'll be. And best of all, it's adults only! No ghastly screaming kids to ruin the ambience and fill the pool with inflatables.' Evidently inflatables in a pool were on a par with used condoms. 'Just glorious peace and quiet, wonderful food, grown-up conversation, and fine wine. What could *be* more idyllic?'

By grown-up conversation, needless to say, she meant endless discussions about which celebrity had the best face-lift. Right, here we go. Brace, brace. Zack said, 'Honestly? It doesn't sound that idyllic to me. My idea of a great holiday is going home to Cornwall and piling down to the beach with my nephews and nieces. We play volleyball and dig holes in the sand, we eat ice cream, we throw each other into the sea, and we make a lot—and I mean a lot—of noise.'

'Oh!' Louisa sat back, startled. 'Oh… sorry, I had no idea.' Mentally regrouping, she said hastily, 'But that sounds nice too! Look, maybe we could pop down to see your family before we go to Italy…'

'I really don't think you'd like it,' said Zack. 'There are babies, there are dogs, there are whoopee cushions. There's fish and chips, and games on the beach, and fairground rides.' He shook his head. 'And there's very little in the way of grown-up conversation.'

'But—'

'In fact, anyone attempting even *that much* grown-up conversation'—he held up his hand, his finger and thumb a couple of millimeters apart—'gets wrapped up in seaweed and chucked into the sea.'

'OK, OK, I get it. You like noisy holidays. So what are we going to do?' She fixed him with a let's-negotiate smile.

'I think you should go to Tuscany,' said Zack. 'You'll have a great time.'

The smile faltered. 'You mean… on my own?'

'We don't like the same things.'

Louisa's eyebrows had gone right up. 'On my *own*?'

'Look, we need to talk.' Zack put down his cheese knife; God, he hated this bit. 'The thing is, I really think you'd be happier with someone else.'

'I'd be happier with someone else,' Louisa echoed, dumbfounded. 'On holiday?'

'Not just on holiday. In general. In your life.'

'You mean… instead of you?'

'No, no… well, yes.' He was rubbish at this. How did other people do it? Please don't let her start crying.

'You're finishing with me?'

'Not *finishing*. I just think it would be better if we… you know, called it a day.'

Louisa put down her spoon. 'But it wouldn't be better for me. I don't want to call it a day.'

OK, this wasn't getting them anywhere. Zack took a deep breath and said steadily, 'Yes, but I do.'

She let out a wail of anguish. 'Zacky, *why*?'

He cringed. She'd just called him *Zacky*. Could he cite this as reason number one?

But that would be cruel. He didn't want to be cruel. 'Look, you're great. It's not you, it's me. I work too hard. You deserve to be with someone who'll make you happy.'

'You make me happy.'

'I wouldn't.' Zack shook his head. 'Not in the long term.'

'But I thought we were in it for the long term!' She was crying now, trying to reach across the table for his hands. 'I'm thirty-five, Zack. This was our future. I thought we'd end up having kids together, the works!'

This was the first he'd heard of it. 'You don't like kids,' Zack pointed out. 'The whole point of going to Tuscany was because there wouldn't be any kids there to ruin the holiday.'

'*Other* people's kids. That's completely different. I still want some of my own!'

Some?

'I'm sorry.' Zack stood up. 'I should go. You'll be fine…'

'I can't believe this. I cooked you dinner.' Louisa flung out her arm in the direction of the kitchen. 'Boulangère potatoes and rack of lamb! From a proper butcher!'

'I know, and it was *great*.' Maybe he should send her flowers tomorrow to say thanks. God, it was all so complicated and fraught. Why was it so much easier to walk away from a rocky business deal than from a no-hope emotional relationship?

'Are you seeing someone else?' She searched his face.

Zack kept his expression carefully neutral. 'No, no one.'

'Sure? Because that would make sense. More sense than you just deciding out of the blue that, hey, we like different holidays so let's break up.'

'I'm not seeing anyone else.'

'Not even whatshername? That cute little PA of yours?' Mascara was leaking into the creases around Louisa's carefully made-up eyes. 'Ellie?'

'No.' He shook his head. He saw Ellie almost every day. But not in the way Louisa meant. It killed him to see her and not be able to do anything, but it would be even harder to bear not seeing her at all.

At least they were in Louisa's flat, meaning he could be the one to leave. In the hallway, she tried to throw herself into his arms. He gave her one last apologetic hug.

'How about Disney World?' She mumbled the words damply into his shoulder. 'We could go there if you like.'

He didn't reply.

Louisa pulled away and gazed miserably up at him. 'No?'

'Sorry.' Zack shook his head; it was time to get out of here. 'Bye.'

Chapter 25

OK, WAS THIS SNEAKY? He didn't resort to underhand tactics as a rule. But if they helped, why not?

Zack bent down, unclipped Elmo's lead, and pushed the front door shut behind him. Elmo, tail wagging, trotted down the hallway to greet Ellie.

'Hello, baby! Did you have a lovely walk?'

Wouldn't it be great if she could be saying that to him?

'Morning.' By the time he reached the office, Elmo was up on her lap. 'On a diet?'

'No.' She looked at him, mystified.

'Good. You can have one of these, then.' Zack opened the lid of the cake box to show her. 'I had to get them. We were walking past the deli and they were in the window.'

'Calling out to you.' Ellie grinned. 'Beckoning and whispering your name. They do that sometimes. Especially those naughty strawberry ones.'

He loved the way she instinctively mimed the beckoning and whispering as she said it, without having the remotest idea how irresistible it made her look. He could watch her forever.

'You like them?'

'Just a bit!'

'I'll get us a couple of plates.'

'Thank you,' said Ellie when he came back from the kitchen. She tipped Elmo off her lap and helped herself to one of the pastries, biting into a glazed strawberry with relish. 'Mm, gorgeous.'

A little gentle bribery never hurt. Zack took another cake for himself and pulled out the chair opposite.

'Just so you know, you won't be seeing Louisa around here anymore. We broke up.' He said it casually but kept a close eye on her reaction; wouldn't it be fantastic if her face lit up, betraying the feelings she'd worked so hard to keep hidden from him all this time...

'Oh no, I'm sorry.' Ellie put down her cake. 'Are you upset?'

So much for hidden feelings.

'No.'

'Was it her decision or yours?'

She looked genuinely concerned. For a split second he considered going for the sympathy vote. But no, that would be too underhanded. Zack smiled briefly and said, 'Mine.'

'Oh, well. In that case, I'm glad.'

'Really?' Hope flared.

'She wasn't right for you.' Picking her cake back up, Ellie licked a swirl of cream. 'She *definitely* wasn't right for Elmo.'

'I know.'

'And she was suspicious of me too. Like, she didn't trust me working with you.' Ellie sucked strawberry glaze from her index finger. 'I mean, that was just downright embarrassing.'

OK, you can stop now...

'Anyway, she's gone.' Zack pulled the diary across the desk towards him. 'So, if she wasn't right for me, who would be?' He sat back, feigning amused detachment. 'What kind of girl should I go for next?'

'Seriously? Someone fun. With a good sense of humor. Outgoing. Likes dogs. Doesn't like Liquorice Allsorts.'

'But... I *like* Liquorice Allsorts.'

'Exactly. If she liked them too, you'd end up fighting over the good ones. Far better that she doesn't.'

'You're really giving this some thought, aren't you?'

Ellie swallowed another mouthful of puff pastry and cream. 'It's in my best interests to get you matched up with someone nice. Stop you being grumpy.'

'I'm never grumpy,' Zack protested. Cheek!

'Ah, grumpy people always say that.'

'Fine, then. I'll look out for a liquorice-hating, dog-loving, fifty-years-younger version of Joan Rivers. But in the meantime...' idly he turned over a few pages in the office diary. 'I may need to ask you a favor.'

Ellie didn't hesitate. 'No problem. What kind of favor?'

Oh yes, he was brilliant. This could make all the difference. It had only occurred to him this morning that he might be able to use the situation to his advantage... maybe socializing with Ellie outside the office environment would enable her to view him in a different light.

Who knows, it could ignite the spark.

'There are evening events I have to attend. Sometimes I need to take along a partner. It's just that everyone else does, so it messes up the numbers if you go on your own... anyway, they're usually OK, not too boring...' *Shut up, listen to yourself, you sound like an idiot.* 'So how about it? Does that seem like something you wouldn't mind helping me out with sometimes?' *Jesus, never mind an idiot, you sound like a complete dick.*

'Why not? Sounds like fun. Yes, great.' Ellie was smiling at him as if he wasn't a dick. But sadly not as if she found him completely irresistible either.

'Great.' *No, she just said great, you don't say great too.* 'Right, well, this is the first one, let me tell you about it.' He tapped the page he'd stopped at. 'It's being held at the Dorchester next Wednesday and—'

'Wednesday?' Ellie's hand flew to her mouth. 'I can't do next Wednesday! Sorry!'

'Oh. Shame.' It wasn't really vital to take along a partner but he was still disappointed. So much for the grand plan.

'Isn't that typical? The one thing I really can't get out of. Any other evening and I could have done it.'

'No problem, I'll manage. So, something nice?'

Ellie hesitated. After a moment, as if debating whether or not to tell him, she said, 'Hope so. It's a party for my boyfriend's mum.'

Well. That was a bolt from the blue. Taken aback, Zack wondered what had prompted it. Was she really coming clean after all this time about her relationship with Tony Weston?

Plus, if that was who she was talking about, how old must his mother be? A hundred and forty?

Aloud he said, 'Well, you can't miss that.' OK, seeing as she'd raised the subject, he'd keep it going. 'Where's the party?'

'In her garden. It's a barbecue.' Ellie was busy playing with Elmo's lopsided ears. 'Which means it'll probably tip down with rain, but never mind.'

'And is it a special birthday?'

'Oh yes. She's sixty.'

Not Tony Weston's mother, then. Zack's heart was hammering against his ribs. 'So what's this boyfriend's name?'

She turned pink. 'Todd.'

'You've never mentioned him before.' It was hard work, keeping his tone casual.

'No. Well, it's all pretty new. We've only been seeing each other for a couple of weeks.'

'Going OK?'

Ellie nodded and said brightly, 'Going great!'

Damn. Damn you, Todd, whoever you are.

'And was there someone else before that?' Was he asking too many personal questions now? Possibly, but he needed to know.

She hesitated. 'What, you mean *ever*?'

'I meant since you've been here in Primrose Hill.'

Ellie shook her head. 'No, this is the first for a while.' She looked puzzled. 'Why?'

Always keep your lies as close as possible to the truth. Zack said, 'It's just that someone happened to mention they thought they'd seen you with Tony Weston.'

Ellie's flush deepened significantly. 'Oh.'

'And then I realized, that time I called you at home a while back, he was the person who answered the phone.'

'Right. Yes, it was.' She clicked her fingers at Elmo, inviting him to jump back on to her lap. Classic distraction technique.

He'd started, so he may as well finish. 'And you did say you were living rent-free in your friend's flat.'

'Oh *God*.' Half laughing, half mortified, Ellie buried her face in Elmo's furry ears. 'He's a *friend*. He's not my boyfriend! I can't believe you thought that!'

'Sorry. I'm sorry.' He'd jumped to conclusions and got it oh-so-wrong. Zack said, 'I can't believe I thought it either. Blame it on Michael Douglas and Catherine Zeta-Jones.' Right, so the good news was that Ellie had never been romantically involved with Tony Weston. The bad news was that he appeared to have missed his window of opportunity and she was now ecstatically happy with someone else.

Seriously, did someone up there not like him?

'He's just a friend.' Ellie was still cringing and shaking her head.

'And what a great friend to have.' To change the subject, Zack said, 'How did you come to meet him?'

Ellie swallowed, then gazed out of the window, visibly psyching herself up. On the desk, the phone started to ring. 'Well, er…'

'Leave it,' Zack stopped her as she moved to lift the receiver. 'If it's important they'll call back.' Too intrigued to give up now, he said, 'Carry on with the story.'

Because there was a story, he knew that much for sure.

The phone stopped ringing. Ellie was still holding on to Elmo for dear life. Elmo, reveling in the attention, was now reclining like a hairy mini-Cleopatra in her arms.

'Tony's my father-in-law. Well,' Ellie amended, 'he was my father-in-law.'

'So you were married.' The moment the words were out of his mouth, Zack made the connection. *He knew.* Hadn't he Googled Tony Weston that very first day, after seeing the two of them together at the Ivy? Hadn't he read on Wikipedia that Tony Weston's real name was Tony Something-else? But back then, the fact that his surname was Kendall hadn't been significant enough to remember, which was why it hadn't rung any bells when Ellie had eventually come into his life.

And hadn't he also read in the same entry about the tragic loss of Tony's only son in a car accident?

Oh God.

'I was married.' Ellie dipped her head in agreement, acknowledging the fact that he'd figured it out. 'His name was Jamie. He was… lovely.' She carried on gently stroking Elmo's head. 'But he died.'

'I'm so sorry.' Zack couldn't begin to imagine what she'd been through. 'I didn't know.' He watched the play of her fingers against Elmo's ears.

She shrugged. 'I'm sorry too. I should have told you. I kind of wanted to start off with a clean slate.'

'Understandable.' Did this explain her lack of reaction towards him, or was he just not her type anyway?

'Can I just say something? I don't want you to start being nice to me now.'

'You don't want me to start? Does that mean I've *never* been nice to you?'

Ellie glanced at her empty plate and smiled briefly. 'You know what I mean. I'd just like everything to carry on like before.'

'OK.' More than anything, Zack hoped everything *wouldn't* always carry on like before. At some stage in their future, please God, their situation would change. Because now, knowing what he did about her history, he was daring to allow himself the first faint flicker of hope.

It was still a shame, though, about Todd.

'So, does this father-in-law approve of this new chap of yours?'

Say no, say no.

'Tony? Oh, he's delighted. You'd think he'd planned it himself. He couldn't be happier.' Ellie's eyes were shining.

'Right. Excellent.' Zack nodded as if he was delighted too.

Damn.

'Look, you need to get to your meeting.' Bringing the subject to a close, Ellie said, 'But about next Wednesday, I could ask Roo if she's free to come with you to the Dorchester. Would that help you out?'

The mad friend with the risqué past and outrageous taste in T-shirts?

'I don't think so,' Zack said firmly. 'But thanks.'

———

Phew. Well, that was that cat out of the bag. When Zack had left the office, Ellie heaved a sigh of relief. She hadn't planned for it to happen, but now that it had, she was glad. Hopefully, she and Zack had evolved a strong enough working relationship by this stage that his discovering the truth about her past wouldn't alter the way he treated her. Plus, two other good things had happened. She hadn't cried, which was a definite step forward.

And she'd described Todd as her boyfriend. This had been a bit of an experiment, saying it out loud, feeling how the word felt on her tongue. And it had felt, frankly, weird. But it was bound to, the first time. Call it a practice run for next week, when she would be meeting so many of Todd's relatives. After being introduced as his girlfriend and casually dropping the *b*-word into conversation, it would—hopefully—start to sound normal and no longer as weird as, say, *banana*.

'As I was saying the other day to my banana…'

'Oh, I know, my banana's mad about rugby too…'

'My banana and I *loved* that film…'

'Oh yes, I bought my banana a new shirt on Saturday…'

Anyway, the point was, she'd get used to saying boyfriend soon. Stop thinking about it.

Shame about the timing, though. A night out at the Dorchester with Zack would have been fun. Still, it couldn't be helped.

The birthday barbecue would be good too.

Abruptly Ellie's eyes stung and she blinked back tears. Sometimes it still happened without warning.

Don't cry, don't cry.

Oh, Jamie, where are you? Are you still there? Am I doing OK?

Chapter 26

TONY SLOWLY MASSAGED HIS aching temples; this was definitely a side effect of growing older he could do without. Back in the day, half a dozen large Scotches would barely have affected him. They definitely wouldn't have given him a hangover of this magnitude.

But his headache was the least of his worries this morning.

What was that invention thingy he'd heard about? Some kind of dexterity test connected to your computer that you had to pass before it would allow you to access the Internet. So that if you just happened to down, say, half a dozen large Scotches during the course of the evening then be seized by a burning compulsion to send the kind of email you wouldn't dream of sending if you were sober, you wouldn't be able to send it.

Except you always could, of course, because this was Beverly Hills. You'd just call someone up, a member of staff or some employee from Geek Squad and arrange for them to come over to the house and for a small fee perform the necessary dexterous task in order to allow you onto your email account.

But since he hadn't had that particular invention thingy installed, he hadn't even needed to do that. Instead he'd opened his laptop, entered Martha's email address, typed out his message, and pressed Send.

There, done. As easy as that.

Stupidly easy.

And he hadn't been so trolleyed that he couldn't remember what

he'd written, either. Lacking in literary excellence his words may have
been, but they'd come straight from the heart. His wounded, lonely,
desperate, and inebriated heart.

> *Oh Martha,*
>   *I know I shouldn't be doing this but I just have to.*
> *I miss you. I miss you so much, Martha, all the time. I*
> *know I shouldn't, but that only makes it worse. I'm doing*
> *my best to get over you. Guess what? It's not going so well.*
>   *I hope all is well with you. Have you sold lots of*
> *paintings? Not given any more away, I hope. And how*
> *is Henry? And are you doing OK? I won't ask if you miss*
> *me too.*
>   *Right, I'm off to bed now. Will you even read this?*
> *Maybe you just delete my mails without looking at them.*
> *But don't worry, either way I won't expect a reply.*
>   *Sorry. Just needed to say it.*
>   *I love and miss you, beautiful Martha, more than*
> *you'll ever know. But I do understand.*
>   *Be happy.*
>   *All love,*
>   *T x*

Tony watched the computer screen shimmer into life. Had he
gone over the top this time? Might there be a letter waiting in his
inbox from Martha's solicitors, warning him that his messages consti-
tuted harassment and any more would result in his immediate arrest?

Then his heart did a flip, because there among the list of emails
that had come in overnight was one from Martha. For the first time
in weeks, she'd sent a reply. Tony concentrated on keeping his breathing under control. For several seconds he couldn't bring himself to
open it, in case her reaction was too cruel to bear. If she announced

that she was blocking his address he would have to accept that he must never attempt to contact her again.

How could he bear that?

His hand shook as he moved the mouse.

Click.

And there was Martha's email up on the screen.

Very short and to the point, she'd written:

I miss you too.

———

'Ooh, I've missed you *so much*!'

'I can't breathe.' Niall was grinning at her, his hair slick with rain. 'You're choking me.'

Roo loosened her grip on him; when he'd come through the front door she'd launched herself at him like a monkey. 'I can't help it. I'm excited. Did you have a miserable weekend too?'

'What do you think?' He'd been forced to spend it at a business conference in Southampton. 'I've had sales targets and expansion strategies up to here. God, let's not talk about it now. *You*'—his fingers deftly unfastened her navy satin bra—'are looking spectacular.'

'Not so bad yourself.' Roo retaliated by sliding off his suit jacket and removing his tie. She wasn't going to ask him how Yasmin and Ben were. She wouldn't even think about them. It was Monday lunchtime, Niall had rushed over from work, and they only had forty minutes before he had to race back. They had no time to waste. Hence the fact that she was wearing scarcely any clothes in preparation…

Thirty minutes had passed in the most glorious way imaginable. Her skin sheeny with perspiration, Roo lay on her back in the bed and stretched pleasurably, like a cat. In the bathroom across the landing, Niall had already jumped into the shower. In ten minutes he would be on his way back to work but she wasn't going to whine about it. He'd be over again tomorrow evening. She would be cheerful and understanding, the kind of reaction that would *make* him want to see her again, then maybe in a few months when—

De-dee-doo-ding.

Roo stopped breathing and turned her head. It was a muffled sound, quiet but instantly recognizable, signaling that Niall's mobile had received a text.

Which wasn't unusual in itself. But in all the months she'd known him, it was the first time Niall had left his phone unattended. Normally it went everywhere with him, even into the bathroom. The two of them were never parted. Now, like a child glimpsing Father Christmas and finding herself unable to resist investigating further, Roo slithered out of bed and followed the direction the noise had come from.

And there it was, in the pocket of the trousers he'd so hastily discarded earlier. She held the phone in her hand and saw that the text had come from a contact listed only as V.

V… V… Offhand, all she could think of was Vivica, one of his former co-workers. She had left the company a couple of months back; Niall had gone along to her leaving party. He'd also mentioned in passing that she was a bloody good saleswoman, single, and hardworking.

Roo stood there, naked and clutching his mobile, her mind in a tizz. Partly because it was the first time she'd been able to clutch his mobile. But also partly because some sixth sense was telling her she really should be opening this text.

Her thumb hovered over the button. If she pressed it, the message would appear.

If she pressed it, Niall would know she'd pressed it.

The next moment, in the bathroom, the shower was turned off. A jolt of adrenaline coursed through her, because now she had less than a minute left. If she was going to press the button, she had to press it now.

On the one hand, Niall might hate her for spying on him. He might be furious.

On the other hand, she had to know what the message said. *Had* to.

Oh please don't let it be bad…

She pressed it.

> *OMG, best weekend ever!!! When can we do it again? (And again and again!!!!!) Call me asap.*
>   *Lots of love, V xxxxx*

No, please no. Roo whimpered with fear, her brain struggling to take in the significance of the words. She felt sick… as if she might actually *be* sick. Across the landing she could hear Niall opening the shower door, stepping out onto the tiled floor. She couldn't confront him; her head wasn't ready yet. There was a loud buzzing in her ears, he'd be out of the bathroom in less than forty seconds, there wasn't time for anything now, he had to be back at work…

OK, get rid of the message. Breathless and fumbling, her fingers suddenly as huge as sausages, Roo pressed and pressed the necessary buttons. She clutched the phone to her chest to mute the tinkly notes it emitted with each new action. Finally the message was deleted, vanished, gone forever. *Almost as if she'd imagined it, except she knew she hadn't.* Clumsily and in the nick of time she slipped the phone back into Niall's trouser pocket. Then the bathroom door opened and he re-appeared, vigorously toweling himself dry with her favorite lilac towel.

Roo blurted out, 'I need the loo,' and hurried past him.

By the time she re-emerged, he was fully dressed and ready to rush off.

'I don't want to go.' He planted a perfunctory kiss on her mouth, at the same time patting his jacket pockets. 'But I have to. Shit, where's my phone?'

She stood there and let him find it, saw the momentary look of anxiety change to one of relief as he pulled the mobile out of his trouser pocket and instinctively checked the screen. No new messages. Cool. He shot her a confident smile and said, 'Right, I'm off. I'll see you tomorrow, OK?'

'Yes.' Her voice sounded high and strange, but Niall didn't notice. He ruffled her hair then raced downstairs, let himself out of the house, and—*woop, click, clunk*—jumped into his car.

Frozen to the spot, Roo listened to the sound of it disappearing off up the road. Her brain was still fizzing over, making rational thought impossible. Less than ten minutes ago, she'd had a boyfriend that she adored. OK, so he had a wife and baby, but other than that he'd been close to perfect.

And now, thanks to one little text, her whole world had been turned upside down. Because try as she might, she was having trouble coming up with a convincing explanation as to how it might not mean what it appeared to mean.

Five minutes later, still perspiring but no longer in a good way, she'd managed to track down Vivica on Google. Yet another example of the miracle of technology doing something incredibly clever, yet you couldn't help wishing sometimes that it wouldn't. Life had surely been simpler, easier, and less wracked with pain before the advent of the Internet.

Vivica + 'Broughton and Wingfield Associates' on Google Images had brought up three photos of Vivica Mellon being presented with a trophy for achieving outstanding sales figures last year. She *looked* like a saleswoman too. Her shiny dark hair was cut in an efficient bob, she used red lipstick and lipliner, and she was wearing a navy crimplene trouser suit.

OK, the crimplene bit probably wasn't true but it made Roo feel better to think it. The look of stop-at-nothing triumph on Vivica's heart-shaped face told her all she needed to know about her character.

If she worked in a shop and you wanted a pint of milk, she wouldn't let you out again until you'd bought the fridge.

Was it her?

Was she sleeping with Niall?

Was it all happening again?

Shaking, Roo switched off the laptop. She couldn't bear it. All her life she'd fallen for men who started off perfect and morphed into bastards. Time after time, one way or another, they'd let her down and broken her heart. *Trampled on it.*

Meeting Niall, she'd really thought she'd hit the jackpot. This time, at last, it would be different.

Then, once he'd captured her, he'd told her he was married.

Which wasn't great, admittedly, but there were excellent reasons why he was being unfaithful to his wife.

Or were there?

And now this.

She didn't know it for sure, but it was looking as if Yasmin wasn't the only one Niall was cheating on.

Roo felt panicky and nauseous and horribly alone. One way or another, she was going to have to find out.

Chapter 27

NIALL'S NAME CAME UP on the screen and Roo braced herself. This was it. She picked up the phone and pressed Answer. 'Hello?'

'Hi, it's me.' His voice was cautious. Which, on its own, pretty much confirmed her worst fears.

'Oh, hi.' Roo kept her own tone cheery. Last night she'd barely slept. Today her stomach was still churning and she hadn't been able to eat a thing. But it was important to sound normal, normal, normal…

'Everything OK?'

'Everything's fine! Why wouldn't it be?'

'No reason.' Pause. 'Um, did you look at my phone yesterday?'

'Your phone?'

'It's just that someone says they sent me a text as a joke, but I didn't get it.'

He'd worked out the timings, hadn't he, found out exactly when it had been sent. Roo waited, then said evenly, 'Would that be someone beginning with *V*? And ending in *kiss kiss kiss*?'

His silence told her everything she needed to know. That was it, then.

'It was just a joke,' said Niall. 'One of the guys at the office was messing about, winding me up—'

'Niall, it wasn't a joke. Why don't you just be a man and admit it? You've been sleeping with Vivica Mellon.'

More silence. The final confirmation.

'I suppose some people are just greedy,' Roo went on. 'Why settle for one mistress when you can have two?'

'Look, it's not the same thing. I swear to God, she's just someone I used to work with.'

'And now you're sleeping with her.'

'Once. One weekend, that's all it was. She made all the running. She *chased* me.'

He was still lying. All of a sudden she could tell. It was like a one-way mirror suddenly, magically, becoming two-way, revealing everything. 'Oh my God,' said Roo, 'you are unbelievable.'

Another pause.

'Well, fine then.' Niall abruptly switched gear. 'So that's it, is it? You don't want to see me again. All over.'

Fear and panic engulfed her. Fear and panic and… a strong sense of déjà vu. Of course, that was it, the good old double bluff. It was a ploy she'd encountered before, designed to frighten you into backing down. And she *had* backed down, because it was the equivalent of seeing a rather nice handbag in a shop and idly trying to decide whether or not to buy it, then hearing someone else exclaim, 'Oh, wow, look at that amazing bag, I have to have it!' The threat of losing something instilled terror and desperation into your very soul…

But not today. She wasn't going to fall for those tactics again. This time she was going to do the right thing.

'Yes, it's all over.'

'Roo.' His voice softened instantly. 'Babe, you know you don't mean that.'

'Oh, I do.' She was shaking but determined. 'I really do.'

'You want to give up what we have together, all for the sake of a silly… blip? That's crazy. I told you, Vivica means nothing to me. Look, I'm stuck here at work but I'll come over this evening. I'll be there at eight, then we can talk properly, sort everything out.'

'Don't come over. I don't want to see you again. Or speak to you again. I can't believe I ever trusted you. But that's me, I'm just stupid.'

'Roo, we need to—'

'And I won't be changing my mind either.' She had to get off the phone now, before she lost all control. 'Goodbye, Niall. Tell Vivica her lipliner really doesn't suit her. And tonight, just for a change, why don't you try going home to your wife?'

'How does it look?' Ellie emerged from the bedroom and did a twirl, showing off her new red dress with the spaghetti straps and floaty hem. She'd bought it from Wallis, especially for tomorrow night. 'Good enough to meet your family?'

'Perfect.' Todd held out his arms and came towards her. *Oh God, here we go again, he's gearing up for another kiss.* She got out of it by puckering her lips and turning it into a jokey one instead.

'Mwah! And if it gets a bit cold I can wear it with my purple silky jackety thing. Right, let me just change out of it now, then we'll be off.'

Escaping his grasp, she headed back to the bedroom. Tonight a whole group of girls from Brace House were going out to a show. Paula, who had arranged the evening, had insisted she went along with them and stayed the night on her sofa to avoid a late journey back across town. 'Oh, Ellie, you *must* come, it's ages since we saw you! How are you coping over there? How *are* things with you?'

Paula, bless her, was like a young mother hen. But she meant well and she had a good heart. Anyway, it would be lovely to see everyone again and catch up with all their news. Ellie was looking forward to it. And Todd, who had come over to show off his new car, was giving her a lift into the West End.

Ellie stepped out of the dress and changed into white jeans and a khaki tank top. As she was looping the spaghetti straps onto a hanger, the doorbell went and she called out, 'Can you see who that is?'

Moments later Todd called back, 'It's Roo. She's on her way up.'

'I'll be out in a sec. Did she say if she wants something?'

'Not really. I think she's crying.'

Ellie put down the coat hanger. '*What?*'

Roo was crying. But trying hard not to. Her bleached white hair looked as fraught as she did and her eyelids were puffy. When she saw that Ellie was made up and dressed up for her night out with the girls, she said, 'Oh, you're going out…'

'Here, come and sit down. What's happened?'

'It's Niall.' Roo was clutching a balled-up tissue. 'It's all over.'

Todd raised an eyebrow. 'He finished with you?'

Honestly, men. Ellie shook her head at his lack of tact.

But Roo said, 'No, I finished with him. I can't believe I did it. You know what? He was seeing someone else.'

Ellie gaped. '*Besides* you and Yasmin?'

'Oh yes. Some girl he used to work with. They spent the weekend together.' She wiped her eyes as a couple more tears seeped out. 'He's such a bastard.'

'But you already knew that,' Todd announced. 'Good riddance, that's what I say. You're better off without him.'

'I know.'

'So I don't get why you're crying.' He looked genuinely baffled.

'Because I loved him. Because I thought he loved me.' Roo sniffed and said miserably, 'Because it's the story of my stupid, pathetic, useless life.'

'Oh, Roo…' Torn, Ellie checked her watch; they really should be leaving now.

'And he might come over,' Roo went on, 'to try and make me change my mind. I don't want to be there in case he turns up. But you're going out.' She gazed beseechingly at Ellie. 'Could I stay here, just for a couple of hours? Would that be all right?'

Ellie made up her mind. 'Look, I'll cancel. Let me just call Paula and explain, then I can stay here with you.'

'No, no.' Roo shook her head vehemently. 'No way, that's not fair. You're not giving up your night out because of me. That'd just make me feel worse.'

'Well, I'm not leaving you here on your own.' Equally adamant, Ellie folded her arms. 'I *can't*.'

'Look, I'll stay with her.' Todd picked up the keys to his precious new Toyota and turned to Roo. 'OK?'

She blinked, taken aback. '*You?*'

Ellie had always been aware of the slightly tricky atmosphere between them. Todd had made no secret of the fact that he disapproved of Roo's relationship with Niall. Roo, in turn, had reacted by becoming flippant and defensive.

'I don't know if that's a good idea,' said Ellie.

'Come on, it's the only way. I'll drop you on Shaftesbury Avenue then come back and keep her company.'

Roo said warily, 'And give me hassle all night? Because I'm telling you now, I'm not in the mood to be lectured to by Mr Morality.'

'He won't. He'll be nice. *Won't you?*' Ellie pointed a warning finger at Todd. He was right, though; she was the main reason Paula had organized tonight's get-together. It wouldn't be fair to let her down now.

Todd said evenly, 'Of course I'll be nice.'

Fresh tears leaked out of Roo's eyes as she picked at a loose thread on the frayed knee of her jeans. Clearly not trusting him for one minute, she mumbled, 'And you're not allowed to say you told me so, either.'

Todd didn't reply.

'Oh *God*.' Roo let out a wail of despair. 'What the hell, I deserve to be miserable. Just go ahead and say it.' She shook her head in defeat. 'It's all my own fault.'

— ∿ —

It was eleven o'clock and the most bizarre and powerful thing was happening. In her whole life, Roo had never known an experience like it. For the last three hours, she and Todd had talked nonstop. He had told her all about growing up with Jamie, their deep friendship, his past girlfriends, his family, and his career. In return she had told him about her music, her childhood, and her lamentable history with the opposite sex. And somehow, over the course of the evening, her perception of Todd Howard had undergone a complete sea change.

Or… or… *his* perception of her had altered and the fact that he was now viewing her differently meant she was able to relax and stop being so prickly and defensive.

Or something. Either way, it had been the most unbelievable transformation. Out of nowhere, a kind of electricity had sprung up. Each time she looked at Todd she could feel it. And from the way he was looking back at her, gazing unwaveringly into her eyes, he was feeling it too.

Not that either of them had said as much. But it was right there, hovering in the air between them like smog.

And, also like smog, it was breathtaking. She was finding it harder and harder to breathe…

'OK.' Todd abruptly broke the silence that had fallen. 'Are you waiting for me to go first?'

'What?' Roo's glass was empty but she picked it up and took a nervous pretend sip anyway. Her teeth clanked against the rim.

'Hey. You know what.' He took the glass and placed it on the coffee table. Then he reached for her, cupped her face in his cool hands, and said, 'I never thought I'd be doing this, not in a million years. But I have to.'

Their mouths were just inches apart; any closer and she'd go cross-eyed. On his way back to the flat, Todd had stopped at the liquor store and bought a single bottle of wine; that was all they'd had between them. Roo knew she wasn't drunk but she'd never felt so powerless.

'What about Ellie?' Her voice caught in her throat, came out as a croak.

'Oh God, I know. I don't want to hurt her. But... it's not right.'

'I know it's not right! We can't do this! I have to leave... that's it, I'm going home.' Roo struggled to pull away, scrambling clumsily to her feet. But Todd was shaking his head, standing up too, not releasing his grip.

'I didn't mean it like that. It's me and Ellie... our relationship's not right. I've tried and tried, but it just isn't working. It's not even a proper... *thing.*'

'We still shouldn't be *doing* this.'

'I know.' He pulled her close to him, wrapped his arms around her, and just held her tightly. Without moving. For twenty, thirty seconds they stayed like that. The longer Todd didn't kiss her, the more desperately she wanted him to. Her skin was buzzing, her whole body had never felt so alive. Finally, he released her and gazed deep into her eyes. 'Well? Shall we stop now?'

Roo couldn't speak. Was this how it felt to be on death row and hear that your final appeal had been turned down? All she could do was gaze back in wonder and drink in the details of his face, of those features that had seemed so ordinary before yet had become, in the space of just a few hours, *extra*ordinary... the broad forehead, those curly eyelashes, and the gray eyes that, close up, were flecked with sparks of amber. His face was just the right shape for his features, his mouth was irresistible... oh God, she had to back away but she couldn't do it, she just *couldn't...*

'No.' Todd smiled slightly, reading her mind. 'Me neither.' He reached for her hand again—*electricity, more electricity than she knew what to do with*—and led her to the doorway. 'Come on, we can't stay here.'

Together they left the flat and made their way across the road. The tingling skin was still happening. Roo felt as if she were in a dream… she was no longer responsible for her actions…

Oh, for crying out loud, how utterly pathetic, of course she was responsible. Who else was she hoping to blame it on? She stopped dead on the pavement outside her own house and dug her heels in. 'This is wrong. It's not going to happen.'

'Roo.' Todd took a deep breath. 'Just so you know the truth. I need to explain about me and Ellie.'

She clapped her hands over her face; it was Niall and Yasmin all over again. 'I don't want to hear it.'

'You must. What did I tell you before? Listen to me. It's not a proper relationship. There's no sex,' said Todd. 'There's no intimacy. It's not real, it's not working. I thought it would, but it hasn't. And now I'm trapped. I've got myself into a situation that I can't get out of.'

'So you're telling me you don't want to be with Ellie.' Roo gripped the black wrought-iron railings. 'But she wants to be with you.'

'I don't know. I think so. But I can't honestly tell.' There was genuine pain in his eyes. 'And I was the one who started it, so what can I do? On paper we're perfect for each other. We had Jamie in common. I knew how much she was missing him and I wanted to make her feel better. And I've tried, I really have tried my best, but it's just not happening.' Todd shrugged helplessly. 'If it was anyone else, I'd finish with them, but how can I do that to Ellie? She's been through so much. I'm not going to be the one who hurts her again.'

Talk about a close call. Thank goodness she'd come to her senses in time. Filled with self-loathing, Roo said, 'Of course you can't. Oh God, and look what we almost did to her tonight. I can't bear it.'

'But you did it to Niall's wife.'

Was that how Todd thought of her? As the lowest of the low? Her fingers ached now from gripping the railings. 'That's different.' Even if it was still despicable. 'Ellie's my friend.'

'It's not just sex, though. You and me.' He gazed at her with genuine emotion. 'This... thing between us. I know it's come out of nowhere... but it feels *real*.'

'Forget it. None of it's real and nothing's going to happen. You're leaving now, and I'm going to bed.' Awash with shame, Roo said, 'Will you tell Ellie about any of this?'

Which was like asking Prince Charles if he enjoyed eating boiled kittens. In disbelief, Todd said, 'Of course not.'

'Right. Bye, then.' Roo watched him turn away. The guilt almost more than she could bear, she didn't tell him that she might.

Chapter 28

'WHAT ARE YOU DOING?' said Todd.

Ellie carried on texting. They were on their way to his mum's barbecue in Wimbledon. 'I've been trying to get through to Roo all day. She's still not answering her phone. I hope she's all right.'

'She'll be fine. You look nice.'

'Hmm?' Her fingers flying over the keys, Ellie finished her message:

> Roo, call me back. Are you OK? Worried about you!
> Love, Ellie xxx.

She pressed Send, then glanced up and said absently, 'Oh, this dress? Thanks.' Now why was he looking at her like that? Had she done something wrong? Quick, think… right, she was his girlfriend, maybe he was waiting for her to come up with a compliment in return. She smiled brightly, touched Todd's crisp cotton sleeve, and said, 'Your shirt's very nice too!'

—⁓—

'Here they are! Oh, will you just look at this?' Maria Howard's excitement knew no bounds as she turned and saw them coming through the French doors that opened on to her back garden. Her arms flinging wide like an angel's wings, she sent a mini wave of Pimm's cascading into the herbaceous border. 'My wonderful son and his beautiful girlfriend! Come here, come here… oh, Ellie, it's so lovely to see you again! And don't you look perfect together!'

'Sorry,' Todd murmured in her ear. 'I did warn you.'

He had, but there was still no escape. Ellie found herself smothered in Maria's Lauder-scented, flowery-bloused embrace. She was touched by the welcome, even if it did mean she felt a bit of a fraud. Everyone was going to think she and Todd were a proper couple in a normal relationship. Whereas in reality she was feeling more and more like an alien doing her best to pass herself off as a human being.

'You don't know how happy it makes me.' Maria was now holding her at arm's length, surveying her with pride. 'Seeing the two of you like this. Poor Jamie, we all loved him so much. But he'd want you to move on with your life.'

Ellie nodded and said, 'I know,' a lump springing to her throat. The last time she'd seen Todd's mum had been at Jamie's funeral and her memories of that day were hazy. Before that, they'd met a few times. It was slightly intimidating, though, that Maria was gazing at her as rapturously as a future mother-in-law. Hastily, she handed over the card and present she'd brought along and changed the subject. 'Anyway, happy birthday! You're looking fantastic!'

'Am I? Oh, you're so sweet!' Maria gave her another hug. 'We're going to have such fun… we can go shopping together! Now, come over and let me introduce you to everyone. They've all been longing to meet you. Todd, get Ellie a drink and something to eat… Sue, Sue, where's Tanya? Look who's here!'

The next hour was a whirl of new faces, struggling to remember everyone's names, and being told over and over again what a lovely couple she and Todd made. People also gave her sympathetic looks, told her she'd been through so much, and murmured encouragingly how brave she was, before brightening and moving the conversation on to the much happier future. Maria's sisters, cousins, friends, and neighbors meant well and they were nice people. There was much jolly talk about her and Todd, and jokey speculation about whether it was time to start looking out for a new hat. When Ellie ate a chicken drumstick and asked Maria what had been in the marinade, Tanya had exclaimed, 'Ooh, bit of a cook, are you? Lucky old Todd!'

When she'd admired Sue's necklace, Sue had clutched her arm excitedly and said, 'I got it in Venice. Have you ever been there? Oh, you and Todd must go, it's the most romantic place in the world.' Prompting Dave and Hazel from over the road to chime in that Venice was where they'd spent their honeymoon, whereupon bouffant-blonde Rita from next door beamed at Ellie and said, 'Now *that's* an idea, isn't it?'

Ellie smiled and did her best to dismiss it as harmless fun, but it was too unsubtle, too often, too much. It was like being trapped in a 1970s sitcom. Maybe if she and Todd had been a proper couple she'd love all the saucy double entendres and wedding talk, and it would be giving her a nice warm glow of belonging. But this was just making her feel claustrophobic. They couldn't carry on like this; she was going to have to do something about it.

But not now, during Maria's birthday party. That would just ruin everyone's night.

Instead, she concentrated on being cheerful, enjoying the food, dancing along with everyone else to the music, and having fun.

At midnight, Ellie shared a minicab home with Brendan and Judy, friends of Maria's who lived in Hampstead. Before leaving the party Maria hugged her and said squiffily, 'You know what? I love the bracelet you gave me, but you're the best birthday present I could have wished for. You and Todd getting together has made my year!'

Ellie had refused Todd's earlier offer of a lift home, to enable him to relax and have a drink. When they said their goodbyes he kissed her and whispered, 'Thanks. I'll call you tomorrow.'

In the minicab on the way back to Primrose Hill, Judy insisted on getting her phone out and showing off a seemingly endless selection of blurry, postage-stamp sized photos of their three grandchildren. 'Oh yes, they're the light of our lives, aren't they, love?' She gave Brendan a dreamy smile. 'Wouldn't be without them for the world, would we? Bless her, Maria's always asking after them; she's been desperate to become a granny for years.'

Oh good grief.

'When Todd moved to Boston she was petrified he'd meet someone out there and settle down in the States for good,' Brendan chimed in. 'She was so relieved when he decided to come home.'

'And now he's got you,' said Judy. 'Is it any wonder she's over the moon? I tell you what, love, you'd never want for a baby-sitter with Maria around.'

Help...

It was past midnight and Roo's stomach was in knots. Guilt wasn't an emotion that had ever featured largely in her life.

Until today, this morning, when it had seized her in its viselike grip and changed everything. Oh yes, it was making up for lost time now.

And she, Roo Taylor, was going to change as well.

Moreover, this wasn't a whim. It wasn't like waking up one morning and deciding to have a bit of a spring clean or go on a diet. It was so much more than that. Because to date she'd led a charmed, stress-free, *selfish* life. And let's face it, she hadn't always been a nice person. Worst of all, she hadn't even realized it, had simply carried on regardless, pleasure-seeking and doing things that had the potential to hurt others. She had drunk too much, taken too many drugs, slept with men she should never have slept with. And if they'd happened to have wives or girlfriends at home... well, she'd still gone ahead and done it anyway, because why the hell shouldn't she? God, looking back on it now, she'd been a disgusting, despicable human being. Her behavior had been abysmal and she should have been thoroughly ashamed of herself.

Gazing out of the window at the empty darkened street, Roo dug her nails into her palms. Well, now she was. And she was determined to make amends. Her old life was behind her and the new one had begun.

She hadn't even drunk any coffee today. Just tap water. That was how serious she was.

No more alcohol either. *Ever.*

Just lots and lots of visits to… church. Oh yes. If that was what it was going to take, she'd even keep doing that. She'd paid one a visit this afternoon, in the desperate hope that God would speak to her. It had been cool and musty smelling inside, with overtones of wood polish. The wooden pews had been slippery and uncomfortable. Dust particles had danced in the colored beams of sunlight shining through the stained-glass windows. A fly had buzzed around like a mini fighter jet. God hadn't spoken to her, as it turned out, but that didn't matter. Instead, her conscience had. In fact, actually hearing God's voice might have freaked her out completely, so she was glad it hadn't happened.

This way was better. She was going to do it herself.

Roo stiffened as headlights rounded the corner, lighting up the street. The minicab pulled up opposite and she held her breath.

Ellie was back.

Please let her be on her own. Yes, she was. Throwing open the window, Roo stuck her head out and called, 'Ellie?'

Ellie swung round and looked up as the cab moved off down the road. 'Oh, sweetie, I've been so worried about you! Are you all right?'

Was she about to lose her friendship for ever? Was she even right to be doing this?

Yes. She had to be honest. It was the only way.

Her chest tightening with fear, Roo said, 'I'm OK. Look, I'm sorry, I know it's late.' Her voice cracked. 'But can you come over?'

Chapter 29

'...So that's it. Todd didn't want me to tell you, but I had to. And you mustn't blame him. It was all my fault. But I promise on my life it'll never happen again. And I'm going to make it up to you, if you'll let me. I know you must hate me. I hate myself. But I've changed. I'm a different person. I'm going to make up for every bad thing I've ever done. But I just want you to know I'm so, so sorry.'

Ellie shook her head. She'd listened in silence while the whole confession had come tumbling out. She could have said something sooner, but Roo was so desperate to get everything off her chest it would have been wrong to jump in and stop her in her tracks.

Now she said, 'I can't believe it.'

Roo hung her head. 'I'm sorry.'

'Thank God.'

'What?'

'This is the best news I've heard in months.'

Wrong-footed, Roo said, 'How can it be good news?'

'Because it wasn't working for us. It felt all wrong and I kept pretending it didn't, but it *did*. And I couldn't hurt Todd's feelings. I couldn't tell anyone, not even you. I started off thinking it was just because I was out of practice, but it wasn't. Todd and I were never meant to be anything but friends. And now he knows that too. Oh thank God, this is fantastic, you have no idea!'

Roo's face was a picture. 'Are you just saying that?'

'No.'

'You really aren't angry with me?'

'No!'

'But I did a terrible thing.'

'Hello? Did I miss something?' said Ellie. 'Did you have sex with him?'

'No!'

'Did you even kiss him?'

'No, but I wanted to! I *nearly* did.'

'Well, now you can. You can do anything you like with him. As often as you want.'

'No.' Roo vehemently shook her head.

'No what?' Honestly, how many more times could they say the word?

'I'm not going to do anything with him.'

'But I *want* you to.'

'Ellie, I told you. I've changed. I made a pact with myself today. First, no more lies. I had to tell you the truth, even if it meant losing you as a friend. Second, if I didn't lose you, I'd make it up to you somehow. And third'—Roo was counting on her fingers—'either way, nothing's going to happen between me and Todd.'

'But that's stupid. You like him. And he likes you.'

'All the more reason. It's my punishment. If I promised that nothing would happen between me and Woody Allen, it wouldn't be much of a punishment, would it?'

'You don't have to punish yourself.' Ellie frowned; was she not making herself clear here? 'I'm *glad* it happened.'

'Maybe, but that's irrelevant. The point is, I didn't know you'd be glad, did I? I just went ahead and did it.'

'But you didn't do anything!'

'I let him put his arms around me.'

'Big deal.'

'OK, what if it hadn't been Todd? If it had been your Jamie,' Roo stated bluntly, 'you wouldn't be saying that.'

Ellie looked at her. She had a point. Then again, hopefully Jamie wouldn't have put his arms around Roo in the first place.

Would you?

Are you kidding? No way, not in a million years, not even if we were in Antarctica.

OK, don't overdo it.

Anyway, speaking of husbands...

'What about Niall? Please tell me you aren't planning to break it to Yasmin that you've been doing a lot more than just putting your arms around her husband.'

'You know, I was wondering about that.'

'Don't even think it!'

Roo looked torn. 'Not a good idea?'

'Hideous, *terrible* idea. You can't do that, no way.' Ellie shuddered at the thought. 'She has a baby and a husband who cheats on her. Isn't that bad enough? You mustn't tell her.'

'Oh. OK.'

'Promise.'

'I promise.'

'Right. Good. Now come here.' Ellie stood up and gave her a hug. 'Everything's going to be fine.'

Roo promptly burst into tears. 'Oh God, you're being so nice and I don't deserve it. I'm such a horrible person.'

'You aren't, you aren't.' Her spiky gelled hair felt like Astroturf. 'You made a mistake and now you've learned your lesson. I'm happy you're not going to see Niall anymore. I'm even happier that Todd and I don't have to pretend to be a couple anymore. We can just go back to being friends. Look at me.' Pulling back, Ellie regarded Roo's wet, miserable face. 'Don't cry. I'd love it if you two got together.'

But Roo was already shaking her head, clearly dead set on punishing herself. 'No way. That's not going to happen. I won't let it.'

'How was the party last night?' Zack, between appointments, came into the office eating a slice of toast.

Well, he was bound to ask. Ellie said, 'It was great! No rain, everyone was lovely, food was fantastic. I ate seven chicken samosas. How did your posh do at the Dorchester go?'

'Probably a lot more boring than your barbecue. And sadly lacking in samosas.' He finished his toast. 'There's another event on Monday evening at Claridge's. Could you make that, do you think?'

Claridge's? Wheeeee!

'Monday? No problem, that's fine.' As Ellie nodded enthusiastically, the doorbell went, signaling the arrival of his next appointment.

'Good. Excellent. I'll get that.' Looking pleased, Zack swung out of the office to let the client in and take him upstairs.

Ellie went back to her typing. She hadn't been able to bring herself to tell him about Todd. It was only last week that she'd mentioned him for the first time, boasting to Zack about how happy they were. What kind of an idiot would she look like if she were to announce, just days later, that it was all over? If she tried to explain that she was delighted, Zack wouldn't believe her. He'd think she'd been heartlessly dumped. Worse, he'd feel sorry for her. She'd be back at square one all over again, the poor widow to be pitied and handled with kid gloves.

No, far easier for now to not mention it. There was no reason at all to tell him the truth.

Speaking of the truth, there were still things to sort out with Todd. Oh dear, his poor old mum. Maria was going to be devastated when she heard her son was single again.

All the more reason to persuade Roo to change her mind and abandon her pledge.

—⁓—

Todd came over straight after work. He couldn't have been more penitent. 'I'm so sorry.'

'Oh, don't you start. I told you, this is good news! It wasn't working out. We both knew it. We were just too polite to say so. Now we can relax and stop trying to make it work. We don't have to do any more of that yucky kissing stuff!'

Todd visibly relaxed. 'Oh God, wasn't that weird? I had no idea it could be like that. I couldn't figure out why it felt so... so...'

'Gross,' Ellie supplied helpfully. 'No offense. It wasn't you.'

'It wasn't you either.'

'It was just wrong. Like a Marmite and strawberry sandwich. We're both nice, we just don't go together.'

'Piccalilli and chocolate.' Todd nodded in agreement.

'Liquorice and bacon. OK'—she waved her hands—'we have to stop now. I'm starting to feel sick.'

'We'll go back to being friends.'

'You know what? I'm feeling so much better already.' She pulled a face. 'Will your mum be upset?'

'Well, yes, but she'll get over it.'

'Wait till she meets Roo.'

Todd raked his fingers through his hair. 'I swear to God, I had no idea that was going to happen. I've gone over and over it in my head and there was no hint of it before.'

'I know. Isn't it incredible how it can happen like that? I didn't think you even liked her that much.'

'That's just it.' He gestured in disbelief. 'I *really* didn't like her. Because she was sleeping with a married man. But then on Tuesday... I don't know... she was just being so hard on herself and somehow everything changed. These feelings came up out of nowhere. And it was the same for her too. We both just knew it. I didn't want her to say anything, because I couldn't bear the thought of you getting hurt.'

'You're so sweet! Thank goodness Roo told me. We could have carried on being all wrong for each other for months.' Ellie fanned herself with relief. 'In fact, you need to get yourself over there now.'

Todd hesitated. 'She said we couldn't see each other.'

'Oh, that was then. She'll be over it by now. Come on, I'll come with you so she knows it's OK.'

He looked uncomfortable. 'Couldn't you call her and say it? Then I'll go over on my own.'

'No way! I want to see this thing with my own eyes. All this amazing chemistry that's sprung up. Don't spoil my fun,' Ellie begged. 'This is going to be so romantic. I can't wait!'

———

'No.'

Ellie tried again. 'Roo, come on, just open the door.'

From the upstairs window, Roo shook her head. 'I will not.' Her hair was standing on end; she resembled an electrocuted white cat and there were smudges on her face. She was focusing all her attention on Ellie, refusing to even glance at Todd. 'He isn't coming in.'

'But everything's OK. If you want to make me happy, you'll get together.'

'Not going to happen. In fact, I'm quite hurt that you think you can get me to give in. This isn't a whim, you know. It's a whole new me. With morals. And scruples.'

'And a messy T-shirt,' said Ellie, because there were gray smudges across her front as well. 'What have you been *doing* up there?'

'Clearing out. Decluttering. Detoxing my life. Actually, has he got his car here?'

'I can hear you,' Todd pointed out. 'And yes, I do have my car.'

'Right. Wait there.' Roo disappeared from view.

'See?' Ellie said encouragingly. 'I told you it'd be OK. She's on her way down.'

'No I'm not.' Roo's head popped out again. 'Stand back, my aim isn't that great.'

'What are you going to do?' said Ellie. 'Shoot us?'

Ffflump. Ffflump. Fffflumppp. Three fully loaded bin bags landed on the pavement. One of them, not properly tied, had a pair of leopard-print jeans poking out of the top. 'If you want to make yourself useful,' Roo called down, 'drop these off at the charity shop.'

Ellie bent down and checked the label on the jeans. 'What's going on? These are your favorites!' Plus they were Vivienne Westwood.

'I know. Now they can be someone else's favorites.'

Her beloved purple suede jacket, the black lacy top with the red velvet trim, the white skirt, the silver leather belt... scrabbling through the contents of the bag, Ellie said, 'Oh, Roo, this is everything you love best. You can't do this.'

Ffflump, fffflump-flump. Ellie darted out of the way as the next lot of bags came sailing through the air. It was like being dive-bombed by giant seagulls.

'I can,' Roo retaliated. 'I have to.'

'Oh my God,' Todd muttered. 'Two days ago I fell in love with the girl of my dreams. Tonight I find out she's insane.'

'You fell in *love* with her?' Ellie turned and gaped as Todd realized what he'd just blurted out.

His ears went bright red and he began to furiously backpedal. 'Look, I didn't mean that, I meant fell *for*, don't read things into—'

'Your subconscious said it. That means your brain knows how you feel.' She clutched his arm. 'Don't be embarrassed, just go with it.'

'Like I said, that was before I found out about the insanity.'

'Roo? Let Todd in now. He's in love with you!'

'He's not coming in. I want him to go.'

Ellie carried on arguing his case but Roo refused to budge. Her mind was evidently made up. Since there was nothing else he could do, Todd loaded the many bin bags into the car and drove off. When he'd gone, Roo unlocked the front door and said, 'Don't try and make me change my mind, because it's not going to happen. Here, try this.' She aimed the nozzle of the atomizer skywards and squished perfume into the air.

The mist fell like fine snow around Ellie's face. The scent was divine, Mediterranean lemons in a bottle. 'It's your Annick Goutal.'

'If you want it, it's yours. Come on up, I've got loads more stuff upstairs.'

She wasn't kidding. The place was full of boxes and half-filled bags. 'You can have all my makeup,' Roo gestured carelessly. 'I won't be needing it anymore.'

She was bare-faced, wearing just the dusty old T-shirt and a battered pair of jeans. Ellie said, 'OK, this is getting too much now. You can't give away your makeup.'

'If you don't want it, I'll find someone else who does. And I've given up drinking too. There's a couple of bottles of New Zealand Sauvignon Blanc in the fridge, if you'd like them.'

'Roo, you don't have to do this.'

'I want to. It makes me feel better. And I've got a job.' She beamed. 'I start tomorrow.'

Oh good grief. 'What kind of a job?'

'I'm volunteering at the charity shop on Ormond Road. The hospice place next to the travel agents.'

'That means you'll be standing up all day. It'll make your feet hurt.'

'If little old ladies can do it, I'm sure I can too.'

This was debatable; little old ladies who volunteered in charity shops tended to be made of sterner stuff than Roo. She was something of a hothouse flower.

'Have you heard from Niall?'

'No. I've blocked his number.'

'You could be a nicer person and still see Todd, you know.'

'Don't keep on. Not seeing Todd is my punishment for having been bad. I *deserve* to be punished,' said Roo.

'OK, fine.' Ellie paused. 'Shall we go to the pub now?'

'This isn't funny!' Roo took a swipe at her with a pair of gold lamé trousers. 'No!'

'Are you giving those to charity?'

'Probably.'

Ellie danced out of reach. 'Good.'

Chapter 30

'Jamie? Are you there?' She didn't say it out loud, just in her head. But he heard her anyway.

'I'm always here.' He appeared in the living room, grinning and barefoot. 'I'm like Lurch in *The Addams Family*. *You rang?*'

'You're better looking than Lurch.' Ellie waited. 'Which is your cue to tell me I'm looking pretty good too.'

'You already know that. That's my favorite dress.'

They'd spotted it three years ago in the window of a little shop in Totnes. Simply styled in slippery, matte silk, it was peacock blue with swirls of emerald green and gold handprinted around the neckline and hem. It was a beautiful dress and she'd worn it when they'd gone out to dinner on his last birthday.

'The main reason it's your favorite is because you discovered you could undo the zip with one hand.'

Jamie said good-naturedly, 'Just as well I'm staying home tonight. Wouldn't want your dress coming undone while you're out at your fancy do with your boss.'

Ellie pumped her tube of lip gloss. 'I hate to break it to you but you aren't really here. Your zip-unfastening days are over.'

'I know.' He watched her apply a layer of gloss to her lips. 'Is that the one that tastes of apricots?'

'Yes.' Ellie's throat tightened; he used to kiss it off her, deliberately getting it all over his own mouth.

'Don't cry. You'll wreck your makeup.'

Easier said than done. She threw the lip gloss into her evening bag and said, 'I'm going now.'

'Have fun.' Jamie's expression softened. 'I mean it. I want you to enjoy yourself.'

A glitzy dinner at Claridge's in Mayfair. What wouldn't she give for her and Jamie to be able to spend the evening there together? *OK, stop this, don't think about it now.* 'I will. Bye.'

⁓

Zack wasn't Jamie but he created quite an impression. As the taxi pulled away down Brook Street, Ellie glimpsed their reflection in the window of Vidal Sassoon opposite Claridge's. She was looking like a better than usual version of herself and Zack, in his dark suit, was quite literally turning heads. One girl, too busy ogling him to look where she was going, slipped off the curb and almost toppled into the gutter.

Zack, not realizing why she'd stumbled, rested a protective hand in the small of Ellie's back and said, 'Careful, these pavements aren't great.' He steered her across the street towards the hotel and she caught sight of them both in another window.

Yee-ha, look at us, heading towards the entrance to Claridge's like a proper glamorous couple in a Chanel ad, if girls in Chanel ads have ever worn emerald-green shoes from Topshop and jeweled hair combs from Primark. Well, you never know, they might.

They reached the other side of the road. Ellie paused to gaze up at the row of flags hanging outside the hotel entrance. Heads of state stayed here. Royals stayed here. Think how many famous people had passed through those revolving doors and—

'Oh, hello! It's Ellie, isn't it? How funny, I was just admiring your dress and then I recognized you from the salon! You came in with your friend the other week.'

It was Yasmin Brookes. Time did that thing of simultaneously speeding up and going into slow motion as Ellie took stock of the situation. And she'd never met Niall but Roo had shown her a picture of him. The man with Yasmin was definitely Niall. Heavens, out with his own wife, what was he thinking of?

'Oh yes, hi.' Yasmin was glancing at Zack; hastily Ellie leapt in before she could come to embarrassing conclusions. 'This is my boss; we're off to a business event.'

'At Claridge's, how fab! I really do love your dress. This is Niall, my husband.'

As Niall nodded affably at them, Yasmin said to him, 'We had a lovely chat in the salon, the three of us. I told you about Ellie's friend. She was the one who looked like that pop singer, Daisy Deeva. Remember from the Three Deevas, years ago? It wasn't her, of course. But she was still nice!'

Niall's expression had frozen; his eyes darted from Yasmin to Ellie, a muscle tensed in his jaw, and his neck went blotchy as he realized who she was. Ellie smiled back at him, reveling in his discomfort. Was this schadenfreude? Excellent!

Aloud she said, 'She is nice,' and saw Niall's Adam's apple bob up and down like a rubber duck in a choppy sea.

'And is she looking after your baby while you're out this evening?'

Yeek, this was schadenfreude coming back to bite you on the bum. Ellie said quickly, 'Yes, yes she is. So where are you off to tonight?'

'Oh, just meeting up with friends in a bar on South Molton Street. It's a treat, isn't it, getting out in the evening? Ellie has a girl,' Yasmin explained to Niall. She turned back to Ellie. 'I'm so sorry, I've forgotten her name…?'

Oh bugger bugger bugger… Ellie's heart began to gallop, she couldn't remember, she had no idea and Zack was now giving her a quizzical look… oh help, for crying out loud, *what was her baby's name?*

'Got it! Alice!' Yasmin mimed relief that didn't begin to compare with Ellie's. 'Honestly, I hate it when that happens. This is what having babies does to us, isn't it? Gives us nappy brain!'

The narrow escape had left Ellie feeling sick. Alice, that was it, thank heavens one of them had remembered. She managed a smile and said gaily, 'Tell me about it. I can't remember my own name sometimes!' She pointed to Zack. 'Or thingamajig's.'

Once inside, Zack said, 'So I take it your friend Roo isn't baby-sitting tonight.'

'No, she isn't.' Could he hear her heart, still clattering away in her chest like a monkey trying to get out?

'I hope that doesn't mean you've left Alice home alone.'

'Oh, she'll be all right. As long as she's got a bottle of rum and the TV remote in her hand, she's happy. She's very advanced for her age.' Ellie looked over her shoulder, double-checking that Yasmin and Niall hadn't followed them through the revolving doors. No, it was safe. She exhaled and said, 'Thanks for getting me away from them.'

'Don't mention it.' Zack had skillfully intervened, explaining that they were late and needed to get inside. 'Although I have to say, for a few seconds you had me there. I was starting to wonder if this was another family member you hadn't told me about.'

'I don't have a baby. I promise.'

'I gathered that, when you couldn't remember its name.'

'Oh *God*.' Ellie winced. 'Was it obvious?'

'Only to someone who was fairly certain you didn't have a baby. I don't think they noticed.'

'Phew. Anyway, I'm never going to see them again.' She checked her watch. 'Are we late? Shall we go up now?'

'We have a few minutes.'

'You mean you want to hear all about how I managed to acquire an imaginary child?'

'Want,' said Zack, 'would be an understatement.'

'OK, I'll tell you, but it's not pretty.' Ellie took a deep breath. 'Niall's the married man Roo was having an affair with. She found out where his wife worked and made me go along with her to see if Yasmin was the nightmare Niall said she was. At the time it seemed like a good idea if I had a baby, so we'd have something to talk about. Which was great until it got to discussing childbirth.'

Zack said gravely, 'I hear it hurts a bit.'

'It does, but I was very brave. Anyway, you've just met her. Yasmin was lovely. But Roo couldn't bring herself to admit it. Except last week she found out she wasn't the only mistress. So she's dumped Niall and now she's busy turning herself into a nun.'

'And he's one of those men who isn't happy unless he's cheating on his partner. Nice.' Zack's expression made his feelings on the subject clear. 'I hope your chap's not like that.'

'No, he isn't.' Since she still hadn't come clean about Todd, she could hardly tell him about the Todd-and-Roo fiasco.

'He doesn't mind you coming here this evening with me?'

'He really doesn't mind.' This much was true at least.

'Good. Well, we'd better head on up there.' As Zack ushered her towards the lift, his hand brushed against her arm and Ellie's skin tingled. Weird; she'd never noticed that happen before. The next moment, the lift doors glided open and he tilted his head, indicating with a brief smile she should go in ahead of him. For a split second she felt a squiggly response in the pit of her stomach. Oh God, stop it, she was hopelessly out of practice on the man front and her first attempt at a comeback had been a disaster. Don't say she was about to launch into a desperate rebound crush on—of all people—her own boss. How embarrassing. How pathetic. How completely, humiliatingly inappropriate.

Right, this wasn't going to happen. Mind over matter. She was going to put a stop to it before it could take hold.

Just… don't let it start.

Chapter 31

THIS EVENING'S DINNER WAS more pleasure than business. Bob Nix was a big, brash, Texan billionaire financier with whom Zack had done deals in the past. Looking to extend his circle of contacts, he had invited a dozen business people plus their partners along for drinks and dinner in the Clarence Room, one of the sixth floor's private suites.

The atmosphere was noisy and relaxed. If you took J. R. Ewing and pumped him full of air with a bicycle pump, you'd end up with Bob. Red-faced and looking about to burst at the seams, he was as loud and jolly as you'd expect of a Texan billionaire. In his late fifties, six foot five without his Stetson, and with glow-in-the-dark veneers, he towered over his wife Bibi, who was young and super-glamorous in a Dolly Partonish way. But she was as welcoming as Bob. Within minutes of complimenting Ellie on her hair combs, she'd discovered they were exactly the same age; in no time they were chatting away about fashion, music, shoes, and makeup.

'So are y'all a couple?'

'No, no, I just work for Zack.' Luckily Zack was deep in conversation with someone else by the fireplace.

'Hey, you can work together and still be a couple.' Bibi's eyes sparkled. 'That's how I met Bob! I was his personal trainer.'

Ellie wiped the mental picture of Bob in tight shorts doing grunty sit-ups from her mind. 'Well, that's not going to happen. Zack only hired me because he knew it wouldn't. Plus I have a boyfriend.'

'Oh right. Sorry. Zack's pretty cute though.'

I know he is. Aloud Ellie said, 'So's my boyfriend.'

Bibi laughed. 'Hey, don't mind me, I'm just a hopeless romantic! Bob and I are so happy together I spend all my time trying to fix other couples up.' She caught the glimmer of surprise in Ellie's eyes. 'Ah, see? Y'all thought I was a gold-digger, didn't you! But I'm not. He's the love of my life. And I've signed a prenup. If we break up, I walk away with nothing but my pride.'

'Good for you.' Inexplicably, Ellie's eyes began to prickle. Oh God, she was a hopeless case.

'And the keys to the safe, obviously. Joke!'

Over dinner, another businessman's wife asked Ellie if she could recommend a good Botox doctor in Harley Street.

Ellie said, 'Sorry, I've never had Botox.'

The wife, whose name was Kara, said, 'Oh my God, why *not?*'

'I'm twenty-nine.'

'Jesus, you're leaving it late! I started when I was twenty!' Kara, who had a face like a boa constrictor, leaned forward and flared her nostrils with difficulty. 'By the time I was your age I'd had six procedures… eyes, ears, plus a full face-lift!'

'And you had your knees done,' her husband chimed in. 'What is it you always say? Nothing worse than a woman with pudgy knees.'

'You're telling me.' Kara mimed gagging. 'I mean, we were in Tuscany with the Mainwarings over Easter and you should have *seen* Kizzy's knees. So pudgy and gross, I felt nauseous every time I looked at them!'

'OK, darling, calm down,' said her husband. 'Some people prefer the natural look.'

'Well, they shouldn't.' Kara shuddered. 'It's just wrong. They should have more consideration for others.'

She actually meant it. Ellie longed to ask Kara's husband if he'd had his knees done too. Across the table she caught Zack's eye and struggled to keep a straight face.

The conversation turned to Tuscany, where everyone else appeared to have holidayed. Several of them owned villas there. Bob said, 'How about you, Ellie? Where d'you like to vacation?'

'Has everyone visited San Gimignano?' Kara was on a roll now, her snake eyes with their barely-there lids flickering around the table. 'It's fifty kilometers from Florence, a completely feudal medieval village with this massive *wall* around it. We stayed at a farmhouse nearby and just did nothing for a month. Totally idyllic.'

'Ellie?' repeated Bob.

She smiled at him. 'I like Cornwall best.'

'Corn-waaaall?' He made it sound like a wall made of corn. Mystified, he shook his head. 'Bottom left-hand corner of England, am I right? Can't say I've ever been there.'

'Oh, you should.' Ellie put down her wine glass. 'It's beautiful. My favorite place is Looe, it's just—'

'Loo?' Bibi clapped her hands in delight. 'You mean like the *toilet*? Oh, wow!'

'That's exactly how I'd describe it,' Kara drawled. 'We were invited down there once. What a nightmare. The place was full of oiks.'

The fork in Ellie's hand was loaded with seafood in a saffron sauce. The temptation was enormous. 'I go there.'

'So you'll have seen them. Wearing knotted hankies on their heads and drinking cans of lager on the beach. Screaming babies, kids dropping ice creams, souvenir shops…' Kara's upper lip did its best to curl.

'Well, I've never been to Italy.' Ellie looked at Zack, wondering if she should be saying this. 'But I'm fairly sure they have souvenir shops in Florence. And babies that cry.'

'Oh well, we're all different.' A thin smile of satisfaction stretched itself across Kara's face. 'Some of us are probably just suited to Tuscany more than others.'

Bibi said, 'We tried it once, Bob, didn't we? Bored the backside off us. Give me Disney World any day.'

Ellie could have hugged her. Kara looked as if she'd been bitten by a mongoose. The waiter arrived to refill their glasses. Across the table, Zack's mouth was twitching.

Hopefully this meant she wasn't about to be sacked on the spot.

At the end of the evening Bibi hugged her goodbye. On impulse Ellie stepped back and removed the jeweled combs Bibi had admired earlier. 'Here, you said how much you liked them. I want you to have these.'

'Oh God, I can't believe it, that's so kind of you! Hang on…' Bibi said, 'let me give you something too.'

Hastily Ellie stopped her. 'No, you can't do that.'

Well, she could, but the item Bibi was struggling to unfasten was a multicarat diamond tennis bracelet, which was a slightly embarrassing exchange for a couple of combs from Primark that had cost one pound fifty each.

———

They left the hotel at eleven fifteen. In the taxi Ellie said, 'Sorry about the thing with Kara. I hope I haven't got you into trouble.'

Zack was finding it almost impossible to tear his gaze away from her. In this light her eyes were huge. Her hair, no longer fastened up in a semichignon, now framed her face and her chin was tilted at a determined angle. Her expression was unrepentant; she was apologizing for possibly causing problems in the business sense but not for saying what she'd said.

'Doesn't matter a bit. She's a crashing snob, and I wasn't wild about her husband either. I didn't know you were such a fan of Cornwall.'

'Oh God, I love it. Ever since we started going down there when I was a kid. We used to stay on a caravan site between Looe and Polperro. Then after that it was camping holidays with friends, sometimes on the south coast, sometimes in Newquay. Other people were flying to Spain and Greece, but I still preferred Cornwall.' The cab swung around a sharp corner and Ellie clutched the door handle to stop herself sliding against him.

Zack wished she would. 'And then you met Jamie.'

'I did. And he loved Cornwall too. We used to get down there three or four times a year. It's where we spent our honeymoon, in this brilliant little hotel in St Ives. We used to talk about moving down there one day. It was our dream.' She paused for a moment. 'But that didn't happen.'

More than anything, Zack wanted to comfort her. Never mind that problem-solving was his thing; this wasn't a problem he could magic away. For a second, as Ellie shook back her hair and he breathed in her now-faded perfume, he wondered what she'd do if he kissed her.

Jump out of the cab, probably.

OK, better not try it.

Aloud he said, 'Anyway, you were right about Florence. It might be a beautiful city but it's boiling hot and crawling with tourists.'

'Is it?'

'Oh yes. And you get hassled by beggars. Really smelly ones.'

They were heading along Portland Place now. He'd managed to make her smile again. Thank goodness he'd taken control of himself and hadn't gone for the kiss. That would have ruined everything.

Ellie tilted her head. 'So how about you? Ever been to Cornwall?'

'I have.'

'OK, silly question, everyone has at one time or another. Did you like it?' She waved a hand in apology. 'Sorry, bit abrupt. It just drives me demented, people like Kara criticizing the place when I love it so much.'

'I did like it. I still do. It's where I grew up.' He saw her expression change, her mouth fall open.

'Seriously? You never told me that!'

'I didn't know I had to.' Something relaxed inside him; *at last, a connection, and it had been there all along.* 'My family still live there. I head down whenever I can.'

'Whereabouts?'

'Perranporth.'

'I know Perranporth! Just down from Newquay! Oh my God, I know Perranporth!' Her eyes were shining, her whole face was lit up.

'And I know Newquay. I used to spend whole weeks at a time on Fistral Beach.'

Ellie clapped a hand to her chest. 'I love Looe to bits, but Fistral Beach is the best for surfing. Full of oiks, obviously.'

'Oh, I like being an oik.'

'Me too. Better an oik than a lizard.' She pulled a face, mimicking Kara's stretched skin and yanked-back, reptilian features.

Zack said, 'Shall I tell you why I finally broke up with Louisa? Because she wanted us to join some friends at a villa in Tuscany for a child-free, fun-free, oik-free fortnight.'

'No!' Ellie burst out laughing. 'Is she *related* to Kara?'

'You know, it wouldn't surprise me. Anyway, that was it. That was my breaking point.'

'I call it a narrow escape. Start going on holidays like that and you'll end up reading books by Salman Rushdie. OK, I'm being a bitch now. Tell me to shut up.'

'Not only reading them,' said Zack. 'Discussing them. In interminable detail.'

'When you're not talking about wine-tasting and vintages, and how your favorite Montepulciano has undertones of Marmite and top notes of Shredded Wheat.'

'With just a touch of peanut butter and a dash of deodorant.'

'Will you just listen to us?' Ellie's eyes were dancing. 'We are *complete* oiks.'

'Thank God for that.'

'Tell me about your family in Perranporth.'

'My parents still live in the house where we all grew up. It's far too big for them now, but they don't want to move.'

'Sea views?'

'Oh yes.'

'I wouldn't want to move either. What are their names? Sorry,' Ellie flapped her hand. 'Being nosy. You don't have to tell me that.'

He wanted to tell her, almost as much as he wanted this cab ride to go on forever. 'Why wouldn't I want to tell you about my family? They're embarrassing, but they're not that embarrassing. My mum's Teresa, but everyone calls her Tizz. My dad's Ken. They ran a landscape gardening business up until they retired a couple of years ago. And I have three sisters who all live in Cornwall. Claire's in St Ives, she's married with three children. Steph's living with her chap in St Austell and they have twin girls. And Paula's in Helston with her two, a boy and a girl.'

Ellie was suitably impressed. 'Wow. So you're an uncle, big time.'

'Just a bit. Five girls and two boys aged between three and eleven. When we all get together it's not what you'd call peaceful.' Zack could feel himself smiling; it was the effect even thinking of his noisy, hyperactive, extended family had on him. 'And there are dogs too. You should see us when we hit the beach.'

'I hope you hand out earplugs to all the poor people trying to read their Salman Rushdie books in peace.'

'Nobody reads Salman Rushdie on Fistral Beach, that's the joy of it. We're all oiks together.'

'I could have seen you there.' Ellie was shaking her head, marveling at the idea. 'We could have been there at the same time. Isn't it weird to think that? You might have thrown our ball back to us when it landed in the middle of your sand castle.'

'I might have kicked sand over your picnic.' Zack didn't believe this. The first time he'd seen her outside the Ivy that day, his reaction had been so intense he was pretty certain their paths had never crossed before. But the idea that they could have been in such close proximity was still a heady one. OK, not heady, because back then she would have been with her husband, and he would more than likely have had some girlfriend or other in tow. Still, as she'd pointed out, it was a surreal thought.

As if reading his mind, Ellie said, 'I've got loads of photos at home of us down there. Wouldn't it be incredible if your family was in the background?'

They were almost home now, heading along Albany Street; in a couple of minutes they'd be back in Primrose Hill. Zack wasn't feeling remotely casual but thank God it came out that way. 'I don't know what Jamie looked like.'

Ellie smiled. 'He was lovely. I can show you photos.'

'I'd like to see them.' *Casual, relaxed, no pressure.*

'You mean tomorrow? Or tonight? Because you can come back now if you want. I could get the albums out, show him to you. You can see what he was like.'

'Would that be difficult? I don't want you to feel pressurized.'

'I just invited you, didn't I?' Her face softened. 'I love talking about Jamie, telling other people about him. He was my husband, he existed, I was so proud to be married to him. Just because he isn't here anymore doesn't mean pressing a delete button and forgetting he was ever here.'

God, she was beautiful.

'If you're sure,' said Zack.

Ellie nodded. 'But you have to promise me one thing. When you see him, no laughing at his skinny legs.'

Chapter 32

IT WAS THE FIRST time he'd visited her flat. Well, Tony Weston's flat. Ellie had already explained that Tony was in LA. She apologized for the Lindor truffle wrappers on the coffee table, the empty Coke can on the arm of the sofa, and the assorted shoes she'd tried on and discarded before coming out tonight. Having kicked off her emerald-green stilettos and made coffee, she pointed him towards the sofa and handed him a small gray leather photo album.

'Here you are. No jokes about my hair either.'

The faint scent of her perfume still hung in the air. He didn't even know what it was. Zack turned the pages of the album and took in every detail in the photographs. This had been her life. Ellie and Jamie at someone else's wedding. The two of them dancing at a party. Jamie jumping into a swimming pool, Jamie lying on a rug with a beer can precariously balanced on his bare chest, Ellie and Jamie sitting outside a sunny restaurant with Tony Weston, the three of them radiating health and fun and happiness.

Jamie had surfer-blond hair, an open, friendly face, and a killer smile.

'He looks pretty cool.' What else could he say? Could he ask her if she liked guys with dark hair too?

'That's only because you haven't seen his legs yet.' Ellie tucked her hair behind her ears. 'By the way, I'm allowed to make fun of them. You're not.'

'Wouldn't dream of it.' Zack didn't tell her about his knees; attempting to compete with a dead man for oddities in the leg department would be just cheap. 'Can I ask one thing, though?'

'Go ahead.' She leaned across the arm of the sofa to see which picture he was pointing to.

'Who's the teenage boy in the skirt?'

'Hey! What did I tell you? No teasing.' Ellie made a grab for the album. 'The hairdresser said having it short would suit me.'

Zack grinned. 'Sorry. It did suit you. I just think having your hair longer suits you more.'

Was he doing a good job? Friendly but not flirty, ironic but not idiotic? He sat back with his coffee while Ellie perched next to him on the arm of the sofa. Her tanned bare feet with the toes painted iridescent pink were visible in the outer corner of his field of vision. God, even her toes were irresistible…

'This is us two years ago,' said Ellie. 'On Fistral Beach.'

Zack looked at the photo. An energetic game of volleyball was in progress. Ellie was wearing a lemon-yellow kaftan over a white bikini. There was Jamie, leaping in midair to knock the ball over the net, above the head of his opponent.

'Who's that?' Zack pointed.

'Todd.'

Todd. The one who had taken Jamie's place. In fairness, he looked perfectly OK, wearing a gray Superdry T-shirt and red board shorts. His brown hair was short and tufty, his smile broad.

'Who are the other people?'

'No idea, they just joined in our game. Todd's girlfriend Anna was taking the photos.'

'What happened to her?'

'They broke up a few weeks later. Anna wouldn't play volleyball because she didn't want to get all sandy.' Ellie smiled and turned the page. 'Hang on, this next one's funny…'

A large dog had come bounding out of the sea and was racing towards the camera. The picture was blurred and taken at an angle.

'He shook himself all over Anna. You should have heard her screaming,' said Ellie. 'She didn't like getting wet either.'

'Has she ever considered a holiday in a farmhouse in Tuscany?' said Zack.

The next snaps showed Jamie, having hoisted Ellie up onto his shoulders, racing down the beach into the sea. He had thin legs and they were both screaming with laughter. The bond between them was clear to see. The final shot, a close-up, captured the look being exchanged between Jamie and Ellie as Jamie lovingly lifted a long strand of wet hair from her cheek. It was a look of pure love, to the extent that Zack realized with a jolt he'd never been in a relationship and shared that depth of feeling.

All these years, this was what he'd been missing out on.

'That's it.' Ellie closed the last page. 'You get the gist. That was Jamie. You've seen him now.'

He saw her casually wipe the corner of her eye, where a lone tear had escaped. 'I can see how happy you were.'

She nodded. 'We were happy.'

'Ever argue?'

'Oh God, yes, all the time. And over the silliest things. That's something else I miss. We used to argue about toast. Jamie liked butter on hot toast, I like it on cold so it doesn't melt. He used to make me his kind of toast because he couldn't be bothered to wait for it to cool down and it drove me nuts. Or he used to go mad when I refused to listen to the GPS because I was always convinced I knew a shortcut. And I miss it.' Ellie's voice cracked as she struggled to maintain control. 'I really miss all that stupid stuff. And the thing is, we had a camcorder and we used to record all the good times on film, but it never occurred to us that we should be recording the fights and the arguments because one of us might die soon and the other one might want to sit down and watch them again.' She stopped and took a deep breath. 'Sorry, just ignore me. Stupid, isn't it? And I'm lucky really, because hundreds of years ago people didn't have photos or camcorders so if someone died they didn't have any way of remembering them, except in their heads.'

Zack so badly wanted to make her feel better. 'When it's someone like that, someone important, you never forget them.'

'Probably not.' Ellie shrugged. 'But I worry that I will.'

'Have you argued with anyone since Jamie died?'

She thought about it. Slowly her expression changed. 'I hadn't realized until now. But I really haven't. Everyone's always too busy being nice to me... I haven't had one single argument. God, isn't that weird? It's *abnormal*.'

'Not even with Todd?'

Ellie shook her head in wonder. 'Not even Todd. I got cross with him after the accident, but we never argued.'

Zack hated himself for getting his hopes up. 'Why did you get cross with him?'

'Oh, I blamed him for everything.'

'Was it his fault?'

'No, of course it wasn't. I blamed myself too.'

'OK. Well, you need someone to argue with. Have you thought of phoning your local tax office? Or a car towing firm? Maybe heading over to the council offices for a good old rant about roadworks?'

She looked thoughtful. 'You mean I should ease myself back into it gradually. Practice on strangers to begin with. Start with a bit of trolley rage, something like that?'

'We could try some bickering in the office if you like.'

'That's very kind. But you'd have to promise not to sack me.'

'I won't sack you.' Zack rose to his feet; he wanted to stay but it was time to leave. 'Thanks for tonight. And for showing me the photos.'

'Thank you for being interested.'

At the door Zack wanted to kiss her but he couldn't do that either. Even a peck on the cheek would be inappropriate. He said, 'What happened to those comb things you had in your hair? You didn't lose them, did you?'

'No, I didn't lose them.' She opened the door. 'Bye. See you tomorrow.'

On her own again, Ellie stood at the window and watched as Zack headed off down the street. Having given away the hair combs on a whim because Bibi had said how much she liked them, she was now worrying that it had been a foolish thing to do. They'd been so cheap, Bibi had most likely only said it to be polite. She'd never actually wear them.

Excellent, you just made yourself look like an idiot.

Oh well, at least Zack didn't know.

'Jamie?'

'I'm over here.'

Ellie turned and there he was, stretched out on the sofa.

'Hi. I miss you.'

His gaze softened. 'I know, sweetie. But you had fun tonight, didn't you?'

'Yes. It was good.'

'And your boss is nice.'

'I know. He likes Cornwall too. It's where he grew up. In Perranporth. Get your feet off the sofa.'

'Why?'

'You're wearing trainers. I don't want the cushions getting dirty.'

He looked outraged. 'My trainers are clean!'

'Oh, for God's sake, just *do* it, will you?'

'But I'm comfortable where I am.'

'And you don't care about making a mess because you aren't the one who has to clean it up, you just bugger off and leave it all to me.'

'What's this? Are you trying to start an argument?'

'Stop laughing at me.'

'You are, though, aren't you? You haven't argued with anyone for ages so now you're getting grumpy with me. But I don't want to argue with you. I won't do it.'

'Well, that's just selfish. I can't argue with you if you're not going to argue back.'

He shrugged. 'Sorry.'

'Typical. You just do what you want to do and you don't care about me, do you?'

'I do care. You know that.'

This wasn't working at all. There was a ball of grief like an unexploded grenade in her chest. Ellie looked at him. 'If you cared, you'd still be here. You'd still be alive, you wouldn't have left me on my own, it's not *fair*...' She broke off as something in the region of her rib cage gave way. Her dress hadn't been tight before, but it was less tight now. Gazing down, her hands went to the zip that had somehow unfastened. It wasn't broken; it had just come undone.

She stared at Jamie. 'Did you do that?'

But he simply shrugged, the picture of innocence. 'It wasn't me.'

Chapter 33

IT HAD BEEN A toss-up between Claridge's and the Berkeley, but in the end Tony had gone with the Berkeley. Ellie had no idea he was even over here in the UK; as far as she was concerned, he was still in LA. Crazy, of course, to buy a London pied-à-terre then not use it, but with Ellie and Todd's relationship still in its tentative early stages, he didn't want to be in their way. And if it had progressed to the next level… well, then he really didn't want to be in the way.

Those were the altruistic reasons, anyway. The third one, skewed rather more in his favor, was that if all went well on this visit over here, he wouldn't want Ellie to be the one left feeling awkward.

This way they all had their privacy.

Right. What was the time? Could he go downstairs and wait now?

Should he put on more cologne or was he already wearing too much?

Would she be early? Would she be late? Was it possible to feel any more like a teenager than this?

Downstairs, ten minutes later, Tony's breath caught in his throat as she walked into the lobby, exactly on time. Oh God, and even more beautiful than he remembered, despite the fact that she'd taken up practically permanent residence in his head. Now he committed every last detail to memory and opened his arms wide.

Martha, wearing a fitted lemon-yellow dress and matching shoes, held his face in her hands and said hesitantly, 'This is wrong, it's the wrongest thing I've ever done. Last time it wasn't planned, but this is premeditated.'

Which sounded promising. Inwardly marveling that the sensation of her skin touching his skin could create a reaction of such intensity, Tony said, 'It's so good to see you again.'

Good was the understatement of the year. Seeing her made him feel properly alive. He squeezed her hands and saw the maelstrom of emotions in her amber eyes.

'Oh, Tony.' Martha's voice was unsteady. 'What have you done to me? I used to think I was a nice person. Honest and decent.'

'You are. Hey, this isn't such a big deal. All we're doing is meeting for lunch.'

'I know. Just lunch.' She exhaled.

'Two friends seeing each other again, catching up.' This had been the agreement; obviously he was hoping for more. But if nothing else happened, that was OK. He wasn't going to put any pressure on her. Seeing Martha again, gazing into her eyes, and hearing her voice was enough.

Nearly.

Oh, but we're so much more than just two friends catching up.

'I've already had to lie to Eunice. She wanted me to go along with her this afternoon to visit Henry. I told her I couldn't, said I had to meet a client.'

'Well, that isn't a lie. It's true. I am a client. I'm your biggest fan.' He tried to lighten the atmosphere and dissipate her guilt. 'Do you want me to buy another painting? I'll buy another painting. I'll buy as many as you like.'

And this time she did smile. 'Oh, Tony. What are you doing to me?'

There were all sorts of answers to that, but he didn't voice them. Instead he gave her hand a squeeze. 'Come on, let's go through to the restaurant. I'm buying you lunch.'

The next three hours flew by. They drank Prosecco—but not

too much—ate wonderful food—Tony was barely aware of it—and talked nonstop. The connection was still there, stronger than ever. They had privacy, they could relax, he never wanted it to end. When the restaurant closed, they moved through to the Blue Bar and carried on, enclosed in their own private bubble of bliss. Upstairs he had a room with a bed in it, but they stayed where they were. It was OK. No pressure. He was over here for three days. Oh, would you look at those eyes. That perfect mouth. The way her dimples flashed every time she smiled. He loved every inch of her, every last glorious caramel curve. And to know that she'd been missing him as desperately as he had missed her… it gave him such hope. Somehow, somewhere, surely they could be together in a way that was miraculously guilt-free…

'Are you listening to a word I'm saying?' Martha leaned forward and tapped his arm.

'Sorry. You're making it hard to concentrate.' He captured her fingers between his own, wondering if he'd be able to kiss her before she left. Would she let him? 'What is it?'

'I was telling you about my trip to Blockbuster the other week. Henry likes to watch the old *Dad's Army* TV shows but he managed to sit on his DVDs so I'd gone along to get him some more. I was just standing by the counter when I heard you saying, "What are you *doing* here?" Well, I jumped a mile. I couldn't believe it, I thought you were right behind me. I nearly had a heart attack on the spot!' She fanned her face at the memory. 'So then of course I turned around and there you were, up on the TV screen in that film you did last year. I felt like such an idiot… oh, hang on, that's mine.' Reaching for her bag, she pulled out the ringing phone and grimaced. 'Oh Lord, it's Eunice.'

'Leave it.' Tony already knew she wouldn't.

'I can't. Won't be a second.' She jumped up and made her way out of the Blue Bar, away from the noise. Tony watched her go. From a distance he saw her answer the phone, then freeze. Oh great, what was it? Please don't let Eunice be putting pressure on her, playing the guilt card. Martha's hand had flown to her mouth now. Something was wrong. Of all the afternoons, why did it have to happen on this one?

'Henry's lost.' She was back, searching agitatedly for her purse. 'He's gone missing on Hampstead Heath. They can't find him... anything could happen to him... I'm sorry, I have to go.'

How could he let her go alone? Outside the Berkeley, the doorman flagged down a black cab and together Tony and Martha jumped in. Ensconced inside the hotel, they hadn't even realized it had begun to rain. Now as they made their way to Hampstead, the taxi's windscreen wipers struggled to cope. Thunder was rumbling, the sky had darkened to slate gray, and lightning crackled overhead.

'There's no point in you coming with me.' Martha's face was taut with anxiety. 'You can't look for him. Eunice mustn't see you.'

'I can keep out of her way.' He wanted to hug and reassure her, but it wasn't the time. 'How did it happen anyway?'

'Henry's always loved the heath. Sometimes we take him there for a walk. Eunice took him today. It was still sunny when they got there. They sat down on a bench and she dozed off.'

'Dozed off?'

'She's exhausted. You can't blame her; she never stops. Anyway, it was only for a couple of minutes. But when she woke up, Henry was gone. No sign of him anywhere. And then it started to rain. Oh God, this is my punishment for not going with them. I came to see you instead and now he's lost.'

'Stop it, don't panic, nothing's going to happen to him.' Tony was firm. 'Trust me, he'll be found.'

But when they eventually reached Hampstead, Henry was still missing. The taxi driver stopped at the bottom of Millfield Lane, close to the Highgate ponds. Martha, on the phone with Eunice, ascertained that she was up by the most northerly of the ponds.

'I'll head on up there. She's distraught. There are park rangers out looking for him.' She opened the door of the cab and was drenched within seconds. 'Please, Eunice mustn't see you. Leave this to me. You go home.'

'OK, I'll do that. Call me as soon as you can.' Any kind of kiss would be hideously inappropriate now. Tony let her go. The moment she was out of sight, he paid the driver and jumped out of the taxi. Where Martha had turned right, he checked that no glimpses of her lemon-yellow dress were visible through the trees and turned left.

The rain was hammering down like gunfire. There wasn't anyone else about and the branches of the trees were being wrenched this way and that, whipped into a frenzy by ferocious gusts of wind. Martha had told him that Henry had gone missing on Parliament Hill, but his favorite section of the heath was where the ponds lay. Getting wetter by the second, Tony headed towards them. His shoes, unaccustomed to the terrain, slipped and slid as he made his way through mud and stones and wild undergrowth. Right, here he was at the water's edge. Still no one else in sight, and the pond was less than enticing, gray and cold-looking, the surface whipped up and pitted with rain. Even the ducks had done the sensible thing and taken shelter. Grasses, long and rough, clung to his trouser legs like seaweed. The next moment he stopped dead in his tracks as something dark bobbed up in the water in the center of the pond. But it wasn't a head; it was a discarded carrier bag. Panic over. God, his heart was thudding now. It could have been Henry. Trudging on, Tony blinked water from his eyes and kept searching. At one stage, in the far distance, he saw a tiny figure up on the hill and heard a voice, barely audible, yelling Henry's name.

Ten minutes later it happened. Did he hear a noise or was it sheer chance that he turned and looked to one side and saw a bare foot sticking out of the undergrowth ten yards away? Back came the fear, because what else did that mean he was about to find? Stumbling across the uneven ground, Tony saw the leg attached to the foot, clad in sodden brown trousers. Then a long thin body, long arms, the head… yes, it was definitely him…

'Hello?' Tony approached with caution. Henry was half-sitting, half-lying beneath a tree with his eyes closed and his mouth slightly open. He looked like a carved wooden statue, abandoned in the rain.

Then the eyes opened and Henry was looking at him. 'I'm wet.'

Alive, then. Not dead.

'Henry? Are you OK?'

'Yes, thank you. I'm wet.'

'I can see that. What happened to your shoes?'

Henry gazed in bemusement at his bony bare feet. 'I don't know. I'm sorry. I'm quite wet.'

'Are you able to stand?'

'I'm quite hungry. Is it time for breakfast?'

Henry's voice was gentle, bewildered, educated. Obediently, he held out his hands and allowed Tony to help him to his feet. His clothes were as sodden as if he'd been in the pond. Maybe he had.

'Been for a swim?' said Tony.

Henry blinked slowly. 'I'm wet.'

They stood and gazed at each other for several seconds in the rain. Then Tony watched as Henry searched in his trouser pockets and produced a gray sock. He proceeded to put it on his left hand like a glove. This was Martha's husband; he had been an accountant. God, Alzheimer's was a brutal, disgusting disease. It crossed Tony's mind that there was no one in sight. No one even knew he was here. If he were a character in a film, he might be tempted to lead Henry to the water's edge and push him in. It was deep here. He wouldn't be able to climb out. He could be gone, removed, *eradicated*…

But this wasn't a film. And he may have done some things in his life that he was less than proud of, but he wasn't a murderer.

Tony smiled slightly and reached for his mobile.

'I'd love a cup of tea,' said Henry, brushing water from his springy gray-white hair.

'We'll get you one.' His finger hovered over the phone. 'Henry, who's Martha?'

He saw a flicker of recognition in the silver-rimmed brown eyes. 'Martha? I think she lives next door, doesn't she?'

Tony said gently, 'Martha's your wife.'

'Ah yes. Yes, that's right.' Henry looked at the sock on his hand. 'A cup of tea and a biscuit.'

'Do you love Martha?' Did this make him a truly despicable person? 'Henry, do you love her? Your wife?'

'Oh yes. Where are my shoes? I love her very much.' He was nodding earnestly now. 'And a ham sandwich. That would be nice. I'm quite hungry, you know.'

Tony made the call. 'I've got him, he's fine.'

'Oh thank God!' Martha let out a sob of relief. 'Where are you?'

He told her, adding, 'Don't say anything to Eunice, just get yourself straight down here.'

It took Martha less than five minutes to reach them. The rain had begun to ease off slightly, but they were all so soaked through now it no longer mattered.

'Hello!' Henry's face lit up at the sight of her heading through the undergrowth towards them.

'What's her name?' said Tony.

'Oh my goodness, I do know it. Let me think… she's my beautiful wife.'

'Oh, Henry, we were so worried about you. We didn't know where you were.' Martha clutched his hands, one of them still encased in the gray knitted sock. 'Where are your shoes?'

'Harrods, I think. Or Sainsbury's. I'm wet.'

'I know, darling. It doesn't matter, we're going to get you home now.' She looked at Tony and said, 'Thank you so much. You have to go. But thank you.'

As Tony turned to leave, Martha was already calling Eunice to tell her that everything was OK, Henry was safe.

Henry, carefully examining the sock on his hand, said to no one in particular, 'Or roast chicken would be nice.'

Chapter 34

OPENING THE DOOR AT eight o'clock in the morning, Roo wasn't that surprised to find Niall on her doorstep. Ellie had told her all about the recent encounter with him and Yasmin outside Claridge's.

But to show willing, she said, 'What are you doing here?'

'You've blocked my number. I need to talk to you, find out what's going on.' He wasted no time. 'You went to see Yasmin.'

'And?'

'I want to know why.'

'Just curious, I suppose. I was interested to find out what she was really like. And guess what? She was lovely. Better than you deserve, that's for sure.'

'Well, don't do it again, OK? Leave her alone.'

'Don't tell me what I can't do,' said Roo.

Niall exhaled. 'OK, please don't go there again. If you tell her, you'd break her heart.'

Fancy that. She'd be the one who broke his wife's heart. Aloud she said, 'You think?'

'Roo. *Please.*'

* * *

Working in a charity shop might not be glamorous but it was undoubtedly a good thing. People gave away stuff they no longer wanted, and it was bought by people who did want it, and the money raised went to a worthy cause.

It was just a shame that sometimes people gave away stuff they no longer wanted without first making sure it was clean. This was Roo's first morning in the shop and she was discovering that rubber gloves were a necessity. Already, unpacking the mound of plastic bags left outside overnight, she had lifted out a pair of jeans with boxer shorts still inside them. Neither of them had been washed. For a good long while. If ever.

But it didn't matter, because she was atoning. Making up for a lifetime of hedonism and selfishness. She wasn't going to throw a diva tantrum and demand to be given something easier and less gross to do.

Besides, it had all been worth it to see the look on Niall's face this morning when she sent him packing with the words, 'Anyway, I have to go now, I mustn't be late for work.'

Stunned, he'd said, 'What d'you mean, *work*?'

And she'd got a real kick out of replying, 'Oh, didn't Ellie mention it? I've got a new job.'

The other upside to having turned over a new leaf was discovering how buzzy and clear-headed it was possible to feel when you gave up drinking. She hadn't realized before what a difference it made when you didn't even have a hint of a hangover fuzzing up your brain.

''Scuse me, love, this one's too small for me, d'you have it in an eighteen?'

The customer was in her forties and had one of those tartan shopping trolleys on wheels. She was holding up a pink cardigan and looking hopeful. The old Roo would have said, 'Hello? We're in a charity shop, darling. This isn't Harvey Nicks.' Or she might have said, 'If you lost a couple of stone, it'd fit you.'

But she wasn't Old Roo anymore, she was New Roo. *Sans* makeup, *sans* snarky attitude. She made a conscious effort to envisage this customer's life: poverty-stricken, unlucky in love, lots of daytime TV… *oh God, apart from the poverty bit, that's me!*… and said, 'I'm so sorry, we don't. But a lovely pale green one just came in this morning, I'm sure it's an eighteen and the color would really suit you. Shall I pop out to the back room and find it?'

Pat, who was the manageress, told her it was to be priced at six pounds fifty. Roo brought the cardigan out and it fitted the woman perfectly. She'd been right about the shade too; it really brought out the color of her eyes.

'Oh dear, six pounds fifty, though.' The woman hesitated, visibly torn. 'That's more than I can afford.'

God, imagine not being able to afford six pounds fifty. Roo leaned forward and whispered, 'It's all right, you can have it for one pound fifty.' What the hell, she'd make up the difference herself.

'OK.' The woman beamed, as well she might. It was a lamb's wool cardigan from Jaeger, in pristine condition. 'I'll take it!'

Three minutes later, glancing up as the woman was about to leave the shop, Roo saw her deftly removing a pair of Russell and Bromley stilettos from a display stand and sliding them into her tartan shopper. She blinked in disbelief as an armful of scarves and handbags followed them.

'Hey!' yelled Roo, outraged.

The woman looked up, gave her a one-fingered salute, and shot out of the shop faster than Usain Bolt, the tartan trolley bouncing at her heels. Roo, cursing this morning's unwise choice of four-inch zebra-print stilettos with multiple ankle straps, yelped, 'Stop her! She *stole* stuff!'

But this clearly wasn't going to happen. She was the only person in the shop under eighty. By the time she managed to unbuckle the fiddly straps and get her shoes off, the thief and her tartan trolley would be in Camden.

Pat, emerging from the back room, shot her a disapproving look. 'Didn't you chase after her?'

In reply, Roo pointed to her bondage heels.

A disparaging sniff, then Pat said, 'In future, wear something you can run in. And what was that I overheard about you letting her have the cardigan for one pound fifty?'

Honestly, were there secret listening devices hidden under the counter? Roo was forced to bite her lip, hard. 'It's OK, I hadn't forgotten. I owe the till five pounds.'

After six hours of breathing in the stale air of the charity shop— clearly not choosing to volunteer in one of the many clean ones had been a mistake—entering the beauty salon was sheer heaven. The luxury, the gorgeous expensive smells, the relaxing atmosphere, the absence of ungrateful shoplifters...

'Oh, look at your poor nails!' Having examined them, Yasmin said sympathetically, 'And this one's broken right down. That must hurt. How did it happen?'

Roo shrugged. 'Humping heavy boxes around. Picking duct tape off a hundred-piece chandelier. Carrying an electric cooker up two flights of stairs.'

'That'll do it.' Yasmin was already preparing to get busy with her manicurist's equipment. She kept her attention focused on the badly torn nail. 'So what's all this in aid of? Are you moving house?'

'No. I've just started as a volunteer in a charity shop. If I smell funny, that's why.'

'Oh, you don't smell! And what an amazing thing to do, giving up your time and working for nothing... that's so generous. You must be a really nice person.'

On the one hand, this was just what Roo wanted to hear. On the other hand, if only Yasmin knew.

But she wasn't going to tell her. Niall could relax; that wasn't why she'd come back here. She wanted to make amends to Yasmin without her finding out the truth.

'Thousands of people do voluntary work.' She showed Yasmin her zebra heels. 'I wore the wrong shoes. Got told off.'

'But they're beautiful.'

'We had a shoplifter.'

'A shoplifter?' Yasmin pulled a face. 'That's just *low*.'

Speaking of low... 'Anyway, how's your family?'

'They're good, thanks. Did your friend tell you we bumped into her the other night?'

'Oh yes, she did mention it.'

'How did the baby-sitting go?'

'With Alice?' Roo wasn't stupid; she'd made a point of learning the name. 'No problem. It was great!'

'Any more teeth yet?'

'Sorry?'

'Teeth? The baby?'

'Oh... well, maybe a few more.' OK, now she was out of her comfort zone. 'I didn't count them. Babies aren't really my thing.'

Yasmin smiled. 'Alice hasn't made you broody then. Not planning on having one yourself.'

'Ew, no chance.'

'You say that now.' Niall's wife's eyes sparkled. 'But you'll end up changing your mind. Give it a few years and it'll happen. Are you with anyone at the moment?'

Roo watched her cuticles being skillfully pushed back with an orange stick, felt the warmth of Yasmin's fingers cupping her hand. 'No, no one. I'm all on my own.'

'Well, that must be your choice. You're so pretty you could have any man you want.'

Don't think about Todd. Definitely don't think about Niall.

'It doesn't work like that, though, does it? It's not that simple. To be honest,' Roo blurted out, 'I've never had much luck with men.'

'Oh, don't worry, you'll get there in the end. You'll find the right man, settle down together, have a baby... sorry, are you OK? Have I said the wrong thing? Here, have a tissue, I'm so sorry, I didn't mean to upset you...'

'No, really, I'm fine.' It was the guilt and the shame that had done it; Roo hastily used her free hand to wipe away the tears that had sprung up out of nowhere. 'It just sounds so lovely. Is that what happened to you?'

'What, with my husband?' Yasmin paused for a moment. Then she said ruefully, 'Well, I hadn't actually planned on getting pregnant, but these things happen, so you just make the best of it, don't you? And now Ben's here, I wouldn't be without him for the world.'

When her nails were finished, skillfully repaired and buffed, and made shorter than before in deference to her new job, Roo paid the bill and added a twenty pound tip.

'Wow.' Yasmin's eyes widened. 'Are you sure?'

'Of course I'm sure. You fitted me in at short notice. And you've done a great job,' said Roo. 'You deserve it.'

'Well, thanks.' Yasmin grinned. 'You can come back again.'

And the weird thing was, she almost couldn't wait. Roo picked up one of the salon's glossy pink and cream brochures detailing the treatments on offer and wondered which of them to have next. 'I will.'

The phone rang that evening just as Ellie was getting ready for bed.

'Oh, hi! Is that Ellie? Ellie, hi there, honey is Tony with you?' Tamara, Tony's personal assistant in LA, had one of those singsong super-sweet voices that made you feel as if you were swimming through treacle.

'No. He's not here.' Ellie frowned; what an odd question. 'He isn't in Britain. He's in LA.'

'No, honey, he's not here. He's definitely over there with you.'

'He isn't, though. And he would have told me if he was coming over.'

'Well, he asked me to organize it. I booked the plane tickets myself and drove him to the airport. OK, don't worry, I just need to ask him about fitting in an interview but his cell's switched off. No problem, I'll keep trying. Bye, honey, bye!'

OK, this was officially strange. Ellie tried Tony's number. Tamara was right; it was switched off. She left a message asking him to call her and said, 'If you're here, why didn't you tell me?'

Most odd. But he must be all right, surely. There had to be a simple explanation.

Ellie yawned, brushed her teeth, and went to bed.

Chapter 35

HE GOT BACK TO Ellie while she was at work the next day.

'Tony! Are you all right?' She'd actually started to worry when his phone had still been switched off this morning.

'I'm fine, sweetheart.'

'Where are you?'

'At home in LA.'

God, who'd ever trust an actor? He was such a plausible liar. 'No you're not,' said Ellie. 'I spoke to Tamara. You're over here.'

'Oh. Damn. OK, you're right. I knew I should have returned Tamara's calls first.'

'Your phone's been switched off!'

'Battery was flat. I forgot to pack my charger, that's all.'

'Why didn't you come to the flat?' *Where you have a perfectly good spare charger.*

Tony paused then said, 'I thought you and Todd would appreciate having it to yourselves. I was being discreet, giving you a bit of space.'

'Are you serious?'

'Really, it's not a problem. I took a room at the Berkeley. You and Todd don't want me hanging around and—'

'Oh, Tony, that's over, it didn't work out. It just wasn't right.' Ellie lowered her voice; Zack was only in the kitchen and she didn't want him to overhear. 'We tried, but we're happier as friends.'

'Oh, sweetheart, I'm sorry.'

'Don't be. We're both fine about it. So you can check out of that hotel right now and get yourself over here. You won't be a third wheel, it'll just be us.'

'Except I'm heading back tomorrow. It was just a flying visit. It's hardly worth it now.'

He sounded… sad. 'Are you busy tonight?'

'No, no, nothing planned…'

Something definitely wasn't right. 'Come over, then. I haven't seen you for ages. I'll cook dinner,' Ellie volunteered. 'I've learned how to do Thai green curry.'

'Really?' It was his favorite.

'Really!'

'Is it nice?'

Honesty forced her to prevaricate. 'It *might* be nice.'

'Or it might not?'

'I'm still practicing. Come over and let me give it another go. If it all goes horribly wrong, we'll order a takeaway.'

Sounding slightly more cheerful, Tony said, 'Or shall I just order it now?'

Zack came into the office a couple of minutes later, dressed in a suit and jangling his keys.

'All OK? I've got a lunch meeting in Piccadilly. Can you take Elmo out for a run at some stage? I'll be back by four at the latest.'

'No problem, that's fine.' He was wearing a new turquoise shirt and it was on the tip of her tongue to say how much the color suited him, but Ellie felt the speeding-up sensation in her chest that meant she was finding him attractive again. Dammit, and she'd worked so hard to squash those feelings, had thought she'd succeeded in getting them under control. OK, just don't mention it, *keep it zipped*.

But she must have looked as if she were about to say something because Zack had stopped in the doorway and was looking expectant. 'Anything else?'

Yes, that color's fantastic against your tan, you look unbelievably gorgeous, you're making me think things I shouldn't be thinking…

'No,' Ellie flashed him her busy smile, 'nothing else. Have a nice time!'

At two thirty she gave Geraldine a call. 'Hi, it's me. Do you want to send Elmo over?'

'Oh hello, darling, absolutely! Sweetie, up you get, it's for you.'

Ellie heard snuffling and said, 'Elmo! Coming for a walk?'

'There you go,' Geraldine said with satisfaction. 'He's on his way.'

Moments later Ellie looked out of the kitchen window and saw Elmo launch himself over the wall. He burst through the dog flap, tail wagging furiously and paws skidding across the tiled floor.

'Come here, baby.' She bent to clip his lead on, but the doorbell simultaneously rang and Elmo gave her the slip. Finally she managed to scoop him up and answer the front door.

'Oh.' Louisa, on the top step, recoiled from the sight of Elmo at unexpectedly close quarters. 'I've come to see Zack. Is he upstairs?'

'He's not here.'

'You're just saying that.'

'I'm not.' What was this about?

'His car's over there.' Louisa pointed across the road.

'He took a cab into town. He really isn't here. Was he expecting you?'

'No. I just need to talk to him.' Louisa's hair and makeup were perfect; she was wearing an apricot linen dress and ultra-high, ultra-pointy cream shoes.

'Well, he's in a lunch meeting now. Why don't you try phoning him later?'

'I've *tried* phoning him. It's not the same, and most of the time he doesn't even pick up.' Louisa's voice began to wobble. 'Look, can I come in?'

Elmo was wriggling like an eel, keen to get on with the business in hand. Ellie hesitated. 'The thing is, we were just about to go out for a walk.'

'Fine then. I'll come with you.'

'But—'

'Please let me. I need to talk about Zack. There, there, good doggie.' Gingerly Louisa patted the top of Elmo's head, which had to be a first. Even Elmo looked astonished. 'He's quite sweet really, isn't he?'

'Who, Zack?'

'No, the dog.' She watched as Ellie attached the lead to Elmo's collar and put him down. 'The last few weeks have been horrible. I've missed him so much.'

'Who, Elmo?'

'*Zack.*' Once the front door was closed, Louisa followed them down the stone steps. 'So how's he been?'

'OK. The same, really.' Oh dear, was that insensitive? 'I'm sure he's missed you too,' Ellie said hastily. 'You know what men are like. They hide it well.'

But it was too late; Louisa's face had crumpled. 'It's so unfair. I've never been so miserable in my life. Does he talk about me?'

'Um… not really.'

'He must do. He must have said something! We were *perfect* together.'

They made a strange little procession, heading past the shops along Regents Park Road. Elmo led the way, straining against his lead and desperate to reach grass. Ellie was second, walking fast in her sparkly flip-flops. Bringing up the rear, hobbling slightly and struggling to keep up in her too-high heels, was Louisa.

'He hasn't said anything to me,' Ellie called over her shoulder. She waved to Briony, who worked in the cake shop.

'Is he seeing someone else?' said Louisa.

'No.'

'How can you say that? How do you know?'

'OK, he hasn't told me he's seeing anyone else. And last week I had to go along as his plus-one to an event, because—'

'Oh God, the dinner at Claridge's? He invited *you*? That's so unfair!'

Ellie increased her pace; this was getting awkward now. Louisa's voice had risen and people were turning to stare at them. At last they reached Primrose Hill itself and she was able to let Elmo off his lead. Finding a stick, she threw it as far as she could and watched him tear after it.

'I bet you're glad we broke up, aren't you?' Louisa's hands were on her hips as she struggled to get her breath back. 'You've got Zack all to yourself now.'

Don't blush, don't blush. 'I work for him. That's all.'

'Urrgh!' Louisa let out a panicky screech and kangarooed sideways as Elmo came hurtling back with the stick in his mouth. Her heels sank into the ground and she struggled to regain her balance. Accusingly she said, 'But you must fancy him.'

'OK, enough. I do not fancy Zack.' Ellie prayed her nose wouldn't suddenly extend by a couple of feet. 'I have a boyfriend. His name is Todd.' Todd wouldn't mind her borrowing him again; it was all in a good cause. 'And I don't need to listen to this rubbish, so you can stop following me now. Bye.'

Louisa promptly buried her face in her hands and shook her head in defeat. 'Oh God, I'm sorry. I didn't mean it. I just d-don't know what to *do...*'

People were definitely paying attention now. A small girl tugged at her mother's arm and said in a loud voice, 'Mummy, is that big lady crying?'

This only made Louisa cry more. She clenched her fists and wailed, 'I'm not *big.*'

'Come on.' Ellie ushered her over to a free bench. 'Sit down. Here, I've got a tissue somewhere.'

All the makeup, so carefully applied in Zack's honor, came off on the tissue. For several minutes Louisa sobbed noisily. Ellie sat next to her, let her get it out of her system, and threw the stick twenty or thirty times for Elmo to chase after and joyfully retrieve. Like a girl with hopeless taste in men, getting her heart broken over and over again, it evidently never occurred to Elmo to stop and wonder if maybe it was all a bit pointless.

'Have you got any more tissues?' Louisa mumbled finally.

'No.'

'Do I look a mess?'

Mess was an understatement. How to be diplomatic? 'A bit.'

'Oh Goddddd…' Louisa rose to her feet. 'I need to clean myself up. Can we head back to the house now, so I can use the bathroom?'

Ellie hesitated but didn't have the heart to refuse. Oh well, she could make it up to Elmo with a top-up walk later. Whistling and calling him back, she re-attached his lead and said, 'OK, let's go.'

Elmo registered his protest by waiting until they'd reached Ancram Street before squatting and depositing a pile of poo on the pavement.

'How can you do that?' Louisa shuddered as Ellie bent and did the inverted nappy-bag trick to pick it up. 'That's *so gross.*'

Did she think poo-collecting was her favorite hobby? Ellie said evenly, 'I don't love it. It's just something that has to be done.'

'What time did Zack say he'd be back?'

'He didn't.' Oops, another lie. 'He could be gone for hours yet.'

'Or he might not. I could stay and wait.'

'I don't think so, I have to work,' said Ellie.

'I wouldn't be a nuisance. I'll just wait for him upstairs.'

'Really, it's not a good idea.'

'Oh, for God's sake, you're not very sympathetic, are you?' Louisa's emotions rose and her face reddened. 'You just don't get how important this is! I love Zack and I want him back. He means everything in the world to me. My heart is breaking, I'm going through hell here... you can't *begin* to understand how I feel!'

Just for a microsecond Jamie appeared without warning, leaning against a parked car with his arms casually crossed and his blond hair glinting in the sunshine. He surveyed Louisa with amusement. Then, as if sensing that Ellie was teetering on the edge of retaliation, he turned and shook his head at her. 'Don't do it.'

He was right. It would be the cheapest form of one-upmanship. Ellie exhaled. Then a taxi drew to a halt and Jamie, in his pink T-shirt and jeans, simply vanished. Elmo let out a volley of barks as Zack jumped out of the cab.

Chapter 36

'WELL, WELL, WHAT A surprise,' Louisa jeered at Ellie. 'You were lying. Fancy that.'

'I told you, I didn't know when he'd be back.' Ellie bristled; Zack was welcome to take over now.

'Hello? Do I look stupid? You were just trying to get rid of me because you're after him yourself.'

It had evidently slipped Louisa's mind that she did look stupid. Well, hooray for that. Zack finished paying the cab driver and strode across the road towards them.

He took in the situation at a glance. 'What's happening here? What's been going on?' He moved towards Ellie. 'Are you all right?'

Which was nice in one way, but succeeded in sending Louisa into paroxysms of jealousy.

'Zacky, I've missed you so much! I need to see you.'

Zacky? Oh good grief, did she actually call him that?

'Seriously.' Zack carried on addressing Ellie. 'Are you OK?'

'I'm fine.' His hand was on her arm. *It felt amazing...*

'Zacky? We have to talk!'

He turned to look at Louisa. 'Really, there's no point.'

'Oh my God, I don't believe this. Look at the two of you together. And you're *protecting* her!' She swung round, her swollen piggy eyes homing in on Ellie like lasers. 'I asked if there was anything going on between you two and you denied it. You sneaky, lying, little—'

'I'll leave you to it.' Ellie headed past her to get to the house. Zack kept a firm grip on her arm and went with her. Enraged, Louisa let out a howl and lashed out wildly in an attempt to separate them. The tissue-thin handles of the nappy bag were torn from Ellie's grasp. The bag hit Louisa's ankle with a wet thud and this time her reaction was ear-splitting, her screams reverberating down the street as she jerked back and kicked it like a football into the air.

'Ugh… *eurgh!*' The bag hadn't burst but the fact that it had made contact was enough. Louisa hopped around, looking as if she'd quite like to amputate the offending leg. Elmo, entranced by another opportunity to play fetch, scooted along the pavement and joyfully retrieved it. Carrying the bag back by its handles, he deposited it at Louisa's feet and waited for her to do it again.

'You filthy disgusting animal, *get away from me!*'

'OK, enough.' Zack unlocked the front door, ushered Ellie past him, and whistled at Elmo to follow her. 'I'm sorting this out now. Get inside.'

Ellie pulled the door closed behind her and headed on through to the kitchen. She watched Elmo slurp noisily from his water bowl. Moments later the phone rang.

'Well, this has brightened my day no end,' said Geraldine. 'It's like *Sex and the City* on my very own doorstep.'

At the sound of her voice, Elmo pricked up his ears and disappeared through the dog flap.

'Elmo's on his way over,' said Ellie.

'Are you in the kitchen? Why aren't you watching the fun? Come on, get the binoculars out! Louisa's on her knees now, she's going to ruin those smart shoes of hers. Or you could come over here and we'll watch it together… oh hello, sweetie, did the nasty lady not want to play catch with you?'

'I can't come over,' said Ellie. 'I've got loads of work to catch up on.' Not true, but she'd already witnessed enough misery for one day.

'Shame. So what's it all about?' From the tone of her voice it was plain that Geraldine already knew.

'Don't you have the window open?'

'Of course I have! What d'you expect me to do? Lip-read? She's convinced there's something going on between you and Zack.'

Ellie's mouth was dry. 'I know. But there isn't.'

The front door slammed twenty minutes later and her fingers on the keyboard went into overdrive... *Dead Mr Mackenzie, Many thinks for your letted...* aargh, Ellie hurriedly deleted the errors before he could see them.

But Zack didn't glance at the computer screen. He put his head round the door and said with a sigh, 'Come on, I think we could both do with a drink.'

He seized a bottle from the fridge, Ellie collected two glasses, and they headed upstairs to the living room. The icy white wine sent little wavelets of relaxation through her stomach but did nothing to dissipate the Zack-related emotions. She took another swallow. At least he didn't know *they* were there.

Zack raked his fingers through his hair and said, 'Well. Sorry about that.'

'Not your fault.'

'Isn't it? I hate ending relationships. God, it's the pits. Maybe I did it wrong.' He paused and rubbed his forehead. 'But I never expected that kind of reaction. Not Louisa. You wouldn't think she was the type.'

'I know. Too cool, too much of a grown-up.' Poor thing, Ellie did actually feel sorry for her; in years to come, Louisa would look back on this day and be appalled by her own loss of dignity.

'And I'm sorry she said all that stuff to you. She's really got it into her head that there's some kind of thing going on between you and me.' Zack's gaze was fixed on her, his tone quizzical. 'I don't know *where* she got that from.'

OK, was this an unspoken accusation? Was he implying that *he* hadn't given Louisa the idea but someone certainly had, and could she by any chance have hinted at it herself? Mortified, Ellie said, 'Well, it wasn't me! Why would I do something like that? The only reason you hired me for this job in the first place was because you knew for a fact I wasn't interested in you and that's the truth, I swear on my life.'

And she wasn't lying; it was true. When she'd first come here, she hadn't been interested. No need to mention the recent change of heart.

'I know, I know that. I didn't mean for one minute that you'd said anything to her.' Zack was equally horrified. 'It's just Louisa, she's upset and looking for someone to blame. Anyway, it's over. She's gone and she won't be back. But I feel bad that you had to put up with all the hassle.' He knocked back the last of his wine. 'Are you seeing Todd tonight? I hope he'll be OK with it.'

'I'm not seeing him tonight.' Ellie had already started shaking her head before the final sentence. 'But he'll be fine.'

'Good. But I'd still like to make it up to you.' Zack thought for a moment. 'Look, if you're free this evening, why don't we go out for something to eat?' He spread his hands. 'Just my way of saying sorry and thanks. How about that? Sound like a plan?'

If everything wasn't as it was, if the situation could have been completely different, Ellie would have loved nothing more. If she didn't work for Zack and they'd just met for the first time, she'd have said yes like a shot.

But she did and they hadn't, and she wasn't going to, even though it was an innocent offer and she was tempted.

She couldn't anyway.

'Thanks, but I can't. I'm cooking for Tony tonight.'

Somehow, against all the odds, a tiny miracle had occurred. The Thai green curry had turned out well. The chicken was tender, the jasmine rice fluffy, and the spices took the roof off your mouth, but in a good way. Having finally overcome her terrible phobia of fish sauce, Ellie had plucked up the courage to buy a bottle and it had made the world of difference. The curry had been magical as a result.

Which was just as well, seeing as Tony was desperately in need of cheering up. To begin with he'd asked her about Todd and she'd told him how relieved she was to be free of the fear that she was trapped in a relationship that was all wrong. Tony was sad but sympathetic; he understood. Then she talked about today's kerfuffle with Louisa and he nodded and said, 'Poor girl,' a couple of times, and helped himself to another beer.

OK, enough. Ellie said, 'Tony? Are you going to tell me what's wrong?' She waited, watching him pour the beer slowly into his glass. 'Because otherwise I'm going to start worrying that you're ill.'

Tony put the bottle down. The laughter lines around his eyes weren't getting much exercise today. His misery was tangible. 'I'm not ill, sweetheart.'

He was an actor. She watched him closely. 'Sure?'

'I'm sure. I promise. It's not that.' He rested his elbows on the table. 'OK, I'll tell you. Remember those paintings I bought, months ago? The ones by the artist I met on Primrose Hill…?'

Chapter 37

ELLIE'S THROAT WAS ON fire, her body was a dead weight, and she couldn't stop shivering. It was almost too painful to turn over in bed. Was this how it felt to climb Kilimanjaro? *Oh God, Jamie, this is horrible, where are you when I need you? Can you not even get me a glass of water?*

She woke up again three hours later. It was sunny outside and the light hurt her eyes. It was even an effort to lift her head and peer at the alarm clock. Eight thirty. Oh no, what about work? But there was no way she could go in today; this wasn't a cough or a cold, it was full-blown flu. She'd experienced it twice before in her life and now it was third time unlucky. But at least she didn't need to wrestle with her conscience; work was out of the question. This wasn't man flu, it was the proper kind. She'd have to call Zack and let him know.

It took superhuman strength to crawl out of bed. Unbelievably, all she'd felt last night was extra tired and a bit hot. Now it was all she could do to make it to the bathroom for Tylenol, a glass of water, and a wee. Then through to the living room to collect her phone.

Back in bed, breathless and weak with exhaustion, Ellie pressed buttons until Zack's name came up. Then she heard his voice telling her he was busy right now and could she leave a message.

'Zack, it's me. Sorry, um, I've got flu.' Even holding the phone was sapping her energy; the pain in her head was indescribable. 'Can't come into work.' Her throat was burning and she was croaking like a frog. She sounded ridiculous, like the worst kind of malingerer putting on one of those feeble I'm-so-sick voices that didn't fool anyone. 'Sorry, but I can't, I really am ill. It's flu… OK… bye.' She ended the call and hauled herself with difficulty over onto her side. Her eyes closed, which could only be a good thing. Sleep would take the pain away, wouldn't it?

The next time Ellie woke it was four o'clock and her skin hurt so much she could hardly bear the duvet to touch it. Her bones ached, and she'd never felt hotter in her life. But two minutes later, having pushed the duvet to one side, she was shivering uncontrollably once more. Her mouth was dry too, and she was thirsty beyond belief. Pushing strands of damp hair off her face only caused more pain. This was worse than Kilimanjaro in size-three high heels. OK, reach for the glass, drink the water. She managed it without spilling too much down the side of her chin. It wasn't until the glass was empty that Ellie realized she'd forgotten to take the next two Tylenols. She couldn't swallow them dry. But this now meant climbing out of bed to get more water. Tears prickled at the back of her eyes. This was when she missed Jamie the most. And she couldn't have picked a worse time to be ill if she tried; Tony had flown back to LA last week, Todd was away at a business conference in Edinburgh, even Roo had taken off for a few days to pay a long overdue visit to her mother in Marbella. If she were truly desperate she could call Paula, but she didn't want to do that; it wouldn't be fair.

Jamie? Jamie, are you there?

But her brain was so fogged with pain and exhaustion and cotton wool that she was unable to conjure him up. And even if she could, he wouldn't be able to bring her another glass of water. The brutal reality was that she was here on her own. If she wanted anything, she was going to have to get it herself.

Ellie shuffled through to the kitchen, careful not to move her head, and filled a pint glass from the tap. There was a carton of orange juice in the fridge; fumbling to get it out, she pushed the bottle of olive oil to one side and watched helplessly, with the reaction times of a slug, as it overbalanced and toppled off the shelf. The bottle smashed on the white tiles and a great pool of extra virgin olive oil glinting with glass splinters spread across the floor.

Ellie hung on to the fridge door and gazed at the mess. You knew you were ill when you didn't have the energy to say, 'Fuck.'

Since there was no way she could clear it up, she took the pint of water and shuffled back to bed. Took two more painkillers. Closed her eyes and began to doze fitfully, her feverish brain conjuring up disjointed, unrelaxing dreams…

And now she was suffocating, being smothered by a big grizzly bear, and the phone was ringing, ringing, ringing…

OK, so it wasn't a bear. Ellie freed herself from the depths of the duvet and managed to locate the phone on its fifth and final ring.

Dozily she croaked, 'Hello?'

'Did I wake you?' It was Zack's voice. 'I just wanted to make sure you're all right.'

'Oh.' Her throat felt as if it were being squeezed by a giant fist, she could barely swallow. Was he calling her to see if she was really ill or just faking it? He sounded concerned but maybe that was to catch her out. 'Um, I don't think I'll be able to come into work tomorrow…' She began to cough feebly, the pain slicing through her brain. '*Ow*, sorry…'

'Don't apologize. Of course you can't work. Have you seen a doctor?'

'No…' Stupidly, she hadn't yet got around to registering with a local doctor's office. What were the chances of her old GP trekking over from Hammersmith?

'Is there someone to look after you?'

Another fit of coughing seized her. 'No.'

'Where's Todd?'

'Away at a business conference.'

'Can you get out of bed?'

'Yes…'

'Right. I'm coming over.'

'No, no… I'll be OK. You don't want to catch this.'

Zack ignored her. 'Is there anything you need?'

I need Jamie. She closed her eyes and whispered, 'Painkillers. Strong ones. I've run out.'

'I've got some. I'm on my way.'

Ellie rubbed a hand over her face; had she ever looked worse than this? Oh well, too ill to care, she swallowed with difficulty. 'Thanks.'

The doorbell duly rang fifteen minutes later. She pressed the buzzer to let him in and collapsed back into bed.

Zack entered the flat and heard a voice call out weakly, 'I'm in here.'

The door to her bedroom was open, the curtains drawn across. The faint smell of her perfume hung in the air. Huddled under the duvet, Ellie lay shivering and deathly pale. She waggled the fingers of her left hand at him and murmured, 'Don't come any closer.'

'I'm never ill.' Ignoring her, he approached the bed. 'Have you been here on your own all day?'

She nodded fractionally and winced. 'It's only flu.'

'I've brought Ibuprofen, Tylenol, and Night Nurse.' He placed them on the bedside table and picked up the empty glasses. 'I'll get you some fresh water. Or how about a cup of tea?'

Ellie shook her head. 'Just water.' She stiffened, remembering something. 'From the bathroom. Don't go into the kitchen, there's a mess. I had an accident.'

Zack wanted to hold her, take her in his arms, scoop her up, and carry her home. Instead, he left the bedroom and pushed open the door to the kitchen. For a horrified split second, greeted by the sight of a golden puddle, he thought she'd had *that* kind of accident. Then he saw the broken glass and realized it was olive oil.

'Here.' He went back with a glass of water. 'Now let's sort out your pillows.'

Ellie rolled over to the side of the bed and he plumped up the flattened pillows. Then he helped her into a semisitting position so she could take two tablets and wash them down with water. It was the most physical contact they'd ever had and it felt incredible. Ellie was ill and he loved being able to help her. He even loved that her skin was shiny and pale green and her stringy hair was all over the place. She was wearing a dark blue jersey nightdress that was slipping off one shoulder and he wasn't even going to think about the fact that this might be the only item of clothing she had on.

Returning to the bedroom twenty minutes later, he said, 'How about some fruit juice?'

Ellie shook her head fractionally, 'Don't go into the kitchen.'

'It's OK, all cleared up.'

'What?' She frowned. 'The olive oil? Oh God, you didn't.' It had actually been a nightmare job; every time he'd scrubbed the floor and wiped it dry, stepping on it had revealed that the tiles were still as slippery as an ice rink.

But he was keen to impress, so Zack shrugged and said easily, 'Not a problem.'

'I can't believe you cleaned my kitchen floor.' She looked mortified.

'Hey, it's done. Don't worry about it.' He picked up the tissue box on the bedside table. 'This is almost empty. Do you have any more?'

'No. It's OK, there's loo roll.'

'You can't use that. I'll get you another box. I need to go now but I'll be back in a couple of hours.'

'You don't have to come back.'

'I'm not leaving you on your own like this. You're ill. Get some sleep now.' Zack leaned over the bed and straightened pillows that didn't need straightening. 'Do you want to give me the key so I don't have to ring the bell?'

She nodded. 'In my handbag in the living room. Could I have a…? No, it doesn't matter.'

'Say it. Anything you like.'

A faint smile lifted the corners of her mouth. 'Great, I'll have a red Mercedes and a diamond tiara.'

'Right.' In that moment Zack knew he loved her, *he actually loved her*. 'Well, that might take a couple of days to organize. Anything else in the meantime?'

'A can of Sprite would be fantastic.'

'Now you're just being greedy. But you're the invalid, so OK.'

Another smile. 'Thanks.'

Chapter 38

ELLIE SLEPT AGAIN, WAKING up two hours later to the sound of Zack letting himself into the flat. God, brave of him to come back. So kind. A grateful tear squeezed out of the corner of her eye; when you felt this ill, it was so lovely not to feel abandoned and alone.

She probably needed a shower but that was impossible; the thought of drops of water pummeling her skin was too agonizing to contemplate. Ellie prayed she didn't smell.

But when he came into the bedroom with a can of Sprite and a pink bendy straw so she didn't spill it down her front, Zack didn't appear to be holding his breath. Maybe she was OK. He did her pillows again, smoothed out the duvet, and re-tucked the corners of the bottom sheet that with all her tossing and turning had come untucked.

'It's dark outside.' The Sprite, ice-cold and delicious, soothed her burning throat.

'Ten o'clock. Time for more Ibuprofen.' He popped them out of their foil packet and handed them over before tearing the perforated cardboard oval from the lid of the new box of Kleenex. 'Can you manage anything to eat?'

Ellie closed her eyes, contemplated food, shook her head. 'No thanks. Not hungry. This Sprite is perfect.'

'Good. Now, do you want to lie on the sofa and watch TV for a bit?'

Television. Needing to concentrate. Having to keep her eyes open. 'I think I'm too tired.'

'OK, you go back to sleep. I've brought my laptop with me. I'm going to do some work for the next couple of hours. If you need anything, just give me a shout.'

'You don't need to stay. I'll be fine.'

'You might be fine. But what if you're not? Look, it's not a problem. It makes no difference to me whether I'm working here or at home. And just so you know, there are plenty more Sprites in the fridge.'

So kind, so thoughtful. And he didn't need to be doing any of this. Ellie turned onto her side and drifted off again, comforted by the knowledge that there was someone else in the flat, for the time being at least.

It was four thirty when she next came to, nudged into semi consciousness by her bladder. For several seconds she couldn't work out if it was morning or afternoon. Right, still dark outside, that had to mean morning. Blurrily she felt her way out of bed and across the room to the en-suite. That was better. OK, now she was upright, how about a trip to the kitchen for another cold Sprite?

Shuffling along the hallway she saw the living-room door was ajar and prodded it open. The lights were low and Zack's laptop stood open on the coffee table. Zack was stretched across the sofa, fast asleep.

Fuzzy-headed and weak-limbed though she was, Ellie couldn't stop looking at him; it was literally impossible to tear her gaze away. She'd never seen Zack sleeping before. In the warm glow of the table lamp his face was relaxed, softened. His dark lashes cast shadows beneath his eyes and his cheekbones were enhanced. There was stubble on his chin. He was lying on his back with his feet crossed at the ankles and one hand resting on his chest. His breathing was even. Best of all, he wasn't making a sound.

A non-snorer. Always nice to know.

OK, stop that. You're ill.

Ellie turned away and headed for the kitchen. He'd done a good job on the floor; it wasn't slippy at all. Feeling more awake now, and fractionally better than before, she opened the fridge and took out another can of Sprite. It took three goes to get the ringpull off. Zack had also bought yogurts, strawberry mousses, jellies, and various bottles of freshly squeezed juice. Her stomach growled; she hadn't eaten anything for over twenty-four hours. She closed the fridge and left the kitchen, unable to resist another peep into the living room on her way back to bed.

But this time Zack's eyes were open, her fridge investigation evidently having woken him up. He turned his head to look at her and said sleepily, 'You were supposed to give me a shout. I'd have got that for you.'

'It's OK, I needed a wee anyway.' *Oh God, I can't believe I just said that.*

'How are you feeling?'

Ellie hung on to the door. 'Embarrassed that I just said *wee* in front of my boss.'

He laughed. 'Don't be. It's what all my sisters say. I'm quite used to it.'

'I thought you'd gone home ages ago.'

'I'm not fussy where I sleep. This is a comfortable sofa. You're looking a bit better.'

'That's hard to believe.' Ellie raked her fingers through her hair. Glancing down, she double-checked that the nightie came to just above her knees. That was OK; she didn't want to give him an inadvertent flash of her pink knickers. If she'd realized he was still here, she would have put on a dressing gown. But it was too late now, he'd seen her in her deeply unglamorous nightwear and bare legs.

Zack stretched and sat up. 'Is there anything else you want?'

She hesitated. After so much sleep she was actually feeling a tiny bit better. 'Maybe… could you do, um… cheese on toast?'

Zack grinned. He rose and pointed to the sofa. 'Here, you sit down. Are you asking me if I know *how* to make cheese on toast?'

She managed a brief smile in return. 'It's OK if you don't. Just Shredded Wheat would be fine.'

Ellie sat with her feet up on the sofa, her head resting on the cushions Zack's own head had rested against minutes before. It was silent outside the flat. Here they were in the middle of the night and it felt as if they were the only two people awake in Primrose Hill.

Then Zack came back with two plates of cheese on toast, grilled to perfection. He'd cut hers into strips to make them easier to eat. He'd also made himself a cup of strong black coffee. Together in the living room they shared a mini picnic in weirdly companionable near silence. When the toast was finished, Zack brought her a strawberry mousse. Somewhere in the distance a siren wailed. As dawn broke, birds began to sing to each other in the trees at the back of the house. Car sounds started up. Ellie's eyelids grew heavy and the exhaustion overtook her once more. From what felt like a great distance she was aware of Zack adjusting the sofa cushions to make her more comfortable. It was like being five years old again, cared for and cosseted. Her head was pounding but it didn't matter. She smiled and murmured, 'That feels nice… you're so lovely…'

…And awake again, hours later, with a start. Still on the sofa, alone in the flat and suffering the most hideous of flashbacks.

That feels nice… you're so lovely…

Oh God, had she really said that? Had those words actually come out of her mouth whilst she'd been in her enfeebled, almost-asleep state? She hadn't meant to say them, had possibly thought that it had *felt* lovely and he had *been* so nice, but it had all got hopelessly muddled en route from her brain and she'd never intended him to hear any of it anyway.

Investigating some more, Ellie discovered she was wrapped in her duvet; at some stage Zack must have fetched it from the bedroom and covered her with it. And there on the coffee table, secured by her phone, was a note in his distinctive handwriting:

> *Morning. How are you feeling? I've gone to take Elmo for*
> *his walk and catch up on some paperwork. Back by eleven*
> *at the latest. Anything you need, just give me a call.*
> *See you soon,*
> *Z.*

The *Z* ended with a little squiggle that might or might not have been a cross, a cartoon fish, or a kiss. Ellie found herself concentrating on it, studying it, trying to work out which of these he could have meant it to be. OK, stop it and get a grip, he hadn't written her a love note. It was just a squiggle.

Also on the coffee table was her alarm clock, the packet of Ibuprofen, a glass of water, and another unopened can of Sprite. He'd thought of everything. After her inane burblings last night it was a wonder there wasn't a straitjacket.

Ellie swallowed the painkillers and drank some water. Everything still hurt and dozing off again was a tempting option. But it was nine thirty, Zack could be back in an hour, and she needed to get clean.

The water hit her skin like bullets, the pain was intense, and she hadn't realized standing up in the shower could be such hard work. Even lifting her arms to shampoo her hair was exhausting...

Right, concentrate, just get through it, let the shower rinse out the shampoo. Her legs were feeling weak and the heat of the water was making her head muzzy... oh, and now there were dots dancing in front of her eyes, this wasn't good, dots getting bigger... OK, out of here, sit down before you fall down... *oof.*

'Oh God, how did this happen? What did you do?' Zack was looking at her in horror.

Ellie told herself it could have been worse. She might have been knocked out completely. Zack could have let himself back into the flat and found her lying in a wet naked heap on the bathroom floor. At least she was wearing her dressing gown and had made it back to the safety of the sofa.

'I fainted in the shower. Well, half out of the shower.' She pressed the handful of tissues to her temple; the bump had swollen to impressive proportions but the bleeding, thankfully, had almost stopped. 'I hit my head on the edge of the radiator. It's OK, I don't need stitches or anything.'

Zack closely inspected the injury. 'I think we'll get a second opinion on that. I can't believe you thought having a shower was a good idea. For crying out loud, you've got the *flu*.'

'Sorry. I just wanted to feel better.'

'And didn't that work well. You could have cracked your skull open. Right, that's it, I'm not leaving you here on your own again.'

'It's OK, I promise I won't have any more showers.'

He probably wouldn't want to know this, and she wouldn't dream of telling him, but he was gorgeous when he was exasperated. Ellie lay back as he disappeared into the kitchen, and listened to the rattley noises emanating from the freezer.

He returned moments later with a packet of frozen sweet corn wrapped in a clean tea towel. 'Here, don't move, let me do it. You're as white as a sheet.'

'Are you always this bossy?' She closed her eyes as the icy parcel covered the egg-sized lump on her temple.

'Always.'

'But you can't stay here all the time.'

'I know. But you need looking after.' Zack wiped a trickle of water away from her neck. 'That's why you're coming back to Ancram Street with me.'

—⁓—

Zack brought his car round, double-parking it outside the flat and not even allowing her to make her own way down the staircase. Instead, he lifted her up and carried her in his arms.

Who said the flu didn't have its compensations?

'I feel like I'm being kidnapped.' God, it felt fantastic. Ellie had to keep her eyes averted in case he could tell what was going through her mind.

'Can't have you falling down the stairs and breaking your neck.' Zack's tone was brusque. He was just being practical. Her head felt like a bowling ball; it was a struggle to keep it upright. Giving in, Ellie rested it against his shoulder. That was even better. The sensation of his soft cotton shirt against her hot cheek was just blissful.

'I hope I'm not heavy.'

'You're fine. We're almost there. Mind your feet.' He reached the downstairs hallway and maneuvered her with care out through the door.

Two minutes later they arrived at Ancram Street and the process was repeated in reverse. Ellie closed her eyes, remembering the time after their wedding when Jamie had ceremoniously carried her over the threshold of the Hammersmith flat. He'd pretended to buckle under her weight, she'd jabbed him in the ribs, and they'd ended up laughing so much he'd almost dropped her.

OK, don't think about it. She didn't have the energy to get emotional now. She was carried over a whole different class of threshold and up the stairs. Past the living room. Along the corridor and through the door at the end.

Twenty minutes later there was a knock at the door, then it was pushed open.

'Only me.' Geraldine came in, leaning on her walking stick. 'Oh, my darling, you do look poorly. Zack asked me to come and check you over. That's a pretty impressive bump you have on your head there.'

Ellie was wiped out. She allowed herself to be examined. Zack's spare room was all pale green and white with a summery feel and billowing leaf-green curtains. The queen-sized bed was comfortable. Her temple throbbed. She said, 'I'm being a real nuisance, aren't I?'

'Not your fault, is it? OK, all done. Nothing sinister. Just rest and keep up the fluids. You'll be feeling better soon.'

'Poor Zack, being landed with me.'

'Some people like having someone to look after. It brings out the best in them. And it's nice to see Zack like this.' Geraldine waggled her eyebrows. 'I always think a good bedside manner is a lovely attribute in a man.'

Chapter 39

WAS THIS WRONG? SHOULD he have done it? Zack only knew that having Ellie stay here in this house made him feel complete. He'd canceled a couple of meetings this afternoon without even hesitating. He simply didn't care. For so long he'd put all his efforts into the business, had practically devoted his life to it. But it no longer seemed important.

No, that wasn't true. Work was still important. It just wasn't his number one priority.

He knocked at the door and said, 'OK to come in?'

Ellie was sitting up in bed, wearing a clean white T-shirt. Her face was pale and there were violet shadows beneath her eyes but to him she still looked lovely.

'Hi. Thanks.' She reached for the mug of tomato soup he'd brought up to her. 'I can't believe I woke up wanting soup.' She smiled and took a sip. 'That tastes fantastic. I must be over the worst.'

Which was good news, of course it was. But a small, selfish part of Zack didn't want her to be over the worst. Until this evening Ellie had been so unwell it had made absolute sense to insist she come to stay. But as soon as she was better, she would return to her own flat. And Todd would be back from his conference in Glasgow. He hadn't said so to Ellie, but personally he thought Todd could have made more of an effort; his girlfriend was ill and he wasn't exactly inundating her with phone calls. I mean, did he not care how she was? Was he not even bothered? Would it kill him to send her some flowers?

Then again, maybe this was a hopeful sign, a hint that their relationship might not be going such great guns after all. He leaned over to clear empty water glasses from the bedside table and said casually, 'Heard from Todd today?'

'Oh yes. He called earlier.' Ellie nodded and looked defensive. 'And he's been texting me.' She indicated her mobile, lying face down on the duvet. 'I've had loads of texts from him.'

Was she embarrassed by the lack of attention he'd been paying her? Excellent. 'And he's OK about you staying here?'

She nodded. 'Absolutely. He's grateful to you for looking after me.'

'No problem. You can repay me when you're better.' Zack smiled briefly. 'I've got another favor to ask you.'

'Oh? Go on then, fire away.' Ellie was definitely on the mend; she was drinking her soup with relish.

'I've just had an email from Steph.'

'Your sister, the one who lives in St Austell,' said Ellie. 'Twin girls.'

He felt absurdly touched that she'd remembered. 'That's the one. Well, Steph and Gareth have been together for seven years but they've just decided to get married.' He paused. 'In September.'

'*This* September? Wow.'

'That's Steph all over. No patience. Once she decides to do something, that's it. Basically they heard that a wedding had been canceled at the village church and grabbed the chance while it was there.'

'Like Lastminute.com,' said Ellie. 'Why not?'

'And they're having the reception at Mum and Dad's. A hundred guests.'

'Crikey.'

'It'll be fine. Mum's in her element. They had Claire's wedding at home too; it was a triumph.'

Ellie finished her mug of soup. 'So where do I come in? You want me to help in some way? Oh, is it the invitations, d'you need me to—?'

'Not that kind of help. Actually, it's more personal.' Zack sat on the end of the bed. 'The thing is, Steph's asked her friend Mya to be one of her bridesmaids. I used to go out with Mya, years ago. Now, she's nothing like Louisa,' he added hastily. 'Mya's more like a Labrador, all bouncy and enthusiastic. According to Steph, she's already getting overexcited about me being there. If I go on my own I'm just going to be fending her off the whole time. It'll be awkward. She's a nice girl and I don't want to hurt her feelings.' He hesitated. 'So what would really help would be if I was to take someone else along with me. Then she'd understand and leave me alone. No more hassle.' This wasn't some story he'd made up; it was all true. But he was the one ruthlessly taking advantage of the situation and using it for his own purposes. With a bit of luck. 'So, up to you. I know it's a big ask, but you'd be really helping me out. And it'll be a good do.' Another pause. 'If you think Todd wouldn't mind.'

Zack McLaren, you have a nerve.

Ellie's eyes were bright and a flash of color had returned to her cheeks. For a couple of seconds she thought it through. Finally she swallowed and said, 'I'll explain it to him. I'm sure he won't mind.'

'OK, good. Thanks.' His heart was actually thumping against his ribs. Ellie had just agreed to come down to Cornwall with him to attend his sister's wedding.

Result.

Lovely though it had been to be looked after by Zack, Ellie was aware she had imposed for long enough. It was now Sunday, she'd been here for three days, and no longer qualified as an invalid. The aching, the shivers, the raging temperature had all subsided. Her appetite was back, she no longer looked like a bit of old road kill, and the utter exhaustion had receded too. She felt human again, albeit a bit on the fragile side.

'Now are you sure you'll be OK?' Zack had insisted on driving her the few hundred yards home. 'What time's Todd getting back?'

'Very soon.' Ellie climbed out of the car; it was three o'clock in the afternoon. 'Any minute now. Thanks for looking after me.' She kept a firm hold of her overnight case as he moved to take it. 'Don't worry, I can manage. And just… well, thanks for everything. I'll be back at work as soon as I'm up to it. Wednesday or Thursday.' He'd done so much for her, she didn't know how to express her gratitude. At least being riddled with flu germs meant a polite kiss on the cheek was out of the question.

And anyway, he was her boss. She was his employee. It would be wrong.

Instead Ellie said, 'Bye,' and did an awkward little wave before fitting her key into the lock and letting herself into the house.

—m—

'Why didn't you let me know you were ill? I'd have come straight back! I could have looked after you!'

Oh dear, Roo was offended.

'You were visiting your mum,' Ellie pointed out. 'Anyway, you wouldn't have been so happy if you'd caught my bugs.'

Roo visibly bristled at the slur. 'I'd still have done it. I *owe* you, remember? How am I ever going to make things up to you if you won't let me do stuff?'

'You don't owe me, I've told you a million times. You did me a favor.' Ellie sighed; Roo was still sticking obstinately to her newfound vow of saintliness. No caffeine, no alcohol, no makeup, endless do-goodery, and a stubborn refusal to answer Todd's calls and messages. It was getting a bit wearing, to be honest; she wished the old fun-loving irreverent Roo would make a comeback.

'Right, let's do a list.' Roo whipped a notebook from her bag. 'Tell me what you need and I'll go out and get it. Food, toiletries… anything you want.'

'OK. Thanks.' Ellie watched her perch, pen poised, on the arm of the sofa. 'I've nearly run out of deodorant, so you could get me a can of spray.'

'What make?'

'Anything, it doesn't matter.'

This clearly wasn't good enough. 'But which one would you like *most*?'

'OK, Dove.'

Roo wrote it down. 'What else?'

'Apple juice. And some more bread. White, medium sliced.'

The pen flew over the paper. 'Got it. Next?'

'Call Todd.'

The pen abruptly stopped. 'And say what?'

'Tell him you'd like to see him. Just put him out of his misery. All you're doing is cutting off your nose to spite your face.'

Roo jutted her chin. 'Maybe my nose deserves to be cut off.'

'You said you'd do anything I want.' This flu had weakened her; Ellie knew her powers of persuasion weren't on top form. 'This is what I want, for you and Todd to get together.'

'Not going to happen.'

'But you're making *me* feel guilty. If it wasn't for me, you'd be a couple by now. So it's all my fault!'

'Nice try,' said Roo. 'But the answer's still no. Your hair's looking a bit manky, by the way.' She changed the subject. 'How about if I call my hairdresser and get her over here to give you a nice cut and blow-dry?'

Always good to know your hair was manky. 'Thanks, but no thanks.' Her whole life, Ellie had never once emerged from a salon comfortable with the blow-dry she'd had inflicted on her; they always made her feel like a Stepford wife.

'How about a manicure, then?'

'No.'

'Massage?'

'Really, no.'

'Fake tan?'

'*No.*'

Roo narrowed her eyes in frustration. 'Stubborn.'

'Pot. Kettle,' said Ellie.

'But I'm trying to help you!'

'Same here!'

'Ooh, you're so annoying,' cried Roo.

Ellie kept a straight face. 'Ditto.'

—⁓—

Roo returned with the shopping then headed off to Ormond Road for her shift at the charity shop. Ellie lay on the sofa and dozed. She woke up with a start an hour later, to the sound of laughter in the street below.

It was Jamie's laugh. There was no mistaking it. Ellie listened, stunned. It was him… oh God, he was back… she leapt off the sofa and stumbled to the window, her skin prickling with joy and disbelief. *Jamie, I'm here…*

Lack of blood caused her head to spin. The man outside on the pavement was burly and shiny-bald, in his forties, and displaying an impressive paunch as he climbed into his car and carried on chatting on his mobile to whoever had just made him laugh in that spookily Jamie-like way.

Don't be so stupid, how could you even think it would really be him?

The car sped off and Ellie slumped back on to the sofa. Being momentarily fooled always made the crashing-back-to-reality bit harder to bear. She reached for her mobile and pressed the familiar series of buttons.

'Hi, I can't speak to you at the moment.' This time it was the real Jamie saying it.

'Well, try a bit harder,' said Ellie.

'…But just leave a message after the beep and I'll get back to you as soon as I can. Bye!'

Ellie waited for the beep, then said, 'Hi, Jamie, is that a promise? Because I keep leaving messages… I've left loads and loads of messages and I'm *still* waiting for you to call me back.' She'd told him this before too. She swallowed hard, annoyance giving way to guilt as it invariably did. Poor Jamie, it wasn't his fault he couldn't call her back. 'Sorry. Just wanted to hear your voice. I love you, OK? Miss you. Bye.'

She hung up and had a cry, using her sleeve to wipe her wet face rather than get up and find a tissue. Because there was no need; no one to see her and no appearances to keep up.

'Eurgh.' Jamie wandered into the living room as she was wiping her nose. 'That's not very ladylike.'

'Guess what? I don't care.'

'Oh, sweetheart. I thought you were feeling better.'

Ellie hauled herself off the sofa and went to fetch the tissue box. Flu-wise she might be feeling better. Jamie-wise her defenses were down, her emotions muddled, and she was riddled with guilt. 'I wanted you to look after me. You weren't here.'

'Sorry. But Zack came to the rescue. He did a pretty good job, didn't he?'

'I suppose. But he wasn't you. He's my boss.' Noisily she blew her nose and lay back down. Jamie's hair was longer today; it needed a cut. And he was wearing sand-colored Havaianas with his jeans and Ramones T-shirt.

'You like him though. Is that what's making you feel guilty?'

Ellie lobbed the balled-up tissue at the bin. It missed. 'I don't know. Maybe. Yes.'

'And in a few weeks you'll be going down to Cornwall with him for his sister's wedding. I expect you're feeling a bit funny about that too.'

'No.'

'Sure?' Jamie looked mildly surprised. 'You won't find it weird, putting on a show and essentially pretending to be his girlfriend, when all the time you do actually have a bit of a secret crush on him and wish it could be happening for real?'

'Oh…' Ellie closed her eyes; what was the point of trying to hide something from Jamie when he was already inside her head? 'Fine, yes, it'll be weird. But I have to do it and I can't back down. All Zack wants is a stooge, a stand-in to get him out of an awkward situation. So long as he doesn't know how I feel about him, it'll be fine.'

Chapter 40

'...Thanks, yes, I'll let him know about that. Bye!' Ellie hung up and scribbled the message on the notepad next to the phone. Zack was upstairs conducting a conference call. Her recovery was now complete; it was Thursday and she'd been back at work for a full week. The flu was now so much a thing of the past that the thought of feeling too ill to take even a sip of water seemed bizarre.

The doorbell rang just as the office phone went *ting*, indicating that the conference call upstairs had ended.

Ellie opened the front door, her heart sinking slightly at the sight of the Kerrigans on the doorstep. Zack had already said he couldn't do anything. It really wasn't fair of them to turn up again and pester him like this.

'Hi,' Kaye said eagerly. 'It's us! We're back!'

OK, the job of a good PA was to make her boss's life easier. Much as she'd liked the pair of them, they needed to learn that no meant no.

'Hello.' Ellie's smile was brief. 'Look, I'm afraid Zack's *really* busy—'

'It's OK, we aren't here to see Zack.' Joe Kerrigan took a step towards her and, with a flourish, produced a bunch of enormous yellow orchids. 'These are for you. Because you have been... magnificent! And we'll never be able to thank you enough for what you've done.'

'Hold on.' Ellie took a step back as he jiggled the orchids and a spray of bright orange pollen threatened to land on her white shirt. 'What have I done?'

'We've sold our script. Two studios battled each other for the rights.' Kaye looked as if she was ready to burst with excitement. 'Our dream director wants to work with us on this and future projects. And it's all thanks to you. You made Tony Weston read our screenplay and you've changed our lives!'

In shock, Ellie hadn't even heard Zack come down the staircase. Appearing beside her, he said, 'I didn't know about any of this.'

'Me neither.' She shook her head. 'I had no idea Tony even looked at the script. I tried my best to make him read it, but he said he wasn't interested if there wasn't a part in it for him. It's still at home somewhere… in the magazine rack, I think…' She tailed off at the sight of Kaye and Joe both grinning and shaking their heads at her.

'Well,' said Zack, 'however it happened, it's fantastic news. And you can't stand out there. Come on in and tell us everything.'

Which was how Ellie learned that the screenplay wasn't, in fact, still lurking at home in the midst of the overstuffed magazine rack. Between them, Joe and his wife relayed the story of how Tony had taken it with him on the plane, then piqued the interest of his own agent Marvin, who had in turn piqued the interest of Stephen, a leading screen agent at the talent agency where they both worked. A buzz around the script had duly been created, several studios had been keen to option it, and frenzied negotiations had ensued.

'It was unbelievable,' Kaye exclaimed. 'They flew us out there. First class! We had champagne and little slippers and everything!'

'And then we had all these meetings,' Joe took over. 'You can't begin to imagine what that was like. They're talking budgets and ideas and A-list stars… they're telling us our script is brilliant—'

'I knew it was brilliant,' Ellie blurted out. 'I knew it!'

Joe's teeth were white and endearingly crooked; he still looked like a scruffy tennis player, but today he was a scruffy tennis player who'd just won a Grand Slam tournament and couldn't believe his luck. His eyes crinkling, he rubbed a hand across the golden stubble on his jaw. 'We know you did. So anyhow, the contract's been signed. Our feet have hardly touched the ground, but we're back in London. So now you understand why we had to come and see you.'

Ellie was overwhelmed. 'I'm so glad you did.'

'Ellie?' There were actually tears of happiness swimming in Kaye's eyes. 'Is it OK if I give you a hug?'

Ellie laughed and got herself enthusiastically hugged. Meanwhile Joe shook hands with Zack, then Kaye let go of Ellie and gave Zack a hug too. This was followed by a slightly awkward moment when Ellie swung around and held out her arms, expecting it to be her turn with Joe. But it didn't happen; he was too busy looking at Kaye, waiting for her hug with Zack to be over.

Never mind. It was sweet. They were so madly in love.

'OK,' said Kaye, when they'd finished. 'Well, that's it!' She gave Joe's arm a light tap. 'I'll wait outside.' Turning to Ellie, she added, 'Joe wants a quick word with you. Is that OK?'

Joe in turn glanced at Zack. 'A quick private word, if you wouldn't mind. It's just something about Tony Weston... kind of private...'

'Of course. No problem.' Zack opened the office door and indicated for Joe's wife to go ahead of him. 'I'll show Kaye out.'

The door closed behind them.

'I lied,' said Joe.

'In what way?' Ellie really hoped he hadn't made up the whole sold-the-film script story. Kaye would disembowel him if he had.

'This isn't about Tony Weston.'

'No?'

'OK, of course we wanted to thank you. But I also had an ulterior motive for coming here today.' He exhaled. 'Bringing you those flowers is my way of saying I think you're gorgeous and I've fancied you rotten since the first time I saw you.'

Ellie did a double take. Was he serious? '*What?*'

'Oh yes. So how about it? Fancy meeting up one evening?' Another pause, then Joe said with an easy smile, 'You look pretty shocked. I'm not that bad, am I?'

Were all men like this? Ellie felt herself flush with anger.

'What about Kaye?'

'What about her?'

'You're married!'

'I'm not married! Who would I be married to? *Kaye?*' His eyebrows disappeared up under his tousled blond bangs. 'Oh my God, I can't believe you thought that. Kaye's my *sister.*'

Oh.

Oh.

Well.

'Oops,' said Ellie. 'I got it wrong. Just kind of assumed. You have the same name. You look married.'

Alarm mingled with horror. '*How?*'

'I mean, you aren't anything alike.' It was an understandable mistake, surely. Joe had messy blond hair and green eyes; he was tall, thin, and gangly. Kaye was small and dark and neat. She also wore a wedding ring. Together they were the Kerrigans.

'I'm like Mum, Kaye takes after Dad. She's married. No kids. We write together, that's all, I promise. I'm completely single. So shall I ask the question again?'

'Hang on, just let me think this through.' Seeing someone in a whole new light took a bit of adjusting to. Joe Kerrigan wasn't married to Kaye. He'd just asked her out on a date. He was physically attractive but not in an obvious way. His nose was beaky, he had a ready smile and a scruffy, laid-back approach to clothes which she found captivating. Basically, he wasn't the kind who'd intimidate you.

'Just so you know,' said Joe, 'I'm starting to get nervous now.'

'Really?'

'Oh yes, really. The worst thing is, Kaye said you'd turn me down. And I hate it when I'm wrong and she's right.'

'Is she unbearable?'

He shook his head mournfully. ''Kaye's a gloater. She could take it up professionally. You can't imagine what it's like, having her as a sister. Actually, I've run out of nerve. Can we forget this ever happened? I'd rather back out now than get turned down.'

'Can I just ask a question?'

'Feel free.'

'How do you know I'm single? I might not be,' said Ellie. 'I could be living with someone.'

'I asked Tony Weston. You're not. You broke up with some guy recently. But you're definitely not heartbroken about it,' said Joe. 'I checked.'

Ellie relaxed. He was funny, unthreatening, and good company. Now that she was trying to weigh up the pros and cons, she was finding it hard to muster any cons. The more she thought about it, the more attractive the proposition seemed. And the more attractive Joe Kerrigan was becoming. The indefinable spark that had so resolutely failed to appear between her and Todd was actually showing discernible signs of life.

Best of all, Joe wasn't her boss. And if there was one thing she knew she needed badly right now, it was an opportunity to get over her embarrassing crush on Zack.

What better way of diverting her attention?

'OK,' said Ellie.

Joe looked cautious. 'OK what? You're agreeing I should back out now? Or that you'll come out with me?'

'That one. The second one.'

'Seriously? Wow, fantastic.' His whole face lit up. 'When would suit you?'

'Any time.' Recklessly, Ellie said, 'I'm free. How about tonight?'

He shook his head in admiration. 'You are my kind of girl. I knew I liked you. Ha, come on, it's my turn to gloat. Wait until I tell Kaye.'

Out in the hallway, Zack and Kaye were talking about dogs. Kaye turned to look at them. 'Well?'

Joe looked proud. 'She said yes.'

'Did she?' Kaye beamed at Ellie. 'Did you? Damn, I said you'd say no!'

'Sorry.' Ellie was aware of Zack's gaze upon her.

'Sorry about what?' said Zack.

'I asked Ellie out on a date,' Joe explained cheerfully. 'Kaye didn't think I stood a chance. Ha, we're going out tonight.'

Zack looked as if he'd been secretly electrocuted. A muscle twitched in his jaw. 'Oh.'

And Ellie realized she'd been so distracted, she'd completely forgotten about Todd.

———

Kaye and Joe left. Zack disappeared into the kitchen to make coffee. When he entered the office minutes later, he said evenly, 'So am I allowed to ask what's going on? Are you building up a collection?'

Ellie stopped typing and felt a prickle of perspiration on the back of her neck. She'd lied to him; no wonder he didn't sound amused. Worse, she'd lied in order to not look like an idiot...

'Will you be telling Todd, or weren't you planning on him finding out? Not that it's any of my business,' Zack went on. 'I'm just surprised.'

'Look, Todd and I aren't seeing each other anymore. It didn't work out. We broke up, but we're still friends. Sorry I didn't mention it.' She didn't need a mirror to know she'd gone bright red. 'I didn't want to bore you, banging on about my personal life.'

'Right. Well.' He clearly wasn't pleased that she'd neglected to tell him; maybe he was wondering if he could trust her after all. 'So now you're going out with Joe Kerrigan. Tonight. Are you sure about this?' He frowned. 'I mean, isn't it all a bit sudden?'

OK, he was telling her she was desperate. And maybe she was, but not for the reason he thought. Ellie sat up straight. 'Why can't it be sudden? Haven't you ever met someone and felt an instant connection? Because that's what happened today. I really like Joe. I think he really likes me. Who knows, maybe it was fate that brought him here with that screenplay.'

'I'm just—'

'No,' she broke in, 'let me say this. I didn't agree to meet him because I'm desperate for any old date; I did it because I think this could be special. I'm looking forward to it. In fact,' Ellie said with emphasis, 'I can't wait.'

⁓

Zack headed upstairs, ostensibly to work on a business proposal ahead of tomorrow's meeting in Milan.

In reality, one word was going round in his head. *Fuck, fuck, fuck…*

How had this happened? How *could* it be happening? Why couldn't Ellie have told him before that the thing with Todd was all over? And now it was too late, because she was in the grip of an instant connection and there was nothing he could do about it.

Fuck.

Chapter 41

ELLIE PRESSED HER HANDS against the washbasin and leaned forward, gazing at her reflection in the bathroom mirror.

This was it then. She wanted it to happen and it was going to happen. Her mind was made up.

Who'd have thought it? Looking back, it seemed inconceivable that life could alter so drastically. The last seven days had passed in a whirlwind of activity. It was like being inside a snow globe that had suddenly been picked up and shaken. This time last week she had been just another boyfriendless PA with a hopeless, humiliating crush on her boss. Then Joe Kerrigan had turned up and changed everything. On their first date he'd taken her out on a boat on the Thames. On their second date they'd gone Rollerblading in Hyde Park. The third date had been a picnic in Kensington Gardens, the fourth a trip on the London Eye. Joe was fun, he was funny, they had a fantastic time together, and when he kissed her she enjoyed kissing him back. The chemistry that had been so painfully absent between herself and Todd was here in spades. The prospect of taking things further no longer made her feel panicky and slightly sick. Her libido, after nineteen months in deep-frozen hibernation, was back.

And the time had now come to take things to the next level.

Here, tonight, in just a few minutes' time.

Ellie peered more closely at her reflection. Did she look different already? Were her pupils more dilated than usual? Was this really OK?

Quite often when she looked in this mirror, she would see Jamie in the bathroom behind her. But there was no sign of him tonight and her mind skittered away from the idea of conjuring him up. What for, so she could ask him if it was all right? So she could make him tell her not to worry, he didn't mind, it was fine?

No, this was her night. It was only fair that Jamie should stay away, leave her alone to get on with it.

Get it over with.

That wasn't fair. It was just a big step emotionally. As soon as the first time after Jamie was out of the way, it would be easier.

Anyway, it was nice to have these kinds of feelings again. A small part of her had secretly worried sometimes that they might be gone for good.

There was a light knock on the door.

'Hello?' said Joe from the other side. 'Are you still in there? Or have you jumped out of the window?'

Ellie smiled and opened the door. 'I'm still here.'

He wrapped his arms around her. 'Nervous?'

'Kind of.'

'We don't have to do anything if you don't want to.'

'I do want to.'

'Well, that's good. So do I.' Joe kissed the tip of her nose, then rested his forehead against hers. 'Just so you know, I'm a bit nervous too.'

Maybe she shouldn't have told him he'd be the first since Jamie. It was bound to put him under pressure. Ellie led him across the hallway towards the bedroom. 'Come on, let's do this thing.'

Joe grinned. 'Get the first time over and out of the way.'

See? He understood.

'Exactly.'

And then, hopefully, they could do it again.

It was a stunning morning, sunny and warm with a cloudless sky overhead, the kind of morning that made you feel glad to be alive.

Zack, walking Elmo, wasn't feeling glad about anything. The last week surely ranked among the crappiest of his life. In between his trip to Milan and another flying visit to Dundee, he had been forced to watch Ellie fall in love with another man. Or in lust. Whichever, it had been a hideous experience. There was a new light in her eyes, she always seemed to be on the brink of smiling, and there was an aura about her that definitely hadn't been there before. It was fizzing out of her like an out-of-control Alka-Seltzer.

Nor was she capable of keeping her newfound happiness to herself. The namechecks had been coming thick and fast. When Zack had made a comment about his flight back from Milan, Ellie had launched into something funny that had happened to Joe when he'd been on his way over to LA. If he made her a coffee, she retaliated with a Joe-related anecdote about coffee. When he asked her if she'd watched *Dragons' Den* last night, Ellie said, 'No, we were out, Joe took me to a salsa bar, it was *brilliant.*'

As if he was remotely interested. Each fresh detail was like lemon juice in a wound but Ellie simply couldn't help herself; she carried on regaling him with stories about Joe Kerrigan and in return he had to listen and nod and smile as if he were pleased for her.

Elmo danced on the end of his lead, snuffling at a candy wrapper on the pavement. Zack pulled him away, carried on walking, and checked his watch. Half eight.

As a rule, the journey from Primrose Hill to Ancram Street didn't take in Nevis Street. But today, he told himself, he just happened to feel like heading in that direction. Coincidentally he'd felt the same way yesterday. OK, and the day before.

Well, a bit of extra exercise never did any harm, did it?

But in the same way that listeners never hear good of themselves, less than two minutes later Zack saw what he really hadn't wanted to see. He and Elmo stood at the upper end of the road and watched as the front door of Ellie's house opened and Joe Kerrigan came out.

Looking as if he'd spent the night having sex.

Zack's jaw tightened. He felt as if he'd been punched in the stomach. Was it any wonder Joe's hair was disheveled and he looked the way he did? He was leaving Ellie's house at eight thirty in the morning. Of course they'd had sex.

As he watched, Joe turned and gazed up at the first floor. Then he broke into a grin and called out, 'See you later.'

The window was flung open and Zack heard Ellie say, 'What was that?'

'I'll see you later.' Joe's grin broadened and he blew her a kiss. 'Missing you already.'

OK, he'd heard enough. Zack moved out of sight before Joe had a chance to turn round and recognize him.

Back home now.

Served him right for having come this way in the first place.

———

Ellie arrived at the house dead on nine o'clock, her hair still damp from the shower. She was wearing a pale pink shift dress, pink and silver sandals, and a thin silver bracelet Zack hadn't seen before.

'That's nice.' Busy adding a new appointment to the diary, he indicated the bracelet.

'This? Thanks! It was a present from Joe.'

Another sucker punch. Great. Aloud Zack said, 'Right.'

'Isn't it pretty?' Ellie was turning her wrist this way and that, so it caught the light. 'He gave it to me last night. I love it!'

Oh, Joe, do fuck off.

'Excellent. Well, I'm off to Monte Carlo on Tuesday, so I need you to book me a flight to Nice. The meeting's at midday.'

'No problem. I'll do that now.' Her eyes were sparkling; she might not have got much sleep last night but she was running on adrenaline. 'Leave it with me.'

But by midafternoon the lack of sleep was catching up with her. Twice while he was in the office he caught Ellie yawning. Three times her phone chirruped to signal the arrival of a text and she stopped typing in order to read the messages and reply.

The last straw came when Zack attempted to return a call and discovered she'd written down the wrong number.

'Look, I'm sorry if I'm keeping you up, but you need to be paying more attention.' Marching into the office, he found her sending yet another text. 'I'm trying to make an important call here and this isn't the number.' He pushed the piece of paper across the desk, his annoyance ratchetted up to the next level by the fact that Ellie finished composing the text and sent it before looking at the number she'd written.

'OK, let me try. That's definitely the one he gave me.' She held out her hand for his phone and reeled off the numbers. 'Oh-two-six-seven-three…'

'No, you've written oh-two-oh-seven-three.'

'That's a six.' Ellie pointed to it.

Unreasonably annoyed, Zack said, 'It looks like a zero.'

'It might look like one of your zeros,' she retaliated, 'because you don't always bother to close yours. But I do close mine. This one isn't closed, because it isn't a zero. It's a six.'

Unfairly, the figure was now looking more and more like a six.

Zack took back his phone, unwilling to concede defeat. 'And you haven't stopped yawning all morning.'

'I might have yawned a couple of times.' Ellie was defensive. 'But it hasn't stopped me working.'

'Maybe not, but all the texting's certainly managing it. I'm just saying, it's not very professional, breaking off from whatever you're doing every few minutes to read a new text from your boyfriend, then send one back.'

'Hey, hang on, you're annoyed with me because *I* wrote a number down correctly and *you* got it wrong?' Ellie's eyes flashed. 'And I've yawned maybe twice, because I've been so busy I haven't had time to stop and make myself a cup of coffee yet?'

'Don't forget the texting,' said Zack.

'Fine. Here you go, help yourself.' She reached over, grabbed his left wrist and slammed her phone into his upturned palm. 'Have a good look, scroll through the texts I've sent today. Read them.'

'No.'

'Yes.'

'I don't want to read your texts.'

'And I don't care whether or not you *want* to.' Ellie was breathing rapidly, her chest rising and falling as she snatched the phone, pressed a few buttons, and shoved it back at him. 'You're going to.'

Which meant Zack was forced to stand there and read each of the texts in turn.

None of them were from Joe Kerrigan. Instead, Ellie had been in contact with the PAs of two of the other business people due at the meeting in Monaco. Thanks to her negotiations, the journey from Nice airport to Monte Carlo would no longer be by car; they were to be whisked there by helicopter instead.

'Oh God. I'm sorry.' Zack handed the phone back.

'Good.'

'I mean, *really* sorry.'

'That's OK. You've been a bit twitchy today. In a funny mood.'

'I know.'

Ellie was looking at him. 'Is something wrong?'

What could he say? *Yes, something is wrong, and it's all your fault?*

'No.' Zack shook his head. 'I shouldn't have had a go. I'm not usually like that.'

'I know you aren't. Anyway, thanks.'

'For apologizing? That's the least I can do.'

'Not for the apology,' said Ellie. 'For the argument. My first proper one in a long time.'

'Oh.' He began to relax. 'Did you enjoy it?'

'Very much. Especially the bit where I won. In fact…'

'In fact what?' She was eyeing him thoughtfully.

'Was this all part of the plan? You knew I missed having arguments so you decided to start one?' A slow smile was spreading across Ellie's face. 'Oh my God, am I right? Did you do it on purpose?'

Zack briefly considered the alternatives. Talk about a moral dilemma. *Bloody morals.*

'OK,' he said finally, 'I'd love to be able to tell you that was true. But I'm afraid it wasn't. I was just being a bad-tempered old git.'

Ellie's smile broadened. 'The thing is, you say that now. But I'm still not sure I believe you.'

Zack couldn't speak. All he wanted to do was kiss her.

And he wasn't allowed to do that either.

Chapter 42

THE IRONY OF THE situation didn't escape Roo. Here she was, lying in a reclining chair allowing her ex-lover's wife to inflict pain on her.

Pain is good.

She wouldn't even mind more pain than this, but Yasmin was a pro. Swiftly, skillfully, she manipulated the twirled-together threads, whisking out tiny hairs and leaving perfectly sculpted eyebrows in their place. Well, hopefully she was. Roo imagined sitting up at the end, gazing into the mirror, and discovering that one eyebrow was arched and the other one flat. Or missing altogether.

'So,' Yasmin said cheerfully, 'how's everything been going with you?'

'Not so bad.' Between the razor-sharp *ting ting ting*s as each hair was tweaked out, Roo updated her with the latest goings-on in the shop. Yesterday a man had donated a portrait in oils of the ugliest woman any of them had ever seen. This morning he had returned explaining that it was a painting of his late wife and he'd missed her too much, could he please have it back? His relief when he learned that it hadn't been snapped up had touched the hearts of everyone in the shop. When they'd handed over the hideous portrait, he'd wept tears of joy.

'How about you?' Roo changed the subject.

'Me? Oh, I'm getting a divorce.'

'*What?*' Roo's eyes had been closed. Now they snapped open. 'You mean, you and your... husband?'

'That's generally how it works.'

'But... why?' Was she sounding too shocked? Oh God, this was awful. But she had to ask.

'Nothing very original, I'm afraid. Same old story. I found out he's been having an affair.' Yasmin stopped threading, raised the back of the recliner slightly, and handed Roo a mirror. 'Here you are. Have a look and see what you think.'

Roo gazed at her reflection and saw a selfish, marriage-wrecking harlot with stunning eyebrows.

'Is that about right,' said Yasmin, 'or do you want them narrower?'

'This is fine.' It was hard to look at herself. Roo put the mirror down.

'OK, the skin's a bit red. I'm going to put some aloe vera gel on there to cool it down. You just lie back and relax.'

When the gel had been applied, Roo said, 'Who was it?'

'Who was what?'

'The other woman.'

'Oh, they used to work together. She's a sales rep with another company now.'

'That's awful.' What would be *really* awful was if she were to accidentally mention Vivica's name. Roo clamped her mouth shut so it couldn't slip out.

'It is awful, but I'm doing OK. Oh, bless you for looking so upset.' Yasmin gave her shoulder a grateful squeeze. 'You've come here to be pampered, you don't have to put up with me bleating on about my marriage.'

'You aren't bleating.'

'If I get tedious, just tell me to change the subject.'

Roo needed to know. 'So what happened? How did you find out?'

'Total cliché. Came home unexpectedly and caught them at it.'

Oh God, that could have been me. It couldn't have, because she'd never visited their house, but Roo covered her mouth in horror anyway. Swallowing with difficulty, she said, 'Then what?'

'Actually, I was quite proud of myself.' Yasmin's cheeks dimpled. 'I threw a can of super strength hair spray at him. I'm usually rubbish at throwing, my friends say I throw darts like harpoons. But I got him on the forehead. It was one of those brilliant moments when you wish there'd been someone there to video it. I'd love to have put it on YouTube.'

She appeared to be taking it incredibly well. Far better than Roo, whose heart was going twenty-six to the dozen.

'So you've kicked him out of the house?'

'No, I didn't want to stay there. Me and Ben are back at my mum's.' Yasmin's dimples deepened again. 'It's lovely.'

'You don't seem that upset.'

'Truthfully? I'm not. Being married to Niall was like being a single mother anyway. He never made any effort. He's selfish. I ended up doing everything. I'll let you into a secret.' Yasmin lowered her voice as another client headed past on her way to the tanning room. 'I'm pretty sure this one wasn't the first. I think he's had other affairs.'

For a terrifying second, Roo felt the backs of her eyes prickle with tears. *Stop it, stop it, don't you dare do that...* mentally she ordered the tears to sink back in.

'You do?'

'Oh yes. Anyway, never mind. I've only myself to blame. Niall was never what you'd call good husband material. I kidded myself we'd be OK.' Absently Yasmin smoothed more aloe vera gel on to Roo's eyebrows. 'My friends tried to warn me, but I wouldn't listen. It's funny, isn't it? I was so sure I could change him. I thought loving him would be enough. But it wasn't. And he didn't want to change. Why would he, when he could carry on having his cake and eating it and helping himself to chocolate biscuits too?'

Roo swallowed. She'd been one of the chocolate biscuits.

'So... is he still seeing this girl?' she ventured. 'The ex-work colleague?'

'No idea. He says not. But that's the thing with Niall; he says lots of things. I just don't listen anymore. There, the redness is fading. Do you want to sit up?'

Roo did as she was told. Was Yasmin putting on a brave front or was she genuinely taking the breakup in her stride?

'Can I ask you something?' said Yasmin.

The ground tilted. *Oh God, what now?*

'Go on.'

'The first time you came here, you had a ton of makeup on. But since then, you haven't worn any at all. It's not a criticism,' Yasmin said hastily. 'You're still really pretty. I just wondered why you'd stopped, that's all.'

At last, she could be honest.

'I wanted a change. To be a different person.' Roo stood up, followed her across to the pay desk, and took out her purse. 'I didn't like what I'd become. And makeup was my armor. I used to spend a fortune on eye shadows and mascaras… it was crazy. So I decided to give them all up and go back to being just me.'

'Wow, good for you. Gosh, thanks.' Yasmin's eyes widened as Roo handed her the money for the threading plus a twenty pound tip. 'Are you sure?'

It was guilt money, pure and simple. But it made her feel better; it was one of her prime reasons for coming here. And she had a lot more giving to do yet.

'Absolutely,' said Roo.

Zack was in Monte Carlo. Ellie had just received a text from him: 'Helicopter fantastic. The only way to travel. Thanks for thinking of it. All OK at the office? Z.'

Smiling to herself, she pictured him in the helicopter, circling Monte Carlo, as excited as a small boy as he picked out the multimillion-pound yachts bobbing in the glittering aquamarine water of the harbor.

Ellie texted back: 'Have sold your company and run off to Barbados with the proceeds. Byeeeee…'

She pressed Send, then began a second text: 'OK, maybe I haven't. Knew you'd love helicopter. No need for thanks, I am your brilliant PA. All fine this end. Have fun!'

As she was sending it, the post clattered through the letter box out in the hall. Ellie went to pick it up. Anything business, she opened and dealt with if necessary. Anything that looked personal, she left for Zack. But among today's delivery was a postcard. On the front was a picture of boxing kangaroos. The lady kangaroo, complete with lipstick and pinny, was raising her front legs in victory. The man kangaroo, clutching a can of beer and a bush hat, lay flat on his back.

On the back of the card was a scrawled message:

> *Hi Zack, I'm coming home! Lost my phone, so don't have your number. Call me at Mum's any time after the 29th August. Missed you so much and can't wait to see you again.*
> *All love, Meg xxxxx*

Meg. The mix of emotions she was becoming all too familiar with reappeared. Zack had mentioned Meg once or twice when they'd talked about past relationships. He'd been busy building up his business, Meg had worked as a journalist on a glossy magazine and their affair had ebbed and flowed over the course of several months, until Meg had been persuaded by a girlfriend to take off on a round-the-world trip. And that was it, she had gone.

When Zack had told her, Ellie had said, 'Did you miss her terribly?'

And he replied, 'Yes, I kind of did.'

'What would have happened if she'd stayed here?'

Zack had shrugged. 'Who knows.'

Ellie gazed at the postcard and wondered what might happen now that his former girlfriend was on her way back. What was she like? Had she changed while she'd been away? Did she deserve him?

Would Zack say casually, 'Oh, by the way, you don't need to give up your weekend to come down with me to my sister's wedding. I'll be taking Meg now instead.'

Just imagining him saying those words made Ellie want to stick her fingers in her ears and go, 'La-la-la-can't-hear-you!' whilst inside she felt sick with disappointment because, Joe or no Joe, the trip down to Cornwall with Zack was something she'd been looking forward to more than she would admit to a living soul.

Or Jamie.

Rrrrrrrrrrrinnnnnnnggggg.

Glad of the diversion, Ellie lobbed the postcard at Zack's in-tray. It helicoptered through the air, skidded across the envelopes already sitting there, and slid down the back of the radiator.

Was that *meant* to happen? The temptation to leave it there, to pretend she hadn't seen it disappear out of sight, was huge. What if this was fate's way of letting her know that Zack and Meg shouldn't get back together?

OK, front door first. Opening it, Ellie came face to face with a dumpy woman in her late fifties, with pale eyes and bushy caterpillar eyebrows. She was wearing a peach crimplene blouse and a turquoise pleated skirt, and it was probably safe to assume this wasn't another of Zack's former girlfriends.

At least, she hoped not.

Chapter 43

'HELLO, DEAR, IS ZACK at home?'

'Sorry, he's away. Maybe I can help you.'

'Oh, I do hope so! I'm Christine, dear. I used to be Zack's PA.'

Ellie had heard all about her. Nicknamed Crimplene Christine by Zack, her skirts invariably reacted with the nylon in her tights and petticoat, creating a build-up of static charge each time she moved. Shaking hands with her, Zack had gravely explained, was a positive health hazard. Poor Elmo had been too terrified to venture into the office.

'Come along inside. I'm Ellie. It's lovely to meet you,' said Ellie. At least, it was lovely so long as she wasn't here to ask for her old job back.

'Ah, there it is. You still have it, thank heavens for that!'

Christine was pointing to the largest of the plants on the window ledge, some temperamental creature with bright orangey-pink flowers and glossy heart-shaped leaves that was always threatening to keel over and die.

'This one?' Ellie moved towards it. 'It's yours?'

'Not the plant. The pot it's in. My bossy sister gave it to me for Christmas,' Christine explained. 'You have no idea what she's like. Anyway, she's coming to London tomorrow to stay for a couple of days. Before she got off the phone this morning she said, "And I hope you're using that lovely plant pot I gave you; it had better not be hidden away in the back of a cupboard." Well, I'm telling you, my poor heart nearly jumped out of my throat.' She flapped her sausage fingers in dismay. 'For a couple of seconds I couldn't remember for the life of me what I'd done with the thing. Then it came back to me. I'd left it here. Now look, I know it's a bit of a cheek, but do you think Zack would mind awfully if I took it home?'

Ellie managed to reassure Christine that Zack wouldn't mind a bit. Relieved, Christine asked chattily how she was enjoying working for him. Then she started asking how Zack was, and if he was still seeing Louisa. The next thing Ellie knew, Christine had made them both a cup of tea and settled herself down for a nice chat.

Oh well, she wasn't rushed off her feet. She could spare ten minutes.

Christine was gratifyingly pleased to hear that the relationship with Louisa was now over. Leaning forward in her chair, she confided, 'Always felt as if she was looking down her nose at me. I brought in some homemade shortbread one day and offered her a piece. My goodness, you'd have thought I was offering her live newts!'

Ellie warmed to her. 'She was a bit iffy with me as well. Accused me of chasing after Zack.'

Christine's pale eyes twinkled. 'And were you?'

'No!'

'I wouldn't blame you, mind. He's definitely got it, hasn't he? If I were twenty-five years younger I'd have made a play for him myself!'

Oo-er, missus. Maybe it hadn't just been the crimplene causing those sparks to fly.

'And how are things with you?' Ellie changed the subject, struck by how cheerful Christine seemed. 'Zack told me about your husband not being very well. It must be so much easier for you, not having to work full-time anymore.'

'Well, actually, I am working.' There was an audible crackle of static as Christine shifted in her chair and rested the saucer in her lap. 'It was all quite fortuitous really. You see, the day care place couldn't cope with Eric anymore. Now, I love my poor hubby to bits, but the two of us being at home together was too much. I don't mind telling you, it's a lonely old business. Anyway, my doctor suggested considering some respite care and I did a bit of research. We ended up going to look at a nursing home not far from us, then while we were there I happened to see a notice up on the board saying they were looking for part-time staff. Well, I spoke to the lady who runs the place and we reached an agreement. I'm working there three days a week and Eric comes along with me. And once or twice a week he stays overnight so I can go home and have an evening out, or just a rest on my own and get a proper night's sleep. It's working out really well, all things considered.' Christine smiled bravely. 'It's nice to get to know other people in my situation. And Eric likes it too. Just because he's losing his memory doesn't mean he can't enjoy other people's company. It's a good place, Stanshawe House. The staff are wonderful, and everyone's so understanding. No one minds if Eric starts a game of chess then wanders off halfway through.'

Stanshawe House, Stanshawe House, why did that ring a distant bell? It only took a couple of seconds to make the connection. Should she mention it? Or keep quiet?

'I think a friend of mine knows someone who lives there.' For a moment Ellie couldn't remember the surname; she had to conjure up a mental image of the painting in the flat, hanging above the mantelpiece in the living room. Having pictured it, she concentrated on the signature in the bottom right-hand corner: Martha Daines, that was it.

Christine took a sip of tea. 'One of the residents? Who is it?'

'Mr Daines.'

'Henry?'

'That's the one.'

'Oh, my dear, I'm sorry. Didn't your friend tell you? Henry died a few weeks ago.'

Ellie sat back. 'Oh, right. I didn't know. Well, that's... sad. What happened?'

'Nothing dramatic.' Christine shrugged. 'Bless his heart, he was such a dear gentle soul. He just passed away in his sleep, which isn't the worst way to go. He wasn't in any pain. Do you think your friend knows he's dead?'

Ellie shook her head. Tony had called for a long chat last night and he would have mentioned it. 'I don't think he does.'

'Oh my goodness, I hope I haven't spoken out of turn.' Looking worried, Christine said, 'Maybe he should speak to the family... Henry's wife...'

'Martha.' Ellie needed to double-check that they were talking about the same man.

'Yes, Martha. Poor darling, she took it very hard.'

'It must be a terrible time for her.' Ellie nodded in agreement. 'I'm sure he'll do that. I'll let him know.'

They chatted for a while longer about Zack, then Ellie lifted the plant in its blue pot and carried it outside to Christine's little car.

'Bye then, dear. Thanks so much for the plant. And I'm glad you've settled in here. Give Zack my regards.' With an unexpected twinkle, Christine said, 'You can give him a kiss from me, if you like.'

Which was slightly alarming, and ironic to think that Zack had hired Christine in order to be safe, when it was becoming scarily apparent that she'd had a crush on him all along.

It just went to show, no matter how unprepossessing the exterior, a flirty soul could still lie beneath.

Back inside the house, Ellie leaned against the office door and gazed at the radiator.

For quite a while.

No, it was no good, she couldn't do it. She just wasn't that kind of person.

Dammit.

She had to use the plastic flyswat to reach across the desk and poke around behind the radiator until the postcard from Australia slid out. On her hands and knees, Ellie retrieved it from the floor under the desk, then straightened up again and put it in Zack's in-tray.

A loose splinter from one of the oak floorboards had managed to rip a hole in the knee of her tights, new on this morning.

Great.

This was her reward for doing the right thing.

Chapter 44

HONESTLY, YOU TRIED YOUR best and sometimes everything worked out perfectly.

Other times, it all went horribly wrong.

Ellie blamed the alcohol. Or more to the point, the lack of it. When she'd invited Roo over for dinner, the plan had been to soften her up and make her realize that the time had come to give in. And a couple of bottles of Barolo might well have done the trick. Then, when the doorbell rang and Todd appeared, the metaphorical violins could start to play and in years to come they would fondly remember the night when Ellie had managed to persuade them they really should be together.

Plus, she would be a bridesmaid.

Whereas the reality, minus alcohol, meant that Roo was stone-cold sober and Todd at his wits' end.

'I'll go.' Roo put down her glass of water.

'No.' From the doorway, Todd shook his head. 'I will.'

'Can't you both stay?' Was this how it felt to be a relationship counselor? Filled with frustration, Ellie said, 'Couldn't we just have a nice evening together?'

Todd looked at Roo. 'I've sent you letters and texts and emails and you've ignored them all. Now that I'm here, can we at least talk?'

'About us, you mean? I'd rather not.' Roo was breathing rapidly. 'No point.'

The air was thick with sexual tension, like extra-crackly cel-lophane. Ellie said, 'OK, how about both of you staying and *not* talking about any of that stuff?' She turned to Todd. 'You're one of my oldest friends. And you'—she swung back to Roo—'you're my newest. I don't want to be stuck in the middle. So how about we give it a try?'

Silence.

Followed by more silence. Apart from that almost-audible zing of sexual tension.

'Please,' Ellie tried again. 'Because why should I be the one to suffer? Haven't I been through enough?'

Oh yes, she could be shameless when she wanted. Jamie wouldn't mind.

'I can't believe you just said that,' said Roo.

Todd shook his head at Ellie. 'Talk about low.'

'Fine. Are you staying or not?'

'I'll stay.'

But the next couple of hours weren't easy. The tension didn't let up for a second. On the surface Roo and Todd were eating and talking, but their feelings for each other remained the elephant in the room.

Finally Todd cracked and said, 'This is crazy.' He put down his beer and said abruptly, 'Roo, can I talk to you in the kitchen?'

'No.'

His eyes blazed with emotion. 'Just for one minute.'

'Not even for one second,' said Roo.

They glared at each other across the table. It was almost unbear-able to watch. Ellie pushed back her chair and said, 'I'm just off to the loo…'

'Stay where you are!' Roo blurted out.

'Hello? I need a wee. And no'—Ellie rose to her feet—'you're not coming with me.'

She didn't need a wee, but she loitered in the bathroom for a couple of minutes. Honestly, was this a ridiculous situation or what?

Finally there was a knock on the door.

'If you're being discreet, you can come out now,' said Todd.

Ellie emerged from the bathroom.

The living room was empty.

'Where is she?'

'Gone.'

'Oh God, I'm sorry.' Ellie collapsed back down on her chair.

He rubbed his hand over his head. 'She said thanks for the dinner, by the way.'

'Right.'

Todd indicated the table, strewn with plates and the remains of the tiramisu. 'Me too.'

'No problem.' She'd have the rest of it for breakfast.

'And for doing your best. Nice try.'

'It would have been better if it had worked.'

'This whole business is killing me.' Todd looked defeated.

'I know. I'm sorry.'

'I feel like Bridget bloody Jones.' He gave a huff of annoyance and flipped the top off another bottle of beer. 'I'm like a *girl*, all churned up inside. I tell you, it's doing my head in.'

'Same.' Ellie nodded.

'Do I sound like a girl?'

'A bit.'

Todd's lip curled. 'If Jamie was here now, I'd never hear the last of it. Right, let's stop.' He mimed zipping his mouth shut. 'No more about me. We'll talk about you. Still going OK with Joe?'

Ellie smiled and nodded; she had been through this earlier when Roo had asked the same question. Except Todd was less likely to want to know if the sex was good.

'We're having fun. I feel normal again.'

'That's fantastic. Brilliant.' Todd clearly meant it. 'I can't wait to meet him.'

They'd get on well together. Ellie nodded. 'We'll do it. I'll set something up.'

Todd left at eleven. There were two things she hadn't shared with him. The first was what she'd found out earlier today from Christine. Tony had confided in her about Martha, but Todd didn't know about any of that, and there was no reason to tell him.

Ellie, though, felt the need to do something about it. Even if she wasn't sure what.

She cleared the dinner table and loaded the dishwasher, then sat down on the sofa and switched on her laptop.

Sending an email to Tony was off the agenda. Telling him his lover's husband had died would be just so wrong. If Martha had wanted him to know, she would have contacted him herself.

And she hadn't. Of course she wouldn't. Her guilt would be as all-consuming as her grief.

Ellie typed Martha Daines into Google and up came the link to her website.

There was the home page. There was the gallery of paintings. There was the email address.

She wrote the email straight from the heart, without stopping once.

> *Dearest Martha,*
>
> *I have just heard, via someone who works at Stanshawe House, about the death of your husband, Henry. I'm so very sorry, please accept my deepest condolences. My father-in-law Tony is a great admirer of your work. I haven't told him about Henry. I was married to his son Jamie, however, and do know how it feels to lose a husband, so I understand some of what you're going through and how*

*you might be feeling now. If you ever feel you'd like to
email or speak to me, please do so at any time.*

Ellie gave her phone number and home address and the link to
an online forum for widows that she had found helpful last year when
the grief had been at its most overwhelming. She concluded with:

*Love, Ellie Kendall. P.S. I mean it about contacting
me. You don't have to if you don't want to, but it does
help to talk.*

Then she leaned back against the sofa cushions and made Jamie
walk into the living room.

'Well? Should I send it?'

Jamie stayed by the door, his hair glinting white-blond from the
light behind him in the hallway. He was wearing a pale yellow shirt
and the usual jeans.

'Go for it.' He shrugged easily. 'You obviously want to.'

If she tried hard enough, she could even conjure up the smell of
him. 'I know, but is it the right thing to do?'

'Sweetheart, you want to help her. You've got something in
common.' Jamie paused for a moment. 'And not just the obvious.
Do it.'

By *not just the obvious*, he meant the burden of guilt.

He knew. Of course he knew.

Ellie pressed Send and the email went hurtling off into cyber-
space. She might hear back from Martha. Or she might not.

There was now a mischievous glint in Jamie's eyes.

'I don't want to talk about the other thing,' said Ellie.

'Sure?'

'Quite sure, thanks.'

His grin was playful. 'OK. But I know anyway.'

'Well, you would.'

'Don't worry, I won't tell anyone. Bye!'

Jamie left with just a hint of a jaunty swagger. Ellie closed her eyes. This was the second secret she hadn't shared with Todd this evening. And Roo didn't know either. It wasn't the kind of information she would dream of passing on to anyone. Not whilst she was in a relationship, at least.

How would any self-respecting man feel if he were to find out that while he was making love to his new girlfriend, she was busy pretending he was someone else?

Chapter 45

'YOUR BOYFRIEND'S WAITING OUTSIDE.'

Was there a particular reason for Zack looking ever so slightly pissed off about it? Ellie checked her watch: three minutes to five.

'He asked me what time I'd be finishing work. It's OK if he meets me here, isn't it?' She heard herself sounding defensive; Zack hadn't been in the sunniest of moods recently. 'Is there anything else you need me to do, or can I go?'

He shot her a look of impatience mixed with a hint of an eye roll. In retaliation Ellie shut down her computer and pushed back her chair.

'Right, well, I'll be off then. See you tomorrow. Have a nice night!' She flashed him an extra-bright smile to cover up for the fact that having to sidle past him in order to reach the door was having its habitual heart-galloping effect.

Evidently bored now, Zack turned his attention to the calendar on the wall as she left. 'You too.'

Outside, Joe held out his arms and gave Ellie a huge hug.

'I've been waiting for ages.'

'I know. Zack said you were out here.'

'I saw him at the upstairs window. Thought he might have invited me in.'

Overhead the sky was leaden and it was spitting with rain. Slightly embarrassed that Zack hadn't asked him inside, Ellie said, 'Sorry, he's been a bit funny lately.'

'Speaking of funny. There's something I have to tell you.'

'Oh God, is it my hair?' She knew she shouldn't have cut her bangs last night. Ellie's hands went up to tug at the ends. 'Is it crooked?'

Joe shook his head. 'It's not your hair. Listen, this is pretty major.'

Where was this going? Ellie couldn't imagine. 'Major good or major bad?'

'Major good.' He gazed at her in his beaky, intense way. 'Well, I think so.'

It was raining properly now. They were standing on the pavement outside Zack's house, getting wet. Was Zack still there, in his picky mood, watching them and wondering what was going on?

'Come on, let's get home.' Ellie began to walk up the road. 'Tell me on the way.'

'OK.' Joe loped alongside her, his arm around her shoulders, his baggy khaki jacket flapping at his side. 'Here goes. I've just had a call from Stephen in LA.'

Stephen was the agent they'd signed with at the agency in LA. 'And?'

'Mac Zeller's been in touch.'

'Right,' said Ellie. Mac Zeller was the producer-director who had bought his and Kaye's film script.

'He wants us to work exclusively with him on a new screenplay...'

'Wow, fantastic!'

'...And he's also produced a sitcom that's breaking all records in its first series in the States. *The Afternooners*. It's set to be bigger and better than *Friends*.' The words were tumbling out now. 'And Mac wants us to join the writing team. Me and Kaye! It's just unbelievable. I could hardly breathe when Stephen told me... to think he has that much faith in us...' Joe stopped walking and gripped her hands, his silver-rimmed glasses speckled with rain.

'That's great.' Ellie reached up and wiped them clean, so he could see. 'It'll mean going back out there for a bit.'

'More than that.' Joe's Adam's apple bobbed as he swallowed. 'It means going out there for a while. Six months, minimum. A couple of years, preferably. It's just not something we can do from over here. We have to move to LA.' His hands were trembling. 'Ellie, he's made us an offer we can't refuse. It's the chance of a lifetime. There's no way we can turn it down.'

He was searching her face for a reaction. Ellie hugged him. 'Of course you can't! Move to LA and work with Mac Zeller? It's amazing. And you deserve it.'

Joe pulled back, his own expression unreadable. 'Seriously?'

'God, yes!' Why wouldn't she mean it?

'OK, here's the thing. I was kind of hoping you might be a bit more upset, so that I could say, "And I want you to come with me."'

'Oh.'

His crooked smile flickered like a lightbulb struggling not to go out. 'Well? How would you feel about that?'

Fifty yards away, in his first-floor living room, Zack watched from the window as Ellie and Joe stood and faced each other, oblivious to the increasing rain. He'd have a better view if he flung the window wide open and leaned out, or if he happened to have a handy periscope, like the ones he'd bought his nephews last Christmas so they could spy round corners.

But that wasn't really on. He couldn't hear what they were saying, but Ellie had just hugged Joe and he was now stroking her cheek. She was smiling up at him. Zack turned away, slightly despising himself. As he did so, his phone rang in his pocket.

Taking it out, he saw the caller's name. Meg.

~~~

Back at Nevis Street, Ellie took off her wet jacket and put the kettle on, prevaricating while she worked out what to say.

But Joe wasn't stupid. He already knew.

'So you're not tempted?'

She turned to look at him. 'I can't, sorry, no.'

'That's a real shame. I have to go,' said Joe. 'You do understand that, don't you?'

Ellie nodded. 'I do.'

'I'll really miss you.'

'I'll miss you too.'

'But not as much.' The lopsided smile was back. 'Otherwise you'd come along.'

OK, here goes. 'Joe, the last few weeks have been brilliant. We've had a fantastic time.'

He spoke with rueful resignation. 'That means you really aren't going to change your mind.'

'You wouldn't want me to. Listen, can we be honest with each other? Marks out of ten for how you feel about me.' Ellie held up her hands. 'And don't say ten. You have to be *completely* honest.'

Joe raked his fingers through his damp hair. 'Nine. OK, not nine. Eight and a half. But that's good, that's really good.'

'Thank you. Now it's my turn.' Ellie had been going to say eight. To be kind she said, 'You're an eight and a half too.'

'They sound like pretty high marks to me.'

'They are. But not high enough. If you're planning to live with someone, it has to be tens all the way.'

His eyebrows went up. 'You told me not to say ten.'

'Because it wouldn't have been true.' Ellie reached for his hands. 'But you've given me my confidence back, and that's the best present in the world. Thanks to you, I know I can feel normal again, do all the stuff that normal people do, have sex and enjoy it.'

Joe said gravely, 'It's a special talent of mine. I've always been excellent at sex.'

Everything was going to be OK. She felt herself relax. 'You're great in bed. And out of it.'

'In an eight and a half out of ten kind of way.'

Ellie broke into a grin. 'When you meet your perfect ten out of ten woman, I want you to phone me up and say, "Now I get it, now I understand. Ellie, I'm sorry. You were right and I was wrong."'

'Come here, you.' Joe pulled her into a hug. 'It's OK, I already know you're right. I'm just going to miss you, that's all. We've had a good time, haven't we?'

'The best.' She planted a fond kiss on his mouth. 'Thank you. For everything.'

His face softened. 'Trust me, it's been a pleasure.'

'For me too.' It had stopped raining. Ellie said, 'Come on, we have to go out and celebrate. My treat. You're going to Hollywood!'

'You're feeling normal again.'

'We've had a fantastic fling,' she agreed happily.

'And some fantastic sex,' Joe modestly reminded her.

Ellie smiled and kissed him again. It had been good. Inside her own head, though, it hadn't always been Joe she'd been having the fantastic sex with.

But she wouldn't tell him that. There was no need for him to ever know.

Chapter 46

YASMIN FINISHED CLEANING THE old polish off Roo's toenails and began massaging her feet with exfoliating scrub. 'Go on then, tell me more!'

Roo smiled; Yasmin loved hearing about the bizarre goings-on in the charity shop. 'OK, yesterday this girl came in. Early twenties. Skinny, huge boobs, blond extensions, big blue eyes. She gave us two huge bags of clothes. Really good stuff, all size eight. Said she hoped we'd get a good price for everything.'

Yasmin looked up expectantly. 'And?'

'So first thing this morning she came back. Except this time she wasn't smiling. Mad as a box of maggots. I waved to her and she said, "Has that bitch been in here?" Then all of a sudden she saw one of her dresses and went berserk, started screaming and swearing and trying to rip it off the mannequin…'

'Why?' Yasmin sat back, mystified.

'Yesterday morning she had a massive fight with her sister,' said Roo. 'Her identical twin sister.'

'Oh…' Yasmin started to laugh. 'That's brilliant! We had a pair of twins here last year; they were retired schoolteachers but they still argued about what color they were going to have their nails painted. One of them wanted pearlized pink and the other had her heart set on glossy plum, but—'

'Yaz?' Jackie, one of the other beauticians currently manning reception, was peering out of the window. 'Sorry to interrupt, but he's back again. He's on his way over.'

Roo's blood ran cold; there was something about the urgency

in Jackie's voice that gave it away. And Yasmin had frozen too. It couldn't be him, surely not... and if it was, what could she do?

'He's got flowers!' Jackie hastily backed away from the window. 'OK, here he comes...'

Roo heard the door swing open behind her. Yasmin scrambled to her feet. Oh God, oh God, this was a nightmare, Roo's heart was galloping out of control, her head was spinning, she felt sick...

Then everything went dark and for a surreal split second Roo thought she'd passed out. Except, hang on, that couldn't be right, her brain was still going. The next moment she felt the soft folds of the towel being patted into place over her face and head, for all the world as if she'd just had a nice relaxing steam facial.

Which she hadn't.

Which kind of implied...

Except how could it?

'Niall, this is silly.' Still winding the ends of the towel behind Roo's head, ensuring that none of her hair was visible, Yasmin said, 'I've told you before, you can't just turn up here. I'm busy.'

The galloping in Roo's chest was so thunderous it felt as if horses were about to burst out. She was lying back in a reclining chair with her jeans rolled to her knees, her feet slathered in gritty gunk, and her whole head wrapped in a dark blue towel. Less than six feet away from Niall. She could smell his aftershave. Sense his desperation. Hear the tremor in his voice.

'...but you won't let me into your mother's house and you refuse to come home, so what else can I do? Yaz, I'm sorry.' He was gabbling now. 'I've told you a thousand times. I made a mistake and I'm going to spend the rest of my life regretting it. But you're the one I love. You and Ben. We're a family and we should be together... here, at least take these, they're your favorite.'

From beneath the swathes of soft towel Roo heard the crackle of tissue paper and florist's cellophane.

'Just leave them on the desk, Niall.' Yasmin sounded as uninterested as if he were the FedEx man dropping off a delivery. 'I'm not going to let you do this in front of my client. It's unprofessional. Plus, you're making an idiot of yourself.'

'Yaz, don't you understand? I don't care! I want you to forgive me.' Niall's voice cracked with emotion. 'I want to win you back, and I don't think anyone would begrudge me a couple of minutes to try.' A hand came to rest on her shoulder and Roo, aghast, pressed herself back into the reclining chair so hard the plastic covering squeaked. 'Would you?'

Rational thought was still a struggle but she was stingingly aware that this was Yasmin's situation. This was her workplace, she was the one in control. *And she was the one who had covered Roo's face with a towel.*

Did this mean… oh God… that she *knew*?

Either way it wasn't her place to sit up and reveal her identity by whisking the towel off her face, *Scooby-Doo* style.

Which was probably a good thing anyway.

Instead, Roo shook her head and heard herself adopt a kind of strangled Cockney growl. 'Nah, s'alright.' Heavens, she sounded like Dame Edna with bronchitis.

'Look, we're a family.' The hand left her shoulder; Niall was addressing Yasmin again. 'I miss you so much. I miss Ben. I'll do anything you want.' He was pleading now. 'I'm never going to see Vivica again and I swear that's the truth. Baby, it was one mistake, that's all. Just give me another chance, *please*.'

'OK, three things.' Yasmin remained calm. 'I don't like it when you call me baby. I never have.'

Ouch. Niall sounded as if he was shaking his head. 'Sorry, sorry.'

'Plus, I don't want to give you another chance.'

'But—'

'And the third thing is,' Yasmin continued as if he hadn't

interrupted, 'you're still lying to me now. One mistake, you said. But that's just not true, is it? Vivica isn't the only woman you've had an affair with.'

Ohmygod. The buzzing in Roo's ears was like a jumbo jet. This was why Yasmin had covered her face with a towel, so that she could be the one to perform the triumphant unveiling. A part of Roo had to admire her. It would be a magnificent moment, the coup de grace to signal the death of their marriage. All they needed now was a drum roll…

'I swear there hasn't been anyone else.' Niall was adamant.

Roo bit her lip.

'Yes there has, Niall. You know there has.'

'Baby—um, Yaz, honest to God, I'm telling the truth!'

OK, here it comes, here it comes. Roo's nails dug into her palms. *Here comes the big reveal…*

'Are you? OK, fine, have it your way. But our marriage is still over,' said Yasmin. 'And I have work to do here. So now that you've had your little say, could you go and leave us in peace?'

Hey? What? What about me?

There was a long silence. Finally, Roo heard Niall's exhalation of defeat. Then footsteps as he made his way out of the salon. The door opened, then closed.

Everyone waited.

At last Jackie announced, 'He's back in his car. Driving off. Gone.'

And the towel was lifted away from Roo's face.

Yasmin gazed down at her. 'Oops.'

Roo's mouth was as dry as the Sahara. She unstuck her tongue. 'How did you know?'

'OK,' Jackie broke in. 'For a start, you're Daisy Deeva.'

'What?' Roo's head whipped round; Jackie was standing behind the reception desk with her arms crossed beneath her jacked-up bosom. 'You mean *all* of you know about this?'

'Of course we do.' Jackie's tone was cool. She glanced out of the window again. 'Yaz, Mrs Simpson's here for her appointment. She's just paying the taxi.'

'Right.' Yasmin indicated Roo's unpainted toes. 'Shall we clean you up and give these a miss for today? After this next appointment it's my lunch break. How about if you wait in the café up the road and I'll join you in twenty minutes?'

She was giving nothing away. Roo swallowed and said, 'Right.' What other choice did she have?

———

It wasn't twenty minutes. More like forty. It felt like forty hours. Roo couldn't stop shaking. Her stomach was all churned up. Was she sitting in the wrong café? How could she possibly have known?

Finally the door opened and Yasmin came in. She chatted to the waitress at the counter, ordered herself a latte, then made her way over to the table in the corner where Roo was sitting.

'I'm so sorry,' Roo blurted out. 'Really I am. I hate myself. And I know it should never have happened in the first place, but it's all over now, I promise.'

'I know it is,' said Yasmin.

Roo's palms were damp; she surreptitiously wiped them on her jeans. 'How did you find out?'

'OK, from the beginning? Over the years I've got to know my husband pretty well. And I know he's a good liar. Apart from one thing. The lying might be good, but he can't control his neck.' Yasmin patted her own neck. 'Maybe you noticed it yourself. It goes kind of blotchy. Dead giveaway. Anyhow, the first time you came into the salon we thought you were Daisy Deeva but you said you weren't. So that night I was telling Niall about you and the weirdest thing happened. His neck went blotchy!'

For heaven's sake, was she serious? 'That was it? Just his neck?'

'Well, I wasn't sure. But you'd lied,' Yasmin pointed out. 'So that made two things to be suspicious about. Then there was the evening we were out and we bumped into your friend Ellie. It did seem slightly strange that she couldn't remember the name of her own child.'

Roo licked her lips, she still had no idea where this was heading. 'So then you knew.'

'Well, the neck thing happened again. Worse this time. It was pretty obvious that Niall was wondering what the hell was going on!'

'It was all over by then. I'd finished with him.'

'OK.' Yasmin nodded, mentally piecing events together. 'So was he also seeing Vivica then?'

'Yes.'

'And that's why you stopped seeing him?'

Roo flushed and nodded, awash with shame.

'Out of interest, did Niall tell you where I worked?'

'No. I found a list of things you'd asked him to buy. Written on salon paper.'

'Ah. That makes more sense.' Yasmin leaned forward and took a sip of her latte.

'Why didn't you tell me you knew?'

'Honestly? I've no idea. I was just so curious. You kept coming back to the salon. And you seemed really nice, which was confusing. I had no idea what you were up to. None of us could work out what was going on. But I didn't want to confront you, because then you'd disappear.' The corners of Yasmin's mouth lifted. 'And this might sound mercenary, but you're the best tipper I ever had.'

Roo was busy pleating the edges of the blue and white table-cloth. 'You must hate me so much.'

'You'd think so, wouldn't you? That's the weird thing, though. I don't. I never have.'

'The first time we came, it was to find out what you were like.'

'To see if I was as awful as Niall said I was, you mean? Nagging, moaning, bad-tempered, and always shattered? I can imagine what he told you. And sometimes it was true.' Wryly, Yasmin went on, 'Having to work and look after a baby and run a household while your husband does bugger all can have that effect.'

'I'm sorry.'

'So you keep saying.'

'I should have chucked him the moment I found out he was married. I'm a bad person.' Roo's eyes filled with tears. 'I'm doing my best to make up for it, I promise.'

'Oh God, please don't cry! I didn't mean to upset you.' Yasmin hastily shoved a paper napkin at her. 'Listen, you heard me when Niall came in today. I don't want him back! I'm better off without him. If he's still seeing Vivica now, you can bet he'll be chasing some other piece of skirt by Christmas. I don't think one woman will ever be enough. He'll always be on the hunt for the next adrenaline rush.'

The paper napkin was scratchy. Roo blotted the tears and willed herself to get a grip. 'I think you're right. But I'm still sorry. And I'll never *ever* do it again.'

'How did you find out about Vivica?'

'I read a text from her on his phone while he was in the bathroom.'

Yasmin shook her head and tut-tutted. 'Basic schoolboy error. He won't be doing that again in a hurry.'

'I thought you were going to whisk the towel off my face when he was in the salon.'

'It did occur to me. But then Niall would just blame you for wrecking his marriage. No'—Yasmin smiled briefly—'I prefer it this way. It's like a bit of one-upmanship on my part. And I want you to carry on coming to the salon.' She checked her watch. 'In fact, we could head back there if you want. I can give you that pedicure.'

Roo checked her watch. One fifteen. 'I can't. I have to start my shift at two.'

'This is what we haven't been able to work out.' Yasmin looked puzzled. 'You're Daisy Deeva. Why are you working in a charity shop?'

'I told you. I'm trying to become a better person. I'm making up for all the bad things I've done.'

'Seriously?' A thought occurred to Yasmin. 'Is that why…? No, sorry, doesn't matter.'

'Is that why what?'

'The makeup thing. I just wondered.'

Roo nodded. 'I gave it all away. And my good clothes.'

'My God.'

Speaking of God… 'And I've been to church. Twice.' She'd stopped after the second visit when a bossy woman had told her off for click-clacking in her high heels across the echoey flagstoned floor.

'Crikey.' Yasmin looked suitably impressed. 'All because of Niall.'

'Not all. There was something else too. I nearly kissed Ellie's boyfriend.' There, she'd said it. Now Yasmin knew everything, every last bit of bad stuff.

Yasmin's eyes widened. 'Does she know?'

Roo nodded wearily. 'Oh yes. I told her.'

'Did she go crazy?'

'No, she was relieved.' Oh God, the tears were back. 'She'd been wondering how to break up with him. But that's beside the point; I didn't know that at the time. And I still nearly did it.'

'OK, don't be offended by this.' Ready to leave now, Yasmin reached for her pale blue leather bag. 'But when I do eventually find myself another man, I probably won't introduce him to you.'

Yet another wave of shame engulfed Roo. 'I wouldn't do anything, I swear I wouldn't. This is what I'm trying to say.' She was desperate to explain before Yasmin left. 'I'll do anything, *anything* I can to make it up to you—'

'Roo.' Yasmin stopped her in her babbling tracks. 'Calm down. It was meant to be a joke.'

Chapter 47

LITTLE VENICE. THE SUN was blazing down out of a cloudless blue sky, glittering on the surface of the water and making Ellie wish she hadn't sat on her sunglasses last night.

She'd walked from Camden Lock along the Regent's Canal. Now here she was at last, at the intersection where it met the Grand Union Canal and Paddington Basin. Brightly colored narrow boats bobbed up and down, ducks swam between them with insouciance, and people were sitting out on their decks, drinking wine. It was a beautiful afternoon and the towpaths were busy with tourists and locals enjoying the unexpectedly good weather. Weeping willows blurred the outlines of the white stucco Nash houses beyond them. Shading her eyes, Ellie surveyed the scene and scanned the opposite bank.

There she was, wearing a flowing emerald-green dress and with her easel set up on the towpath. Ellie made her way to the blue iron bridge and headed across it. Would meeting Martha be strange? Would it be awkward? Would they struggle to find things to talk about?

No one had been more surprised than Ellie when Martha had replied to her impulsively sent message. Brief and to the point, she had thanked her for the email and insisted that she most definitely *didn't* want Tony to be told about the death of her husband. That had been all.

Until two days later when, out of the blue, another mail had arrived in Ellie's inbox:

Dear Ellie,

Was I rude before? A bit abrupt? If so, I'm sorry.
Many thanks for your kind offer. I don't feel it would be
appropriate to come to your flat, but I shall be painting in
Little Venice on Sunday afternoon. If you happened to be
free and in the area, it would be nice to meet you.
Best wishes,
Martha.

At close quarters, Ellie saw that the easel might be up but no painting was getting done. Martha was sitting on her stool holding a piece of charcoal but only the most basic outlines were in place. Tony had described her as voluptuous and glowing. Well, that wasn't currently the case. Attractive she might be, with her striking cheekbones and beautifully shaped head, but her face was drawn, there were dark circles beneath her eyes, and any glow was conspicuous by its absence.

But when she turned and saw Ellie standing a few meters away watching her, she broke into a smile that made a difference.

'Hello. Is it you?'

'It's me,' Ellie agreed.

'Thought so. Hello, darling, nice to meet you.' Martha sighed and gestured with an air of helplessness at the few lines sketched on the artist's pad in front of her. 'I think I'll give up on this. Shall we go and find somewhere we can have a cup of tea?'

'Can't we stay here?'

'But there's nowhere for you to sit...' There was a moment of hostess panic. 'Oh dear, I didn't think this through.'

'Hello? Are you suggesting I'm ancient and decrepit?' Ellie was wearing old jeans and a white shirt with the sleeves rolled up. She sat down cross-legged, out of the way of passers-by, just to the right of Martha. 'I'm fine like this.'

'Only if you're sure. Let me know when your bottom goes numb. I keep trying to paint,' said Martha. 'But I can't seem to do it anymore. I want to, but it just won't happen.' She looked stricken. 'I might never paint again.'

'How are you feeling? You can tell me. And I mean properly tell me,' said Ellie. 'That's why I'm here.'

'Darling, I know. And bless you for coming. Truthfully?' Martha paused and rolled the stick of charcoal between her thumb and forefinger. 'I feel like a rabbit that's been hit by a car and left in a ditch to die. I feel like an empty house with all the windows flung open and a cold wind whistling through. I feel guilty and alone and sometimes I wonder if Henry's in a better place now, and then I hate myself for thinking that... actually, I hate myself pretty much all the time. And I miss him, I miss him so desperately I could rip out my own heart because it couldn't hurt as much as this. How does that sound?'

'Truthfully?' echoed Ellie. 'It sounds familiar.'

'You know about me and Tony? You must do.'

'Yes. He told me.' Was Martha aware that she was turning her wedding ring round and round? It was loose on her finger; she had evidently lost weight.

'And while you were married to Jamie, did you have an affair with another man?'

'No.' Ellie shook her head. 'I didn't.'

'Well then. You didn't have that to feel guilty about.'

'I know. It must be awful. But the guilt still gets you, one way or another. I blamed myself for not forcing Jamie to take the train instead of the car.'

'That's just part of the whole grieving process, though.' Martha sat back. 'I've read the leaflets. But I do actually have a valid reason to hate myself.'

'Your husband wasn't himself.'

'That's not good enough.'

'Look, there's nothing I can say that'll make you feel better.' Ellie watched a pair of swans glide past. 'But it's only been a few weeks. Things will get easier in time.'

'That's what everyone tells me. I can't imagine it happening.'

'It will. Look at me. I couldn't ever imagine getting involved with someone else. But I did,' said Ellie.

'Oh yes. Tony told me.' A smile flickered across her face. 'He was so pleased for you. Jamie's best friend. I heard all about it. That's lovely.'

Oh dear. 'Actually, that was never a proper thing. It didn't work out. But then someone else came along,' said Ellie, 'and it was great. I felt normal again.'

Martha looked interested. 'And are you still seeing him?'

'Well, no…'

'Why, what happened?'

'He's moving to America.'

'So he dumped you?' She was outraged.

'No, he asked me to go with him. But I didn't want to.'

'Why not?'

Why not indeed?

'Because he was nearly right,' said Ellie. 'Just not exactly right.'

Martha said, 'You know what being an artist means? It means noticing every last detail. The kind of tiny details other people might miss.' She paused. 'So what I'm interested in finding out is, why did you start blinking really fast just then?'

Ellie swallowed. 'You mean when I looked at the water and the sun made my eyes sting?'

'No. Come on, what aren't you telling me?' Martha pointed with the stick of charcoal. 'And that big gulpy swallow you just did? I saw that too.'

For heaven's sake, what was she, some kind of witch?

Oh well, they were here to be honest with each other. Ellie pushed her bangs out of her eyes and said, 'You could get burned at the stake for doing that, you know. But OK, just between us, there's someone else. But it's embarrassing and nothing's ever going to come of it.'

'Why not? Is he married?'

'No! It's just... he's my boss.' There, it was out. She'd said it.

'Well, that's been known to happen. It's fine. Oh,' said Martha as something else occurred to her. 'Unless he's gay?'

Ellie smiled; it would almost be easier if he was. 'He isn't gay.'

'Well then, what's stopping you?'

'He's not interested. And the last thing he wants is that kind of complication. He only hired me in the first place because I made it clear nothing like that would ever happen. Because at the time,' Ellie said evenly, 'it was true. I didn't feel anything at all.'

'Oh, sweetheart, but you've changed your mind. He's won you over. Isn't that a good thing?' Martha looked hopeful. 'Maybe he's changed his mind too.'

'Believe me, he hasn't. And he's never going to know how I feel. If he did, I'd have to leave.' Ellie shook her head. 'Which would be awful, because he's a fantastic boss. And I love my job. Apart from the pathetic yearny crush bit, obviously. What are you doing?' Oh God, Martha was on her feet, folding up her easel and packing everything in her bag. Had she upset her?

'You're cheering me up. And I'm not going to get any work done today. I'm not a great drinker,' said Martha, 'but I think I'm in the mood for one now. Come on, it's so lovely to meet you. Will you let me buy you a glass of champagne?'

─◆◆◆─

'You're late.' Roo pulled open the front door. 'I said to be here by six. It's six thirty.'

'I know. I'm sorry.'

'Where have you been?' Roo's nostrils quivered. 'Are you drunk?'

'No, I've just had a lovely afternoon,' Ellie protested.

'Drinking! I can smell the fumes!'

Roo's newfound teetotalism had its drawbacks; she was in danger of turning into the no-fun alcohol police. 'It was only going to be a glass each. But it was cheaper to buy a bottle. We sat outside a bistro in Little Venice and just talked and talked for ages. I didn't notice the time.'

'Who were you with?'

The inside of the house smelled of roast beef and gravy. Ellie's stomach growled in anticipation; she wasn't going to complain about this aspect of Roo's attempts at self-improvement. She wasn't going to tell her the truth either. There was no need for Roo to know about her meeting with Martha. It had been a perfect one-off, not to be re-peated. She had promised never to tell Tony about Henry's death and Martha in turn had promised to keep the story of the Embarrassing Hopeless Crush to herself.

'Dinner smells fantastic. Have you done Yorkshire puddings?'

'I did, but they look a bit burnt.' In the kitchen, Roo peered critically through the smoked-glass front of the oven. 'It's your fault for being late.'

'Sorry.' Ellie gazed at the pans bubbling away on the hob. There were carrots and broad beans. Next to them on the granite worktop sat bowls of roast potatoes, balsamic braised onions, and what ap-peared to be... no, surely not...

'What's that?' She pointed.

'Sage and onion stuffing.'

'With roast beef?'

Roo was defensive. 'I *like* sage and onion stuffing.'

'So do I.' Ellie hid a smile; with her blue and white stripy apron and her hair spiked up in all directions, Roo was half domestic goddess, half frazzled chicken.

'And why won't you tell me who you've been with?' As she spoke, Roo picked up a whisk and began vigorously stirring the gravy.

Ellie thought for a moment. Todd had always been mad about gravy; he and Jamie had once knocked a pint of it back in one go for a bet. She said, 'I was with Todd,' and saw a little spray of gravy hit the splashback.

'Oh right. Don't tell me, let me guess.' Roo's voice was brittle. 'He's still going on about how he wants me to stop being stubborn so we can get together.'

The great thing about alcohol was, it had a talent for rearranging your mental processes and making you think about things in a way you might not have thought about them before.

'He didn't say that. Actually, he didn't mention you once.' Ellie reached past and stole a single crunchy roast potato from the blue dish. 'Between you and me, I'm pretty sure you can relax now. He's over it.'

Splitt went the gravy. Just a tiny bit. Not turning her head, Roo said casually, 'Oh?'

'Mm. Mmmmm.' Ellie flapped her hand to signal that she couldn't speak with her mouth full. Roo's cooking skills might be hit and miss but she'd got roast potatoes down to a *T*. She chewed and swallowed and saw that Roo was still waiting for her to carry on.

'He's met someone else,' said Ellie. This was great; like a magician pulling ribbons from his mouth, little white lies were tumbling out. 'That's what we were talking about. He couldn't stop. Her name's Lisa. You know what? He's completely smitten!'

'Oh. Well, good for him. That's… great.' Roo flashed a bright, couldn't-be-happier smile.

'And he says she's really pretty!'

'Can you pass me the gravy jug? It's in the cupboard behind you.'

'She's a math teacher. Isn't that amazing? Did you ever have pretty math teachers when you were at school? Because we definitely didn't.'

'OK, nearly ready now.' Bustling around the kitchen like a hyper-active rabbit, Roo said, 'Why don't you go and wait in the living room? I'll bring everything through in a minute.'

'Wait until you hear how they met,' said Ellie. 'Guess how it happened!'

'I don't know. Here, take my glass of water.'

'Her car broke down in Fulham. She was waiting at the traffic lights and they went green and her car just died on her. Everyone was tooting their horns and getting really annoyed. And it was raining too. Anyway, nobody was helping her. But Todd had just come out of the Tesco Metro and he saw what was going on. He put down his carrier bags and pushed the car round the corner out of the way—'

'Right, is that enough roast beef? Do you want mustard with it?'

'So then he went back to pick up his shopping and guess what? Someone had come along and run off with it! Can you imagine? But the funny thing is, it's like they ended up doing him the most massive favor, because when he told Lisa, it really broke the ice. He waited with her until the breakdown people arrived, they were chat-ting away in the rain, and then Lisa said seeing as it was her fault someone had run off with all his food, the least she could do was buy him dinner. So that's what happened, and it's all gone on from there! Isn't that just incredibly romantic?'

'Yes, it is. Now can we change the subject?' Roo practically shooed her out of the kitchen. 'I'm really not interested.'

It was a wonder her nose hadn't telescoped itself forward and crashed against the opposite wall. Satisfied, Ellie carried the glasses of water through to the other room. Leave it now, don't say another word. Job done.

Chapter 48

ELLIE WAS ON THE Internet putting together a complicated travel schedule for Zack's upcoming trips to Copenhagen and South Africa. So far, the chief problem seemed to be that there were two meetings already arranged, leaving him with roughly twenty minutes to fly from Cape Town to Johannesburg.

Basically, it wasn't a plane he'd be needing, more like a Tardis.

Zack came downstairs and into the office. 'Have you seen the email from Bob Nix?'

'No, but we need to do something about this. Come and have a look.' She tapped the list of times and dates on the writing pad next to the PC. 'You organized this meeting and they organized that one. Shall I see if I can shift Cape Town back?'

'Ah, I see what you mean.' One hand resting on the desk, Zack leaned over her shoulder in order to study the schedule. 'Yes, give Anika a call and ask if we can meet first thing in the morning. Do it in a minute,' he went on, reaching for the mouse and minimizing the site on the computer screen. 'There's something else I want to show you.' Speedily he went to his email account and clicked on the message that had come in just a few minutes earlier.

Ellie focused her attention on the screen. Being so physically close to Zack was causing all kinds of inner havoc. She should be used to it by now but, if anything, it was getting worse. OK, don't think about the smell of him, the heat from his body, the play of muscles and tendons in his hand as he maneuvered and clicked the mouse…

> *Hey Zack,*
>
> *Great job with the SpencerInc deal last week—heard about that from Ted. Impressed.*
>
> *Bibi asked me to send you the attached photo. She says hi, and can you show Ellie? Sure hope she's still working for you!*
>
> *Bob.*

'Go on then.' Ellie nodded, indicating that he should open the attachment.

A page from a magazine filled the screen. Bob and Bibi had been photographed at a glitzy charity ball in Dallas. Their teeth were dazzling. Bob looked like a huge jovial bear in a dinner suit. Bibi was wearing a silver lamé dress that showed off her spectacular bosom and tiny waist. Her turquoise eyes sparkled. Her hair, piled up in an explosion of curls and ringlets, was fastened in place with silver jeweled combs.

Across the bottom of the photo, Bibi had scribbled: 'Ellie! I've never had so many compliments!'

Ellie smiled. Behind her, she was intensely aware of Zack's warm breath on the back of her neck.

'Those hair things.' He sounded puzzled. 'They look like the ones you wore that night we met them.'

'They do a bit.'

Zack peered more closely, his arm brushing her shoulder. 'They're exactly the same.' He shifted position, looked round at Ellie. 'Are they yours?'

'Yes.'

'You gave them to Bibi?'

Ellie flushed; was he cross with her? Embarrassed that she'd given the wife of a billionaire such cheap combs? 'She said she liked them. I didn't think she'd actually wear the things.' She indicated the photo on the screen. 'Especially not to something like that.'

'Hey, I'm not complaining.' Zack straightened and swung her chair round so she was properly facing him. Searching her face, he said, 'Did you think I was?'

'I don't know.' Ellie felt herself getting flustered; when Zack was looking at her like this, it was hard to concentrate. 'After I got home I thought I probably shouldn't have done it.' God, *really* hard to concentrate. 'I mean, you wouldn't believe how cheap they were... I just hope no one lets on to Bibi... people might laugh at her for wearing them and then she'll be mortified.'

'Can I just say something?' Zack cut through her babbling. 'Bibi's a smart lady who knows her own mind. She wears whatever she wants to wear and I wouldn't want to be the one who tried to laugh at her. Apart from anything else, she has a black belt in karate.'

'Haven't we all,' said Ellie.

He did a slight double take. 'Have you?'

'That's for me to know and you to find out.' She didn't have a black belt but had got as far as green at the age of fourteen. Once you'd got that far you could always fake the rest.

'Now I'm scared.' He smiled briefly. 'Anyway, it was a nice thing to do. Bob and Bibi liked you very much.'

'I liked them.' Ellie shifted in her swivel chair; had the atmosphere changed? For the past few weeks Zack had been distant and businesslike. But now he was leaning against the desk, his leg inches from hers, and it was as if all the tension had melted away. There was a softening in his manner, a return to the laid-back, relaxed Zack who had cared for her and been such easy company while she'd been ill with the flu.

In fact, maybe even more than that. Was it her imagination or was he looking at her almost as if there was something he wanted to say but didn't know quite how to say it? Or did she just wish there was? Oh Lord, was she doing it again, conjuring up fantasies like a deluded Take That fan?

'You never know, something like this could make all the difference.' Zack picked up the diary and idly flipped through the pages.
'Bob's looking for a partner in a new electronics company. He might
ask me to go in with him. If he does, I'll need to fly out to Texas
for a week or two, probably early December.' He frowned, deep in
thought. 'You know, it'd be pretty hectic. Lots to do, workwise and
socially. I might need you to come out with me.'

Eeeeeep, yelped a little voice in Ellie's head. A trip to Texas with
Zack! Oh God, what if they took an overnight flight and had to sleep
next to each other on the plane?

Except that wasn't actually likely to happen, was it? He'd probably be cocooned in luxury up there in business class, while she'd
be squashed into economy at the back of the plane, surrounded by
screaming kids.

Aloud she said, 'That's fine.'

He was watching her intently. 'Sure it won't interfere with your
plans?'

He thought she was still seeing Joe. Was this the moment to
tell him it was over? But if she did, would he just assume she'd been
dumped again? Ellie shook her head. 'It's my job. Not a problem, no
problem at all.'

'Good, good.' He carried on turning the pages of the diary. She
saw him check his appointments for September. There at the end of
the month was the weekend of his sister's wedding. He flicked on
past without saying anything. It hadn't been mentioned since the
day he'd asked her to go with him. Had he forgotten about inviting
her? Was he hoping *she'd* forgotten? Had he made arrangements to
take someone else?

Was this why he was in a better mood? Ellie's stomach clenched
with anxiety. Just because Zack hadn't talked to her about it didn't
mean it wasn't happening.

Right, ask him.

'Er…' Bugger, her throat had gone funny and her mouth was dry. Pushing back her chair, she said, 'Cup of tea?' It would be easier to ask the question when he wasn't so close.

'Thanks.' But when she went into the kitchen, he followed her. Right, just get it over with. Ellie threw tea bags into two mugs. 'So what's happening with your sister's wedding?'

'Utter chaos.' Zack visibly relaxed. 'A million things to do and not nearly enough time to do it in. The twins are refusing to be bridesmaids unless they can wear trainers that light up. Plus, they want the dogs to walk up the aisle with them. Steph's tearing her hair out. But it'll all get sorted out in the end.'

The tea bags fizzed and filled with air as Ellie poured boiling water on to them. 'Look, if you don't need me for that anymore, it's fine.'

'Why?' Zack stiffened. 'Don't you want to come?'

'No… I mean yes…' Stirring too vigorously, she sploshed tea over the worktop.

'Is it Joe?'

'No, I just thought you might have someone else you'd rather take.' Honestly, did he have any idea how hard it was to sound casual when he was looking at her like this?

'Someone else like who?'

She may as well say it. 'OK, I saw the postcard that arrived for you the other week. From Australia. I wasn't being nosy,' Ellie went on hurriedly, 'I just couldn't help seeing what it said.'

'The one from Meg.' She caught a glimmer of a smile. 'What makes you think I'd want to take her along to Steph's wedding?'

'Well, she used to be your girlfriend. And she seemed pretty keen to see you again.' OK, she sounded *so* nosy. 'Look, sorry, but it makes things easier if I know what's going on.'

'Nothing's going on.' Zack took the milk out of the fridge and passed it to her. 'You're right, Meg was pretty keen. I met up with her for a drink at the Queen's Head the other evening. It was nice to see her again, catch up with her news, but that's as far as it goes. There's no way we'll be getting back together.'

'Oh. Right.'

'And I definitely won't be inviting her to come along to Steph's wedding.'

Milk. Slosh. Milk. Bigger slosh. Whoops. Flustered, Ellie said, 'So you still want me?'

Oh God, did I really just say that?

After a moment, Zack replied evenly, 'Yes. If you still want to go.'

Oo-er. Was it her or was it getting hot in here?

'I do want to. I'm looking forward to it.' The way he was watching her was having a strange effect on her knees. 'Meeting your family.'

'It'll be good fun. You may need earplugs,' said Zack, 'but you will like them. You'll get on really well together.'

And now he was looking at her mouth. Was this how it felt to be hypnotized? Barely able to think straight, Ellie murmured, 'They sound great,' and wondered if she'd said it right or if her lips had gone all rubbery and completely lost control of themselves. Was she making any sense or was it all coming out as blah-blah-blah? And still he was gazing at her in such a way that it was almost as if—

'Woof! Woof-woof!'

Chapter 49

ELLIE LEAPT A FOOT in the air as the dog flap clattered and Elmo erupted into the kitchen. She heard Zack exhale with what could have been frustration. Or was that just more wishful thinking on her part? Mentally dragging herself back to the real world, she picked up a rag and gave the granite worktop a wipe down where she'd spilled the milk.

'It's not time to go out,' Zack told Elmo, who was still barking and leaping around like a landed salmon. He shook his head at the dog, then gave in and said, 'Oh, what the hell, come on then.' He reached for the red lead, hanging on a hook by the back door. This was Elmo's cue to stop fooling around and stand still, allowing Zack to clip it to his collar. As Zack bent down to do this, Elmo scuttled into reverse, did a speedy three-point turn, and hurtled back out through the dog flap.

'What's he playing at?' Zack frowned and hung the lead back up.

Ellie went to the window. Elmo was dancing around in the garden, jumping up onto the wall then down again. The next moment, still yapping noisily, he launched himself back into the kitchen. Ellie picked up the phone and called Geraldine next door.

'No reply.' She looked over at Elmo, then at Zack. 'Did she say she was going out?'

He shook his head. 'No.'

'Where's the spare key?'

'She asked to borrow it last week when her sister came to stay. Hasn't given it back yet.'

'Let's see if she's there.' Ellie opened the kitchen door. The three of them jumped over the low wall. There was nothing to see through Geraldine's kitchen window but Elmo was still yelping in a state of full-on agitation. Yelling Geraldine's name provoked no response.

'OK, I'll give it a go.' Ellie slid her arms out of her pink cotton cardigan, handed it to Zack and eyed the dog flap in Geraldine's back door. *Think yourself thin, think yourself thin.*

'Can you get through?' Zack was looking doubtful; it was a flap designed for a medium-sized dog.

'Thanks for that vote of confidence.' She took a swipe at him. 'If I get stuck, it's your fault for buying so many doughnuts. And no videoing this and putting it on YouTube. Right.' She kicked off her shoes. 'You'll have to do the thing with the sensor.'

Was this wise? If she did get stuck, would the fire brigade have to be called and the entire door dismantled? Might she have to be crowbarred out? Ellie knelt down and waited for Zack to disconnect the sensor from Elmo's collar. He held it right next to the flap, enabling her to push it open.

'You'd better not be laughing at me.' No longer able to see him, Ellie went through arms first and began wiggling her shoulders through the tight bit.

Above her, Zack said, 'Wouldn't dream of it.'

He was definitely laughing. She prayed her skirt hadn't ridden up. OK, halfway through now. Hips and bottom next. It was going to be a tight squeeze. Bracing herself, Ellie said, 'And if I can't manage this, don't go calling the fire brigade. Just leave me here until I've lost enough weight.'

But she eventually got through. Just. As she scrambled to her feet, it occurred to her that they may have overreacted. Geraldine had probably gone out to visit a friend. Either that or she was upstairs having a bath or an afternoon nap, and Elmo had been doing his Superdog-to-the-rescue impression for a laugh.

'Geraldine?' She raised her voice as Elmo dived in through the dog flap behind her. 'Hello? *Geraldine?*'

And then she heard Geraldine, very faintly, calling out, 'Ellie? Thank God. I'm up here.'

Ellie turned, unlocked and unbolted the kitchen door, and opened it to let Zack in. 'She's upstairs.'

They followed Elmo up to the top floor. Geraldine was lying in the doorway to the bedroom, a curled-up copy of *World Medicine* magazine to the right of her and her walking stick to the left.

'The cavalry's arrived.' She managed a faint smile at the sight of them. 'Don't touch me. I've fractured my right femur.'

Zack was already calling an ambulance. Elmo licked Geraldine's hand and she fondled his ears with gratitude. 'Clever boy. Did you bark at them in Morse code?'

'Put it this way, forcing him to watch all those *Lassie* DVDs really paid off.' Ellie knelt on the carpet beside her. 'How did it happen?'

'There was a massive spider up on the wall and I tried to splat it with my rolled-up magazine. But it scuttled off to one side. So I went to whack it again.' Geraldine sounded exasperated. 'That's when I lost my balance and came crashing down like a bloody tree.'

'That's karma for you,' said Ellie.

'You're telling me. I've been lying here for the last twenty minutes and it's been smirking down at me the whole time.'

Ellie followed the line of Geraldine's gaze and let out a squeak; the spider was indeed up there, malevolent-looking and measuring a good three inches in diameter.

Zack ended the call. 'Right, ambulance is on its way.'

'Thanks for coming to the rescue. Oh Lord,' Geraldine sighed. 'They're going to cart me off to the hospital.' She looked at Ellie. 'Could you be an angel and help me get a bag packed?'

'No problem. Zack, kill the spider, would you?'

'What, and end up like Geraldine? Let him live. I'll go down and keep an eye out for the ambulance.'

When he'd left them, Geraldine murmured with amusement, 'Just like my husband. Scared of them but would die rather than admit it.'

For a precarious moment Ellie found herself wavering; could she confide in Geraldine? Then she saw the mischievous glint in the older woman's eye and came crashing back to her senses. Sharing her feelings for Zack would clearly be insane; Geraldine had *no* self-control.

'Don't worry about Elmo. We'll take care of him.' Rising from her kneeling position and mentally zipping her mouth shut, Ellie said, 'Tell me where your overnight bag is and what you want me to pack.'

Zack accompanied Geraldine to University College Hospital and waited with her until she'd been seen in the ER, then admitted onto a ward. Surgery to pin and stabilize the intracapsular fracture was scheduled to be carried out first thing tomorrow and the pain was under control. As he made his way home, a text came through from Ellie:

> *Travel schedule sorted, meetings rearranged. Taking Elmo for a run, back by six. Give Geraldine our love xx*

The kisses, needless to say, were for Geraldine, not for him. But that hadn't stopped him looking at the text three times already. On a whim, as the taxi reached Primrose Hill and Regents Park Road, Zack told the cab driver to stop. The hill itself was bathed in sunshine and there were still plenty of people about. Heading up to the top, he kept a look out for Ellie. This afternoon he could have sworn her attitude towards him had changed; just thinking about the incredible longing he'd experienced brought it all back. He'd so badly wanted to kiss her, had been right on the verge of doing it, right up to the moment when Elmo had come crashing through the dog flap.

And then he saw her. Having reached the brow of the hill, Zack saw a flash of pink. There they were, Ellie with her long dark hair flying and Elmo's tail wagging in joyful anticipation as she hurled his red ball into the air and he launched himself after it. Ellie waited until he'd reached the ball before haring off in the opposite direction. By the time Elmo caught up with her, she was lying on the grass pretending to be asleep. With a giant leap, he landed on her stomach and dropped the ball on her chest. She doubled up laughing and lifted him into the air, causing Elmo to bark with delight and paddle his legs furiously. The next moment Ellie had thrown his ball and the two of them were off again, chasing after it.

She had no idea he was there. Zack didn't want to move. He could stand here and watch her forever; her complete lack of self-consciousness was irresistible. Gripped by a surge of longing, he made up his mind. After the events of today, surely he had the perfect excuse to invite her back to the house for dinner. They could talk about what had happened to Geraldine, discuss the care of Elmo in the weeks ahead, maybe recapture the moment that had felt as if it might have been about to happen before bloody Elmo had come bursting into the kitchen and interrupted them. When he'd checked with Ellie earlier that she could look after Elmo if he was held up at the hospital, she had said it was fine, she wasn't seeing Joe tonight.

Which could only be good news. Wherever Joe might be this evening without her, it served him right.

⎯⎯

'Hey!' Spotting the figure heading her way, Ellie waved wildly with both arms.

When they reached each other she said, 'I can't believe you're making me do this.'

'Don't be like that. It'll be great.'

'It won't be great! You've already told me it's going to be horrendous. You just want me there to share the agony.'

But Ellie was smiling; she couldn't help herself. Roo had called her twenty minutes ago, desperate for support. Brian, in his late forties and terminally dandruffy, was the kind of person you really hoped wouldn't sit next to you on the bus. A fellow volunteer at the charity shop, he was a nonstop chatterer and somewhat eccentric; he also drove everyone insane with his misplaced enthusiasm for... well, just about everything you could possibly think of.

'OK, it's true,' Roo admitted. 'But he doesn't have any friends. He joined this amateur dramatics society to try and make some, and it didn't work. What could I say?'

It was the opening night of Brian's first play, being held in a crumbling church hall in Crouch End. This afternoon he'd proudly presented Roo with two tickets for the performance. 'They're his friends and family tickets,' Roo had explained during her begging phone call, 'and there's no one else he can invite. Please, *please*, say you'll come with me.'

Vowing to become a good person was all very admirable, but Roo wasn't above taking other people down with her. 'Because if it's just me,' she'd pointed out, 'Brian might get it into his head that it's some kind of date. And he'll insist on walking me home afterwards.'

Ellie shielded her eyes from the sun, watching as Elmo wrestled playfully with a pair of terriers for control of his ball and ended up rolling down the grassy slope. 'What time do we have to be there?'

'Eight o'clock, curtain up. But Brian says if we want good seats to get there by seven.' Roo was tilting her head to one side. 'Now is this who I think it is?'

Ellie followed the direction of her gaze and felt her stomach give a little squeeze. Seeing Zack unexpectedly had that effect on her.

Then again, it had also been known to happen when it wasn't unexpected.

She nodded. 'That's Zack.'

'I guessed. And that's what I call a body.' Roo raised a mischievous eyebrow. 'Don't look so shocked. I'm not going to do anything.' She grinned. 'Just pointing it out, in case you hadn't noticed.'

In case she hadn't noticed. Oh God, wouldn't *that* have made life easier. 'Hi!' said Ellie over-brightly as Zack approached them. 'How's Geraldine?'

'Pretty good, all things considered.' He nodded at Roo. 'You're Roo? We meet at last. I've heard all about you.'

'Same.' Roo perched her sunglasses on the top of her head and beamed at Zack. The next moment Elmo came racing up, his tongue lolling and his tail going like a propeller.

'You said you were bringing him for a walk,' said Zack, 'so I thought I'd meet you here.'

'And am I glad you did,' Roo exclaimed. 'If you hadn't made it back in time, Ellie might have said she had to stay at home and look after your dog. But you're here, so it's OK, we can go out tonight!'

'So much for my get-out clause.' Ellie looked at Zack. 'Thanks.'

There was the tiniest of pauses. Then Zack said, 'Where are you going?'

'To the theatre. To see a play. It's going to be awful.'

'We don't know that for sure,' said Roo.

'We kind of do.' Ellie shook her head. 'You said Brian was playing the part of a singing Spanish juggler. You also told me he's pale blue, tone deaf, and can't juggle.'

'Well, we're going and that's that.' Roo put her dark glasses back on. Taking Elmo's lead from Ellie, she handed it to Zack. 'We need to go home and get changed first too. Bye then.' She flashed him another smile. 'See you again sometime.'

'I bet you're jealous.' Ellie rolled her eyes good-naturedly at

Zack. 'If only we'd had a spare ticket you could have joined us, but apparently they're *very* in demand.'

'It's a sell-out.' Roo called over her shoulder as she headed down the hill.

Ellie bent down to ruffle Elmo's ears. 'Bye, sweetie, see you tomorrow.'

And another plan hits the rocks.

'Bye,' said Zack.

Chapter 50

'WE'VE BEEN TRYING TO think of ways to raise money for St Mark's Hospice,' said Yasmin. 'They looked after my auntie before she died last year. It's the most amazing place, but they're desperate for more cash. If they can't reach their target by Christmas they might have to close.'

Roo said, 'That's terrible. *Ow*.' Yasmin was good at leg waxes but not that good. It still hurt.

'Sorry! So anyway, we've decided to have a raffle here at the salon. And seeing as you're one of our celebrity clients, we wondered if you'd donate a prize.'

More pain. Roo flinched. 'Of course I will, but I'm not a celebrity.'

'I know, but you used to be. Maybe you could give us a signed photo or something. Or one of your old stage outfits. Anything really.' Yasmin carried on ripping merrily away at the little hairs on Roo's legs. 'It's just to raise as much money as possible. The last time we held a raffle we raised two hundred and eighty pounds!'

Roo felt bad. She didn't have any stage outfits she could donate. Nobody would want a signed photograph of her. Wasn't there any other way she could help? *Ow*.

'Who else are you asking?'

'Gosh, pretty much everyone! We're offering prizes of sessions here at the salon, obviously. And quite a few of the clients have offered to bring in boxes of chocolates, homemade cakes, that kind of thing. Everyone's being great,' said Yasmin. 'They all want to chip in.'

Which was all very lovely but it wasn't going to save a hospice on the brink of closure. Roo said, 'Who are your other celebrity clients?'

'Well…' Yasmin pulled a face, 'we're not really the kind of salon that gets celebrities.'

Jackie, ever the optimist, said, 'Gary Barlow walked past our window the other week.'

'That doesn't really count though,' said Yasmin.

'Ooh, and there was that woman who used to be a weathergirl on TV. Thingywhatsit.' Jackie made twirly can't-remember-the-name gestures with her pen. 'Remember? She got huge. Came in for a body wrap and we ran out of wrap.'

'Funnily enough,' Yasmin carried on waxing, 'she never came back after that.'

Jackie thought for a moment. 'How about that actress who always used to play mad women? Thelma someone. Knobbly elbows and funny teeth. Oh, I've just remembered, she moved to Canada.'

Yasmin rolled her eyes. 'Is it any wonder our celebrity clients emigrate?'

'Whoops, sorry! But we've still got Ceecee Milton!'

Another blast from the past. Roo had met Ceecee Milton a couple of times, back in the day when they had both been experiencing success. Like herself, Ceecee had briefly risen and enjoyed her moment in the celebrity spotlight before fading back again into sepia-toned obscurity. This had largely been down to the fact that her husband, a sleazy operator who doubled as her manager, had managed to alienate most of the big guns in the business. You couldn't fault Ceecee's powerful voice, but when each booking had to be made through someone who created difficulties and complained nonstop about every last detail, it became easier to book someone else for the job. And so another promising career had bitten the dust.

'Who else is there?' said Roo.

'Um, that's it, really.' Yasmin looked apologetic.

'Just me and Ceecee?' Oh dear. Talk about scraping the bottom of the celebrity barrel. 'A couple of old has-beens.'

'She's really nice, though. She'll definitely give us something good for the raffle.'

Paranoid, Roo wondered what that meant. Was Yasmin implying that Ceecee was nicer than her?

'I'll give you something too. I just don't know what yet.' *Ow.* 'Is she still married?'

'Not to that awful one. She dumped him a while back. Got herself a lovely new husband now.' Yasmin broke into a smile. 'See? It can happen. There's hope for us all.'

The rain was hammering down as Roo emerged from the tube station. Within seconds her hair was plastered to her head and her T-shirt had turned transparent. People in the street were actually recoiling at the sight of her, which possibly meant she looked a bit deranged, but Roo didn't care. Her body was exhausted but her heart was singing, her brain fizzy with excitement. It was ten to nine in the morning, she'd had no sleep whatsoever, and this was something she had never experienced before. At least, not without the aid of alcohol or other mind-altering substances.

'Oh my goodness.' Yasmin, arriving to open up the salon, discovered her waiting in the doorway. 'What's happened? Are you OK?'

'I'm great.' Roo wiped her sodden hair away from her face and followed her inside. 'I've been up all night. Writing.'

Yasmin passed her a towel. 'Here, dry yourself off. I didn't know you were doing that now. What is it, an autobiography?'

'Not that kind of writing. I've done a song. It's really good.' Roo shook her head and tried again. 'Actually it's not, it's better than that. It's brilliant.'

'Ooh, how fab! Sing it to me, then!'

At the best of times Roo's singing voice resembled a cat in a vet's waiting room. 'I can't. I need Ceecee to do it. Can you give me her number?'

Yasmin was clearly puzzled. 'Ceecee Milton? Why?'

'Because this is the best song I've ever written. I can't quite believe I've done it, but I have. And I want us to put it out as a charity single,' said Roo. 'For your hospice. If we do this properly, we can make it happen. In a big way.'

'Really? Seriously? Oh my God, how?'

'Scam. Beg. Use every contact we have.' Roo's head was positively bursting with possibilities. 'And get a buzz going.'

'How do we do that?'

'Well, I think mainly we want to use a mixture of rumor and gossip and technology.' Were her eyes shining? Roo thought they probably were. 'And some truly massive lies.'

Ellie had never seen anything like it. Summoned to a townhouse in St John's Wood, it was eight in the evening by the time she arrived. The huge extension at the back of the house had been turned into a recording studio, there were technical types doing technical things at the mixing desks, and the buzz in the air was tangible. Roo was there at the center of things, running on Diet Coke and adrenaline. Having pulled every string she could conceivably lay her hands on, she had brought together a team of experts to weave their magic. Musicians, music producers, and backing singers were milling around the studio, listening and contributing and contacting others who might be able to help their cause. And there was Yasmin with her baby son on her hip, chatting to statuesque Ceecee Milton, who was black and beautiful and balancing her own baby daughter on hers.

'Hello!' Spotting her and beckoning Ellie over, Yasmin said, 'Can you believe all this is happening? This is Ceecee, by the way.'

'Hi there.' Ceecee had a wonderful smile. 'You must be the one with the invisible baby.'

'Sorry about that.' Ellie glanced at Yasmin. 'The good thing is, the nappies are invisible too.' She paused to listen as someone flicked a switch and the opening bars of music filled the room. 'This is just amazing.'

'Wait till you hear the whole thing.' The music stopped. 'Ceecee's voice is fantastic. I can't get over how they've done it all in one day. And the track itself...'

Someone raised their hand for silence, the music began again, and everyone listened intently. Within thirty seconds Ellie knew just how special it was. Ceecee's heartbreaking vocals were making the little hairs on her arms stand on end. As the song continued, the backing singers joined in and Ceecee's own voice began to soar. 'You're the light in my life... you're everything... when it's dark you're my light, you're my world, all I believe in...'

Oh God, there was such emotion in the words, Ellie had to turn away. She was going to cry, how embarrassing. Fumbling in her bag, she surreptitiously pulled out a mini pack of Kleenex. The next moment Yasmin was in need of a tissue as well. Gazing around, Ellie saw they weren't the only ones. The music, haunting and powerful and emotive, was impossible to resist; it gripped you by the throat and didn't let go. Grown men were standing there with tears in their eyes. Yasmin's son Ben, blithely indifferent, wriggled and pulled her hair and kicked one of his booties off. The skinny man with the goatee who had been at the recording desk put his arm around Roo's shoulders and gave her a squeeze as the song reached its crescendo...

Ellie only knew that such an extreme reaction to a song you were hearing for the first time was a rare thing. When the final notes had died away, there was absolute silence for a couple of seconds. Then Ceecee dabbed her eyes and said huskily, 'Damn, I'm good,' and the studio erupted with whoops and cheers and wild applause.

In a daze, Roo said, 'We've done it. Have we? I think we've done it.' She sank down on to a conker-brown leather sofa and buried her face in her hands.

All around her, people continued to celebrate. Within thirty seconds Roo was fast asleep.

By eleven o'clock the video had been completed. It hadn't taken long at all. Quite simply, someone was dispatched to the local Chinese takeaway for a pile of brown paper bags. A camcorder then recorded the process of the track being laid down while everyone wore bags over their heads with just eye holes cut in them to avert unfortunate accidents. Ceecee and the backing singers wore them too. Every last member of the team would be anonymous.

By midnight the video had been edited together and posted on YouTube. Next, the whispering campaign began. Everyone posted links on websites, Twitter, Myspace and Facebook, dropping hints as to who might be involved: Bono, Jay-Z, Elton John, Beyoncé... Next, they called in favors from journalists, TV people, other music contacts, anyone they could possibly think of. Each person contacted was asked to listen to the song just once, then spread the word that it was a) for charity and b) the track of the year.

By one o'clock the word was already spreading like wildfire, the YouTube clip had been viewed almost half a million times, and speculation as to who could be behind it was rife. Goatee man had to contact Bono, Jay-Z, Elton, and Beyoncé and ask them to remain enigmatic, neither confirming nor denying involvement in order to promote the cause.

Ceecee took her soundly sleeping daughter home at one thirty. Yasmin had left before midnight with Ben. At two o'clock Ellie put a hand on Roo's shoulder and gently shook her awake.

'Hey, there's a taxi outside if you want to come home. Or Denny says you can stay here if you like.'

Roo blinked up at her, momentarily confused. Then she swung

her legs off the sofa and hauled herself upright. 'No, it's OK, I'll come back with you.' She rubbed her eyes and peered at her watch. 'I'm working in the shop tomorrow morning. Mustn't be late.'

Chapter 51

HAD IT ONLY BEEN ten days? Roo was incredulous; was it actually possible that it could all have happened so fast? Eleven days ago the song hadn't existed, not even in her own head, yet now it was known to millions, maybe even billions of people all over the world. Talk about surreal.

Roo was in the green room waiting to be called out on set. Live TV was always scary. Well, it hadn't been years ago because she'd generally been off her head and it had all been a laugh, but doing it sober now was in another league altogether. How could you ever be completely sure what might come out of your mouth next?

Logically you knew it wouldn't happen, but there was always that deep-down niggling fear that you might gaze into the camera and start shouting, 'Fuck, fuck, bastard-bollocks-fuck!'

'Everything OK?' One of the friendly runners came up to her. 'Are you sure you wouldn't like a glass of wine?'

'No thanks.' This was an enormous lie, obviously; she'd love a glass of wine. She just wasn't going to have one. Especially since she'd already broken one vow; trying to explain earlier to the bewildered makeup girl that she didn't wear makeup had been a waste of breath.

'Oh no, you have to let me do your face! This is TV!' The girl had stood firm. 'You don't want to look like something that's just been dug up, do you? We can't let you do that—you'd scare the viewers!'

Vanity had vied with exhaustion. Aware that she was promoting a worthy cause and should be making a good impression, Roo had caved in. Just this once wouldn't hurt, would it?

And now that her heinous crime had been committed, it was nice, she was able to admit, to feel pretty again.

The door opened and Ceecee, with no such qualms, came back from the makeup department. In her crimson velvet dress and glossy lipstick to match, she was looking glorious. Batting her shimmering gold eyelids and extravagant false eyelashes at Roo, she did a show-off twirl and said, 'Look at us. For a couple of old rejects, I think we've scrubbed up pretty good.'

'Well, I have,' said Roo. 'You're still looking a bit ropey, if you ask me.'

'Girl, will you look at these eyelashes? I'm smoking hot and you know it!' Blissfully happy in her second marriage, Ceecee shimmied her generous hips. 'I'm telling you, my Nathan isn't going to know what's hit him when I get home tonight.'

In five minutes they were due on. Tomorrow they were booked, along with Yasmin, to do a series of newspaper and magazine interviews. So much for the idea that everyone involved would remain anonymous; that had lasted all of four days. But that length of time had been enough to serve its purpose, piquing the interest of millions and instigating a torrent of speculation. By the time they'd been unmasked—OK, debagged—their work had been done. 'The Light In My Life' had shot to the top of the download chart. The YouTube clip had been viewed seven million times and the song itself was being ranked up there alongside some of the all-time greats. When it became apparent that it hadn't been written and performed by superstars, the general public decided they loved it all the more. This week it was at number one, outselling all other singles many times over.

Already Roo and Ceecee were under pressure to fly to the US to appear over there on the major chat shows. The last few days had been a complete whirlwind. Roo had no idea what would happen next; all she knew was that when the news of her involvement had broken, nobody had been able to get in or out of the charity shop on account of the vast number of paparazzi milling around outside. Nor had the situation improved when the staff discovered she was raising money for a rival charity and not their own. Then people started cramming into the shop, taking photos on their mobiles, and asking Roo for her autograph, and the manageress had lost her temper. This level of disruption simply couldn't be tolerated.

And that was it, she was ordered to collect her things and leave. Sacked on the spot.

From a charity shop. That was the thanks you got for trying to be a good person.

As always, despite her best efforts, Roo found her thoughts drawn back to Todd. What was he doing? Who was he with? Were he and Lisa curled up together on a sofa right now, watching the TV? When she appeared on the screen, would Todd mentally compare her with the perky, pretty little math genius in his arms and thank his lucky stars he'd made the right choice?

Would perky Lisa smile up at him and say, 'So that's her, is it?' Whilst thinking: *Yay, I'm cuter than she is.*

OK, block that, don't think about it now. On the TV screens, the first interview was in the process of being wrapped up and an assistant with a headset was making her way across the green room towards her. Time to go.

———

Ellie had been shopping in Oxford Street searching for something she could wear to Zack's sister's wedding. In a hurry to get back to watch the show, she'd ended up buying three outfits without trying them on. The plan had been to buy something peacock blue, to go with her newest shoes, so of course she'd come home with a crimson wrap dress, a pale gray top and skirt with silver lace overlay, and a bottle-green dress and matching swirly jacket with a shot-silk fuchsia-pink lining.

Because choosing what to wear to a wedding was never straight-forward, was it?

Having drawn the living room curtains and switched on the TV, she stripped down to her bra and knickers and tried the wrap dress first. As expected, it was OK but a bit safe. And leaning forward caused the crossover bit to gape, which wasn't safe but wasn't really what you wanted at a wedding either.

No. Back in the bag.

Silver lacy outfit next. Oh crikey, how was it that you could see something in a shop and think it would look great on, when in reality it made you look like Dr Ruth?

Ellie peeled off the top and skirt and put them back in the second carrier. Sometimes she made really bad decisions when it came to choosing clothes. Right. She picked up the third and final outfit and prayed it would do. Bugger, the dress had the kind of zip at the back that you needed to be double-jointed to do up.

And there, just when you didn't want him, was Jamie, stretched out across the sofa with an arm behind his head.

'Taking a lot of trouble over this,' he observed.

'It's a wedding. I want to look nice.' Having stepped into the dress, she got the zip up as far as she could. Oh, for heaven's sake. She was a size twelve. If this was a size twelve, she was a pencil.

Jamie pulled a face. 'Maybe it'll be better with the jacket.'

As if. She put the jacket on and gazed at herself in the mirror above the fireplace.

'You look like one of those Slimmers of the Year,' he said helpfully, 'wearing your old clothes to show how much weight you've lost.'

'Oh God.'

'Good colors though.' As if that made everything better.

'Disaster,' said Ellie. 'I'll have to take the whole lot back.' It was so frustrating. 'What am I going to *wear*?'

'How about my favorite? The one we bought on our honeymoon.'

'I've worn it before. When we went to Claridge's.'

'Did we? I don't remember that.' Jamie's eyes were sparkling with mischief; he was doing it on purpose.

'When I went with Zack.' Ellie eased herself out of the way-too-big dress and jacket.

'And does that mean you can't wear it again?'

'No. I'd just like to wear something different.'

He looked mystified. 'Why?'

'Because we don't all want to go around in the same clothes all the time, wearing them until they disintegrate.' To make her point, she eyed his frayed jeans with one tanned knee showing through a series of horizontal rips.

'It might be that.' Jamie conceded the point with a grin. 'Or it could be because you don't want to wear your honeymoon dress while you're having a weekend away with another man.'

Was he right? Was that the real reason? Ellie collected up the carrier bags of clothes and marched past him. Dumping them in the hallway, she went into the bedroom and returned wearing a sweatshirt and shorts. On the TV, the ad break was over and the second half of the chat show was about to start. 'OK, you have to be quiet now,' she announced. 'I want to watch this. Roo's going to be on.'

'You mean you'd rather watch her than listen to me?' Jamie pretended to look affronted. He'd always liked being the center of attention.

'She's real,' said Ellie. 'And you're not.'

'…From has-beens to heroes!' Vince Torrance, who prided himself on his cheeky chappie persona and liberal use of irony, was making his introduction. 'From lucked-out losers to record-smashing sensations! From the gutter to the stars… and now right here in this studio… ladies and gentlemen, please welcome Ceecee Milton and Daisy Deeva!'

At home in Primrose Hill, with a can of Fanta and a big packet of Kettle chips to hand, Ellie sat watching the show. Beneath that glib, shiny, exterior Vince Torrance was actually an intelligent man and an astute interviewer.

Reaching across the sofa for her phone, she pressed the call button. When it was answered, she said, 'Are you watching?'

He knew it was on. She'd texted him earlier. 'No,' said Todd.

'Put it on.'

'What am I, a complete masochist?' But he gave a giving-in sigh, not an annoyed one. The next moment she heard the sound of the TV echoing down the line.

'Doesn't she look fantastic?' Incredibly, Roo had been persuaded to wear makeup tonight.

'Yes, she does. Just explain something. How is this supposed to make me feel better?'

'Sshh, I can't hear what they're saying.' Ellie returned her attention to the TV, where Vince was making jokey comments about Roo's time working in the charity shop.

'…and this outfit you're wearing tonight.' He jokingly indicated Roo's charcoal jacket and skinny white trousers. 'I'm assuming that's where you picked these things up.'

Roo nodded. 'Yes, I did.'

'Ah! OK.' Wrong-footed, he laughed. 'Well, that's admirable. So forgive me, but this is quite a transformation for you. In the old days you were a pretty wild child, I think it's safe to say.'

'Oh, I was.'

'And what's brought this change about?'

'I didn't like myself very much,' said Roo. 'I decided it was time to become a nicer person.'

'And now? Do you think you are nicer?' Vince looked genuinely interested.

Roo rubbed her fingers through her spiky white-blond hair and shrugged. 'I hope so. I think I am, yes.'

'And you've written this phenomenal song, with all the proceeds going to St Mark's Hospice. That's something to be incredibly proud of. You must be over the moon, surely.'

Clearly embarrassed, Roo shifted in her chair. 'Well, yes, we're thrilled with the way it's taken off.'

'So is this the happiest time of your life?' Vince was watching her closely, pushing. 'It has to be! You must be unbelievably happy!'

For a moment Roo's huge brown eyes swam with tears; she tilted her head back, gazed up at the ceiling, then back again at Vince. 'The hospice was going to have to close down. Now that isn't going to happen. It wasn't just me; it was Ceecee and everyone else involved in the campaign. And it worked; we've got everything we wanted and more.' Her smile was bright but anyone who really knew her could see that it wasn't quite reaching her eyes. 'Of course I'm happy,' said Roo.

In exasperated unison into their respective phones, Ellie and Todd shouted at the TV screen, 'Liar!'

Chapter 52

THERE WERE DRINKS IN the green room after the show. The first guest, a comedian, was taking center stage, knocking back vodka at a rate of knots and being noisily hilarious.

'Hi, you all right?' Vince approached Roo, who was leaning against a wall checking her mobile. Lots of messages but none from anyone she was in any hurry to call back.

'I'm good, thanks.'

'Sorry about the clothes thing. I assumed they were designer.'

'No problem.' Roo put her phone away.

'Exactly. Just made people love you more.' He paused. 'Are you sure you're OK?'

'I'm fine.'

'You're going to be a star again. From now on you'll be able to do anything you want.'

Roo gave a noncommittal shrug; the last thing she wanted was to be a star again. What's more, it wouldn't enable her to do anything she wanted.

'Hey, how about you and me slipping away?' Vince's fingers were running lightly up her spine in what was presumably a seductive manner. He gave her his trademark saucy grin and moved closer to her ear. 'Where d'you want to go? Anywhere you like. Can I just say something?' he murmured. 'You are one gorgeous lady.' And here it was, a shining example of exactly why she didn't want to return to that world. The old Roo would have been off with him like a shot, neither noticing nor caring that he was a slimy character with a huge ego. The only person Vince Torrance loved was himself; spend the night in his bed and it would be all over Twitter in the morning.

And once upon a time I would have found that funny.

'No thanks.' A great wave of shame at the way her old self had behaved swept over her. 'In fact, I think I'm going to head off now.'

'Oh hey, no, don't do that. You can't leave… the evening's just getting started.'

His hand had moved to her waist now. Roo extricated herself with a sideways shrug and said, 'Mine isn't. I'm going home.'

'Fine, then.' Evidently not planning on bursting into tears about it, Vince said, 'I thought you'd've been up for a bit of fun, but never mind. Tom'll organize your car.'

He beckoned to Tom, gave her a perfunctory kiss on the cheek, and headed over to the comedian who was still holding court in the center of the room.

Roo felt a smidgen better about herself. She put down her fizzy water and reached for her bag as Tom, the transport organizer, came trotting over.

At the same time, she'd never felt lonelier in her life.

The car rounded the corner into Nevis Street and pulled up outside Roo's house. It was ten thirty, a crescent moon hung in the sky at the end of the road, and the stars were out tonight in force. Roo climbed out onto the pavement, thanked the driver, and watched him leave.

Was Ellie at home? Was she awake? Her living-room lights were on but Roo had sent her a text twenty minutes ago saying she was on her way home and hadn't received a reply.

The feeling of overwhelming loneliness was back; it was like being smothered in black velvet. Roo took out her phone again, ready to ring Ellie, then stopped as she saw movement at the window. The curtain was pulled back and Ellie appeared. She waved, flung the window open, and leaned out.

'Hey, I know you! You're that songwriter person I was watching on telly earlier.'

Roo felt herself relax. How could she have got through the last couple of months without Ellie? And to think that if she hadn't left her key in the lock that day, they might never have met. Plenty of people in big cities lived opposite each other for years and didn't so much as say hello.

Then again, if it hadn't been for Ellie, she would never have got to know Todd either. OK, never mind that now. *Don't think about Todd.*

Roo shielded her eyes from the glare of the street lamp. 'Was I OK?'

'You were great. But there was one thing.' Ellie rested her elbows on the windowsill. 'Why isn't this the happiest time of your life?'

Roo had been on her way across the street. She stopped in the middle of the road.

'What?'

'You heard. Except we both know the answer. It's because you're still crazy about Todd.'

Roo's stomach scrunched itself into a tight knot. This wasn't fair; she wasn't up to another lecture, not now, not tonight.

'Don't look at me like that.' Ellie's voice softened when Roo didn't say anything. 'Oh, Roo, haven't you punished yourself enough now?'

Roo's eyes began to prickle. She bit her lip.

'Listen, you did some bad things,' Ellie went on. 'But now you've done good. More than enough good. I *promise.*'

A single tear slid down Roo's cheek and dripped off her chin. *More than enough good;* had the scales tipped in her favor, had she actually redressed the balance at last? She gazed up at Ellie and said hopefully, 'Do you really think I have?'

'Yes.' Ellie nodded. 'I do.'

For the first time Roo found herself able to acknowledge that maybe, just maybe, Ellie was right. She shifted from one foot to the other. But there was still the matter of Todd's girlfriend; it wasn't as if she could just change her mind.

'OK, this is crazy, why am I standing out here like an idiot?' She continued across the street. 'Open the door, I'm coming up.'

'No, you can't.' Ellie's voice stopped her in her tracks. 'Sorry, but I'm so shattered, and Zack's making me go in extra-early tomorrow. I just have to go to bed.'

'Oh.' Stung by the unexpected rejection, Roo said, 'OK.' *Five minutes wouldn't hurt, surely?*

'Hang on, though.' Ellie was straightening up. 'I've got something for you.'

'What is it?'

'Wait a sec.' She disappeared from view. Still feeling put out, Roo guessed she'd been making cupcakes again. A few seconds later, Ellie's front door opened.

And there was Todd. Standing there, watching her. With something like determination in his eyes.

Oh God…

Roo was unable to move. She was having trouble staying upright. Now he was closing the short distance between them and she was mouthing helplessly like a goldfish, which probably wasn't attractive.

'Sshh.' Todd shook his head. 'Don't say anything. Stop it,' he warned as a kind of strangled croak found its way out. 'Not a word.'

But Roo managed it. She had to. 'Wh-where's Lisa?'

'Lisa.' Another shake. 'Don't worry. She's gone.'

Gone, yes, thank you…

The next moment Todd reached her and seamlessly drew her into his arms. His face, the face she hadn't been able to put out of her mind for so long, was now inches from hers. In the glow from the street lamp she could see the amber flecks in his gray eyes, the way his eyelashes curled at the corners, the tiny scar below his left eyebrow. And then there was his mouth… oh God, would it really be all right?

'Come here,' Todd murmured, sliding one hand behind her neck. And then she *was* there. Their mouths met at last and she gave a tiny uncontrollable shiver, because this… *this* was the kiss she'd spent so long waiting for. Except now she was messing it up, making a complete hash of it, because the emotion was too much and she was about to burst into tears, and if there were two things you really couldn't do simultaneously, it was kiss and cry…

Roo drew back in the nick of time as a great braying sob broke out. Anyone listening would think there was a donkey loose in the street.

'Hey, hey.' Half-laughing, Todd held on to her. 'I'm not that bad.'

'S-sorry. I'm just so h-h-happy.' Months of pent-up tension had to escape somehow. She clung to him, overwhelmed and overcome with emotion. 'I can't believe you're here…'

'Me neither.' He was gently rubbing her arms as if she was an accident victim in shock. 'This wasn't planned, you know. Ellie called and invited me over. You weren't supposed to find out I was upstairs.'

Roo kissed him quickly on the mouth then smiled and kissed him again. It was OK, the explosive crying jag had passed. She turned to look up at the window. It was closed now, Ellie having beaten a diplomatic retreat.

'I love that girl,' she said.

Todd grinned. 'So do I.'

'What happened with Lisa?' She needed to know; had there been a huge falling out or had the relationship simply run its course? Had Lisa ended it, or Todd?

'Ah yes, Lisa. The math teacher,' said Todd. 'The one with the unreliable car.'

Roo held her breath. Had he realized there was only one woman for him, and Lisa wasn't it?

'She disappeared,' Todd went on seriously. 'Back inside Ellie's head.'

It took a couple of moments for this to sink in.

'You mean it wasn't true?' Roo searched his face.

'None of it was true. Ellie made her up. She invented the whole thing. Personally,' said Todd, 'I'm never going to believe a word she says again.'

'Nor me.' The irony was that if it hadn't involved Todd and another woman, she would have loved the story of how they'd met.

'But she was right about you not being happy. She saw it on the TV. Well, we both did.'

Roo stroked her fingers wonderingly through his hair. 'And she made me realize I'd done enough. At last. So she's quite clever really.'

'I love you.'

'Me too.' She leaned into him. Their noses were practically touching. How many kisses did they have ahead of them? It was a giddying thought. And not only kisses, either…

'I'm so proud of you.' Todd's expression softened. 'You're amazing.'

'I made some horrible mistakes.' She could feel the heat emanating from his body.

'Everyone makes mistakes. But you stopped and did something about it. Most people don't bother.'

At that moment a white BMW turned into Nevis Street, catching them in its headlights. As it passed Roo and Todd, windows were buzzed down and they found themselves subjected to a good-natured chorus of whistles, helpful comments, and bawdy cheers.

'And to think this used to be a decent neighborhood,' Roo tut-tutted. 'It's going right downhill.'

'On the other hand, they do have a point,' said Todd.

Together they turned and made their way across the street to her house. Roo linked her fingers through his and gave them a squeeze. She could hardly wait.

Aloud she said, 'They certainly do.'

Chapter 53

IT WAS THE LAST week in September and Ellie had that squiggly going-on-holiday feeling in her stomach. The Indian summer had timed itself to perfection, there wasn't a cloud in the luminous blue sky, and she and Zack were on their way to Perranporth. It was happening at last and the hardest part was containing her excitement. If Zack had any idea how much she'd been looking forward to this… well, it would scare the living daylights out of him. He'd probably lean across in a panic, fling open the passenger door of the Mercedes, and push her out.

But he didn't know and he wasn't going to find out. Ellie gave a little wriggle in her seat and sat back, enjoying the feel of the sun on her face and watching the scenery whoosh by as they sped down the M4. Elmo was asleep in the back of the car. Geraldine, out of hospital now and recuperating nicely, had gone to stay with her sister in Exeter. Roo and Todd were so besotted they could barely tear their hands off each other; they were like a couple of magnets who couldn't physically stand to be apart. Best of all, Todd's mum and Roo had met and instantly hit it off. Maria was as crazy about her son's new girlfriend as Todd was, and plans were already in place for a mega party to introduce Roo to everyone she knew.

They'd left Berkshire behind them. Behind her, Elmo was snuffling in his sleep, paws twitching as he chased London pigeons in his dreams. He was such a city dog. Ellie took a packet of gumdrops out of her bag and offered them to Zack. 'Want one?'

'Thanks. Can you find me a green one?'

'Green? What, seriously?' She winced. 'Are you sure?'

'Yes. Why?'

'Nobody likes green! They're the ones you only eat when everything else is gone. You have to be desperate.'

'Green's my favorite,' said Zack.

'Well, that makes you officially weird. But also kind of useful to have around.' Ellie found one and passed it over. 'You can have all the yellows too, if you want.'

He glanced across at her. 'Which are Joe's favorites?'

'No idea. I've never offered him a gumdrop.'

'I haven't asked for a while how things are going with you two.'

'Fine.' Ellie helped herself to a red one. They were the best by a mile.

'Did you see him last night?'

She nodded, glad of her sunglasses and the sweet in her mouth. 'Mmm.'

'OK. That's clever.' Zack waited. 'Because on Twitter this morning he posted a photo of himself taken last night at a party at the Beverly Hills Hotel.'

Ellie stopped chewing. Bugger. Zack added helpfully, 'Which is in Beverly Hills.'

Well, it was bound to happen sooner or later. She finished the wine gum and swallowed it. 'I thought you weren't on Twitter.'

'I'm not. Joe sent me an email yesterday. Just a friendly catch-up letting me know how things are going for him in LA. So after that, I was pretty curious.' He said drily, 'You don't need to be on Twitter to look someone up.'

She heaved a sigh and fiddled with the clasp on her bag. It had only been a little white lie, but she always seemed destined to be found out.

'Handy hint,' said Zack. 'In future, probably better to keep the other person in the loop so they know what they should or shouldn't say.'

'I'll make sure I do that.' The scenery was still whipping past; they were over the border into Wiltshire now.

'You could have told me, you know.' She could feel him glancing sideways at her. 'Why didn't you?'

Because I'm crazy about you and I don't want to make a complete fool of myself. Because it's easier if you think I'm seeing someone else.

Aloud, Ellie said, 'It was just… embarrassing.' It was so hard to find the words. 'You never really seemed to approve of me and Joe in the first place. And that felt horrible. It's like when you're sixteen and your mum warns you against getting involved with the local bad boy. So you go ahead and start seeing him, and it turns out he's a nightmare, a total heartbreaker who treats you like rubbish and cops off with other girls behind your back. But you can't bear to admit to your mum that she was right.'

Zack didn't look amused. 'Did Joe break your heart?'

'No, God no! It was lovely while it lasted, it just wasn't right. Well, not right enough.' Would he understand if she said it? Ellie gave it a go. 'He was an eight.'

'I didn't dislike Joe. He was a good guy.' Zack inclined his head. 'He still is. But I could see he wasn't your type.'

'Oh.' She was instantly on the defensive. 'He didn't dump me, you know. He asked me to move with him to LA.'

'So what stopped you?'

'Well, there's this guy I work for. Pretty hopeless character. God knows how he'd manage without me to organize him.' That was better, she'd made him smile. Ellie felt herself relax. 'Honestly? It was never going to happen. You can't move to another continent with someone who isn't a ten.'

Another sidelong glance, another eyebrow raised. 'And what does somebody have to do to be a ten?'

She raised her chin; he was teasing her now. 'They don't have to do anything. Just be themselves, and be right. Go on then, how about you?' Time to turn the tables. 'What makes a girl perfect?'

They were overtaking an oil tanker. The countryside continued to whoosh past. The corners of Zack's mouth began to twitch. 'It helps a lot if she doesn't call me Zacky.'

'OK, brace yourself.' It was five o'clock in the afternoon, the long journey was over, and they were approaching Perranporth. Zack said, 'Sometimes my family can be a bit overwhelming. If my mother asks any impertinent questions, ignore her.'

Ellie's stomach was in knots; she'd thought his family knew she was just a friend. It wasn't until they'd left the M5 behind them that Zack had explained how it had been easier to tell them they were a new couple. 'It just made sense. I don't know why it didn't occur to me before. My family can't keep a secret to save their lives; someone would be bound to tell Mya. Whereas this way, only we know the truth.'

Fear-fueled adrenaline was now zinging like sherbet through Ellie's veins. The old have-to-pretend-we're-a-couple ploy was one she'd seen in romantic films, but only ever at the beginning of the film when the couple genuinely couldn't stand the sight of each other. Having to do it when you had a Kilimanjaro-sized crush on your boss and he really didn't have a crush on you in return was going to be a whole lot trickier to pull off.

Minutes later they turned a corner and there it was, set back from the road at the end of a curving driveway. A long Georgian farmhouse built of pale gray stone and smothered in ivy, with a silvery slate roof and an elaborate old-style conservatory to one side. The gardens surrounding it were spectacular but not off-puttingly formal. The front door to the house was painted emerald green. Almost all the sash windows downstairs were open. Behind the house a pink and white tent was visible. The overall effect was incredibly welcoming…

'Look at those windows flung open,' said Zack. 'Bet you any money my mother's been burning cakes again.'

He brought the car to a halt. Elmo, on Ellie's lap, gave a bark of recognition and began scrabbling his paws against the passenger window. The next moment the bright green front door opened and a horde of people and dogs began spilling out.

Was this how it felt to be Beyoncé?

'Welcome to my family.' Zack's tone was dry. 'Well? Do you think we can do this?'

If Jamie were watching her now, he'd be laughing his head off at the predicament she'd got herself into. The only way, really, was to go for it, plunge in full tilt, and act her socks off.

Ellie grinned at him. 'Zacky, don't panic, it'll be fine.'

'Darling, how lovely, it's been too long!' Teresa McLaren gave her son an enthusiastic hug then turned to Ellie. 'And you must be Ellie. It's even lovelier to meet you!'

Zack said, 'Mum, call her Piglet. Everyone does.'

'No, they don't.' Ellie shook her head at Teresa. 'Ignore him, he just made that up.'

'He's a shocker. But everybody does call me Tizz, so you must too.' Tizz was beaming; in her midsixties, she had flyaway brown hair escaping from a hastily assembled bun, Zack's dark eyes, and a streak of flour across her forehead. She was wearing a stripy blue and white shirt over crumpled jeans and had a rangy, boyish figure. 'We've been so looking forward to this. Now, let's introduce you to everyone…'

'Mum, why are all the windows open?' said Zack.

'You know exactly why, darling. Too much going on, too much chatter, and I forgot to set the timer on the oven.' Tizz was unrepentant. 'I burned the bloody shortbread.'

By eight o'clock Ellie felt as if she'd known Zack's family for years. Well, apart from not having quite got all the names and faces of the younger contingent matched together. The interior of the house was spacious and comfortable, decorated in an eclectic mix of Gothic, suburban, and shabby chic. Zack's father Ken, returning from a trip to the shops for unburnt shortbread and extra supplies of Bombay Sapphire gin, was tall and suntanned with a loud booming laugh, twinkling faded gray eyes, and a big bumpy nose that Zack hadn't inherited.

Zack's sisters were equally welcoming, each of them possessing a recognizable mix of their parents' genes and a raucous sense of humor. Claire was the blondest, Paula the one with the wickedest, loudest laugh. And Steph, due to be married less than forty-eight hours from now, was the most laid-back future bride you could imagine, especially seeing as her twin daughters Joss and Lily were still dead set on wearing trainers with their bridesmaid dresses.

OK, Joss and Lily, identical twins, tick.

Gareth, Steph's about-to-be husband, tick.

Paula's children were Tom and Zaylie, dark straight hair, dark curly hair, tick, tick.

Claire and her husband Paul—no, *Phil*—had two girls and one boy, Suki and Belle and… hang on a sec, Lewis, that was it. Tick, tick, tick.

As for the dogs, they were a boisterous mix of Labradors, mongrels, and terriers, and Ellie wasn't even going to attempt to work out which of them belonged to which branch of the family. It was enough for now that Elmo was having the time of his life.

So far they'd all been down to the beach to give the dogs a run before sundown, before calling in at the best takeaway in Perranporth. Then, back at the house, they'd sat outside on the lit-up terrace eating fish and chips, drinking gin, and discussing the plans for the wedding.

After a while, even better, the conversation turned to Zack when he was young.

'He made me jump over a wall,' Claire relayed with relish, 'and there were ten million stinging nettles on the other side.'

Zack narrowed his eyes. 'Only to pay you back for tipping live crabs into my wellington boots.'

'But you deserved it,' Paula chimed in. 'You'd hidden whitebait in her schoolbag.'

'Oh God, I'd forgotten about the whitebait.' Claire was outraged. 'They stank!'

The children were shrieking with laughter. Joss, sitting at Ellie's feet, squealed, 'I'm going to do the crab thing tomorrow to everyone in my class!'

'You mustn't.' Zack pointed a chip at her. 'Because it's not funny and it's not clever.'

Belle shook her head. 'It is funny, I think. *And* quite clever.'

'At the time it was hilarious.' Zack's expression was solemn. 'The next day when I put on my wellies and got crabs grabbing hold of my toes, not so much.'

'I could do it,' said Zaylie. 'I wouldn't get caught. Everyone thinks I'm nice!'

'I used to like these children.' Zack scooped Zaylie on to his lap and began tickling her bare feet.

Within seconds she was reduced to helpless giggles. 'Is Ellie your girlfriend?'

'Yes, she is, she's my new girlfriend.'

Ellie's breath caught in her throat. *If only.*

'Has she seen you with no clothes on?'

Oh crikey, just the thought of it. Thank goodness the lighting was dim. 'No, I have not.' Above the laughter, Ellie said with horror, 'Yuk, no *way*.'

'I know where there's a picture of Uncle Zack and he's sitting in a paddling pool *naked.*' Zaylie's face was triumphant. 'It's in a book of photographs in Grandma's room, she was showing us the other day. Do you want me to get it and show you?'

'Mum, I thought I told you to throw that one away.' Zack looked pained.

'Oh, darling, how could I? You were so adorable.'

Ellie kept a straight face. 'Was it taken very recently?'

'Very funny. I was two. And you don't want to see it,' said Zack.

Sometimes an opportunity came along that was simply too good to pass up. And she was supposed to be his girlfriend, wasn't she? 'Actually,' Ellie's gaze was innocent, 'I think you'll find I do.'

Chapter 54

'GOODNIGHT, ELLIE, SLEEP WELL. It's so lovely having you here.' Tizz gave her a fond hug and a kiss on the cheek. Claire and Paula had left with their respective families earlier. Steph and Gareth, who were staying until the wedding, had put the twins to bed hours ago. Now it was gone midnight and everyone was heading upstairs.

'Thanks for everything. Night.' Through the open window, they could hear Zack and Gareth outside, giving the dogs a last run around the garden before turning in for the night. If this had been a film, Zack's mum would at this point have said merrily, 'Now, no spare rooms left so I've put you in together! That won't be a problem, will it?' As a result of which, all manner of embarrassing and comical situations would inevitably have ensued.

But this was a big house, a six-bedroomed one, and Tizz had already said earlier, 'Now then, I did ask Zack if you'd be sharing but he said separate rooms. So yours is along here.' Bending her head closer to Ellie's, her tone conspiratorial, she'd added, 'Good move, by the way. Well done, you!'

Meaning she thought Ellie was playing hard to get, treating her new boyfriend mean in order to keep him keen. Which was a guilt trip, but what could you do?

At least this way she'd get a decent night's sleep.

Zack was coming up the staircase five minutes later as she emerged from the bathroom.

'Enjoying yourself?'

'I am.' Just standing there in front of him in her cotton pajamas felt intimate; this was something that hadn't happened since she'd been a flu-infested invalid.

'You're doing a great job.' He was keeping his voice low. 'Apart from the bit with the naked photo.'

He smelled of faded-down aftershave, cognac, and the seaside. Ellie committed the delicious smell to memory. 'The kids thought it was hysterical.'

Having finished settling the dogs into their baskets in the kitchen, Gareth was now on his way upstairs. Ellie's heart began to gallop as Zack moved closer, for all the world as if they were a proper couple on the verge of exchanging a goodnight kiss. Not a peck, something meaningful. For a moment she thought it was actually going to happen. Then, as if noticing Gareth's presence, he pulled back and called out, 'Night.'

'Night, you two.' Gareth ambled past, raised a hand, and disappeared into the room at the far end of the landing. Leaving them alone once more.

OK, this was crazy, she was standing here waiting, *like someone expecting to be kissed.* Dragging herself out of her dopey trance, Ellie took a deliberate step back and said, 'Right, see you tomorrow.'

Zack gazed at her for a long moment before moving away. 'Yes, tomorrow. Sleep well.'

Ellie closed the bedroom door behind her, sank back against it, and prayed nothing like that would happen again. Talk about torture. If Zack knew how desperately she'd wanted him to kiss her, she'd never be able to show her face again. Oh God, but what would it have been like if it had actually happened?

OK, fantasizing again. Stop this now, get a grip. Go to bed.

When he was in London, hard at work and wishing he could be in

Cornwall, Zack often scrolled down the favorites list on his laptop and clicked on the Perran Sands webcam to remind him of home. Today he didn't have to; he was here, seeing it for himself.

It was Friday afternoon, sunny and breezy, school was out for the weekend, and the good weather had brought people flocking to the beach. The Atlantic Ocean was glittering and whipped up, breakers were rolling in, and the surfers were out in force.

Zack smiled at the sight of two surfers in particular. Joss in her little wet suit was struggling with a crisis of confidence. Ellie had been helping her for the last thirty minutes, showing her how to stay balanced on her board, yelling encouragement alongside her each time she attempted a new wave, then catching and consoling her when she came tumbling off.

Last-minute wedding preparations were occupying his parents back at the house. They had encouraged Zack and Ellie to escape down to the beach with Steph, Gareth, and the twins for a couple of hours. Tizz had taken Zack aside this morning and murmured not so subtly, 'This one's worth hanging on to, you know. She's fab.'

And he had felt torn on so many levels, because on the one hand he hated deceiving his mother, but on the other hand she was the world's most incurable blabbermouth.

Plus, she was right. He knew only too well that Ellie was worth hanging on to. But he was also terrified of making his feelings known and ruining their amicable working relationship. Worse than that, in fact—running the risk of wrecking *everything*. Being scared wasn't an emotion Zack was familiar with, but it had him in its grip now. Last night he had wanted so badly to kiss her; he'd been on the brink of giving in to temptation. Only imagining the awkwardness at the wedding if she rejected him out of hand had stopped him from giving in and just doing it.

And here they came now, racing up the beach together with their boards under their arms and the others following behind.

'I'm f-f-freezing.' Joss, her teeth chattering violently, collapsed to her knees and unzipped her suit.

'Wasn't she brilliant?' Ellie grabbed a turquoise towel and began energetically toweling her dry.

'She was.' Zack loved Ellie's enthusiasm, the light in her gray eyes, the way her skin glowed and the tip of her nose had turned shiny and pink with cold. 'Here, you get yourself warm; I'll help Joss.'

Which was noble of him, because of the two of them he knew who he'd rather warm up.

'Ellie, look at me! I'm not cold!' Lily, who loved nothing more than a bit of sibling one-upmanship, came dancing up to them. 'Can we play volleyball next? Volleyball's my favorite!'

'In a minute, sweetie.' Ellie was now vigorously toweling her own hair; when she'd got herself looking like a scarecrow she pulled a comical cross-eyed face at the two girls.

'Zack, I'm good at volleyball, aren't I?' Joss turned to him, bristling with indignation. 'I'm better than Lily is.'

'Oh!' Lily pointed over Zack's shoulder.

'What?' Zack started to turn, to see what was happening behind him. And that was when everything went black.

———

So this was Mya. Ellie had seen her making her way across the sand towards them, holding a playful finger to her lips. Dark haired, curvily attractive, and wearing a surprising amount of makeup for a trip to the beach, she was sporting a white lace shirt, tight black jeans, lots of silver jewelry, and… gosh, by the smell of it, a good half-bottle of Chanel No. 5.

Well, it was either Mya or one of the Kardashians. But from the way she was now kneeling behind Zack, her hands covering his eyes and her smile beaming from ear to ear, Ellie thought she could probably guess which.

'Surprise!' Mya let him go at last. 'Hi, you! I just dropped in on your mum and she said you were all here, so I thought I'd come on down.' She gave Zack an enthusiastic just-good-friends kiss and a hug before greeting the rest of them with a cheery smile. 'Hey, kids, excited about tomorrow?'

'Ellie, this is Mya.' Zack performed the introductions. 'Mya, my girlfriend Ellie.'

'Yes, hi, Steph told me you were coming to the wedding. Nice to meet you.'

Mya was friendly and cheerful, but Ellie knew she was being given a thorough once-over and most probably found sadly lacking. Oh well, couldn't be helped. She combed her fingers through her Worzel Gummidge hair and said, 'You too,' smiling back in a Yes-I'm-his-girlfriend-aren't-I-lucky kind of way.

'Come on!' Lily was scrambling impatiently to her feet, sending up a spray of sand. 'Let's play volleyball! Mya, you can play too.'

To her credit, Mya was a good sport and she did join in. Bracelets and necklaces clanking like a jailer's keys, hair rock-steady thanks to the impenetrable coating of Elnett super-strength, she threw herself into the game with enthusiasm and on several occasions accidentally-on-purpose threw herself into Zack's path. Ellie couldn't help liking her, though; when Zack had described Mya as a Labrador puppy he'd been spot on.

The game was great fun, noisy and boisterous. Afterwards Zack draped his arm around Ellie's shoulders and planted an affectionate boyfriend kiss on her forehead. 'Well done. If your team hadn't cheated, we'd have beaten you.'

He'd only done it for show, but it still felt fantastic; imagine what it would be like if he were doing it for real. Ellie gave him a girlfriend jab in the ribs. 'I've got news for you. You still wouldn't have stood a chance.'

As they made their way back to the house, Mya caught up with Ellie while Zack was taking control of the dogs.

'Hi. Look, sorry if I was over the top back there. Steph's just told me I was being a bit obvious with Zack. The thing is, I don't mean to be, I just can't help myself. My body language gives me away. When you've had a crush on someone as long as I have, it's hard to keep it under control.'

'It's fine. No problem.' Ellie was charmed by her frankness.

'But you don't have to worry, I wouldn't *do* anything. Not while he's with you.' Mya shook her head vigorously. 'I'm not that kind of person.' She sighed. 'Oh, but he's gorgeous. You're so lucky.'

'I know.' Ellie shifted the stripy beach bag over her shoulder. 'He's great.'

'And you look so happy together.'

'We are.' *Well, I am. Especially when he puts his arm round my shoulder and kisses me on the forehead like an actual proper boyfriend.*

'But were you like me? I mean, when you first realized how much you liked him, did your body language give you away? Were you all googly eyes and touchy-feely without being able to control yourself?' Mya made touchy-feely gestures in the air and her bracelets jangled like sleigh bells. 'Was that how you were with Zack or were you able to keep it all under control?'

'I think I probably... kept it more hidden.' Zack and Steph were coming up behind them now, which was distracting to say the least. Ellie said, 'I was scared of giving myself away, because of working for him. I mean, if it didn't work out, I risked losing my job. Which would have been awful.'

'Oh God, I knew it. You didn't let on and it got him interested. Instead of pretty much jumping up and down, going, "Me, me!" I'm a complete failure.' Mya was looking forlorn. 'I'm just shooting myself in the foot.'

'Maybe, but body language is just being honest. It's nature's way of letting other people know how you feel. I think your way could be best.' *Only in theory, obviously.*

'Do you? Ah, that's nice of you to say.' Without even realizing she was doing it, Mya gave Ellie's arm a grateful squeeze. 'But I'm really going to try and rein myself in. Give it a shot, see how it goes.' Beneath the layers and layers of mascara, her amber eyes were bright with determination. 'After all, your way worked for you.'

Elmo caught up with them. Zack, materializing at Ellie's side, said easily, 'What are you two chatting about?'

'How Ellie stayed cool at work and didn't let on how much she fancied you.' Mya reached across and gave him a nudge. 'I bet you kept your feelings under wraps too, didn't you?'

'Yes.' Zack smiled slightly. 'I did.'

'Ha, I knew it! Neither of you saying anything, no giveaway body language, just all these incredible emotions smoldering away under the surface. Imagine the excitement, the adrenaline buzz, the electricity.' Mya heaved a sigh of envy. '*So* romantic.'

For a moment nobody spoke. Ellie couldn't look at Zack. At last she said faintly, 'Yes, yes, it was.'

'Ellie!' The next second her hand was seized. 'Quick, we're having a race home and we need to beat Zack and Lily.' Joss was already trying to jump up behind her. 'Come on, catch my legs, you have to give me a piggyback!'

Chapter 55

TWO PAIRS OF TRAINERS flash-flash-flashed, changing color with each step taken as Lily and Joss trooped up the aisle behind their mother. They'd won, but so cleverly that no one begrudged them their moment of victory.

Ellie, standing beside Zack in one of the front pews, smiled at the memory. She had been making coffee in the kitchen earlier while the girls gazed dispiritedly at the lilac satin bridesmaids' shoes on their feet. At length Joss had said, 'Mummy, why did you choose to wear that dress for your wedding?'

Steph, fabulous in slinky oyster satin, had replied, 'Because this was the one I liked best, sweetie.'

Prompting Joss to say in a sad voice, 'Oh. I liked my flashing trainers best.'

Ellie and Steph had exchanged a look across the kitchen. And that was the moment Steph gave in. After all, she explained to the rest of the family, the whole point of getting married in the first place was for the sake of the kids.

And now they were. Getting married. In a beautiful fourteenth-century church, surrounded by friends and family. The service was being conducted by a jolly vicar who had known Steph since she was seven. As he pointed out to the congregation, it was highly likely that she'd have been partial to a pair of flashing trainers herself if only they'd been invented that many years ago.

The atmosphere during the service was relaxed and celebratory.

Mya, with flowers in her hair and her lilac dress clinging to every curve, looked amazing. When the vows had been exchanged and the vicar declared that Gareth may kiss the bride, Lily said in a despairing voice, 'They're always doing that,' prompting much laughter and a round of applause when Gareth announced that he was about to do it again.

Zack turned and smiled at Ellie. He reached for her hand and gave it a squeeze. The next moment a bony finger tapped him on the shoulder from behind.

'We were just saying,' stage-whispered an elderly woman with peacock feathers exploding from her hat, 'could be you two next.'

After the service everyone spilled outside into the sunshine. Ellie's high heel skidded on one of the steps and she almost went flying. Grabbing her in the nick of time, Zack held her up.

'Are you OK?' His arm was around her waist. *It felt gorgeous.*

'I'm fine. That was a real slip, by the way. Not a Mya-type one.' She didn't want him to think she'd done it on purpose.

'I know that.'

'Oh my goodness, look at me.' Tizz was dabbing at her eyes with a tissue. 'Crying like a baby, how ridiculous. I'm not used to this makeup malarkey.' She presented her face to Ellie for inspection. 'Have I smudged anything? Do I look like a panda?'

Since neither of them had a mirror, Ellie took control of the tissue and carefully wiped away the mascara spillage. 'There, all done.'

'You're a star.' Tizz leaned in and murmured not very discreetly, 'You never know, it could be you and Zack next!'

'Mum,' said Zack.

'What? I'm just saying it could be!'

'The photographer wants you.' Zack pointed to where a rotund man garlanded with cameras was attempting to corral the main players into a group.

'He'll be wanting all of us. Come on.'

OK, embarrassing. Ellie tried to hang back. 'It's a family shot. You don't want me in it.'

'Don't be silly, of course we do.' Zack was being dragged over by some of the children; as soon as he was out of earshot, Tizz clutched Ellie's elbow and said, 'I have such a good feeling about you. I'm serious, darling. High hopes. We've been waiting so long for Zack to meet the right girl and I really think it's happened at last.'

This was awful. Ellie hated having to lie. 'But it's early days, it's too soon to say…'

'Maybe so, but I see the way he looks at you.' They were approaching the photographer now. 'And let me tell you, Zack's pretty smitten. I'm his mother.' Tizz's eyes were sparkling. 'Trust me, I can tell.'

Then she was seized by the photographer and ushered to her allotted position. Zack murmured in Ellie's ear, 'What's she been saying to you now?'

His mouth accidentally brushed the top of her ear as he said it, causing a fresh attack of the zingers. When they'd died down, Ellie whispered back, 'Basically, you're doing a great job.'

'What does that mean?'

'Your mum's convinced you like me. She says she can tell.' Ellie marveled at her ability to sound amused. 'I'm impressed; I didn't know you were such a good actor. You could end up with a BAFTA for this.'

―∞―

By three o'clock they were back at the house and the wedding party was in full flow. A gypsy punk band from St Austell was playing insanely catchy Russian-style music, violins and balalaikas dueling with the hypnotic beat of the drums. There was wild dancing, there was singing, even the dogs joined in. Then it was time to sit down and eat. On her way to their table in the marquee, Ellie was stopped by the vicar.

'Hello! Having fun?'

'Oh yes.'

'You're Zack's girlfriend, am I right?'

Would lying to a man of God cause you to be instantly struck down by a thunderbolt? Ellie nodded and said brightly, 'That's me!'

The thunderbolt didn't happen. He beamed at her. 'Could be you two next, getting married!'

OK, she couldn't do it. Lying to a vicar was plain wrong. 'Actually, we won't be. It's not really like that with me and Zack. We're just friends.' There, she'd said it.

'Hahahahahaha!' The vicar threw back his head, showing a quantity of amalgam fillings. 'Very good, hahaha. Now, where's my table? Ah, I'm over there...'

The tables were covered in white swagged tablecloths strewn with flowers and silver confetti. The wine had been flowing for the last hour and everyone was nicely relaxed. As the hired caterers began serving the first course, Zack introduced Ellie to the other guests at their table: two long-standing neighbors of the McLarens, three old school friends of Steph's, and a well-dressed man in his early sixties who explained that he was Gareth's godfather.

'So are you going to be next on the list?' The woman who had lived next door to Zack for many years gave him a jokey nudge.

'Who knows? It could be a possibility.' Ellie found herself on the receiving end of the kind of smile from Zack that would have anyone believing him. God, he was brilliant at this. Then again, two could play at that game.

She said playfully, 'You'd have to give me a pay raise first.'

He shook his head. 'You drive a hard bargain.'

'Maybe.' Ellie turned and gazed deep, deep, *deep* into his eyes. 'But I'm worth it.'

Across the table, one of Steph's friends said cheerfully, 'You two, get a room!'

Which brought Ellie crashing back to earth and concentrating hard on her starter of scallops in Pernod.

By the time the plates were removed, Zack had got talking to Gareth's godfather, whose name was Paul. Moments later, Elmo arrived to pay them a visit, scrabbling to be allowed on to Zack's lap. 'Sorry about this. *No*, Elmo. Get down.'

'Oh, let him join us, I don't mind. I love dogs.' Paul gave Elmo's ears a friendly scratch and adjusted the leather collar that had got itself skew-whiff in all the excitement. 'But if your name's McLaren, why does it say Castle on the identity tag?' He looked at Ellie. 'Or is that you?'

Ellie shook her head. 'He's a timeshare dog. Zack and his neighbor have dual custody. Neither of them can manage a full-time commitment. Zack takes Elmo for most of the walks while he's at home. Then when he's away, Elmo goes to live with Geraldine.'

Paul nodded. 'Makes sense. Good plan.' Then he smiled and rubbed Elmo's head. 'Geraldine Castle, that takes me back. I used to know someone by that name years ago.'

'If you met our Geraldine, you'd never forget her. She's a character,' said Zack.

'So was the one I knew. Quite a girl.' Paul leaned back to make room for the waitress who was now serving dinner. 'She once danced with a skeleton at our May Ball.'

Ellie and Zack exchanged a look. Ellie said, 'Our Geraldine's a doctor.'

Switching from fond reminiscence to dawning realization, Paul put down his wine glass. 'So am I.'

There was a tiny pause. Could it really be the same Geraldine? Ellie said, 'Where did you study medicine?'

'Edinburgh.'

'That's it.' Ellie nodded. 'Edinburgh's where she trained. She told me once about a crowd of them having a wheelbarrow race down Princes Street. In real wheelbarrows.'

'Why am I not surprised to hear that?' said Zack.

'Did she mention she was wearing a bikini top and hula skirt while she was doing it?' Paul was shaking his head in disbelief. 'This is amazing. I was there. We'd been to a costume party. It was midnight, there were roadworks going on, and the wheelbarrows had been left out, so we decided to put them to good use…'

'You and Geraldine! Oh wow!' Ellie clapped her hands; was there anything more satisfying than making a connection? 'Were you two a couple?'

'No, no, nothing like that. I had a girlfriend. Geraldine had a boyfriend. Although I must admit, I did have a secret crush on her. She was a stunning-looking girl back then.'

Ellie couldn't tear her eyes off him; his hair might be streaked with silver now, his eyes crinkled and his jawline less than chiseled, but she wouldn't mind betting that in his day he'd been a bit of a looker himself.

Hastily Paul added, 'Don't tell her I said that!'

'We have to call her,' said Ellie. 'This is brilliant.'

'No…' He looked panicked.

But Zack already had his phone out. 'We must.' He pressed a few buttons and waited. The rest of the table had by now fallen silent. 'Hi, Geraldine? Yes, Elmo's fine. No, nothing's wrong, it's all good. Listen, about the time you got yourself carted along Princes Street in a wheelbarrow.' He hit the hands-free button just in time to catch Geraldine's parrot-like squawk of recognition.

'Oh my God, how did you find out about that? I don't believe it!'

'And what was it you were wearing? Not very much, by all accounts.'

'A lei, a red bikini, and a grass skirt. Which in Edinburgh, let me tell you, is pretty intrepid. I still can't imagine how you've got to hear about it.'

'We're here with someone who knew you back then.' Zack's dark eyes glittered with amusement. 'His name's Paul.'

'Paul Fletcher.' Mortified, Paul clearly didn't expect her to remember him by his first name alone.

'Fletcher,' Zack duly repeated so Geraldine could hear.

'Oh my giddy aunt, Paul *Fletcher*? Are you serious? He never knew this, but I had such a crush on that boy! We used to call him the Greek God,' Geraldine exclaimed. 'He was just *beautiful*.'

They all watched a sixty-something doctor blush deeply. Zack switched off hands free and carried on listening. Finally he said, 'No, no, of course I won't tell him you said that. Hang on, let me just go and find him, I'll pass you over and the two of you can have a chat.'

He covered the phone. Everyone around the table was agog. Paul was visibly trembling. 'I can't do this. She thinks I'm a Greek God.'

'It isn't Skype.' Ellie gave his arm a comforting pat. 'She can't see you. Anyway, you're still quite handsome.' *Ach, wrong thing to say.*

'Thanks.' Paul's smile was wry.

'And Geraldine's wheelbarrow racing days are long gone,' Zack chimed in. 'She's currently getting over a fractured hip.' He uncovered the phone and handed it over. 'Here you go.'

Paul took it and pushed back his chair. 'I can't talk to her with you lot listening. You have no idea what this is doing to me. It's like asking me to talk to Barbra Streisand.'

He left them, weaving his way between the tables and heading out into the garden before raising the phone to his ear.

Chapter 56

TWENTY MINUTES LATER, PAUL'S main course had grown cold on his plate and everyone else had demolished theirs.

Strawberry pavlovas arrived. The talk around the table was lively and punctuated with laughter. Ellie had to protect Paul's dessert from being taken hostage by Steph's friend Tara.

Finally, over forty minutes later and just as the speeches were about to start, he reappeared. Trying hard not to look like the cat that got the cream, the prawns, and the Loch Fyne salmon.

'Well.' He shook his head and sat down.

'Couldn't think of anything to say?' Zack offered him a top-up of wine.

'No thanks, I mean, yes.' In a daze, Paul covered his glass. 'No wine. That was amazing. What a woman… yes, thanks, take it away.' He waved at his untouched plate and flashed a distracted smile at the waitress. 'Sorry, I'm sure it was delicious… wow, who'd have thought something like this could happen out of nowhere? We couldn't *stop* talking. No, not for me.' Now the waitress was attempting to refill his wine glass. 'Just water, thanks. She's staying in Exeter, did you know that?'

'Yes.' Ellie nodded. 'Her sister has a bungalow not far from the university.'

'It's only seventy miles from here. Geraldine's invited me to stay.' He was checking his watch. 'I can be there in an hour.'

'You're leaving *now*?'

'I'm fine to drive. I've only had half a glass of wine. Gareth won't mind if I leave early. God, just hearing her voice again was incredible.' His hand went up to smooth his silver-streaked hair. 'Do I look OK?'

He was dazed, happy, as besotted as a teenager.

'You look great.' Ellie smiled; there was a Christmas-morning quality to his excitement.

At the top table, the best man rose to his feet and dinged a glass with a spoon to attract everyone's attention.

'Speeches,' said Paul. 'I'll wait until they're over.' He sounded as if he'd quite like them to be over in the next five minutes. 'Then I'll head off.'

He was as good as his word. Half an hour later, when the speeches had been concluded and the dancing was about to begin again in earnest, he made his excuses to Gareth and Steph. Finally, he shook Zack's hand and kissed Ellie on the cheek.

'Am I glad they put me at your table.'

'Drive carefully.' She hugged him in return. How amazing that he was doing this.

'I will.'

When he'd left the marquee, one of Steph's friends on the other side of the table said, 'Wow, old people don't hang about, do they!'

Tara, next to her, said, 'They can't afford to. Why waste time when you might be about to die?' She turned to Zack. 'You'll have to tell us what happens. We need to know if there's a happy ending.'

'We will.' Zack rested his arm across the back of Ellie's chair and tilted his head. 'Well? Are we getting out onto that dance floor now?'

'Oh yes, we definitely are.' But the wine was taking its toll; Ellie needed the loo. She pushed back her chair and said, 'Just give me two minutes.'

Outside the marquee, the trees glittered with twinkle lights and the air was fresh and cool. Ellie made her way across to the house.

The downstairs loo was occupied so she waited in the hallway for it to become free. There were people chatting in the kitchen. Idly half-listening, she recognized Mya's voice, then realized they were discussing her and began to pay attention.

'I mean, she's nice and everything. I really like her. But the twins told me they're sleeping in separate rooms! Now, is it just me or is that weird?'

'Her husband died, though.' Ellie didn't recognize the second voice and the door was only slightly ajar; another of Steph's girl-friends, presumably. 'Maybe it's something to do with that.'

'Yes, except I've been watching them. They *look* like they're crazy about each other,' said Mya, 'but he hasn't actually kissed her. Not once, not on the lips. And you have to admit, that is *seriously* weird.'

The cloakroom door was unlocked and Gareth's mother emerged. She smiled at Ellie in that way women always smile at whoever's next in line for the loo.

A minute later, Ellie pulled the flush and washed her hands. It was a beautiful cloakroom, spacious and decorated in silver and white, with a black and white diamond-patterned marble floor and a Venetian mirror above the sink.

And Jamie, reflected in the mirror, wearing his pale gray Superdry polo shirt and pink board shorts.

Ellie wasn't surprised to see him. She'd made him appear. Jamie was her conjured-up creation, from his messy sea-salted hair and the smell of his aftershave all the way down to the skinny legs and the dusting of sand on his tanned bare feet.

'It's a wedding.' Jamie gestured at himself. 'If you're going to bring me here, shouldn't I be wearing something a bit smarter than this?'

'You don't like suits. And you're not leaving the loo either. Now listen, what do you think? Should I kiss Zack or shouldn't I?'

'Do you want to?'

'Of course I want to! I'm just worried I might not be able to stop!

What if it turns into a cartoon and my mouth won't let go and he has to wrench me off his face like a sink plunger?'

Jamie looked thoughtful. 'Do you want me to come with you?'

'No!' She definitely wasn't having that.

'So what's brought this on, all of a sudden?'

Ellie exhaled. 'Paul and Geraldine. He isn't wasting time because they're in their sixties and who knows how long they have left? But look at us.' She could feel her heart thudding away like a bass speaker. 'How long do any of us have left? I could die tomorrow. So that's it, I'm just going to go ahead. If it all goes horribly wrong, you can have a good laugh about it later. You can come with me on the bus of shame back to London.'

'Hey, remember how we met?'

He was giving her a playful look. Of course Ellie remembered; how could she forget? They'd each been with their own group of friends at a club in Piccadilly. Having spotted her looking at Jamie, her friend Lisa had given her a nudge and said, 'Dare you to go over there and kiss him without saying a word. If he tries to talk to you, pretend not to speak any English.'

So she had.

The kiss had been amazing. Afterwards, she had talked gobbledygook. 'Ke, mi andzengo. Vamejski.'

'Vamejskiola!' Without missing a beat, Jamie had broken into a grin and lightly touched her cheek. 'Laksadi ja, pelodria. Tibo!'

And that had been it; in those few miraculous seconds they'd both known this was it; they were in it for the long haul. It had been that instantaneous.

Till death us do part.

But that was then. This was now. She was a different person these days.

'Sweetheart, go for it.' Jamie was remembering that night too; she could tell by the smile on his face. 'It worked wonders for me.'

Ellie wished she could reach out and touch him. 'I know we don't do this as much as we used to. But I do still miss you.'

'Hey, no need to feel guilty. I'll always be here if you need me.' His expression softened. 'Five, ten, twenty years from now… it doesn't matter. Well, except for one thing.'

'Which is?'

The irreverent grin was back. Jamie said, 'You're going to get old and wrinkly, sweetheart. But I'm always going to look this good.'

––⁓––

Plans, however, didn't always work out. By the time Ellie returned to the marquee, another determined female had taken advantage of her absence and dragged Zack on to the dance floor.

So much for the sisterhood.

She sat down and poured herself more wine. Then she watched as Zack laughed and joked with her rival. And her heart did that crumpled little squeeze of love because really, was there anything more irresistible than a man not caring that he was making a complete fool of himself in front of everyone, because it was making his current dance partner happy and that was all that mattered?

Zack and Lily were giving it everything they had, dancing like maniacs to 'All The Single Ladies'. Joss barreled across the dance floor and joined in. There was Beyoncé-style foot stamping, hip wiggling, hand clapping, and head shaking. Attitude was the key. The three of them were a team. Then the song ended, everyone applauded, and Zack scooped up a twin in each arm. He pretended to stagger with exhaustion. The DJ, taking pity on him, began to play something slow. And Zack, looking across the room to see if she was back from the loo, saw her at the table and broke into a smile.

Oh heavens, and now here he was, standing in front of her, holding out a hand. 'Our turn now. Sorry about that. I was kidnapped.'

'I noticed. Don't worry, we filmed it. You'll be on YouTube by midnight.'

They reached the dance floor and Zack drew her into his arms. *Heaven.* They began to move slowly along with the music. *More heaven.* Ellie took a breath and said, 'There's something we're going to have to do.'

'What's that?'

She loved him. Everything she was feeling now, this was it, this was love. 'I overheard Mya in the kitchen. She's suspicious.'

'Why?'

His eyes. The way he looked down at her. His hands, one resting on her waist, the other in the small of her back.

'She's been watching us. Paying attention. We haven't kissed.' *There, I said it.* Ellie gazed steadily up at him. 'I think we need to.'

'You do?' His expression was unreadable but she felt the tension in his shoulders. Oh God, was he horribly shocked?

'Nothing too major. Just… you know, a little one.' She no longer trusted herself; any more than a peck might be too much to handle.

'A little one. You mean… right, here, right now?'

'Might be best. So we get it over and done with.' Her heart felt as if it were about to explode out of her chest; no way was she backing down now. 'Sorry, but we should. Look, Steph and Gareth are doing it.'

'I don't know…' He was prevaricating, about to say no and hold her at arm's length so she couldn't get to him. No, that was intolerable, he couldn't duck out, she *had* to do it…

'Don't be such a baby. It's only a kiss, it'll be over in two seconds.' Ellie reached up a hand and curled it around the back of his head. Detecting resistance, she murmured with a touch of desperation, 'Just *pretend*, OK?' and lifted herself up on tiptoe, her face tilted up to his. Her mouth brushed his mouth, a shot of electricity zipped through her body, and her lips parted…

Oh God, was this what heaven felt like? Their mouths were a perfect fit, too much adrenaline was making her dizzy, and what she'd feared might happen was indeed happening, because now she'd started, there was no way in the world she could stop. But somehow it no longer seemed to matter, because Zack didn't appear to want it to end either. He'd evidently decided not to put up a fight and was going along with the game instead. His left hand was in her hair, his right hand in the small of her back, and their bodies were pressed together… oh wow, this was everything she'd dreamed of happening and more… except they were still standing in the middle of the dance floor.

'OK, we're on show.' Tearing himself away, practically causing her to let out a whimper of desolation, Zack seized her hand and propelled her towards the exit. Were people looking at them? Yes they were. Was she managing to walk more or less normally? Well, kind of. Was Mya there? Yes, she was, on the far edge of the dance floor, watching them with a glimmer of disappointment…

Once they were outside he led her round to the back of the house until they were out of sight of everyone. And then they were kissing again… it was like a drug they couldn't get enough of and Ellie was so on fire with longing for more she couldn't even begin to imagine what it meant.

Except, unbelievably, Zack appeared to be feeling it as intensely as she was. His breathing was uneven, his hands were cupping her face—oh heavens, he was a sensational kisser—and it was carrying on and on, even though there were no longer any suspicious ex-girlfriends around to see them.

Which *might* mean…

No, she couldn't let herself think it.

Zack drew back at last and surveyed her. It was dark, but not so dark she couldn't see his face.

'Well?' he said. 'How was that?'

Talk about a loaded question. Was she panting? 'It was… good.'

'I suppose that's better than bad.'

She could barely swallow. 'I don't know what to say.'

'Why not?' There was a glint in his eye, a definite hint of a smile. 'You started it.'

'I wasn't expecting you to join in.'

'Was it just for Mya's benefit?'

'Slightly. She wasn't the whole reason.' OK, just plunge in. 'I wanted to do it.' Ellie paused, still struggling to catch her breath. Impulsively, she said, 'Am I going to get sacked now, for impertinence and sexual harassment?'

His hands were on her shoulders; his thumbs gently grazed her neck, causing shivers of longing to ripple through her body.

'You have no idea.' Zack shook his head. '*No* idea how long I've wanted this to happen.'

Was he serious? 'You haven't.'

'Oh yes, I have.'

'Really? You can't have been.'

'Why not?'

'Because you just wouldn't have! You wanted a PA who *wasn't* going to get all doofy over you. A proper professional working partnership. No shenanigans.'

'True, that is what I wanted.' Zack conceded this point. 'Until you came along and completely got to me.' He paused. '*Doofy?*'

'It just came out. Sometimes only a made-up word will do.'

Her brain had been attacked by egg beaters; it was a wonder she could speak at all. She clung to him in disbelief. 'Did I really? Get to you?'

'Oh yes. And that was before you ever saw me. The time you met Tony for lunch at the Ivy, remember?' Zack's dark eyes glittered in the dim light. 'You passed me in the street in your pink coat and I just felt something here.' He pressed his hand to his chest.

'Nothing else like it has ever happened to me before. But that day it did.'

Ellie was trembling. 'You never said. You never gave any kind of hint.'

'You weren't ready.' He touched her face. 'Not for anyone. Which was fine, I was prepared to wait. Then the Todd thing happened. And that took some coming to terms with, I can tell you. Then you and Todd broke up—'

'But I was too ashamed to tell you. I felt so stupid and hopeless, such a failure.'

'And then along came Joe.' One eyebrow lifted. 'I couldn't *believe* I'd missed my chance again.'

The trembling was stepping up a gear. The backs of her knees had gone all juddery and out of control. That these words could be coming out of Zack's mouth seemed too extraordinary to contemplate.

'And all this time I've been desperately trying to hide how *I* was feeling. I thought you'd be horrified.' Ellie jumped as a daddy longlegs danced past beneath the lit-up branches of the sycamore tree overhead.

'I haven't been able to stop thinking about you. One way or another, you were always out of reach.' He pulled her closer and she felt the heat from his chest. 'I think I'm in love with you.'

Was this a dream? 'Really?'

'Actually, no, that's not true. I know I am.'

Ellie's head was in a complete spin. She'd tried her hardest but things hadn't been remotely right between her and Todd. Then Joe had come along and they'd been better, although nowhere near good enough.

And now this. You could never know for sure, but this just might be… perfect.

~~~

In the marquee, the DJ had taken to the stage in his Status Quo T-shirt. The sound of his favorite band started playing, accompanied by raucous cheers and much stamping of feet as everyone flooded on to the dance floor.

'ROCKIN' ALL OVER THE WORLD!' People with drink inside them were bellowing along at the tops of their voices. In the back garden, Ellie gave herself up to yet another sublime kiss. Zack really was very good at it. The next moment they belatedly sprang apart at the sound of footsteps on the flagstoned path.

'Whoops, sorry…' Having left the house, Tizz was making her way back to the marquee. She stopped and beamed at them. 'Well now, don't you two look happy!'

Zack looked at Ellie. Ellie looked at Zack, struggling to keep a straight face. The silence lengthened. Mystified, Tizz said, 'Come on then, spill the beans! What's up?'

'OK, let me tell her. I told you a bit of a white lie before. Ellie and I weren't actually together before today.' Zack's arm slid around Ellie's waist. 'But we are now.'

'You weren't? You are? Well, that's marvelous news! But you should have asked me if you were perfect for each other.' His mother's eyes danced. 'I could have told you that.' A thought occurred to her. 'Ha, so *that's* why you asked for separate rooms!'

'Sorry.' Ellie grinned. 'And you thought I was playing hard to get.'

'Oh my darling girl, don't apologize, that just makes me love you more. Come along then, let's get back to this party! Don't you just *love* Status Quo?'

That was it then, so much for sloping off. There was to be no early escape. Tizz was insistent and, as it turned out, it didn't matter a bit. If anything, it only served to heighten the delicious anticipation. For the next three hours Ellie and Zack danced and celebrated and socialized with friends and family, all the while enjoying the sizzle of sexual tension that had existed between them for so long but which had only now, at long last, been acknowledged. Adrenaline was zinging through Ellie's veins. It was hard to have eyes for anyone other than Zack. Again and again she thanked her lucky stars, because what if they hadn't found each other?

Finally, just as she was beginning to wonder how much longer she could hold out, Zack murmured in her ear, 'OK, we have to go now. This has been great, but I'm only human.'

Hooray!

Hand in hand, they slipped discreetly away, out of the marquee and back to the house. In through the creaking back door, across the deserted hall, and up the curved staircase.

'People are going to wonder where we've got to.' Ellie pushed open the door to her bedroom.

'They won't notice we're gone,' said Zack as the thud-thud-thud of the music continued to reverberate around them. 'They're having fun without us.'

'I think we might have more fun without them.' Whether or not this worked out, Ellie knew she would never regret it. Sometimes you just had to take the risk. Maybe it would be a brief but wonderful romance, maybe it would last a lifetime. She reached for Zack and kicked the door shut behind her. 'No offense to them, but I know where I'd rather be right now. And it's not out there, dancing to Coldplay.'

At that moment the music faded out and they heard the DJ say, 'OK, Eminem next, the clean version. Now this one was requested by Ellie and I can't see her on the dance floor. Come on, Ellie, get yourself over here, where are you?'

'Oops.' Ellie pulled a face. 'I forgot about that. Should we go back?'

Through the loudspeakers the DJ bellowed, 'And Zack? No sign of you either. Give us a shout, mate—we're all waiting for you!'

'Oh God.' Zack tightened his hold on her and smiled ruefully. 'We're not going.'

'Good,' said Ellie.

Over in the marquee, meanwhile, the realization that they had both vanished from the party was giving rise to laughter and bawdy cheers.

'No? No sign of either of 'em? Honestly, this is a shocking state of affairs,' said the DJ. 'Sloping off for an early night, what's wrong with these people? Disgraceful, that's what I call it. Right then, if they're not here to appreciate my efforts, I'm not playing Eminem. We'll have more Status Quo instead!'

Epilogue

ELLIE LEANED OUT OF the second-floor window and watched the goings-on below. There was Todd, playing soccer with an apple, dribbling it past Zack's nephews as he zigzagged across the manicured lawn and through the croquet hoops. There were Tizz and Ken, chatting with Paul and Geraldine whilst they admired the flowers in the borders. And over there was Steph, kneeling to retie the bows on Lily's shoes. No flashing trainers this time. Lily had found and chosen them herself. These were bright green with sequined butterflies on them; she was currently going through an intensely sparkly stage that had Joss curling her lip in bewildered disbelief.

To think that it had been almost a year since Steph and Gareth's wedding. And now she was having her own. How life had changed in the past eleven months.

Her mobile phone rang and Ellie glanced at it before answering. 'You're five minutes away? Great. Yes, everything's fine. See you soon.'

Turning away from the window, she quickly double-checked her hair was still OK. Not long to go now. It had been Zack's idea to hold the wedding here, at Colworth Manor Hotel where they had spent such an idyllic weekend last November. That had been shortly after he'd sought suggestions for a romantic proposal from Roo, and she had excitedly exclaimed that he must drop the diamond engagement ring into a glass of champagne. She'd seen it done in a film, Roo had told Zack, and it had been so romantic she'd cried buckets.

Ellie's eyes danced at the memory. Zack had nearly cried too, when she'd taken a big swig and almost swallowed the ring.

But the sentiment had been there. It was the thought that counted, and the three dazzling diamonds had glittered proudly on her finger ever since. She knew without a doubt that Zack was the right man for her; in fact, more than that, he was perfect. They were as besotted with each other now as they had been on that first night. These days they laughed, loved, and argued with each other and every day together was a joy. The desolate pain she'd experienced following Jamie's death had lessened and shrunk more than she'd ever imagined possible.

Nor did she see so much of Jamie now, either. The need was no longer there. Occasionally Ellie conjured him up for a couple of seconds, just to touch base and say hi, but these days he didn't occupy her mind to the same degree. Their long conversations were now a thing of the past. It was enough to know that Jamie approved of Zack and the next step she was about to take.

Ellie turned and gazed at herself in the elaborate full-length mirror. Oh my word, would you look at that, she was like an actual proper bride! Her hair was up, but in a tousled rather than a super-glued way. Her dress was ivory silk, bias cut, and full length. Zack's sister Paula had done her makeup and they'd heroically resisted the urging from Lily to add pink glitter. All in all, if she did say so herself, she was looking pretty good.

'Just as well,' said Jamie, appearing in the mirror behind her and flashing his habitual easy grin. 'Otherwise Zack might run a mile, and that would just be embarrassing.'

Ellie smiled. It seemed only fair to have him drop by, today of all days.

'So?' She held up her hands, did a pose. 'Will I do?'

Jamie surveyed her for a couple of seconds. 'You look fantastic. I'm so proud of you.'

'Thanks.' She wasn't going to cry, not today. 'I do still love you.' She needed to say it, to make sure he understood. 'Just because I'm getting married again doesn't mean I'll ever forget you.'

'I know. But you've got Zack now.' Jamie looked thoughtful. 'The only thing I'm not too happy about is his legs. They're not as skinny as mine.'

'I know. But his knees are knobbly. So that makes you even.'

'Glad to hear it. OK, I'm going to go now. Be happy, sweetheart.'

OK, maybe just the one tear. 'Thanks. Bye.'

Ellie carefully blotted her eyes with a tissue. When she looked up again, Jamie had gone.

Moments later there was a knock at the door. She called out, 'Come in,' and Tony appeared.

They hugged each other, hard.

Tony drew back finally and surveyed her with pride. 'Oh sweetheart. I miss my boy so much. And I never thought I'd be saying this, but today is going to be a very good day. It's going to be… splendid.'

Moved, Ellie straightened his pale gray tie. Tony was still smartly dressed but the last year had taken its toll on him. There was a lot more silver in his hair now. The lines on his face were more pronounced. He put on a brave front, but she knew he'd been working hard on various projects in order to take his mind off the emptiness in his own life. He'd kept the Nevis Street flat on after she'd moved in with Zack, but these days it was a seldom used pied-à-terre with most of his work concentrated in the States.

And Ellie was fairly certain she knew why. He had learned of Henry's death through the Internet but had respected Martha's wishes not to resume contact. No one knew better than Tony the power of grief.

'It will be.' She brushed a fleck of lint from the shoulder of his morning suit. 'You're looking very handsome.'

'Flatterer.' Ever the actor, he was adept at hiding his loneliness beneath that ready, charismatic smile. Glancing out of the window, he said, 'By the way, should pregnant women run around like lunatics?'

He was referring to Roo, her topaz-yellow dress plastered to her impressive seven-month bump as she raced barefoot across the lawn with Lily, Joss, and Elmo in hot pursuit. With her shoes in one hand and Elmo's favorite new squeaky toy in the other, she was squeaking it wildly, sending Elmo into a frenzy of excitement. The next moment all four of them had hurtled over a flower bed. It was like a kindergarten version of the Grand National.

'Roo's fine. It's good exercise. Did I tell you, she's got Todd doing 5K runs with her on Saturday mornings?' Ellie had declined their kind offer to join them, but had nothing but respect for their efforts. Once the baby was born, Roo had her sights set on next year's London marathon. She turned away from the window to face Tony again. 'Now listen, can you do me a huge favor?'

His expression softened. 'Anything.'

'Everyone here knows pretty much everyone else. But I've invited a friend along who doesn't know anyone at all.' Ellie pulled a face. 'Which means she's going to feel a bit on her own. I was hoping you could kind of look after her. Would that be OK?'

'Oh God, do I have to?' Evidently not enthralled, Tony hesitated for only a split second before good manners took over. 'Sorry, that's fine, of course I will. Is it someone you used to work with?'

Ellie checked her watch. 'Come on, she'll be waiting downstairs. Let's go and find her, and I'll introduce you.'

Together they made their way down the impressive staircase. Ellie practiced walking like a bride and not falling off her high heels. In twenty minutes the wedding was scheduled to begin. Tony, her beloved former father-in-law, would escort her into the oak-paneled drawing room where the ceremony was being held, and give her away.

But before that happened, there was one other small thing she had to do.

One other small *exciting* thing, hopefully.

She led Tony through the door on the left and there was Martha waiting for them, thinner but still beautiful, wearing a flowing Cadbury-purple dress and jacket, and nervously clutching a tray-sized silver gift bag with curly silver and white ribbons trailing from the handles.

Tony stopped dead when he saw her. Ellie let go of his arm and moved discreetly to one side. Martha did her level best to smile over at her but her attention was being dragged towards Tony, who in turn couldn't tear his gaze away.

'Martha… my God, you're *here*.'

'Ellie invited me. We've been talking things through.' The lilt and the warmth in her voice was unchanged. 'She made me see that it was OK. I couldn't have done it before. Now I can. It's been a nightmare year.' Martha paused, her smile hesitant. 'But I'm on the mend.'

Tony took a tentative step towards her. 'I can't believe this is happening.'

'She was worried you might have moved on,' Ellie put in help-fully. 'Met someone else.'

'No. Never.' He shook his head. 'I'm so sorry about Henry.'

'Thank you.' The necklace of handmade pink pebbles bobbed against Martha's throat.

'And Eunice? Is she well?' .

'Very well. She's living in Carlisle now, close to her daughter.' The twinkle in her eye signaled that whether Eunice's daughter was thrilled with this development was debatable. 'And my son has met a wonderful girl, so fingers crossed there. I keep embarrassing him, dropping hints about how I can't wait to become a granny.' The next moment, remembering the ribbon-strewn silver gift bag in her hand, Martha held it out to Ellie and said, 'Sorry, this is for you.'

'That's so kind. You didn't have to.' They exchanged a hug.

'Oh, darling, I'm just glad I was able to.'

'Right, I'll leave you in peace for five minutes.' Ellie pointed to Tony. 'Then you have a bride to give away.'

The expression on his face told Ellie she'd done the right thing. 'Thank you.'

'You're sure you don't mind looking after her?'

Tony squeezed her hand. 'I'll give it my very best shot.'

Ellie closed the door behind her. Out in the hallway, she lifted the painting out of the gift bag.

There it was, a sunny summer's day in Little Venice. Martha had returned to the exact spot where they'd first met, in order to demonstrate that her ability to paint had returned. Along with her enthusiasm for life.

The next moment another door opened and she heard Zack's voice a split second before he emerged from the drawing room where the ceremony was being held.

'Close your eyes,' Ellie blurted out.

Zack appeared, dark hair slicked back, tanned jaw stubble-free. His eyes were closed.

'It's unlucky to see the bride before the wedding,' Ellie reminded him.

'So move away,' said Zack. 'You'll have to, I can't see where I'm going.'

Well, sometimes a situation arose that was just too good to pass up. Crossing the hallway, Ellie planted a kiss on his beautiful un-suspecting mouth.

'How do I know it's you?' Zack kept his eyes closed. 'It could be anyone.'

'It's me.'

'I'm not sure I believe you.' The beautiful mouth was twitching.

'Put it this way.' She pressed herself against him and pinched his bottom. 'It had better be me.'

Zack touched her face, exploring the various curves and angles, before kissing her again. 'OK, it's you. I recognize you now.' He broke into a slow smile. 'Ellie Kendall, you have no idea how much I love you. Will you marry me?'

Was it possible to feel happier than this? 'Play your cards right,' she ran a playful finger down the front of his cream waistcoat, 'and I just might.'

Acknowledgments

Huge thanks to my wonderful son Cory, who came up with the perfect title for this book.

About the Author

Jill Mansell lives with her partner and children in Bristol and writes full time. Actually, that's not true; she watches TV, eats gumdrops, admires the rugby players training in the sports field behind her house, and spends hours on the Internet marveling at how many other writers have blogs. Only when she's *completely* run out of ways to procrastinate does she write.

READ ON FOR A SNEAK PEEK OF JILL MANSELL'S

nadia knows best

AVAILABLE MAY 2012

FROM SOURCEBOOKS LANDMARK

Chapter 1

'Ooooohh… eeee…' To her horror Nadia realised she was having a *Bambi* moment. A scary, drawn-out, Bambi-on-ice moment in fact. Except unlike Bambi she couldn't make it stop simply by landing with a bump on her bottom.

The car carried on sliding in slow motion across the perilously snow-packed road. Despite knowing—in theory—that what you were meant to do was keep your foot *off* the brake and steer *into* the skid, Nadia's hands and feet were frantically doing all the wrong things because steering into a skid was like trying to write while you were looking in a mirror and—oh God, *wall*—

Cccrunchh.

Silence.

Phew, still alive, hooray for that.

Opening her eyes, Nadia unpeeled her trembling gloved hands from the steering wheel and mentally congratulated herself on not being dead. The car was tilted at a bit of an odd angle, thanks to the ditch directly in front of the wall, but despite the best efforts of the snow she hadn't actually been going fast enough to do spectacular amounts of damage to either it or herself.

Then again, what to do now?

Pulling her hat down over her eyebrows and bracing herself against the cold, Nadia clambered out of the grubby black Renault and inspected the crumpled front wing. Just as well she hadn't borrowed her grandmother's pride and joy for the journey—the teeniest scratch on Miriam's Maserati would have meant being beaten with a big stick and sent to stand in the naughty corner for weeks.

Her face screwed up against the stinging onslaught of low-flying—and actually quite ferocious—snowflakes, Nadia hopped back into the car. At least she had her mobile. She could dial 999 and ask the police to come and rescue her... except if she did that, chances were they might want to know where she was.

Hmm.

Maybe phone home then, and at least let the family know she was in a ditch, in a blizzard, somewhere in deepest darkest Gloucestershire. Or, more accurately, deepest *whitest* Gloucestershire.

Although it would be dark soon enough.

This dilemma was solved neatly enough by the discovery that her phone was dead, which narrowed the options down to two. Should she leave the car and trudge off through the ever-deepening snow in search of civilisation?

Or stay here and hope that somebody else—preferably in a Sherman tank or a helicopter—might come along and rescue her?

Since civilisation could be miles away and her feet still ached like mad from dancing last night, Nadia reached over to the back seat for her sleeping bag, wriggled into it like a giant worm and settled down to wait.

Poor old Laurie, he'd missed a brilliant party. Nadia smiled to herself, thinking back to yesterday morning's phone call. She wondered how hot it was right now in Egypt, if Laurie was remembering to drink only bottled water and if he'd managed to squeeze in a visit to Tutankhamun's tomb before flying on to Milan.

Gosh, she was hungry. Easing a hand from the cocoon of her sleeping bag, she flicked open the glove compartment. A packet of Rolos and a half-empty bag of wine gums. Should she ration herself, like people trapped on mountains, to one Rolo a day? Or give in to temptation and guzzle the whole lot at once?

But she wasn't trapped on a mountain and she wasn't going to starve. Compromising, Nadia ate three Rolos and half a dozen wine gums, then switched on the car radio for company, just in time to hear a DJ cheerfully announcing that there was plenty more snow on the way.

That was the thing about Sherman tanks, they were never around when you needed them.

Less than half an hour later—though it seemed like more—Nadia let out a shriek and abruptly stopped singing along with Sting to 'Don't Stand So Close To Me'. Actually, it was an appropriate song. The person who had tapped on her window *was* pretty close.

Male or female? Hard to tell with that hat pulled down over their face. Wrapped up in a Barbour, thick sweater and jeans, it was either a man or a hulking great six-foot-plus woman.

Hoping it wasn't Janet Street-Porter, Nadia opened the window and promptly wished she could have been wearing something more alluring than a green nylon sleeping bag strewn with bits of gold foil Rolo wrapper.

She also hoped she'd been singing more or less in tune.

Not that this was terribly likely.

'Are you OK?'

He had dark hair, light brown eyes and snowflakes decorating his black, spiky eyelashes.

'I'm fine. Really warm. Skidded off the road,' Nadia explained, fairly idiotically given the novel angle at which she was sitting.

He inclined his head. 'I noticed.'

Nadia peered at the empty road behind him. 'Did you crash too?'

'No, I did the sensible thing.' He looked amused. 'Abandoned the car before that happened. It's at the bottom of the last hill.'

'Rolo?' She offered him one through the open window. Not her last Rolo, obviously.

'No thanks. Look, there's a village half a mile ahead. Do you want to walk with me?'

'You live around here?' Nadia brightened, then hesitated. Hang on, a complete stranger offering her shelter in the middle of nowhere, seemingly perfectly normal and friendly right up until the moment he reappeared from the woodshed with madness in his eyes and a sharp axe?

How many times had she seen *that* film?

He shook his head, scattering snowflakes. 'No, I live in Oxford.'

'So how do you know there's a village?' She didn't want to struggle through the blizzard on a whim.

The mad axe-murderer seemed entertained by the wary look in her eyes.

'I'm very psychic.'

Oh God, he really *was* a nutter.

'That's great.' Nadia took a deep breath. 'Look, have you ever been to this part of Gloucestershire before?'

'No.' Smiling, he patted the pocket of his waxed Barbour. 'But, unlike you, I do have a map.'

'I feel like a refugee,' Nadia muttered as they trudged along the narrow lane, the snow squeaking underfoot. Since hopping along like a ten-year-old in a sack race wasn't practical, she was carrying her rolled-up sleeping bag under one arm and her overnight case in the other.

'You look like a refugee.' Glancing across at her, he broke into a grin and held out an arm. 'Here, let me carry those.'

She knew his name now. Jay Tiernan. He'd introduced himself while she'd been struggling to extricate herself from the sleeping bag. In return she'd asked, 'What does J stand for?'

'Nothing. It's just Jay.'

Hmm, a likely story. It was probably short for something embarrassing like Jethro or Jasper. Or Josephine.

Then again, Nadia could sympathise. School sports days had always been a mortifying experience, with dozens of sniggering boys lined up roaring, 'Go, Nad… GONAD… GO, GO, GO!'

But Jay Tiernan didn't need to know that. Thankfully, Nadia handed him her overnight bag. Her nose was a fetching shade of pink, her eyes were watering and her toes numb. Ranulph Fiennes needn't worry about competition—she'd be hopeless at trekking across the Antarctic.

'You lied,' Nadia panted forty minutes later. 'That wasn't half a mile.'

'Never mind, we're here now.'

'And this isn't a village.'

'It is,' said Jay. 'It's just… small.'

Nadia peered through the tumbling snowflakes at the deserted single street. There were no lights on in any of the cottages. Nor were there any shops. Just a postbox, a bus shelter and a phone box.

And a pub.

'The Willow Inn,' Jay announced, squinting at the dilapidated sign. 'We'll try there.'

The front door was locked. After several minutes of hammering on the wood, they heard the sound of keys rattling and bolts being drawn back.

'Blimey,' slurred the landlord, enveloping them in a cloud of whisky breath. 'Mary and Joseph and the little baby Jesus. Fancy bumping into you in a place like this.'

Nadia, clutching her rolled-up sleeping bag in her arms, realised he thought she had a baby in there. Then again, he was so drunk she could probably get away with it.

'Hi,' Jay began. 'We wondered if—'

'Shut, mate. Closed. Six o'clock we open.' The middle-aged man jabbed vaguely at his watch. 'You could try coming back then. No kids mind, this isn't a family pub. Kids? Can't stand 'em.'

'Look, the roads are blocked, we've had to abandon our cars, we've been walking for *hours*,' Nadia blurted out, 'and we need somewhere to stay.' Hastily she unravelled the sleeping bag to show him how empty it was. 'And we definitely don't have a baby.'

As a rule, batting her eyelashes and widening her big brown eyes had the desired effect, but the landlord of the Willow Inn was clearly too far gone for that.

'Don't do board and lodging neither.' Wheezing with laughter he flapped his arm and said, 'There's a stable down the road, you could try there.'

Nadia briefly wondered if bursting into tears would help. Failing that, hitting the landlord over the head before tying him up and locking him in his own cellar.

Jay, his method thankfully more law-abiding, said, 'We need somewhere to stay and something to eat. We'd pay you, of course.'

The landlord's bloodshot eyes promptly lit up. 'Hundred quid.'

'Fine.'

'Cash, mind. Up front.'

Solemnly, Jay nodded. 'It's a deal.'

The power cut that had left every house in the street in darkness was still going strong at nine o'clock that evening. The pub, illuminated with flickering candles, had gradually filled up with locals driven out of their homes by the lack of TV, as well as half a dozen other stranded drivers in need of a roof over their heads.

By some miracle the landlord, Pete, was still drinking and still conscious. Well, just about. Cindy, the barmaid, confided to Nadia that Pete's latest girlfriend had walked out on him three weeks ago, precipitating this mammoth binge. Now, evidently cheered by the amount of money he was extorting from stranded travellers, he was wavering precariously on a bar stool, leaving Cindy to do all the work.

Dinner, also thanks to the power cut, was thick chunks of bread toasted over an open fire, tinned ravioli, doorsteps of cheese, pickled onions the size of satsumas and stale digestive biscuits.

Nadia, who had given the onions a miss, said, 'Yum.'

'A candlelit meal, what could be more romantic?' Jay indicated their rickety wooden table. 'Never let it be said I don't know how to give a woman a good time. Pickled egg?'

Nadia smiled; he had a nice voice. She'd always been a sucker for a nice voice.

'No thanks. We need to sort the room thing out. You can't sleep down here.'

Pete's insistence on cash in advance for the only spare bedroom had left Nadia with a dilemma. With only fifteen pounds in her purse, it had been left to Jay to come up with the rest of the money. When Pete had shown them the chilly room, cluttered with junk and taken up almost entirely by a lumpy, unmade double bed (A hundred pounds? Bargain!), Jay had murmured, 'It's OK, I'll sleep downstairs.'

But that had been before the others had arrived, turning the small bar into a makeshift refugee camp. Two of them had nasty hacking coughs. It wasn't fair to take the room Jay had largely paid for.

'You should have the bed,' Nadia told him. 'Honestly, I'll be fine down here.'

'You might be fine, but you won't get any sleep.'

'I'd feel guilty otherwise.' She watched him refill their glasses with red wine.

'We could both sleep in the bed,' said Jay.

Nadia hesitated. It was the most practical solution, of course. It was just a shame he couldn't have been nice-but-comfortingly-ugly, rather than nice-and-definitely-attractive.

Dangerously attractive, in fact.

Not that she'd be tempted to do anything naughty, but she didn't want Jay thinking she might be tempted. In her experience, attractive men seemed to take this for granted.

'Just sleep.' Nadia met his gaze. 'No funny business. We'd have all our clothes on. And I'd be in my sleeping bag,' she added for good measure.

'Absolutely.' Jay's mouth had begun to twitch. Oh Lord, did he still think she fancied him?

'I have a boyfriend,' Nadia explained firmly, 'and we really love each other.'

Jay nodded, to show he understood. 'Me too.'